STOLEN DIARY

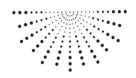

KATHRYN LANE

eBook ISBN: 978-1-7354638-4-1

Paperback ISBN: 978-1-7354638-3-4

Paperback is printed and bound in the USA

Tortuga Publishing, LLC

The Woodlands, Texas

Cover Design by Tim Barber, Dissect Designs

Interior Design by Danielle Hartman Acee, authorsassistant.com

Editing by Sandra A. Spicher

Expert Readers: Rosa Herst, Carol Ann Martz, Harry Martz, Norman Parrish, David R. Stafseth, and Jorge Lane Terrazas

*In loving memory of the two incredible women
that most influenced my life:*

*My beautiful mother, Frances Lane,
who was also the gentlest soul I've ever encountered*

*My childhood friend, Malena González de Rodríguez,
another gentle soul*

LIST OF CHARACTERS

Jasmin – a young math genius that grows up in an overprotected environment

Grandfather – Jasmin's grandfather, Agustín Campos de la Vega, a retired Colonel from the Mexican Army; also called Colonel Campos

Grandmother – Jasmin's grandmother; the Colonel's wife, Anita

Mama – Jasmin's mother – Leticia Campos

Salva Domínguez – Jasmin's father

Lola – housekeeper for the Campos de la Vega family

Lorenzo – stableman at the colonel's stables and general handyman

Teresa – therapist who works with Jasmine on equine therapy

Dr. De la Mota – university professor of mathematics and physics, and Jasmin's private professor

Dr. Arroyo – university professor of archaeology and literature, and Jasmin's private professor

Priest – also called Alfredo

Gabriela – Jasmin's governess and chauffeur in Mexico City

Dr. Rojas – university professor of physics in Mexico City

Akifumi Sato – physics and math PhD candidate at the university in Mexico City; also called Aki

Sebastián – owner of a coffee shop

Dr. Segundo Huerta – professor of communications
Rosana Huerta – Segundo Huerta's sister
Javier – bodyguard and private security detail
González – the Colonel's attorney
Detective Serna – member of the C4I4 security system in Mexico City
El Lencho – extortionist and head of a kidnapping group
Nurse – assisted in Jasmin's delivery
Pistolero – Gunman
PI – private investigator hired by Agustín Campos
Rodrigo Alvarado – extortionist (offstage)
Gustavo Molinari – human trafficker (offstage)
Campos – a young boy named after Colonel Campos

Animal kingdom members of the Campos de la Vega and Dominguez families:

   Alba – a wooden cat, a gift from Dr. De la Mota
   Ixchel – Jasmin's palomino mare
   Sojón, Sancho, and Alonzo – three cats

NOTE: A few readers might find it unusual that a young university student might need a bodyguard to accompany her to class. Unfortunately, in Mexico, where part of the action of this fictional novel takes place, families do hire bodyguards to protect their children and teenagers. The reason is to safeguard their children from possible kidnappings for ransom.

GLOSSARY

Alba—Dawn
bazar sábado—Saturday bazaar
casa chica—a house where a mistress lives, considered secondary to the wife's house
casita—small house, usually a guest house
Chihuahua building at the Plaza de las Tres Culturas—a building, named after the northern state of Chihuahua, in Mexico City's Park of the Three Cultures
chiles rellenos—green chiles stuffed with cheese or meat, covered in egg batter, and fried to a golden brown
Chingados, está loco el hombre. Piensa que es el Quijote—Fuck, this man's crazy. He thinks he's the Quixote
Ciudad Segura—the name of a street surveillance program in Mexico City, the name translates to "safe city"
Federales—Mexican federal police
hijo de puta—son of a bitch
mi pequeña—endearing term meaning 'my little one'
mi pequeña ingeniera espacial—my little space engineer
mole poblano—a traditional dark-red Mexican sauce from the state of

Puebla made with chocolate, brown sugar, and chiles. The sauce is served with chicken, turkey, or wild game

mon amour, ma petite princesse—French for 'my love, my little princess'

Ocotlán—a Nahuatl word meaning a place of pines; the village Jasmin is from is named for its pine trees

papel picado—sheets of colored tissue paper that are cut into festive designs and used to decorate an area

pendejo—stupid

peso—Mexican currency

pistolero—gunman

¿Que mierda estás diciendo?—What shit are you talking about?

¿Qué pasó?—What happened?

Si, señora—Yes, ma'am

Si, yo soy Don Quijote de la Mancha—Yes, I'm Don Quixote of La Mancha

tacos al pastor—Mexican street tacos, also called shepherd tacos

telenovela—television soap opera

tlacoyos—a pre-Hispanic predecessor to the taco made with cactus pads

zaguán—a covered passageway that is open to an interior patio of a home and has a door to the street

NOTE: Words and names that are used in Spanish in this work of fiction carry accent marks. The exceptions are Jasmin's name and the word mama. For the purposes of this novel, these two words are pronounced as if they are in English and therefore, do not carry accents.

PART I

CHAPTER ONE

"**R**un through the chromatic scales one more time. Remember not to bunny-hop your fingers and don't press your thumbs into the sides of black keys."

Agustín Campos de la Vega, a retired colonel, beamed with pride as he watched his granddaughter's little fingers dance gracefully over the keys. Monitoring her technique brought him such joy that he felt his heart reach out to give her an invisible embrace.

Jasmin sat up straighter on the piano bench. He smiled when she positioned her hands over the keys the way he'd explained. She played each half step intuitively finding the correct fingering this time.

"Much better." Agustín stroked his handlebar mustache. He'd first grown it during the years of the Dirty War which culminated with the student uprising in Mexico City in 1968, shortly before the Olympics. "Play it again."

Following his instructions, she glanced at him when she finished.

"That's good. Now I'll play 'Ode to Joy' and you can sing along."

Jasmin seemed hyper-concentrated whenever she sang the lyrics to her favorite piece.

It was getting late. Agustín told Jasmin to put on her sweater. "I'll walk you to the house."

They stepped outside to the zaguán, a covered passageway complete with outdoor furniture, that separated the big house from Agustín's casita. His quarters had served as a guest cottage until his wife, Anita, had decided in a fit of anger, to kick him out of the big house.

The full, yellow moon lit up the patio, casting shadows from the bare branches of the apple trees onto a large fountain. The gurgling water created ripples on the surface. A sudden gust of wind churned the water even more, causing the moonlight reflected on the edges of the swirls to shudder over the surface of the dark water.

Jasmin pulled her sweater up to cover her nose. She stepped closer to her grandfather and grabbed his hand tightly. Despite the chilly air, Agustín felt perspiration on her little hands.

He stopped and pointed to the full moon. It was so big, he thought he could almost smell it. "See that beauty up there? Do you see the image of the rabbit?"

Jasmin looked into the night sky.

"Your ancestors, the Maya, thought the rabbit in the moon was Ixchel's friend and companion."

"Ixchel?"

"The moon goddess," Agustín explained. He started walking again, squeezing Jasmin's hand to bring her along. "Tomorrow we celebrate your birthday. Do you know how old you're going to be?"

Jasmin held up four fingers.

Agustín smiled. Stepping inside the house, they walked to her bedroom. He sat at the foot of the bed while she went to the bathroom to change into her pajamas.

She crawled into bed, pulled the sheet and light blanket up, and tucked the edges under her chin. "Tell me a story."

"Tomorrow is a big day and you need to sleep." He leaned over to kiss her on the forehead.

"Please, just one story," she pleaded.

Agustín sighed and moved a heavy Queen Anne armchair closer to the bed. "The Popol Vuh, that sacred Maya book I've told you about—"

"Yes," Jasmin said, "the story about the Hero Twins."

"That's correct, but tonight I'm going to tell you about the discovery of the maize mountain, deep in the Maya Mountains south of us in Guatemala, where the seeds for corn are hidden. Remember last time I told you that maize is the most important crop and food source for the ancient Maya? Not only important as food, but the Maya also believed a maize dough was used to create the first humans."

He glanced at Jasmin and saw she had already fallen asleep. Softly, he wished her sweet dreams and turned the light off as he left the room.

The next day, Agustín joined everyone for lunch in the main house. Ever since Anita had booted him out, she only invited him to join in family meals on special occasions like today. The seating arrangement kept him as far from her as possible, although he did eat breakfast in the main house. Neither his wife nor his daughter, Leticia, partook of the morning meal.

Most of his dinners were delivered on a platter to his casita, where like a distinguished prisoner, he read from the great books while he ate. On occasion, he liked to imagine himself a modern interpretation of the sixteenth century Spanish military leader, Miguel de Cervantes, who became the giant of Spanish literature early in the following century. Cervantes claimed he wrote the prologue to his famous *Don Quixote* while imprisoned. Not a writer himself, Agustín had started to think, though not seriously enough, about writing a satirical, picaresque novel to justify his isolation and feel even more akin to Cervantes. Exile to the casita did bring one benefit the illustrious Spaniard had not enjoyed while incarcerated. Lola, the longtime housekeeper in the Colonel's household, cooked exquisitely, contrary to what Spain's prison kitchens would have produced four centuries earlier.

At the table, Salva Dominguez, Jasmin's father, broke into a birthday song. The rest of the family sang along softly, knowing that Salva's voice was by far the best. He pushed a plate containing a cake, dripping in purple frosting with four lighted candles, toward his daughter.

"Make a wish," he said, showing her how to blow the candles out.

Leticia, Jasmin's mother, took the cake, removed the candles, and cut six slices, serving a piece to each person in the dining room.

"What did you wish for?" Grandfather asked.

Jasmin fidgeted with the candles, laying them out side by side on the table, then rearranging them again in the same configuration. "A horse. I want my own horse."

"Then we should all go to the stables," Agustín said.

Jasmin led her parents, grandparents, and Lola through the patio to the corral and stables.

As they approached, Anita saw a beautiful palomino horse. Turning to her estranged husband with a look of contempt, she asked, "Agustín, why must you spoil her?"

"But I'm not. She'll use this mare in her therapy. Surely you don't resent a gift like this when you see the miracles her therapy yields."

"She's making progress," Anita conceded. She put her hand to her chest. "But it gives me heart palpitations to know how she manipulates you."

Agustín turned to Jasmin. "She's a mare, a female horse."

Without responding, Jasmin ran to the palomino. She took the reins from Lorenzo, the handyman who had worked for Agustín for nearly forty years. A tall man, Lorenzo's finely chiseled nose, obsidian eyes, square chin, and outstanding posture, a trait he'd learned from the colonel, gave him a dignified appearance. He helped Jasmin put on her helmet. Then he eased her into the saddle, speaking softly to the mare.

Leticia glanced at her father for a few seconds and cleared her throat before speaking in a tentative voice. "Papá, I hope this is the only gift you're giving her."

"Ah, there's another one. I've hired a math tutor. You know she loves the subject. He'll start in January."

"Math tutor?" Anita turned to Leticia and asked if she'd been consulted about the tutor.

Leticia shook her head.

Agustín ignored his wife and stepped toward the birthday girl.

Anita followed him, her voice becoming louder. "Don't shrug me off, Agustín. For god's sake, she's only four years old. We need to talk."

He jumped onto the palomino's rump, adjusting himself behind his granddaughter's saddle. "What will you name your mare?"

"Ixchel."

"Really? Why?"

"Her color reminds me of last night's moon."

"That's appropriate," Grandfather said, chuckling.

Jasmin loosened her grip on the reins and let the mare take them toward the pasture.

Leticia stood next to Anita as they watched Agustín and Jasmin ride away. Anita grabbed her chest and started hyperventilating. Leticia turned toward her mother and saw her lose her balance. She reached out to steady her mother. The woman was speaking gibberish.

"Salva, help me get mother inside." Leticia's voice quavered with urgency.

Salva and the housekeeper stabilized the woman. Lorenzo rushed over to support most of Anita's weight, freeing Salva, who wasn't carrying his phone, to run to the house and call an ambulance. Lola and Lorenzo assisted the matriarch as she took hesitant steps across the yard to the patio. Leticia nervously walked beside them, reassuring her mother, between prayers, that all would be well. She opened the door to the house and they took Anita to her bedroom.

Lorenzo stepped aside as the two women propped the matriarch's head up on pillows. Anita's forehead was wet with perspiration and her shortness of breath alarmed her daughter. Leticia held her mother's hand trying to comfort her.

"It's Agustín…he's killing me. It's affected my heart…since I've suspected…since I told him to move to the casita," she said in a hoarse whisper.

Lola, appearing uncomfortable, left to fetch a moist towel from the bathroom.

"That child, Leticia," the matriarch said, "be careful. That child… she manipulates your father. That child…she should never…"

"Be calm, Mother," Leticia urged. "The ambulance will be here soon. You'll be fine."

"Her ability in math…it's not normal. I have to tell you—" her mother gasped for air. "You know there's something wrong—"

"Yes, Mother, she's different."

"It's more. She's—"

Leticia moved her head closer to her mother's. "She's what? Tell me."

"I've told you a thousand times. You can't trust her—"

"She's only a child, Mother."

"Keep her…at a distance. Promise me." Her mother looked at her with begging eyes. "Promise me."

Leticia promised.

"A letter…you'll find a letter with my jewelry." The woman coughed and gasped for air, like a fish out of water.

Alarmed, Leticia lifted her head and stared at her mother. She glanced at her watch, impatient for help to arrive. She picked up a magazine from the nightstand and used it as a fan to circulate air for her mother. Turning toward the door, she noticed Lorenzo. Looking embarrassed, he backed out of the room, mumbling something about being called if he were needed.

"Find my father. Tell him to come here. Urgently."

The housekeeper returned and wiped the matriarch's forehead with the damp towel. Leticia put the magazine back on the nightstand and went down on her knees. She leaned close to her mother, telling her help was coming.

Salva burst into the room with two men and a stretcher.

"The patient has a heart condition. Right?" a paramedic asked. Not waiting for an answer, he ordered the other medic to get the defibrillator ready.

The medic in charge approached the bed. Feeling for a pulse at the carotid artery, he pulled her off the pillows and laid her flat on the bed. While his colleague peeled the adhesive from the electrode pads, he ripped Anita's blouse open. He grabbed a pad from his helper and attached it on the front of the patient's chest, above the right nipple, and the second one on the left side below the breast. He administered defibrillation.

Leticia moved closer to Salva, praying desperately her mother would be revived.

The paramedics stopped working on Anita. Leticia stared at her mother in disbelief.

The man in charge looked at Leticia. "I'm sorry. We were too late," he announced in a firm but sympathetic voice.

Agustín entered the room, winded by the half run half walk he had taken from the pasture, and humbly approached the bed. The medic moved aside. Agustín kneeled and reached for his wife's hand, holding it, and kissing it, while he leaned his forehead onto Anita's shoulder.

Leticia, dazed, started weeping. Salva took his wife into his arms. Clutching him, Leticia cried hysterically.

CHAPTER TWO

TWO YEARS LATER

After saddling his own horse, Salva moved to the edge of the pasture to watch the end of Jasmin's therapy session. Teresa, the therapist, instructed Jasmin to remain mounted on Ixchel. The therapist broke into a song naming the parts of the body. Jasmin joined in the catchy tune, touching each part of the anatomy— her hair, her head, face, neck, ears, eyes, nose, mouth, teeth, and on through to her legs and knees—as they sang.

Teresa helped Jasmin dismount. They continued singing and Jasmin touched her mare's mane and head, and continued with the ears and face, except for the teeth. They ended the song with Jasmin touching Ixchel's shoulders. Teresa handed her pupil a carrot.

"Remember to look her in the eyes before you give her the treat."

Jasmin spoke gently to her mare and Ixchel obeyed by moving her head down. After a few more seconds, she held the carrot from the back tip until Ixchel grabbed it between her teeth.

With the lesson over, Salva rode up and asked his daughter if she wanted to ride into the village with him.

"Yes."

"I need to speak with you first," Teresa said. "Let me ask Lorenzo to supervise Jasmin. I'll be back."

Salva watched the lithe middle-aged woman walk Jasmin and the mare to the stables and return alone.

"Jasmin's progress is off the charts. I've taught her everything I know. She's bonded with her mare and that should help her socialize with children her age. Perhaps you and Leticia might place her in a private school."

"Private school?" Salva repeated. "Intellectually she's so far ahead of other kids that she struggles to interact socially. Besides, my father-in-law believes Jasmin should be homeschooled to fully develop her abilities."

"It's just a thought," Teresa said, shrugging. "If she were my child, I'd find a school. One with advanced programs to deal with children like her."

Salva nodded. "I'll talk to my wife."

Teresa waved for Jasmin to join them again.

The therapist informed her that today's session was over.

Salva dismounted to open the gate from the pasture to the dirt road that ran along the boundary of his father-in-law's property. Remounting, he anticipated that riding horseback to a mechanic's shop repairing Leticia's SUV would be far more pleasurable than driving his pickup over the hole-riddled unpaved street. Dust raised by an old black Ford Focus hatchback was the only nuisance they encountered.

They continued their ride into the Village of Ocotlán, a suburb of the city of Tlaxcala. Salva smiled when Jasmin fell into her habit of bringing up odd facts. "Daddy, did you know the name of our village means a place of pines? It comes from the Nahuatl word ocotal."

"Named after pine trees, is it? Why not for apple trees?" He gestured to one as they passed.

Jasmin rolled her eyes and let out an exaggerated sigh. "Our original inhabitants didn't have apples. Don't you know the Spaniards brought them after the conquest?"

Salva swallowed. He thought about his daughter's IQ and figured she'd be a human encyclopedia by the time she was a teenager. According to her math tutor, she could solve calculus problems like the best college freshmen.

"How was your session with Ms. Teresa?" he asked.

"Good. I like working with her. And I love Ixchel. Ms. Teresa says Ixchel is my pet soulmate."

"How would you feel if she no longer gave you classes?"

"Will I still have Ixchel?" Jasmin asked, appearing alarmed. She stared at the horn of the saddle.

"Of course. Ixchel belongs to you. It would just be that Ms. Teresa would no longer teach you."

Jasmin stared straight ahead.

Salva recognized that stare whenever his daughter was disappointed. Before he could speak, she asked why.

"She's taught you everything she knows about horsemanship and caring for Ixchel. It's simply time for you to work on your own." He wondered how his daughter could be so intelligent and yet so naïve. But then, she was only six years old.

"I still want to attend my math class."

"Of course," her father said. "You'll continue your schoolwork. Only Ms. Teresa will stop coaching you."

"My tutor says math is the most useful of all subjects. It's good in almost every job I could ever have, especially if I raise horses when I grow up."

The comment rattled Salva. He had never understood mathematics. He'd never liked the subject. In fact, he'd been plain scared of it when he was in school. Algebra was his nemesis. To get as far away as he could from that baffling topic, he had studied history and literature in college. Considering Jasmin's love of the subject, he realized math was not the profanity he'd always thought it to be.

"Raising horses, huh? Why?"

"To sell them," she said. "I'll have a horse farm."

Shortly before they arrived at the shop, the hatchback passed them again, kicking up another trail of dust.

At the mechanic's shop, Salva dismounted, helped Jasmin to the ground, and demonstrated how to tie the reins of her horse to a metal rail. He did the same with his mount and asked her to watch both horses while he went inside the garage-style shop.

CHAPTER THREE

The street was deserted, except for a girl walking toward Jasmin. The girls' eyes met, and they smiled at each other. Older than Jasmin, maybe about ten, the girl carried a cat in one arm and a large plastic bottle of cola in the other.

A car, the one that had passed Jasmin and her father on the road, came to a sudden stop a few dozen feet from where Jasmin stood, breaking the otherwise tranquil setting. A man jumped from the passenger side and grabbed the older girl. Struggling to get loose, she dropped the cat and the plastic bottle.

Jasmin clenched her teeth tightly, watching yet unable to move. The hatchback opened and the man shoved the girl inside, slamming the door closed. He turned and looked at Jasmin.

She stared back. She heard the girl's screams.

"Please don't hurt her," she said meekly, shifting her stare toward the ground.

The man headed for Jasmin, looking past her in the direction of the shop. Stopping abruptly, he turned and ran back to the car, sliding into the front passenger seat. The vehicle sped away before the door closed.

Behind her, Jasmin heard her father yelling.

"Are you okay? What did that man do?"

"Grabbed a girl and threw her in the car."

"Are you sure?"

"Yes."

"Explain what you saw," Salva said.

"The girl was walking toward me. The car stopped. He jumped out and took her."

"Did he do anything to you?"

"No. The girl dropped a kitten and that bottle." She pointed to a spot farther up the path. Jasmin walked toward the cat. It had taken shelter at the base of a large apple tree and moved around the trunk, avoiding her.

"Jasmin," her father said, "I'm talking to you. Tell me what the girl looked like."

"Black hair. Braids."

"What was she wearing?"

"A dress."

"What color?"

"Yellow and white with flowers on it."

"What color were the flowers?"

"Yellow."

"And the man?"

"He smelled."

"What was he wearing?"

"A black shirt. And cowboy boots."

"Describe the car."

"You saw it. The black one that passed us twice. It was dirty, like the man."

"But was there anything unusual about it?"

Jasmin shook her head. "Just old."

"I need to call the police and report what happened," Salva said, taking his phone from a pocket. "Was the girl about six, like you?"

"No, she was older. Like the grandson of our neighbor, Fermín."

"About nine or ten?" Salva asked to confirm.

"Maybe."

On her hands and knees, Jasmin inched her way toward the tree, speaking gently to the feline, coaxing it to stay put, as Ms. Teresa had taught her to talk to Ixchel. She stretched an arm to grab the kitten, only to watch it bolt up the tree into the branches out of reach. Looking up, she decided the only way to catch it would be to climb up after it.

She glanced at her father before jumping to grab the lowest limb. She swung her feet to the trunk and inched them up until she could reach the next branch to hoist herself into the tree. After catching the kitten, she saw her father watching her as she prepared to jump down from the lowest branch.

Walking back to him, she held the kitten up for him to see. "Look, I got her."

Salva had redialed the police and his hand gripped the phone as he waited for the station to answer. He looked at the cat. "I think it's a boy cat. What are you going to do now that you've caught him?"

"Take him home and feed him. I need to take care of him."

"Mama won't be happy. You know she doesn't like cats."

"That's all right. I'll keep him in the casita." Holding the kitten with trembling hands, she gently scratched the area behind his ears, noticing his luminous blue eyes. "Zero, one, one, two, three, five, eight, thirteen, twenty-one," she murmured to her new friend.

The police station finally picked up the call. Salva provided their location and explained what had happened, reporting it as if he'd witnessed it rather than his daughter.

"I asked the man not to hurt her," Jasmin said, staring at the side-walk. Her hands continued trembling and she started whispering the numbers in the Fibonacci sequence again.

Salva picked Jasmin up. "You're shaking, sweetheart. We are going home where we will be safe."

Hugging the kitten against her chest, she rested her head against her father's shoulder.

After a couple of minutes, Salva put Jasmin on the ground and told her they would mount their horses to return home. She handed the feline to him and grabbed a handful of mane. He used a hand to help push her into the saddle, handed the cat back to her, and arranged the reins so she could handle them with one hand.

"You know that man was a bad person," her father said. "If someone ever tries to take you like that, you must scream. As loud as you can. That way someone can come to your rescue."

Jasmin nodded.

———

Without speaking, they rode their horses home. Salva looked over his shoulder repeatedly to make sure they were not being followed. He marveled at his daughter's ability to add those numbers in her head as they rode. She'd told him it was called the Fibonacci sequence. It was simple enough, but he was not sure what was so special about it. It consisted of adding the last two numbers to arrive at each new one. Jasmin had explained to him that the ratio between the numbers in the sequence approximated the golden ratio, 1.618, rounded so he might remember it. She'd told him the sequence converged on Phi, an irrational number presumably known by the ancient Greeks. They had considered it to be a proportion that was balanced and pleasing to the eye.

To Salva, all numbers were irrational. He was lost in the explanation, yet he enjoyed hearing Jasmin talk about the topic. She'd told him the story about the young man, Leonardo of Pisa, nicknamed Fibonacci, who had lived during the twelfth and thirteenth centuries, and had been born into a wealthy merchant family in Italy. He'd discovered the sequence and it was named after him, though that was long after the Greeks had known about Phi. Later, Leonardo of Pisa also introduced the Arabic numbers to Europe, replacing the impractical Roman numerals. With so much knowledge in her young brain, Salva wondered if she would fill it to capacity and reach a point where she would not be able to store new information. His mind automatically returned to the incident Jasmin had witnessed and he resumed worrying about her safety.

CHAPTER FOUR

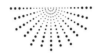

S alva helped his daughter dismount. He felt Jasmin tremble. Clutching the cat close to her chest, she whispered numbers to the feline. They stepped into the patio, interrupting Lola as she trimmed the bougainvillea trellises near the classroom. She turned to look at them and appeared alarmed at seeing Jasmin. She walked toward them.

Asking if Jasmin was okay, Lola embraced her.

"Stay with her, please," Salva said in an anxious tone. "I must speak with Leticia. Jasmin saw a kidnapping." He walked away leaving Lola speechless.

Salva knocked on the casita door and asked Agustín to accompany him to Leticia's office for an urgent meeting. The men interrupted her writing in a black leather-bound book. Her diary, she called it. Closing it as soon as she saw them, Leticia placed it into a desk drawer.

"What are you working on?" Agustín asked.

"A poem, but I can't get the meter or rhythm right. What brings you both to see me?"

"I was inside the mechanic's shop. Jasmin was outside. A car stopped on the street. A guy jumped out and grabbed a girl. Jasmin saw the whole thing."

Hearing her husband's words, Leticia turned pale.

"A kidnapping?" Agustín asked, his upper lip started shaking, which made his mustache quiver.

"It was a young girl. Jasmin was about twelve feet from where it happened. It could be a coincidence," Salva said, "but the car, a black hatchback, was the same one that passed us twice on the dirt road leading to the shop."

"Was he following you and Jasmin?" Agustín asked, pulling on the tip of his mustache.

"It didn't seem so at the time, but now I'm convinced they were. It was a driver with a person in the passenger seat."

"How did Jasmin react?" Leticia asked.

"To the kidnapping?"

She nodded.

"Aloof, but she was trembling." Salva's voice sounded strained. "And there's something else. She rescued a cat the abducted girl had been carrying. I told her she could keep it."

"You didn't." Leticia glared at her husband. "You know I *hate* cats."

Salva glared back at his wife. "Jasmin reverted to reciting the Fibonacci sequence all the way home. You must let her keep it."

Leticia sighed. "Not those damn numbers again."

Agustín appealed to his daughter, emphasizing the cat might alleviate the traumatic event Jasmin had witnessed.

Leticia relented. "As long as it is kept out of doors. And douse it in flea powder. Today."

"It terrifies me," Salva said, "to think Jasmin might have been the intended victim. When I came out of the mechanic's shop, the man was headed toward her. He saw me, turned, and jumped into the hatchback. I didn't get a good look at him. Not sure I'd recognize him if I saw him again."

"We need to talk with the police," Agustín said.

Salva told them he'd already taken care of reporting it, adding that visiting the police chief was a good idea to pressure for an investigation into the young girl's abduction. "It's a poor neighborhood, and it won't hurt for the police to know we're interested in seeing them pursue this case."

Agustín nodded in agreement and suggested they follow up that afternoon. "The two patio gates must be locked at all times for safety reasons. I'll tell Lorenzo to add another five feet of height to the patio walls. Also, he and Lola must never leave Jasmin alone when she's outside, nor Teresa when she's working with Jasmin."

"Speaking of Teresa," Salva said, "she told me this morning that she's taught Jasmin everything she can."

Agustín shook his head. "After what happened today," he said, "we should ask Teresa to stay on longer. Under no circumstances can Jasmin ride her horse in the pasture unless someone's with her."

———

With the meeting over, Agustín headed outside. He saw Jasmin, cross-legged like a yogi, sitting next to Lola, on the concrete surrounding the fountain. She held a metal bowl of milk to the kitten's face, encouraging it to drink. Lola stood up, rubbed the cat's head, and returned to trimming the bougainvillea.

"What's your pet's name?"

Jasmin looked up at her grandfather. "Sojón."

"Where did that come from?"

"I don't know. I just made it up. Sounds nice, doesn't it?"

"It's a perfect name. Let me tell you, mon amour, ma petite princesse, every action has consequences. You brought Sojón here and now that requires that you must take care of him."

She nodded.

"You might feed him in the zaguán to make sure Mama does not object. And you can bring Sojón inside the casita for your piano lesson. Afterward, you can give him leftover chicken as a treat for listening."

"Will they kill that girl?" Jasmin asked.

"I hope not."

"Why do people die?"

"It's the law of nature. The life and death cycle. It's natural for old people to die, not young ones."

Jasmin looked intently at the cat. "Like Grandmother when she died. You told me everyone must die sometime."

"That's right."

"I don't want you to die," Jasmin said, staring at the concrete walkway.

Agustín's stomach felt a ping. He sat on the base of the fountain and faced her. "If I die, it means I go on to another life. Whenever that happens, play 'Ode to Joy' on the piano and sing it, too. Before you know it, you'll feel better."

Jasmin still stared at the concrete.

"Bring Sojón to the casita when he finishes the milk." Agustín stood and walked toward the zaguán, knowing that Salva was right about the kidnapper. He may have been after Jasmin. He wondered who, maybe someone from his past life in the military, might have a vendetta against him, hate him enough to hurt Jasmin. He thought of a soldier he'd disciplined. That soldier had been court-martialed. Later he'd become a criminal. He was in prison, but he could still extract vengeance. A military man always makes enemies. Then there were others, like the family of a young student protestor he'd accidentally killed years ago at a public disturbance that had turned violent. Walking, Agustín felt his knees creaking, the burden of worry bearing on his joints.

After Anita's death, he had decided to stay in the casita, though he now ate most of his meals in the house with his family. He'd grown comfortable in the smaller quarters and that left the house for Leticia and Salva. It would eventually be his daughter's property anyway. Glancing back at Jasmin, his eyes felt moist as he watched her crossing the patio holding Sojón draped over one arm like a rag doll, while she balanced the milk bowl with her other hand.

CHAPTER FIVE

Jasmin tiptoed down the hallway the next morning, stepped onto the patio, and headed to the zaguán to release Sojón from a cage Grandfather had set up to prevent the cat from wandering away. Although the patio was secure, there were spaces under the gates where a feline could easily crawl through. Her grandfather had explained the evening before that he'd informed the police about the cat and told them if the victim's family wanted it returned, they would do so. Jasmin, already loving Sojón, hoped that would never happen.

Long, plaintive meows greeted Jasmin. The cat's cry continued even after she picked him up and walked to the kitchen in the main house. She filled a small ceramic bowl with cooked meat Lola had left in the refrigerator for the new family member.

Sojón purred his approval.

Sitting on the floor next to her new pet, Jasmin heard Lola enter the kitchen. She picked up both feline and dish and scurried toward the door.

Lola stopped her. "Mi niña, it's fine with me that you bring the kitty into my kitchen, but your mama will be furious. Take the meat to the milk bowl you used yesterday and bring this one back to me."

As she walked toward the zaguán, Jasmin glanced at the window of her mother's office. She saw Leticia's shadowy figure, slightly distorted behind the glass panels, looking out at the patio. Facing away, Jasmin continued across the patio carrying Sojón. She feared her mother had seen her leave the kitchen with her pet. Her grandfather joined her on the zaguán while the cat finished his meal.

Together, Jasmin and her grandfather walked to the kitchen for breakfast. They'd left Sojón in his cage. Lola joined them with her cup of morning coffee. Salva arrived commenting on the appetite-opening aroma of the tangy fresh-brewed coffee mingling with the cinnamon fragrance escaping from the oven.

Contrary to her usual routine, Leticia, who never entered the kitchen before noon, came in to grab a cup of coffee and a hot cinnamon roll. She asked Jasmin to go to her office after breakfast.

As always happened when Jasmin was in the same room with her mother, she avoided looking at Mama. Especially when Mama was spitting angry like she was right now.

"What do you think you were doing this morning?" Leticia asked, her stern voice pulsing with displeasure.

"Nothing." Jasmin watched her shoes dangling over the big chair where she sat, concentrating on the Fibonacci sequence, muttering each sum.

"You brought that damned cat into the house. Against my orders."

"Two hundred thirty-three, three hundred seventy-seven," Jasmin murmured each new number in the sequence, ignoring her mother.

"Answer me. Why was that cat in the kitchen?"

Jasmin continued mumbling numbers.

A crystal paperweight Jasmin had given her mother last Christmas hit the hardwood floor with such force, Jasmin plunged to the wooden planks thinking Mama might hit her with something. Stunned, she brought her head up and looked at the glass shards scattered on the floor. Total stillness followed, as if the world had stopped abruptly.

Jasmin slowly rose to a sitting position, contemplating the surreal quiet after Mama's outburst.

"Answer me, damn it," Mama said in a hoarse whisper, interrupting the silence.

"I was feeding Sojón," she stammered, getting back into the big chair, feeling confused. Reeling from her mother breaking the paperweight, she promised she'd never bring him into the house again.

Salva rushed into the room.

Leticia ignored her husband and admonished Jasmin to behave, or the cat would have to go. In apparent exasperation, Mama sighed heavily and tapped her fingernails forcefully on her desk. She ordered her daughter to go to her room and stay there.

Jasmin stepped around the broken glass, seeking safety by her father's side.

Salva picked his daughter up.

Mama yelled for Lola. "Bring a broom and dustpan."

"What the hell's going on?" Salva asked. "What's this broken glass? Is that the paperweight Jasmin gave you?"

"She kept reciting those stupid Frabonacci numbers. I smashed it to get her attention."

"It's Fibonacci," Salva said softly. "Even I know that."

"If only we had a normal child." Leticia sighed again.

Salva shook his head, incensed. "We have a budding female Einstein. And you'd prefer a normal child?"

"You always defend her." Leticia turned away from her husband. "Get out of here. Both of you. And if I ever see that cat in this house again, I'll get rid of it." She pulled her diary out of the drawer and snarled, "Now leave, so I can calm down and finish my poem."

Salva told his wife he was not defending Jasmin. He merely recognized their daughter's talent and wished she would too.

Yelling again for the housekeeper to hurry, Leticia impatiently tapped her nails on the desk.

Lola swooped into the office, broom in hand, like a soldier ready to attack the enemy.

Salva put his daughter down. "I'll be back to talk about this," he said over Lola's intense sweeping of glass fragments.

CHAPTER SIX

I n her bedroom, Jasmin could hear her mother's shouts coming from the office. Her mother was fighting with her father over the broken paperweight.

Jasmin peaked down the hallway at the precise moment her parents were leaving the office. With Mama yelling, they entered their bedroom and closed the door. This routine was typical with Mama engaging in a screaming argument with Salva behind locked doors, pushing and hurling objects, breaking some of them as she'd done with the paperweight. They would remain in their room for an extended nap long after the yelling had drowned out. Jasmin figured they were tired from the exertion. Whenever they emerged, they would both be smiling and happy, that is, until Mama became angry again and the ritual repeated itself.

Right now, Mama's shouting could be heard throughout the house. Her parents would surely follow their typical pattern and remain behind closed doors for a couple of hours. Besides the paperweight, Jasmin had also gifted a miniature replica of a Maya jaguar to her mother, but she had not seen it on the desk. She sneaked into Leticia's office, barefoot to avoid making noise. She looked at the floor to make sure Lola had swept up all the glass fragments.

Not finding the jaguar on the desktop, she opened the drawers. It was not tucked away in any of them. Mama's book, the one she called her diary, the one she always put in the drawer when anyone entered, was also missing. With her curiosity awakened, she wondered why her mother kept it hidden. She gazed around the office to see where it could be tucked away.

A five-step antique library ladder was pushed up against the built-in bookcase. Jasmin climbed to the highest rung to see the books lining the top and middle shelves. She took time to examine them and finally, she stepped down to study those nestled on the lowest shelf. She found no miniature and no diary.

The lower section of the built-in had drawers. When she pulled a knob, she discovered the drawer was locked. All of them were. Wondering where Mama might hide the key, she stepped back to the desk where she'd already seen, in the middle drawer, her mother's set of house keys and those for the patio gates. She examined the keyrings, yet no key seemed small enough for the bookcase.

When she glanced around the room, three objects caught her attention. Each one set on a shelf of the bookcase—a large cup with silver trim, a small painted vase, and a miniature chest. On the lowest shelf, the cup was full of candy.

Stepping on the third rung of the ladder, she peered into the painted vase and found it was empty.

Climbing to the highest step, she stretched and grabbed the little chest, slid the top open, and discovered tissue paper inside. She removed the paper and a key fell to the floor, making a clanking sound. Jasmin held her breath. She climbed down and quickly picked up the key.

When no one responded to the noise, she opened the first drawer. It made a squeaky sound, perhaps a complaint at being disturbed, but there was no book inside.

The next drawer popped open when she turned the key. It displayed a hidden treasure, her mother's leather-bound diary. Removing it, she relocked the drawer. Her heart thumped loudly as she wrapped the key into the tissue paper, shoved it inside the little chest, slid the lid closed, and replaced it on the top shelf.

Four days later, Salva took Jasmin horseback riding. He enjoyed the time with his daughter, and he knew he would eventually pick up the gap that Teresa would leave behind when she no longer guided Jasmin and her mare through therapy. When they returned to the stables, Leticia was leaning against the fence talking to Lorenzo.

"What the hell did you do with it?" she demanded, walking toward them and staring angrily at her husband.

Salva, still mounted on the horse, stared back. "What are you talking about?"

"You know perfectly well. You've been spying on me."

Dismounting, he handed Lorenzo the reins to his horse before turning to his wife. "If you tell me why you're upset, I might be able to help."

"My diary. It's missing. My private thoughts and my poems. You stole it!"

"Ten thousand, nine hundred and forty-six—" Jasmin muttered softly.

"I've done nothing of the sort," Salva responded testily. "Perhaps I should have. What the hell's so secretive that you keep it locked up?"

"Give it back," Leticia said in a menacing whisper.

Moving closer to stand face to face with his wife, he smiled wickedly. "If I did take it, I would know your secrets, your sins, your infidelities, your greed, your envy, your arrogance, your wrath." Salva was combative, setting Leticia off again.

Lorenzo, looking apprehensive and uncomfortable, tied Salva's horse to a post and helped Jasmin. She dismounted and ran to her room.

CHAPTER SEVEN

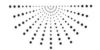

THREE MONTHS LATER

Agustín sat in Leticia's office. "It's none of my business *why* you were unfaithful to your husband, but it is my business to ask why you did not consider the *consequences* of your actions."

"You wouldn't understand," Leticia said, diverting her glance across the room with a peeved expression her father recognized.

"Try me," he said.

"Salva's worthless. He doesn't even have a job."

"That didn't seem to be a problem when you married him. People with PhDs in history don't often find jobs in their fields. Those forced to support a family either drive cabs or open restaurants. Though that's not the issue here, is it?"

Leticia glared at her father.

"Jasmin needs him," he said. "He's such a good father."

Leticia shrugged. "She'll learn to live without him. Besides, she has you."

"It's important to keep a family together," Agustín said. "Why do you think I moved to the casita when your mother asked? Do you think I enjoyed being by myself, missing out on family dinners? No, I did it to keep the peace, sacrificing my own feelings to please Anita."

"That's different."

Agustín scowled.

"Mother had good reasons. You caused her heart condition. On her deathbed, she told me you'd made her sick. So don't you lecture me."

Agustín ignored his daughter's recrimination. Instead, he thought about the abduction Jasmin had witnessed. He'd asked the equine therapist to stay an extra three months to help calm Jasmin's anxiety. It had taken that time for her apprehension to subside. Now her parent's divorce could be much more traumatic. It could sabotage the progress she'd made.

Breaking the silence, Leticia told him that Jasmin would not be the only child living with a single parent. "Besides, she'll see her father on weekends."

"Why don't you at least consider marriage counseling? For Jasmin's sake, keep your marriage together."

"What good would that do? Don't forget, it's Salva who claims he's leaving me."

"Wouldn't *you* leave him if he'd been the unfaithful one?"

Leticia grimaced.

Agustín knew Jasmin would be distraught to learn her father would move out permanently. Father and daughter had grown extremely close. They rode horses together almost every day, and they fed Sojón plus the stray they had found one morning. The new cat had crawled under the fence and stayed, probably figuring he'd found a better place to live. Salva had persuaded Leticia to allow one more cat into the patio enclave.

Salva had taught his daughter how to change the litter in the zaguán and inside the casita. When the equine therapist had left, Salva taught his daughter to groom a horse, to determine if thrush or scratches were visible on the skin, and to check for chafing under the tack. *Sure*, Agustín thought, *I'm very close to my granddaughter. I'll pick up the slack if Salva leaves, but it will not be the same. Jasmin needs her father.*

Leticia tapped her fingernails as if she were signaling to her father that their conversation was over.

Agustín headed for the stables to find his son-in-law.

———

Stooped shouldered, Salva leaned against a wooden rail of the corral, one foot on the ground and the other resting on a lower rail.

Agustín's gaze followed Salva's to the land beyond the corrals. He joined his son-in-law and also leaned against the fence. He cleared his throat. "Would you consider marriage counseling to save the marriage?" he asked without looking directly at Salva for fear of embarrassing him.

"I wish for Jasmin's sake we could work it out." Salva chewed on a stem of hay and continued looking across the expanse of pasture. He sighed. "I approached Leticia about counseling. She wouldn't even consider it."

Agustín scratched his head.

"She thinks I stole her diary and found out about her lover. I swear I never touched that book. I got fed up with her accusations that I'd been unfaithful. Three days ago, I turned it on her and told her to fess up to her own betrayal. In a fit of anger, she confessed. She asked me to leave, telling me she no longer wants to live with me. That she no longer loves me."

"I'm sorry," Agustín said, not knowing what else to say.

"You didn't know Leticia found her childhood love?"

Agustín shook his head.

"Since I confronted her, she's talked of nothing else, telling me the two of them meet at that motel, the one at the juncture with the Mexico City highway. Said she doesn't want to sneak around anymore."

"I'm sorry," Agustín said again. "Leticia's over-reaction to situations with aggressive verbal outbursts is remarkably similar to her mother's personality. Anita had intermittent explosive disorder. It's treatable. Leticia inherited it from her mother. Several times I tried to get counseling and meds for both of them, but Anita never allowed it. And Leticia, as an adult, has always refused."

Salva nodded.

"I didn't know it was an old flame," Agustín said. "I've tried talking to Leticia, but common sense didn't work. You know how headstrong she is."

"I've insisted we both sit with Jasmin to explain that I'll be leaving. Leticia would not agree for me to stay till the end of the week, so I'll be leaving tonight. This separation will hurt our daughter, but it's not on my conscience that the marriage is breaking up."

Three horses in the pasture bolted as if something had spooked them. Agustín glanced at Salva in surprise. Both men looked around but detected nothing.

"A butterfly," Agustín said, "That's probably what startled them."

Salva nodded, looking melancholic. "I'm shattered to leave Jasmin. I'll visit on weekends, but you must understand I cannot remain with Leticia. She doesn't want me. Besides, it's time I made my own way in the world."

The two men continued leaning against the wooden fence in silence, staring across the pasture where the horses had resumed their grazing.

"Take good care of my daughter. The man who abducted that child, he's never been caught. He could still pose a danger."

Agustín nodded.

Salva's eyes were watery. "It's time to call Jasmin and give her the terrible news."

CHAPTER EIGHT

Jasmin locked herself in her bedroom. A cramp rose in her stomach from the sad information her parents had given her. It made no sense that her father would move out. She'd asked why he couldn't move into the casita with Grandfather, but the question was met with an angry response from her mother that Daddy was going to find a job and rent an apartment.

Why couldn't they confine themselves to their bedroom and emerge happy a few hours later as they'd always done in the past? Is this my fault?

After a few minutes, she concluded she was indeed the reason Mama insisted her father had to leave. *But what have I done?*

Tears ran down her face. Jasmin considered her recent actions. She had not brought the cats into the house and, after Mama broke the crystal paperweight, she'd been obedient, almost obsequious, to avoid upsetting her mother. Obedient about everything. Then she remembered taking the book, the one Mama screamed about at the stables about three months ago. Scampering toward her closet, Jasmin opened a box of old toys. From the top she removed three dolls, presents from her grandmother, gifts she'd never played with. Taking the diary from the bottom of the box, she sat cross-legged on the floor, leafing through the pages again to see what she'd missed. Most of it was nonsense, poems about love and full paragraphs her mother had written about her feelings with a simplistic embedded code of what appeared to be abbreviations, but nothing that made sense. Neither were they obtuse mathematical notations. Her mother hated math and didn't even understand it.

If her mother was upset about the diary, Jasmin thought she'd better give it back.

She unlocked her door. Before stepping out, she stopped cold. She'd taken it without permission. Mama would accuse her of stealing it and would insist Jasmin leave the house too. And where would she go? Standing there, she couldn't make up her mind whether to return the book and apologize or hide it where her mother would not find it. The meeting with her parents flashed through her mind. Her father had looked so sad. She didn't want to be treated that way.

If Mama discovered the truth and threw her out, she could move in with Daddy, once he rented an apartment, or she could join Grandfather in the casita. *That's what I'll do,* she thought, *because Grandfather needs me more. He's old and, like Grandmother, he could die unexpectedly.* Her stomach churned at the thought of losing her grandfather. No, she couldn't leave him or Lola either. Or Ixchel. Or the three cats—Sojón, Sancho, and Alonso. The latter one, an old stray, had crawled under the fence recently and had refused to leave. His advanced age inspired her to name him Alonso after Don Quixote.

Jasmin locked her door and looked around her room for a good hiding place for the diary. On top of the bureau, she noticed her calculus book. The dust cover would make the perfect decoy. Mama would never investigate anything related to math. Removing the cover from the textbook, she wrapped it around the leather diary and placed it inside a plastic bag in the bottom drawer of her dresser, blanketing it under blouses and sweaters.

That should keep the diary hidden.

That night, exhausted and sad, Jasmin drifted off to sleep after her grandfather tucked her in bed. She awakened, sweating, from a nightmare. Images of the diary jumping out of the drawer and growing legs, eight of them like a spider, terrified her. Eight eyes, two large ones at the front of a black leather body, glowered at her. The beast sprinted out of her bedroom into the hall, growing as it proceeded until it turned into a monster-sized arachnid. Mama, hearing the commotion, stepped out of her room only to be knocked over by the giant spider.

Anxiety froze Jasmin. Her fingers, hands and arms regained their flexibility after a few seconds. With deliberate caution, she crawled out of bed, crept to the bureau, and opened the drawer. She slipped her hand beneath the clothes to check for the diary. Holding her breath for fear that a spider might bite her, she inched her fingers forward to locate it, expecting to be bitten at any point. Much to her surprise, the book lay as cold and dormant as when she'd first hidden it.

CHAPTER NINE

A year had passed since Salva had left. He'd had a teaching
opportunity in Madrid and had relocated to Spain. Agustín
knew Jasmin still missed her father. Only recently she'd
stopped asking if he'd ever return home. Agustín, driving to his
monthly visit to the police station, considered his efforts in becoming
a father figure for his granddaughter. It was not enough in his mind to
provide material benefits, like the mare and paying for home school-
ing. No, he tried to go beyond all that by instilling in her, or at least
attempting to, the values and ethics for living an honest life. Or was
he, like Don Quixote, lost in a past era of chivalric ideals that did not
fit the modern world?

Smiling, he thought about her devotion to her mare and the love
for her three cats. Jasmin engaged in the daily chores of feeding them
and cleaning their litters. She'd built scratching posts that the felines
seemed to enjoy in the late afternoon when they scratched and
stretched the most.

Yet Agustín could not stop worrying. His fear for her safety kept
her confined to the house and the patio, except when they went out on
their horses. Not that she ever complained. She read books and did
research on the computer. Her playtime, she called it. She practiced

the piano and loved her music lessons. Recently, she'd taken quite an interest in Maya archaeology, a topic the current tutor was not qualified to teach. Her interest in mathematics seemed as strong as ever, though Agustín surmised his granddaughter was becoming bored with her assignments and could benefit from a more experienced professor.

His biggest worry continued to be the kidnapping Jasmin had witnessed. Agustín knew his son-in-law always feared they may have been after Jasmin. If they'd known who she was, they could have demanded ransom, as Salva had repeatedly reminded him. Maybe they did know who she was, but now Jasmin was so closely monitored, they couldn't get to her.

The abducted child came from a family of modest means. Kidnapping for ransom had not been the motivation in that situation. Agustín shuddered to think about that young girl's fate.

Parking in the lot behind the police station, he anticipated the chief of police rushing to usher him into his office as soon as he arrived. Today followed the same ritual, but Agustín Campos pressed the issue more forcefully than normal when he asked about developments in the case.

"I'll call you if I get any news," the chief said. "You really don't need to come here. If we make an arrest, I'll ask you to pay the reward you've offered."

"That girl's abduction happened more than a year ago. It's a cold case now."

The chief explained he'd kept it open. "She's not the only victim of this type of crime in our town. We've solved a couple of cases, but those were not related to this incident. It takes time, you know. My department has interrogated suspected traffickers, but we have not received any credible tips. I don't know what to tell you. The girl's family is resigned to the fact their daughter will probably never be found."

Colonel Campos winced. "No family ever accepts that. I'm surprised at you. What if it'd been your child?" Agustín noticed the chief holding his anger. "That poor girl's family does not have money or influence, so they can't pressure you. It's the reason I do this. To keep you searching."

After returning home from the police station, Agustín took Jasmin riding and marveled at the bond she continued to build with her mare. Ixchel responded with calm to Jasmin's soothing voice, qualities the therapist had developed in both student and mare. In any case, he feared the pasture was becoming too routine for her riding lessons and he asked Lorenzo to prepare an obstacle course. Sometimes, like today, they merely rode their horses. On occasion, when they ventured out of the pasture onto the open meadow beyond the village, Agustín would invite Lorenzo to join them. Lorenzo used Leticia's horse, which she rarely rode.

"What new stuff are you learning in your math class?" Grandfather asked as they circled the pasture.

"I'm becoming the teacher and my tutor is becoming the student."

"What's that supposed to mean?" Her grandfather arched an eyebrow, studying her expression.

"He's stupid. I read stuff online that he knows nothing about."

"Like what?"

"Wormholes, tachyonic particles that travel faster than light, and other theories. He says none of it is proven so we should not waste time on them."

"Mi pequeña," Grandfather said, "my little one, don't become arrogant about your abilities."

Jasmin looked at the saddle horn and shook her head.

"If you talked like that about me, I'd feel you were mean. Never be unkind to people, especially those who are good to you."

"Uh, huh," she responded.

"Do you hear me?"

"Yes, sir."

"I've told you before, every action has a consequence. And every problem has a solution. Instead of being disrespectful toward your tutor, we can work on solving the issue. Perhaps by getting a different teacher. Someone who knows those theories."

Gently pulling the reins from right to left to stop Ixchel, the way her therapist had taught her, Jasmin glanced at her grandfather. She straightened up in the saddle.

He recognized the happiness on her face. He'd make a few calls and, when he drove to Mexico City on Friday, he would interview professors from the university. He would hire someone who could teach several subjects just as the local teacher had been doing to meet the educational accreditation standards.

CHAPTER TEN

NINE MONTHS LATER

J asmin sat on a high stool by the worktable in her classroom perfecting her knowledge of the CAD program her new professor, Dr. De la Mota, had introduced into her lessons. Selecting a sphere shape, she manipulated it by inputting diameter and desired mass. Once the design seemed accurate, she'd create a prototype on the 3-D printer. It only extruded plastic parts, yet that would allow her to see and feel the prototype as well as identify mistakes to correct.

Enthralled in her design, she was oblivious to the creaking sound of the classroom door opening or the footsteps of someone in the room.

"Why are you here all alone at this hour?" her grandfather asked, walking up to the worktable.

Without looking up, she said, "Finishing this design. My professor will help me decide what other physical attributes should be added. Then we'll print it during lab day on Friday."

"You'll print it?" Her grandfather, totally captivated, didn't mention that she was breaking the rule about always being supervised in the patio and schoolroom. "It sounds like you'll put the 3-D printer to good use."

Jasmin faced her grandfather. When he smiled, his wrinkled eyelids stretched and folded into crow's feet and the skin of his temples crinkled into lines penetrating deep into his receding hairline. Laugh lines, he'd told her once. Yet beneath the wrinkles, his iridescent brown eyes, with occasional specks of green, sparkled like gold.

"Building a robot starts with a simple shape. Then I manipulate it by adding to it until I get all the components I'll need, like a blueprint. That's the assignment De la Mota gave me, but a robot is too boring. So I'm also designing a spaceship, which takes a lot of systems and working parts."

Her grandfather glanced at the computer screen and asked her to explain how working with rectangles and circles would eventually become a spaceship.

"Taking it step by step. I research each part of a spaceship, like an oxygen tank and the control panel in the cockpit. Then I design each section. We'll need an orbiter and tanks for liquid propellants and oxygen. What you see here, Grandfather, is the orbiter. Though I should call it a capsule because for my spaceship, it will be just that, a small capsule for me to fit in. And maybe Sojón."

Her grandfather smoothed his mustache. "I don't think Sojón would like to be in a cramped space like that."

Jasmin selected a fresh two-dimensional shape and tapped her small fingers on the keyboard. They both watched the screen as it became a 3-D cylinder that she further manipulated into an orbiter, narrowing it at the front into the nose of the craft. Taking two additional forms, she flattened them into delta wings that tapered toward the rear, and with a final shape, she created a vertical tail that spread away from the orbiter like an elongated shark's fin. "The tail serves to stabilize the spacecraft," she explained.

"It's the space shuttle," her grandfather said. He glanced at his watch. "I hate to tell you, but it's midnight and you must get to bed."

"Just a little longer," she pleaded. "I want to show you the capsule like SpaceX's Falcon 9 rocket."

"Tomorrow, mi pequeña. It's too late now."

At one time the classroom served as a warehouse until it was converted to Jasmin's school after her grandfather hired the first tutor.

A drab room with white walls, it was next to the kitchen at the end of that wing of the house, where the house and the high adobe wall enclosing the patio came together. The walls had been made higher after the kidnapping Jasmin had witnessed. They formed a ninety-degree angle with the house. It also created a large, unused space on that side of the patio near her schoolroom. The space, partially hidden by the trellis supporting the bougainvillea vines, gave a nice large area in front of her classroom.

They stepped onto the patio and made their way to the dark house and continued to Jasmin's bedroom. Tucking her into bed for the second time that night, her grandfather touched her face with the back of his hand. "Good night, mi pequeña ingeniera espacial, my little space engineer."

"Tell me a story."

"It's too late."

"Please. I like hearing about the Maya."

"I've run out of stories, but I have an idea. How about getting another professor? One who can really teach you about the Maya?"

"Yes!" she said, showing more emotion than usual.

"Now go to sleep and we'll talk about it tomorrow."

Every night, after grandfather tucked her in bed, she'd get up to make certain the diary was still where she'd hidden it. Her nightmare about the diary growing spider eyes and legs before sprinting down the hallway, growing at every step until the giant ran over her mother standing at the end of the hall, still haunted her. Only after checking the diary in the drawer to confirm it remained immobile could she drift off to sleep.

CHAPTER ELEVEN

EARLY SPRINGTIME

For as long as Jasmin could remember, her grandfather drove to Mexico City every Friday morning. He would return in the afternoon, always refreshed, he'd tell her, from doing volunteer work and visiting former army buddies. Before departing this morning, he stopped to speak with the gardeners doing the annual trimming of the apple trees in the patio and the yard near the stables. On this occasion, Mama had hired an extra man to build a cedar trellis near the zaguán. She said she wanted to grow more bougainvillea to hide the iron gate that led from the zaguán to the street, but Jasmin figured her mother wanted to keep the cats out of sight.

Her grandfather had a heavy coat on today, even though the weather was not overly cold. She hugged him before he climbed into his car. Lola accompanied her to the classroom and remained with her. Jasmin knew it was to protect her.

She added final touches to her robot assignment. Although she had no interest in it, she had to complete it before her professor arrived.

"I see you're busy," Dr. De la Mota said to Jasmin over the cacophony of the gardeners. After removing his jacket, he joined her at the worktable.

The housekeeper left, closing the door behind her, yet the noise still came through.

De la Mota realized his pupil loved math like no other young person he'd known. At her tender age, she showed more mathematical ability than any of his graduate students. Only once before had he encountered a student who loved the subject as much as Jasmin did. He scratched the tidy wing beard on his chin. His new pupil even looked like that grad student, but he dismissed it as his imagination playing a trick on him.

He'd been teaching Jasmin to design and build circuit boards to use in a robot. Studying her intensity, De la Mota tried to analyze the reasons behind her ability. She was gifted, but she also had issues, real issues dealing with people. She'd obviously had the best therapy available. Agustín had told him her social interaction difficulties were mainly with kids her own age. And he could see why. Eight-year-olds did not use cad-cam apps to design complicated circuit boards. Her concentration was beyond his comprehension. She could focus so efficiently that she would close the world out. Her dedication to projects that interested her kept her working for hours.

He asked her to show him the circuit designs for the robot. What he saw instead startled him. Staring back at him from the computer screen was a spaceship complete with solid rocket boosters. Opening another window, she showed him a spaceship that looked more like a Falcon 9.

"This spaceship is better," she said, explaining how the Falcon 9 look-alike used Merlin-engines powered by liquid oxygen and rocket-grade kerosine. "Plus these engines are reusable and much cheaper than the solid-rocket boosters."

De la Mota was speechless. He stared at her, but she was not deterred.

"This is what I want to build," she said, "with everyday materials available on the Internet."

Nodding, the professor studied her project. He scratched his beard lightly as he digested Jasmin's unthinkable proposal. Clearing his throat, he told her they must build smaller projects first, like the robot, where she could immediately see results. A spaceship would take at least four years to build. Even a simple one. And it would be prohibitively expensive.

"But a robot can't fly me into the galaxy," she whined. "I want to see the golden spiral. It's like the Fibonacci sequence, but in the Milky Way structure."

"Photos from NASA will show you the spiral in our galaxy. You can't see it if you're in space. Besides, building a spaceship does not mean you will fly twenty feet in it," De la Mota explained, "let alone take a voyage on it through the Milky Way. After we make a robot, we can design a miniature spaceship and make it worthy of a short flight. Without you in it. To build a ship capable of actual space travel is, well, beyond our capabilities."

"I want to work on a spaceship. Big enough for me and Sojón."

"Don't even think of putting your cat in a space capsule. It would terrify him."

Jasmin talked about American and European companies planning to fly civilians into space. One company was working on a project to fly people to Mars she argued.

"Well, yes, but they have lots of funding. We don't. If you want to become an engineer or a scientist when you grow up, you'll have to apply your knowledge to more than one type of project."

By the look on his young student's face, he could tell she was not convinced. In addition to her innate ability to calculate numbers and manipulate computer apps, he was discovering she also had a stubborn streak.

A handheld chainsaw sounded on the patio.

"Does the noise bother your concentration?" he asked.

"Noise?" Jasmin cocked her head for a second to listen. "Yeah, the chainsaw makes an eerie sound."

"Exactly." Despite the cool weather outside, De la Mota wiped perspiration from his forehead. "Now show me the robot and circuit designs."

She spent a few minutes completing design enhancements De la

Mota discussed with her. Getting ready to print the head and shell or body of the robot, she generated a G-Code, loaded filament in the 3-D printer, and connected it to the computer.

"You don't have to watch the whole process," De la Mota said, observing her from his desk, "only the first couple of layers to make sure the printer runs smoothly."

She seemed mesmerized as the layers built up on the robot's head. "But I want to watch," she said.

He shrugged.

After running the sections for the prototype, she took them to her professor.

He examined them closely. "Excellent job."

"I don't think so," Jasmin said, appearing disappointed. "They grew little legs. I didn't design them in the blueprint."

De la Mota smiled. "It's difficult to get sphere shapes, like the robot's head and central section, to stand on their own. The app adds little legs as balancing components for printing purposes. All you need to do is cut them off and file the rough edges."

She performed the minor task on the balancing components, assembled the parts into a robot model, and brought it to her professor. "I wish my grandfather were here to see it."

"You can show it to your mother and Lola."

Despite the cool weather outside, it was warm in the classroom. De la Mota ran his forearm across his forehead to mop off the perspiration with the sleeve of his shirt.

The gardeners had stopped working and he was glad the noise had ceased.

CHAPTER TWELVE

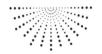

J asmin picked up the plastic robot model to show her mother.

De la Mota, a file in hand, followed her outside just as she'd expected. He leaned against the trellis.

Jasmin looked across the patio toward the zaguán. The gate to the street was open. She headed toward it to close it. The three cats were arching their backs near the chaise longue.

Motion behind the open door to the street surprised her. A man moved swiftly, reaching out to grab her.

Jasmin screamed. Loudly, the way her father had taught her before he'd left.

De la Mota dropped the file. A gust of wind scattered the papers. He sprinted toward her, shouting at the intruder.

Lola, yelling obscenities, rushed from the kitchen carrying a butcher knife. The door banged behind her.

Lunging, the man put a hand over Jasmin's mouth, wrapping his other arm around her. She dropped the model she'd made and kicked the man as hard as she could, hitting him in the shin. Instead of letting go, he held her tighter.

His hand now covered her nostrils. She couldn't breathe.

By instinct, she dug her fingernails into his forearm with

vengeance. She felt a small strip come loose on his arm under her nails, and clutching it with force, she pulled. The man weakened his grip over her mouth just enough that she gasped for air. Then she bit him. Hard.

A pistol fired.

The man dropped her and ran to the street through the open gate.

De la Mota lowered himself to the ground next to Jasmin.

Leticia ran toward her daughter, carrying a pistol aimed at the ground.

The roaring sound of a car speeding away was heard.

Lola, like a mad dog, ran out the open zaguán gate.

Lorenzo, pale and panting, came running from the corrals. "¿Que pasó?"

"What happened?" Leticia snapped. "If you were doing your job, this would not have occurred. Someone tried to abduct Jasmin. Do *not* let any of the gardeners back in. Keep the damned gates locked like you're supposed to."

"Si, señora." Lorenzo moved toward the zaguán gate, looking dejected.

"Stand there until Lola gets back before you lock that one," Leticia said sternly.

Jasmin was reciting the Fibonacci sequence. Lying on the ground, she coughed. She held up her bloody hand and shook it, trying to knock away a strip of moist and slightly sticky tissue she'd pulled off the man's arm. Kneeling next to her, De la Mota was checking her for injuries. He handed her his handkerchief. She cleaned off the blood and tissue and sat up. Using the already bloodied hanky, she wiped her nose.

Jasmin was trembling. Looking at the handkerchief in her hand, she groaned. "Yuk, it's bloody." Grimacing, she used the handkerchief to remove yet another strip of bloody material stuck to one of her fingers.

De la Mota took his handkerchief back and inspected it. "What's this?" He examined what looked like strips of bloodied skin with scabs.

"It came off that man. I ripped it off his arm when I scratched him."

"This is perfect," he said, rolling up his handkerchief and placing it in his pocket. "We'll turn it over to the police to send it for DNA testing."

Lola returned to the patio. Lorenzo locked the gate behind her.

"Did you get the license plate?" Leticia asked.

Lola shook her head. "They were too far away by then."

Leticia who had been pacing, stopped and handed the gun to Lola.

"What color was the car?" Jasmin asked. She remembered her father asking that question when the girl was abducted in the village.

"Black. A hatchback. An old car," Lola said. "There must be dozens like it."

"Not in this rural area," De la Mota said.

Jasmin's breathing became heavy. "That's the same type and color as the one they used to snatch the girl, that time my father and I rode into town." She coughed again and rubbed her neck. "And it looked like the same man. It smelled like him too."

"Smell?" Leticia asked. "How can you remember?"

"It's like he's never bathed."

Leticia suggested they go inside to clean Jasmin up and check if anything needed medical attention.

Lola asked if De la Mota should notify Agustín.

"Good idea, but let's check Jasmin first," Leticia said. "He'll want to know how she is."

The professor helped Jasmin to her feet, confirming she could walk. Next, he picked up the robot model from the ground.

Jasmin and De la Mota followed Leticia to Jasmin's bedroom while Lola took a quick detour to leave the gun in the kitchen before joining them.

The professor sat on the Queen Anne chair while the two women took Jasmin into the bathroom to wash her and check for wounds.

"I'll get a clean blouse for Jasmin to change into," Leticia said.

Jasmin's neck and shoulders stiffened. She held her breath as she resumed the Fibonacci numbers in her mind, afraid her mother would find the diary in the chest of drawers.

Her mother returned with a pink and purple hoodie with horses stamped on the front. She helped Jasmin put it on.

They stepped into the bedroom where the professor sat holding the 3-D model, a model, which for the moment, Jasmin preferred to forget. Instead, she stared at the bottom drawer that her mother had left open. She leaned over to close it and ran her fingers along the bottom, below the clothes, to check for the plastic bag. She pushed the drawer closed. Jasmin breathed and felt herself relax.

"Now you can call my father," Leticia said to De la Mota. "Tell him the two gardeners are people I've had trim the trees for years, but the guy who built the trellis was someone I didn't know. Ask my father to find out who he is."

"Maybe the gardeners went to lunch and left the gate open and this guy walked in off the street," De la Mota suggested.

"Whatever," Leticia said, "I want him to investigate the trellis carpenter."

The professor dialed a number. "Agustín," he said, "we've had a problem."

De la Mota ran the attempted abduction scenario through his head while Lola prepared honey-milk chamomile to calm Jasmin. Then the housekeeper prepared lunch which hardly anyone touched. Eventually, the professor broke the morose silence.

"Shall we spend the afternoon making a list of other materials we need to complete the robot?" he asked Jasmin with hesitation, knowing she wanted to go straight into building a spaceship.

Jasmin's eyes brightened for the first time since the incident. "We can add intruder detection to it. That way, an alarm can go off if an unknown person comes into the patio."

"The alarm would sound whenever any of us stepped on the patio," Leticia said.

"It'll have face recognition software and I'll add all of us to the system. We'll be recognized," she said. "It'll only alert us of strangers."

The professor could tell from Leticia's expression she did not appreciate being outwitted by her daughter.

"And if it rains, then what?" Leticia asked. She looked pleased with her question.

"It's going in the zaguán. It won't get wet."

In class that afternoon Jasmin and De la Mota discussed the materials and made a list, including facial recognition software, for the robot project.

"Remember this is a wish list. Next week we'll price everything and present the project to your grandfather for approval to purchase what we need."

After her professor left, Jasmin walked to her bedroom and found Mama and Lola emptying her chest of drawers and spreading clothes and other contents on the bed. Her legs nearly buckled. Holding her breath, she leaned against the doorframe to catch herself. Slowly she managed to walk to the bed. The calculus dustcover peered up at her through the plastic bag. She heard an agitated heartbeat and imagined the diary transforming into a giant spider as it did in her nightmares. She started to reach for it, but her mother turned toward her. She quickly pulled her arm back.

"You're older and you can use a larger bureau. You're getting your grandmother's and I'll move this one to Grandmother's room. No one uses that bedroom anyway."

By the tone of her mother's voice, Jasmin guessed the diary had not been discovered or else Mama would be screaming for her to leave the house. Though she was still shaking and wanted to snatch up the book, she couldn't attract attention to it. Her stomach cramped. She needed to grab the camouflaged diary and hide it before it was discovered.

Leticia and Lola moved the heavy bureau out of the room. Jasmin took advantage of their temporary absence to grab the plastic bag. Picking it up, she peeled back a corner of the bedspread and pushed the bag out of sight under the pillow before smoothing the bedspread back into place. She took a deep breath and noticed her agitated heartbeat was quieting down.

CHAPTER THIRTEEN

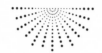

A month after Jasmin's attempted abduction, Agustín crowded everyone, including De la Mota, Lorenzo, and a security expert into the living room of his casita. He smoothed his mustache before speaking.

"The police have not yet found the man who tried to kidnap Jasmin. Based on my granddaughter's description, I reported it was the same man, same car that took that young girl near the mechanic's shop."

"What about the carpenter who built the trellis?" Lorenzo asked. "Did the police follow up with him?"

"They interrogated all three workers. Their DNA did not match the scab Jasmin got off the perpetrator. After questioning them, the police ruled them out."

De la Mota asked if the scab sample had been compared to the DNA database.

Agustín affirmed that it had been, and no matches had been found. He added that he'd installed a security system in the house. He introduced the security expert, saying he would teach them to set and deactivate the system with their personalized codes. In addition, they were all to stay for a chat on security the expert would give after Agustín finished speaking.

"Is there more we can do?" Lorenzo asked.

"The best security is our own awareness," Agustín said. "Report anything unusual, like an unknown person hanging around or a suspicious car." He looked at Jasmin and told the group that she and Dr. De la Mota had built a security robot that would set off an alarm when it detected unknown individuals inside the patio. Jasmin and De la Mota will add your photos to the face recognition app so none of us will set it off.

Jasmin glanced at De la Mota when her grandfather mentioned the robot security.

Lorenzo asked where it would be placed.

"In the zaguán," Agustín said. "On another topic, all of you know Jasmin loves math and science, but she has discovered another love. Maya history. Dr. Arroyo, an archaeologist, will be joining us next week to teach her literature, writing, and history. That will let her and Dr. De la Mota focus on their physics and engineering projects."

Agustín thanked the group and asked the security expert to take over and provide the training.

At the end of her school day, Jasmin walked into the casita for her music lesson. She covered the sheet music arranged on the rack with two printed pages, one of the spacecraft design and another showing the specs in such a tiny font, the page appeared to be covered in miniature spider webs.

Her grandfather grinned and rolled the tips of his mustache to accent their upward-pointing ends. "I must be getting old if this is how sheet music looks now."

"Oh, Grandfather," Jasmin said, flipping her hair behind her ears. "Can't you tell it's my spaceship? It's sized for me. I want to build it and I've estimated the cost. Well, initial costs."

She rattled off so much information, telling him the materials would be everyday products and equipment, that when she glanced at him, she realized her grandfather appeared lost in the details. She slowed down to emphasize the cost containment she'd built into the specs.

"The components will include a regular computer with monitors. They'll be installed above the control panel and will be integrated with applications available off the Internet. Heating and cooling parts, like thermostats, will come from systems used in home construction. The capsule itself will be made from a wide carbon steel pipe used in the oil industry."

He picked up the design page, leaving the one with the specs on the rack. "It's splendid," he said. Appearing lost in his thoughts, he asked her if she realized that if she got it built, she could not actually fly the spaceship.

"My plans," she said, "are to make Maya Explorer worthy of a short flight, one that does not leave the earth's atmosphere."

"Maya Explorer?"

"Yes, my spaceship. Both you and De la Mota have told me I can't fly it into space, even though I've read about a company in Norway that's building rockets from mundane materials and it plans to fly humans in them."

"I'm not letting you sit on top of an explosion about to happen. No way."

"Haven't you told me that every action brings a consequence?" she asked.

Her grandfather looked at her with a perplexed expression.

"I'm building a spaceship. That's an action. Wouldn't the natural consequence be that I'd fly it?"

"You're confusing actions and consequences with your dreams and goals," her grandfather said. "Let me give you an example. I've had a dream of writing a picaresque novel in the style of Cervantes. If I'd acted on it when you first showed me the designs of your spaceship, I'd surely have completed half of it by now. Instead, I've sat on my posterior, twiddling my thumbs."

Jasmin looked at her grandfather. "That's not true. We've done a lot of stuff together. Horseback riding, music, language lessons, and reading books. Since my father left, you're the one who protects me from Mama's outbursts."

"That's right," Grandfather said. "We've read lots of books, even *Don Quixote* twice."

"The best part of reading *Don Quixote* was when we acted it out," Jasmin said in the voice she'd used to portray the squire in their two-person theater. "Grandfather, you played the stubborn knight like I imagined him to be."

Her grandfather chuckled.

"I love the Quixote and Sancho Panza, but not nearly as much as I love you." She got closer and hugged him. She remembered a time when she did not like touching people. But now she loved hugging her grandfather, Ixchel, and the cats.

"And if it were not for you, my petite Einstein, I would have died of sadness and melancholy, like Don Quixote."

"You cannot ever die, Grandfather. I wouldn't know what to do without you."

"Don't forget, mi pequeña, Don Quixote had three deaths. So go build your dream."

"Does that mean I have approval for Maya Explorer?"

"Yes, mon amour, ma petite princesse."

CHAPTER FOURTEEN

Almost a year after Jasmin started studying with Dr. Arroyo, the archaeologist, she had finally convinced him to tackle Cervantes and his masterpiece, *Don Quixote de la Mancha*, in her literature class.

"What do you like about Don Quixote?" Arroyo asked.

"He creates his own reality," she said, turning over the comprehensive copy of the picaresque novel her grandfather had given her. "If he lived today, his adventures would take him to alien civilizations in other galaxies. Instead of his horse Rocinante, he'd ride a quasar motorcycle, his sword would be a proton saber, and instead of tilting at windmills, he'd tilt at nebulae."

"You have quite an imagination." Arroyo seemed caught off guard by her remarks. He cleared his throat. "What's the message in *Don Quixote*?"

Jasmin glanced up. "That an individual person can be correct even if society is wrong."

"Do you know that was a new concept in the early seventeenth century when Cervantes wrote the novel? And a controversial one."

She nodded. "Quixote also had idealistic goals that were not very practical."

"Practical? Can you explain."

"I don't think he knew much about mathematics, and math has been important throughout history."

"Math?" Arroyo asked. He must have sensed an opportunity to regain control of the conversation by changing the topic to archaeology. "The Maya were great mathematicians. They used a base twenty positional system instead of a base ten, like we do. And their system was more elegant. They were able to use only three symbols and positional placement to calculate extremely complex problems."

Jasmin's interest perked up.

He walked to the whiteboard and wrote a dot, telling her it represented a one. Next, he made a bar and told her it stood for five, and last, he drew a shell-shaped symbol that meant zero. He briefly explained the positions on a grid, that zero was also used as a placeholder, one of the reasons the Maya were so adept at amazing calculations, including predictions of lunar and solar eclipses. "I'll show you how the grid works."

"Stop," she said, "let me figure it out." She took the marker from him and set up her own grid, adding dots, bars, and circles. Then she summed up the numbers she'd written and wrote the total. Next to the grid, she scribbled it in the Arabic numbering system, placing the number 2024 on the whiteboard. "It's the year for the next full solar eclipse that we'll see from here."

"You've done this before," Arroyo said, his expression showing suspicion.

Jasmin shook her head.

"You could not have figured it out so quickly."

"Why not?" she asked. "I already know the date for the next solar eclipse."

"That's not what I meant. It's being able to write numbers, using the system. It took the sixteenth century writings of the Spanish friar, Diego de Landa, and the Dresden Codex, one of the few surviving illustrated Maya books, for scholars to decipher the Maya mathematical system. And you're telling me you calculated numbers using the grid when you'd never done it before?"

"Your explanation made it easy."

Arroyo looked as if he didn't believe her. "I didn't explain that numbers after nineteen are written in powers of twenty."

"You didn't have to. You said it was a base twenty instead of base ten, so I don't see the big deal," she countered.

"I don't see how you could calculate it so soon on your own." Sighing, he took a photo of the whiteboard.

Before Arroyo left that afternoon, he asked to speak with her grandfather.

Arroyo handed Agustín his cell phone. "Did you teach Jasmin to manipulate the Maya numbering system?"

Her grandfather looked at the picture. "Not I." He glanced at Jasmin and asked her if De la Mota had taught her principles of Maya mathematics.

She shook her head.

"Will you give me permission to take Jasmin to one of the nearby archaeological sites?" Arroyo asked. "Of course, you would come along. And her mother too. They'll be day trips, like Cholula in Puebla or Cacaxtla just up the road."

"I'm all in favor of hands-on learning," her grandfather said. He smoothed his mustache. "It's the best. We should plan on it. In fact, I'll arrange for us to visit Chichén Itzá in the Yucatán. I'll pay your expenses and we'll make it a three-day trip. Jasmin should see that Maya site."

CHAPTER FIFTEEN

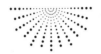

The day Jasmin returned home from Chichén Itzá with her grandfather and Dr. Arroyo, they found the mathematics professor sitting in the classroom working on his laptop.

De la Mota told them he'd forgotten about the change in the day he was supposed to teach. "Since I was already here, I stayed to prepare lesson plans."

Agustín told De la Mota not to worry and invited him to spend the night in the spare bedroom in the main house so he would not have to make the trip from Mexico City again the next day. Grandfather left to notify Lola about the overnight guest.

Dr. Arroyo remarked under his breath that a mathematician would never forget something so elemental as the day he's expected to teach.

"At least I'm not a brown-noser like you," De la Mota said sarcastically.

"Oh, no?" Arroyo asked. "You merely impose yourself for an overnight stay."

"Look who's talking. The man who spent three days mooching off Agustín."

The men exchanged barbs until De la Mota suggested Arroyo get on the road to Mexico City since he'd not been invited to stay overnight.

Arroyo looked at the other man with contempt and walked away.

No sooner had the archaeologist left than De la Mota asked Jasmin about the trip.

"My favorite part was the temple dedicated to Kukulkán, the Maya feathered serpent deity. We stood at the base of the temple to see the reenactment of the slithering serpent bodies crawling down the sides of the steps until they connect with the carved serpent heads on the ground."

"You enjoyed the trip?"

Jasmin nodded. "The whole pyramid is based on the Maya calendar."

"And built with mathematical precision," De la Mota added.

Not long after the trip to Chichén Itzá, Arroyo asked Jasmin if she'd be interested in building a miniature replica of the Kukulkán temple, including a jaguar throne for the interior. A throne where she could sit, like on a small bench.

She responded enthusiastically, remembering the miniature jaguar reproduction she'd purchased years ago for her mother.

"Ask your grandfather for permission to use the empty patio space near the classroom. We'll make the temple large enough for you to go into the interior."

When Jasmin made the request, her grandfather told her to prepare a budget. The project consisted of buying a few simple tools, stones, and lumber, she explained. She also suggested holding concerts on the patio to celebrate the equinoxes. They could reenact the slithering snake bodies coming down the balustrade such as they'd seen at the Kukulkan temple.

"How will you create the illusion of slithering bodies?" Grandfather asked.

"Like they do it at Chichén Itzá for the tourists every evening. By adding dim lights that appear to be crawling slowly down the steps. We'll use an extension cord to get electricity to the replica."

Her grandfather smiled. "Of course, you can build your temple, ma petite princesse."

Jasmin and Arroyo started their field work, as the archaeologist called it, chiseling and hammering crude reproductions, to scale, of the serpent heads and a jaguar throne that would adorn the replica. He allowed Jasmin to chew gum when they worked outside. Her other professor even allowed her to chew it in the classroom, but not Arroyo.

"How did the Maya make the serpents and jaguar so beautiful with far more primitive tools than we're using?" she asked.

"True craftsmanship," Arroyo said.

CHAPTER SIXTEEN

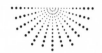

J asmin suspected De la Mota had been happier when he was her only teacher. Ever since Arroyo had been tutoring her, De la Mota seemed unable to contain his jealousy toward his archaeological colleague. As Jasmin's love for archaeology continued to grow, De la Mota seemed obsessed with swaying her back to his areas of expertise. The mathematician's contribution to the replica she was building with Arroyo consisted of biting criticism.

De la Mota eventually must have realized that disapproval of his colleague's temple replica enterprises would not succeed. That is when he unleashed his ultimate weapon.

"Mathematics," he said to Jasmin one day, "is the language of the universe. And physics is the future of science. If you want to build starships, look to the future, not the past."

She and De la Mota spent one day a week designing the interior of the space capsule while she and Arroyo spent time building the Kukulkán replica on another day. Her regular classes were done on alternate days. After Jasmin had spent a year researching the interior components for the capsule and preparing stacks of blueprints, De la Mota told her it was time to build the Maya Explorer.

The capsule's first major hands-on job was sanding the carbon steel pipe. She used an angle grinder to remove saw marks and other surface scratches. During class time, Jasmin worked on technical topics and left the steel polishing for the weekends when she and Lola used face shields and safety goggles while sanding. De la Mota insisted on a mirror like finish, which took a lot of time. By using finer and finer abrasive discs and polishing compounds, the capsule finally looked shiny.

The work had become progressively more interesting. In the past six months, De la Mota had devoted more time explaining the importance of the spaceship seat than almost any other topic.

"It must restrain and protect you," he would tell her enthusiastically, as if it would keep her safe during an actual launch. "The pressure exerted on the cardiovascular system during rocket acceleration is immense. In a horizontal position, the g-forces are spread across the whole body."

Jasmin spent months researching NASA data for seat construction. Her grandfather took her to Puebla to talk to a cardiologist to make sure she designed and produced a safe seat. The final blueprint was a recumbent style to be made from plastic. Using the 3D printer, they had built it layer by layer employing fused deposition modeling. After several trial runs, they were satisfied it met safety requirements while allowing her to operate the control panel.

They'd 3D-printed the wall panels and encasements for the controls and monitors inside the capsule. It was less expensive that way and the printed parts had less weight, an important factor for space travel.

They'd be testing some of their work inside the capsule, including validation on switches they'd installed into the edge of the pilot seat. That way Jasmin could reach the switches easily.

"If the rocket loses power in space, the switches could freeze very quickly," the professor said. "It's critical to keep that from happening. We don't have a backup for that yet."

"How about a battery-powered hairdryer?" she asked.

"Battery powered?"

"Yeah, I'll convert an electric one and use a twelve-volt battery. The heat can keep the switches from freezing."

"I don't see why not. So long as it can be accessed easily," he said. "But surely there's a better way. Of course, when you grow up and work for a space exploration company, you'll have the budget for expensive technology."

For now, they were using regular electricity to power the capsule. Today's experiment would determine if the fuel cells they'd built would actually work. Online, they'd ordered platinum coated nickel wire, nine-volt batteries, sticky tape, a voltmeter, and a few chemicals. By building fuel cells, they hoped to create energy through a chemical reaction. The cells they were testing today were small. If the experiment worked, they would build bigger ones for actual use in generating electricity for the capsule.

CHAPTER SEVENTEEN

TWO YEARS LATER

Since the village girl's kidnapping and her own near abduction, Jasmin had rarely been alone on the patio or anywhere else for that matter. Yet tonight, her favorite cat, Sojón, the one with the luminous blue eyes, the one she'd rescued after the young girl's kidnapping, brought her out onto the patio. He had a habit of scaling the largest of her mother's apple trees. When he tired of his perch, he would yowl to catch Jasmin's attention and wait for her to rescue him.

Before retrieving the feline, she glanced toward the zaguán where Zaggie, the robot, would register her presence. She checked that his green light was on too. She felt satisfied that her robot had discovered several intruders since she'd built him. All three incidents had sent everyone from the big house hustling out to the patio. In each case, the panic ended fine. On the first security breach, her grandfather had brought the postman to the patio. It was her grandfather again who forgot about Zaggie's loud alarm when he had escorted a veterinarian through the patio to the corral. Then Lorenzo had brought a repairman to fix the fountain. Rather than input their identities into the app, Jasmin had turned Zaggie off in each case after the alarm had sounded.

Tonight, Jasmin checked the two outside gates to make certain they were locked. She affectionately touched Zaggie's head as she went past him. Returning to the apple tree, she shuddered at the thought that the abducted girl had never been found. Neither had the perpetrator. *That man should be in prison for life.*

The night sky was cloudless. A brilliant full moon lit the place up like the morning's first light as the sun breaks the horizon. A harvest moon, the people in Ocotlán called it.

Jasmin grabbed Sojón and perched herself on a sturdy branch and leaned against the tree trunk. Mesmerized by the moonlight, she watched it bouncing and shimmering on leaves that fluttered in the breeze. Those silver patches created speckles that pierced the dark walls of the house like diamonds sparkling in a distant galaxy. The illusion captivated her so completely that she imagined herself steering a spaceship through interstellar space. Her back curved against the tree trunk and her legs dangled over the branch. She felt elated in the phantom cockpit. Sojón, her complaisant navigator, was precariously balanced in her lap.

The apple tree was the one spaceship where Sojón could travel with her. Lost in her imaginary world, the sensations of the cool evening air and smell of the sweet jacaranda bushes brought a sliver of reality into her fantasy. The apples would be picked in a few weeks and the leaves would fall to the ground. She pretended to explore the Milky Way's golden spiral from her treehouse spaceship knowing the illusion of outer space would not last.

I'll incorporate a video of the Hubble Ultra Deep Field into my Maya Explorer computer to recreate this feeling. I like the idea of seeing galaxies in our universe from inside my capsule. And soon we might have better videos from the James Webb telescope. The prototype capsule had taken Jasmin and her professor four years to plan, design, and put into production. The carbon steel capsule was more cramped and stuffier than the apple tree. Yet the design incorporated air to be filtered in so the hatch could be closed while she was inside. When finished, her spaceship would offer far more benefits than a backyard tree. Her thoughts drifted to mathematics and theoretical physics, subjects where she dreamed someday of making significant scientific discoveries.

Bright lights came on in the kitchen, shattering her illusion.

Her mother walked regally into the well-lit room. A man dressed in a black robe, accented at the waist with a golden sash, followed two steps behind.

It was not so much the shock of the lights as the fright of seeing her mother that evaporated the magic of her space odyssey.

Jasmin's heart skipped like a pebble falling down a mountain. She panicked. Sojón must have sensed her apprehension for his melodic purring stopped abruptly. Slowly descending the tree to find cover, she lost hold of Sojón and he plummeted to the moist earth. She wrapped her legs around the trunk to ease herself down but lost her grip and crashed to the ground so hard she figured she'd created a small crater. Stunned, she held her breath and shut her eyes tightly for fear her fall had announced their location.

When she did not hear Mama's shrill voice, she squinted one eye open.

The man in the black robe was kissing her mother.

She gasped. The man had her mother pinned against the island in the center of the room. Their intertwined bodies moved in a slow rhythmic motion. Mama's long, thick, black hair was pulled into a fashionable bun. She reached up and released it, causing the tresses to cascade down the sides of her face and flow toward the countertop. The contrast of ebony hair against her pale skin gave her face a ghostly appearance.

Jasmin whimpered. Tears flowed down her face as her father's image came to mind. She missed him and now he was so far away, living in Spain. She hadn't seen him in years. Her mother's outrageous conduct rather than the fall caused her tears. *Why was Mama behaving this way?* She controlled her weeping, picked herself up, and raced across the patio to the zaguán, almost breaking the wooden door to get inside the casita.

CHAPTER EIGHTEEN

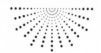

Agustín looked up from the book he was reading and calmly asked Jasmin what had happened.

"I fell out of the apple tree. My knee's broken."

He had her stand next to him and asked her to bend her knee. "You'll survive. Young bones heal quickly."

Then she told him what she'd seen in the kitchen.

He shook his head and stroked his mustache. He adjusted his position in the recliner.

"You're sure?" he asked. He stared across the room.

"Yes, Grandfather."

"Not that devil again. No wonder Leticia hasn't brought him around." He put the Dostoevsky he'd been reading on the side table next to *Jane Eyre*, a novel they'd read together.

"A *devil?*" Jasmin repeated.

Ignoring her, Agustín stood quickly, his bones creaking. He walked to the piano and adjusted the stool after he sat down.

Jasmin stepped next to the piano.

"Flip the switch to the loudspeakers on the patio," he said, thinking the loud music would bring out the neighbors to check what was going on. *When the neighbors return inside their homes, that man should want to sneak away. In that manner, I'll exorcise him right out of my house.* Feeling a little wicked, he smiled. "Go to the window and tell me if the kitchen lights are still on."

"Everything's dark," Jasmin reported. "Only the moonlight is falling on the trees and fountain."

"Tell me if the light comes on in your mother's bedroom."

His fingers glided over the keys with precision and speed, the only bones in his body that never complained when he moved them. His were the fingers of a young man. He pounded out a heavy, dissonant, rhythm-rousing, jazzy sound he knew his granddaughter had never heard him play.

Jasmin turned to the window and stared across the patio. Only a faint light emanated from Mama's room. The curtains in her bedroom parted and her figure appeared at the window, moonlight shining on her perfectly round breasts. Jasmin was shocked. She'd never seen her mother without clothes.

Her mother held her middle finger up in a very explicit manifestation of her displeasure for the music. She yanked the lace curtain around her body before disappearing from the window. The obscene hand gesture reminded Jasmin that her mother had used it when she was angry with Salva. Realizing that her mother was upset made her think back on the diary she'd taken. *If Mama is this indignant over the music Grandfather is playing, then surely, she'd be irate over the diary.* She'd throw Jasmin out of the house despite the years that had passed since she'd taken the journal.

Jasmin watched her mother disappear behind the curtains and pondered what her relationship might be now that her mother had a boyfriend. At best, she and Mama were courteous to each other. Never had they enjoyed the loving closeness most daughters experience with their mothers.

At times like this, Jasmin missed her father the most. She hardly heard from him now that he'd remarried in Spain and was living and working there. He'd always made her feel special. She knew he loved her and so did her grandfather. Her thoughts brought her mind back to the moonlight sparkling through the leaves and bouncing off the surface of the water in the fountain.

Grandfather softened the jazz and spoke over it, inquiring if her mother had reacted yet.

"She's disappeared behind the curtains and bright lights are now on in her room," she reported.

"Good." Then she heard him say under his breath, "that should take the devil away."

"What music are you playing?" she asked.

"'The Black Saint and the Sinner Lady.' Jazz with a message."

Without preamble, he switched to Rossini's "Sins of Old Age."

Or "Péchés de Vieillesse," as Grandfather would have her say when he corrected her French. Jasmin's pronunciation of the language of romance and ancient diplomacy carried such a heavy Mexican accent that it was hard for her grandfather to keep from laughing. They both giggled whenever he coached her to make the correct sound. "Your tongue should rest against the tip of your upper front teeth when you pronounce a French T, like this." He would point to his own mouth and demonstrate. "The tongue should not be behind your teeth as in Spanish. French sounds are softer." She always retorted that Ts, like tigers, are meant to sound strong and forceful.

Turning toward the piano, she watched his fingers at the keyboard again.

"If you're sending Mama a message, why did you select 'Sins of Old Age'? She might think you're hinting at your own sins."

"Very good, Jasmin. You're so clever. But I want your mother to meditate on where sins can take a person."

"Meditate? All night?"

"No, ma petite princesse," he said. "She'd storm over here right now if not for the cats."

"Cats? Oops, I forgot to feed them. I'll do it now."

"Not yet. They're not accustomed to the jazz I played. Let me finish this piece. Then you can see if our cats are ready for a feast tonight."

Lost for a few seconds in the beauty of Grandfather's music,

Jasmin contemplated herself in the large, framed photo hanging on the wall above an elaborately carved buffet table. "My golden girl," Grandfather would say whenever he glanced at that picture. Her dark hair, green eyes, and olive skin came from her Spanish and Maya ancestors, he had always told her. Her grandfather spoke of the Maya people with reverence. According to the old gentleman, they may have been the first ones to discover the concept of zero, and they were very advanced in mathematics centuries before the Spanish arrived.

Jasmin studied the photo to see what could be wrong with her appearance that made Mama so distant, kept Mama from loving her much. At least, that's the way it felt. On the table was another photo of Jasmin as a baby, a small black-and-white picture in a silver standup frame. Her mother was holding her, standing next to Grandmother, on the driver's side of Grandmother's car. Her grandfather had told her that picture was taken about two weeks after she'd been born.

As her grandfather played the last notes, she asked him if he would give her a second music lesson after he scared the man in the black robe away. She could play the guitar this time.

"Not tonight, my darling pequeña. Instead, let's play four hands at the piano. What is your delight?"

"The Rite of Spring," she said.

Grandfather laughed. When he laughed the hardest, like right now, snorts escaped his throat, like breaths his lungs couldn't absorb, and the air had to escape sonorously. The tips of his mustache jumped into the act and vibrated with every snort.

"Jasmin, you're so witty for your age. Stravinsky's pagan ritual is exactly what I need to exorcise that man from my house. Should've thought of it myself."

She didn't understand what he meant when he praised her sense of humor, yet it made her happy when he laughed so strenuously at remarks she made.

Grandfather, still chuckling, adjusted the stool for her height. He nodded to give her the cue to start.

Jasmin lost herself in the music. And her grandfather smoothed over her mistakes to make the music sound beautiful.

"Concert quality," he said after they finished. "In its premiere, 'The

Auguries of Spring' brought on a riot of sorts in the hall. One historian described it as catcalls from an audience upset with the irregular rhythms. I do fear my music will cause your mother to riot tomorrow."

"Catcalls?" Jasmin gasped. She jumped up and pulled two cans of cat food from a cabinet in the kitchenette.

CHAPTER NINETEEN

Agustín sat in front of Leticia's desk prepared to make her realize the folly of her ways through careful handling of the situation. *To confront her directly*, he thought, *would only make her more stubborn in the pursuit of her first love.* That teenage love ended when he and Anita had sent their daughter to study at a private school in Mexico City. Leticia had fallen for the eligible brother of one of her classmates. Her devastated first love entered the seminary when he heard of her betrayal.

"Why the hell did you play that infernally loud music last night?" Leticia asked, getting to the topic she wanted to discuss.

"Just giving my granddaughter an education in music we have not yet covered."

"And you needed to put the loudspeakers on? To bring out the whole town? For all I know some of them may still be snooping around. Some may have seen my visitor leave."

"Visitor? May I ask who that might have been?" Agustín asked sarcastically.

"You old geezer, you are perfectly aware who came here. Jasmin tattled. My visitor came in secret. Until you alerted the townspeople to come out and line up like your stupid cats to listen to the music. They must have thought we had a party."

"Didn't you?" he asked.

"Didn't I what?"

"Have a party?"

Leticia sighed. She energetically tapped her fingernails, polished in blood red, on her desktop.

"Don't you think I did it for your own good?" Agustín asked.

"Inform the town?"

"No," he said, "to keep you from making a mistake. A mistake you may regret later."

"You're a good one to give advice. Mother told me on her deathbed all about the shenanigans you pulled. You killed her, you know."

"And did you not chase your husband away with this nonsense?" he asked, ignoring his daughter's accusations.

"My husband was hardly worth keeping. Besides, I didn't feel like supporting the bastard any longer."

"It was on my money," Agustín said. "Did you ever hear me complain? Do you think a priest will make a better living than a historian?"

Leticia told him not to start on that topic. She reminded him how hard she worked for the money he doled out to her. "In this godforsaken patch of dirt where we live, it's miraculous to get people to pay their rents on time."

"And I'd ask you not to be so harsh on Jasmin," Agustín said.

"For a kid who is gifted, she can be so damned naïve," Leticia blurted out.

"It's hard to be so smart at her age. Stop being critical." He bounced the tip of his cane onto the hardwood floor and waddled toward the door.

Agustín whipped around the corner as he left Leticia's office, almost bumping into Jasmin. Holding an index finger to his lips, he motioned for her to follow him to the casita.

"You mustn't eavesdrop on your mother that way," Agustín said.

"What did she mean that your shenanigans killed Grandmother?" she asked.

"Leticia meant that during my work as a colonel in the Mexican Army, I made certain decisions and took certain actions. Actions that had consequences."

"So her stress over your work killed Grandmother?"

"Indirectly. She claimed it caused a heart condition. She took medication but she still died of a heart attack. Look, she might have developed that illness even if I'd been a model husband. It broke my heart when she died."

They entered the casita and Agustín sat down.

Jasmin took the other chair. "I don't want you to die, Grandfather. It would break *my* heart."

"We must all die sometime. I know you'll be sad when I pass away. But you'll need to accept it. The Maya civilization that you love, they understood the cycle of life and death. And they accepted it. Do you understand me?"

"I guess." She looked distraught.

"Always remember our talks about the Maya," Agustín said, "they had great wisdom." He fidgeted with two books on his side table, placing *War and Peace* on top of Orwell's *Nineteen Eighty-Four*.

Jasmin still looked worried.

"As I said, life's actions bring consequences," Agustín said. "Like the situation your mother was talking about. It's a bittersweet memory. It was one of the best things I ever did, and yet it hurt your grandmother. She became angry and resentful over it."

"If it was so good and yet you have regrets, would you do it again?" Jasmin asked.

"Absolutely. Otherwise, I would not have—" Agustín stopped talking abruptly. Shifting his eyes, he looked across the room. "I have one regret in life. It's when I handled a student uprising in Mexico City. It happened so long ago and yet I still have nightmares over it."

"And that gave Grandmother a heart condition?"

"Not the student uprising. A different incident upset your grandmother..." His voice drifted to a whisper. "Anita never forgave me. And then she died of a heart attack."

"Whenever you die, Grandfather, I'll be sad and won't know what to do. Mama and I don't get along and my father lives in Madrid."

He reached out and touched Jasmin's face and patted it lightly. "You have been the biggest joy of my life. Don't ever forget it. And what have I told you to do, my sweet pequeña, whenever you're sad?"

"To play or sing 'Ode to Joy' and put my whole soul into it. Even if I sing thousands of Odes to Joy, I don't think I'd feel better if something happens to you."

"Then let's practice right now." He sat on the piano bench and adjusted it before Jasmin joined him.

They sang acapella, smiling and laughing through the words of Friedrich Schiller's poem that inspired "Ode to Joy," Beethoven's final movement in the Ninth symphony. They added the piano and sang to the music. Jasmin seemed lost in the words, "Away from our circle, all creatures drink of joy."

Agustín stopped and glanced at the antique clock hanging on the wall. "Your professor should be arriving. You need to get to class."

On the zaguán, she turned to face Zaggie so the robot would catch her identity before she continued across the patio.

Agustín watched her until she entered the classroom.

CHAPTER TWENTY

Jasmin felt excited that she'd turned thirteen. That meant she could do more meaningful projects. She and her physics professor were still making improvements on the spaceship. But today was Dr. Arroyo's turn to teach and she announced her birthday to him as soon as he arrived.

Arroyo immediately asked Leticia for permission to take Jasmin shopping at the crafts store in downtown Tlaxcala. Grandfather, ever eager to participate in extracurricular activities, joined them. He suggested taking a taxi to avoid the parking issues in town center.

At the shop, Arroyo asked her to pick out three large, handcrafted Talavera vases.

"That's my birthday gift to you. And now you'll need to fill them with papier-mâché flowers," he said.

The saleslady explained that local artists made the colorful blooms and people used them for weddings, quinceañera parties, feast days at the church, or simply to liven up a room.

Jasmin had never selected flowers and started picking one after another until her grandfather suggested she pick only the ones she liked best.

"The vases should not look crammed. Flowers need to breathe, like us," he said.

She giggled.

Before they left the shop, Arroyo asked for a packet of colored tissue paper.

Jasmin was carrying the flowers when they stepped into the street while the men carried the vases. They waited at the corner to flag a taxi. She saw an old, gray Ford pickup stopped at the intersection. As the light changed and the truck rolled by, she saw the driver's face.

"That's him, Grandfather. That's the man."

"Who?" he asked, sounding confused.

"The kidnapper. Hurry, before he gets away."

Her grandfather put the vase down and stepped off the sidewalk to take a photo of the license plate.

"Are you sure that was him?"

Jasmin nodded.

Her grandfather flagged a taxi. Instead of going straight home, he told the driver to take them to the police station and wait for them. They went inside and her grandfather spoke to the police chief. Two detectives in unmarked cars were dispatched to the highway leaving Tlaxcala. An alert with the license plate was released to state police. They were to detain the person driving the beat-up gray Ford.

With the reports filled out, Jasmin, her grandfather, and Arroyo returned home.

———

Despite the stress of the beat-up truck incident and reporting it to the police, Jasmin wanted to proceed with the plans Arroyo had suggested for dressing up the classroom for her birthday. They spent the afternoon making papel picado, festive cutouts of cats and guitars from the colored tissue. After they'd completed a dozen sheets or more, they glued strings at the two top corners, carefully folding the paper over to secure the string. Jasmin brought a ladder, nails, and a hammer from the shed and pounded nails into the ceiling's wooden beams as the professor held the ladder sturdy. She looped the strings over the nails.

"Looks like we're ready for a party," her grandfather said.

Jasmin stepped off the ladder and hugged him. "This is the best birthday ever."

"And it's not over yet," he said.

Noise outside the classroom, like people talking, caught Jasmin's attention. She folded the ladder to take it back to the shed. Opening the door, she saw a group of people, mostly kids. They burst into the birthday song, "Las Mañanitas." Further back in the patio, Lorenzo was hanging a pink and purple piñata, a donkey shape in her favorite colors. Lola held a wooden stick, obviously to be used for destroying the piñata.

Jasmin stumbled out the door, dragging the ladder. Her mother rushed toward her, pressing forward, giving her a big hug.

"Happy birthday. You're a teenager now!"

Struggling to breathe, Jasmin dropped the ladder and backed away from her mother. On the patio, Lola was putting final touches on food and drink set out on a long table. And the kids, about ten of them, were lining up to get soft drinks. The patio turned blurry. Jasmin rubbed her eyes to focus on the scene. Her breathing became labored, and she ran back inside the classroom.

Her grandfather took her by the hand and coaxed her outside. She looked across the patio. Lola had the stick in her hand once more and kids were jumping and begging to be first at taking turns on the piñata. The noise level rose in her head.

Lola spotted Jasmin and rushed to her.

"The birthday girl gets the first try," she said, handing Jasmin the stick. Lola walked her, almost pushing her, to the piñata.

Lorenzo pulled the rope, lifting the donkey higher. Lola wrapped a bandana over Jasmin's eyes, twirled her around twice, and led her closer to the piñata. Everyone yelled instructions.

"Higher."

"Lower."

"Swing at it."

"It's in front of you."

"Right now. Hit it!"

She swiped the air with the stick. Yelling erupted. Everyone gave commands and directions. Jasmin had hit the rope. From the laughter and chatter that followed, it must have made the donkey catapult around the rope. Ripping the bandana off, Jasmin handed it and the stick to Lola, stuttering that it was the next person's turn.

Chairs lined the edge of the patio. As soon as she could, Jasmin stumbled toward one and sat down. She crossed her arms. Dazed and lighthearted, she felt nauseous. She had to think. About anything. *Think*, she told herself.

"One hundred ninety-six thousand, four hundred and eighteen—"

Grandfather placed his hand on her shoulder.

"Come, Jasmin, let's go to the stables." He took her hand and crossed the patio, passing her mother on the way.

"What's happening?" Leticia asked.

"We're going to the stables."

"She can't leave. This is her party."

"We need to be alone," Grandfather growled. "It's been a rough day."

Jasmin didn't remember saddling Ixchel, but she did notice when her grandfather helped her into the saddle and handed her the reins. He pulled himself onto the mare's hindquarters, riding double, like they had done many times when she was younger.

She started reciting numbers again.

"Take a deep breath," her grandfather coaxed her. "And let it out slowly."

After a few minutes of concentration on her breathing, Jasmin relaxed, and she loosened the reins. Ixchel took them toward the paddock.

Her grandfather got a call on his cell. When he finished, he told Jasmin the police had found the gray pickup. It was abandoned near the city dump. The license plate on the vehicle was a stolen one. They'd found no fingerprints. At the moment, the investigators had no further leads.

CHAPTER TWENTY-ONE

The day after Jasmin's birthday, De la Mota arrived and handed her a gift box, wishing her a belated birthday. He glanced at the vases with papier-mâché flowers. "A present?" he asked.

"Mama had a party for me."

"A party?"

"She invited kids. They were from the neighborhood, but I don't really know them. Arroyo came and gave me the vases."

De la Mota's expression changed at the mention of the other professor.

Jasmin tore the wrapping paper off the box he had brought. Inside, was a wooden carving of a cat. It was pink and purple, her favorite colors, the same ones as the donkey piñata. The box contained two other packages. One was a video series on exoplanet exploration produced by NASA. The second one was a small helmet for the wooden cat.

She kissed the kitty's nose. "I'll name you Alba."

"Why Alba?" De la Mota asked.

"Dawn—the dawn of a new era. Of civilians traveling in space, maybe even earthlings visiting planets outside our solar system."

"Alba won't complain about being inside a spaceship," he said, chuckling.

She placed Alba on the recumbent seat inside the capsule. "She can travel with me on our next mission." Jasmin took out the video series. "Oh, can I view these on Maya Explorer's monitors?"

"That's the idea," he said.

"Can I see them now?"

De la Mota nodded. "As soon as you climb into the spaceship, Astronaut Jasmin Dominguez."

She felt like Alice in Wonderland about to explore the frontier of space. Instead of going down a rabbit hole, Jasmin would follow Alba into the capsule and together they would explore another solar system. She didn't know if they'd encounter the Cheshire Cat or any of the three queens, but she envisioned a far more fantastical trip than even Alice had experienced in Wonderland.

She put a helmet on her head. It was not complete yet, but she wanted to wear it since she would place one on Alba, too. She selected a video in the exoplanet series and, placing the tiny helmet on Alba, she told her new kitten they would launch soon and explore Alpha Centauri, the closest solar system to our own.

"Our Maya Explorer will produce an infinite amount of energy so we can travel several times the speed of light," Jasmin fantasized out loud.

De la Mota could hear her conversation. He left the hatch open since they did not have the air supply hooked up inside the capsule right now.

"Get ready! We'll circumnavigate Proxima b, the planet in Alpha Centauri most likely to host life forms." She gripped Alba tightly in her hand, intent on the video as the planet came into view. In that moment, it felt like the real thing. She got goose bumps.

After experiencing the Alpha Centaurium solar system on the video, Jasmin climbed out of the capsule and took her helmet off. She hugged De la Mota and thanked him for the wonderful gift. He listened to her as she talked about getting bigger monitors for the control panel.

"That way, I'll see other solar systems even better," she said putting a stick of gum in her mouth.

De la Mota cut the teaching session short, saying he needed to talk to her mother before he left.

The professor sat in the chair closest to Leticia's desk. Jasmin took a seat and peered down at her shoes. Her feet now reached the floor.

"Run along, Jasmin. Go to the stables while Dr. De la Mota and I talk."

Jasmin walked to the hallway leading to the patio, banging the door as loud as she could on her way outside. She crawled to a position under her mother's open window and propped her back against the stuccoed adobe wall. Chewing her gum fiercely for a few more seconds, she took it out and stuck it on the underside of a flowerpot with other wads of used gum. She listened to the conversation flowing through the window. Sojón walked up quietly and brushed against her body.

After a bit of small talk, which was not Leticia's strong point, De la Mota cleared his throat.

"I'm here to recommend that you enroll your daughter at the university in Mexico City. She qualifies for a master's program in the fall. That's only a semester away. She's doing graduate level math and physics. In fact, I've had graduate assistants in the last four years who fall way below her intelligence."

"I won't even consider it," her mother said.

Jasmin heard her mother's fingernails tapping the desktop impatiently. She thought back to her mother's bright red fingernails the night she kissed the priest. She didn't know what to think of her mother being alone in her office with a man, like when Mama had been in the kitchen with the priest. She hoped her mother would not kiss her professor. Before her parents' divorce, she'd seen them kissing. But that seemed okay because they were married.

"Why not?" De la Mota asked.

"She's just turned thirteen."

"Yes, I heard you invited Dr. Arroyo to her birthday party."

"Not really. That was the day he came to teach. The party was for kids her age, but I shouldn't have bothered. She's not a normal kid; she didn't even stay for her own party."

"About the university," De la Mota continued, "that's her environment. That's where she'll excel."

"She excels at music," her mother said. "You've heard her play. And horses, she loves to ride when she's not working on your projects. Archaeology and music are also her loves, not just the subjects you teach her."

"Have you not thought she's happiest with activities that involve math and physics?"

"Listen," Mama said, "she has everything she needs right here, including her grandfather, the most important person in her life."

De la Mota was not deterred. He suggested sending her grandfather to the city with Jasmin. Then he added he'd soon be reaching the limit of what he could teach her at home. Lectures were only half of it. She'd need to carry out experiments in a proper lab.

Sojón meowed. Jasmin held her breath, hoping her mother would not get up and stick her head out the window to scare the cat away. She picked him up and held him in her lap.

"And she loves those dreadful cats," Mama said. "And the horses. She can't take her mare to Mexico City. Besides, my father provides the best one-on-one education money can buy. Right here at home." Her fingernail tapping got louder.

Jasmin exhaled when she realized her mother was not going to get up and scream at Sojón.

"She needs to expand her horizons," the professor said, "and interact with other people."

"Interact?" Mama scoffed. "And who might you suggest? She couldn't interact at her party with kids her own age. They can't pronounce half the words she uses, let alone carry on a conversation on the latest archaeological digs in Egypt or the effects of Mozart's music on the brain. Even I cannot converse with my daughter."

Her mother's words pierced Jasmin's heart. She squeezed Sojón so hard he meowed again and jumped from her lap.

"All I'm saying is she's growing up," De la Mota said, "and maybe you should prepare her for adulthood. Think about it. I'm happy to recommend her for a graduate program. Remember, she finishes her baccalaureate degree at the end of the spring semester. You should find an educational program to further develop her talent."

"Her talent," Leticia said, choking on the words. "That's all I hear from my father. Her damned talent."

De la Mota ignored the comment. Instead, he described a drone Jasmin had built in class. "There's a contest in two weeks. She's designing a new one and I'd like to sponsor her."

"Drones?" Mama asked.

"She builds them from scratch."

"My daughter does that?" Leticia asked, surprised. "I thought they came in a kit."

"She uses the 3-D printer to make the plastic parts and circuitry, materials left over from building the space capsule."

When Leticia learned the drone race was going to be in the city of Puebla, she consented. De la Mota invited her to attend, but she declined. That was the day she had to collect rents on the farm properties. Jasmin heard her mother move her chair to see him out.

Leticia thanked him, telling De la Mota she'd consider talking to her father about sending Jasmin to the university. But added she did not think Jasmin was ready for the big city.

Jasmin crept away from the window. Once she was out of sight, she stood and ran to the casita. When she burst in, her grandfather put his book down.

"De la Mota asked Mama to send me away. And I won't go." Her heart was beating fast, like it did when she had the recurring nightmare.

"Send you away? Where?" her grandfather asked.

"Mama hates me, hates me because I'm smart. What does she want from me? She didn't even know I designed drones. Drones! She obviously didn't know I'd designed a whole spaceship. Did she think Maya Explorer also came from an erector set? That's where she thought my drones came from."

CHAPTER TWENTY-TWO

Early the next morning, Jasmin was exercising Ixchel in the paddock when Lola came running to the stables and flagged her over.

"I'm afraid you're in trouble again," Lola said. "Your mother has summoned your grandfather to her office."

After dismounting, Jasmin handed Ixchel's reins to Lola. Lorenzo would unsaddle the mare and turn her loose in the pasture.

Jasmin raced to the house and entered her room to remove her boots. Scurrying down the hallway, she hid under the stairs.

Over the years, she'd learned that the more indignant and irate Mama became, the more she lowered her voice. Right now, it was approximating a harsh and bitter whisper. She heard her mother say that De la Mota had suggested Jasmin should attend the university in Mexico City.

"At first I didn't like the idea, but after giving it some thought, it sounds like a good plan," Mama said.

"We should consider it," Agustín said, "and other options too. What about the University of the Americas in Puebla? It's so close, I could drive her myself."

Leticia objected. "Neither engineering nor business school are for her." She went on to explain that De la Mota recommended graduate studies in physics and math. "He convinced me, and my decision is final. Even if I'm not close to my daughter, I want the best education for her. Mexico City offers more opportunities."

"It sounds ludicrous," Grandfather said. "Mexico City is not a good place for a girl her age. We've overprotected her, you know."

"As you're always telling me, we need to develop her brilliant mind," Mama said, with a mocking laugh. "What precisely troubles you about sending her to the city?"

Grandfather was silent for several seconds.

Jasmin held her breath and waited, expecting her mother and grandfather to get into a confrontation.

"It's a huge university with too many dangers for her. She's very smart, but she's still a child."

"Ah, I think you're concerned your secrets might come out.

Grandfather's secrets? Jasmin wondered. *What's Mama talking about?*

"She could be kidnapped," Grandfather said.

"That's why you should also move. We'll hire a governess to drive her to class and back, and even manage the household for the two of you. If you prefer a police escort, you still have a few contacts."

"Don't be flippant," her grandfather said. He argued in favor of the nearby university in Puebla so Jasmin could live at home. They offer a mathematics program even if not as prestigious as the one in Mexico City. He emphasized a chauffeur could drive her back and forth, and more importantly, he could continue her music and language lessons.

"If you go with her, you can purchase a new piano in the city."

"You think I don't know why you want to be left alone here?" Grandfather asked. "With us away, you can have midnight visits anytime."

Leticia ignored his comment and said, "There's no reason you can't move there and take care of her. The two of you are so close. You can't live without her, and she can't survive without you."

"Let me think about it."

"Should I assume you'll move with her?" Mama asked. "Or will I have to rely on a governess to take care of her?"

"I'll speak with Jasmin," he said, "and see how she feels about it."

Jasmin did not need her grandfather to catch her listening to them. She raced to her room and put on her boots. When she arrived at the stables, Lorenzo was grooming Ixchel with a hard-bristle brush, using short strokes in the direction of the hair growth on her back.

Jasmin picked up a soft face brush to clean the mare's head. "Mama is trying to send me away," she whispered to Ixchel, "but I won't leave you. We're soulmates. We belong here together. Mama's the one who should go live in Mexico City. And take her priest-friend with her."

When Jasmin and Lorenzo finished brushing Ixchel, she stepped back to admire the mare's shiny golden coat. She picked up the saddle pad and placed it on the mare's back. Lorenzo seemed surprised Jasmin was going to ride again. Yet he heaved the saddle up and cinched it tight.

Just as they finished saddling Ixchel, her mother came out to the stables. Lorenzo's eyes always lit up whenever he caught sight of Leticia. Grandfather had told Jasmin he thought the old gentleman had a crush on Mama.

Jasmin pulled herself into the saddle and took off before her mother could stop her. When she got to the meadow, she looked toward the stables and saw her mother and Lorenzo talking.

CHAPTER TWENTY-THREE

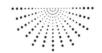

Jasmin and De la Mota invited everyone to the classroom to watch the live transmission of SpaceX's Dragon rocket liftoff from Cape Canaveral, Florida. She'd been reading about it online and could hardly contain her excitement about a spaceship carrying civilian astronauts to the International Space Station. Arroyo was not there that day and Mama didn't show up.

When weather conditions prevented the astronauts from launching, De la Mota made an exception to his schedule and returned the following day to watch the next launch attempt with them.

The aroma of dessert empanadas and coffee Lola had prepared wafted through the classroom. She handed Jasmin a steaming cup of honey-milk chamomile.

They watched the Kennedy Space Center's launch preparations on the classroom monitor. Jasmin could not sit still. She wished she could wormhole herself into one of the Tesla cars carrying crew members. *If only I can throw myself through the live feed.*

Her heart pounded in her ears, and she wiped her sweaty hands on her pants as the launch proceeded through the countdown. She jumped when white smoke spewed from the base.

"It's okay, that's normal," De la Mota said about the smoke.

The rocket lifted and headed skyward.

Leticia stepped into the classroom.

"Look, Mama, if I had the materials to build a better spaceship, I could fly like those astronauts."

Leticia glanced at the rocket racing into the sky on the monitor. "If that means you'd get lost in space, I should reconsider." She laughed.

A chill hit the room. Despite the live feed, everyone's attention turned to Leticia.

"I was only joking," she said, shrugging her shoulders.

"Then stop joking," Agustín said, every word clipped. "You're so cruel."

Leticia's criticism hurt Jasmin. From the expressions on her grandfather's, Lola's, and De la Mota's faces, they seemed upset by the remark.

Jasmin thought about the giant spider of her nightmares. If only it would come to life right now and knock Mama over for that vicious comment. Then she remembered her grandfather telling her not to be unkind to people, so she dismissed the thought.

When the live feed focused on people making speeches, De la Mota turned it off.

The professor stayed for a couple of hours after the launch. He and Jasmin discussed future projects in physics and aerodynamics. As they spoke, Jasmin thought that even simple projects, like building drones, were fundamental to physics and science. These projects could prepare her to work on forward-looking sustainability solutions for the world. Archaeology, though fascinating, was an art of the past.

When Jasmin went to bed that night, she thought of Mama's words about getting lost in space. Her thoughts returned to the rocket launch and soon she fell asleep. In the middle of the night, the recurring nightmare awakened her with a start. The diary sprang out of the drawer, shed the dustcover, and grew eyes and legs. Instead of racing down the hallway and knocking Mama over, this time the leather diary thrust out a head that resembled her mother's. Eyes popped out and spider legs mushroomed from the body. Faceless, sinister figures crowded around the bed. The spider monster grew ever bigger. It came toward her and hovered over the bed. Jasmin wanted to escape, but she was paralyzed. She could feel the monster's breath and she willed herself to run.

The monster was about to devour her, but her body wouldn't move.

She screamed.

The unfathomable monster vanished, and she could move again.

She heard running in the hallway. Scared, she pulled the covers over her head.

Lola ran into the room and turned the light on. Leticia was right behind her.

"What's wrong?" Mama asked. She sat on the edge of the bed and reached for her daughter's hand.

"A nightmare."

"Can you tell me about it?" Leticia asked.

Jasmin sat up and stared at the bedcover, saying she couldn't remember. There was no way she could tell her mother about it. All she said was that it had been very scary. A monster had come for her. And several other dark figures. The afterimages still haunted her.

"There's no monster here," Mama said. "I'll stay until you go back to sleep. I'll sing a lullaby that would put you to sleep when you were a baby."

"But I'm not a baby anymore."

Her mother still sang the lullaby.

Jasmin pretended to fall asleep.

CHAPTER TWENTY-FOUR

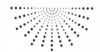

J asmin finished breakfast and Lola walked her to the classroom. They passed the miniature Kukulkán pyramid and Jasmin stopped to admire it, thinking how much she'd enjoyed building it.

"We're going to test the prototype capsule this afternoon. You helped me build it so you must come to watch."

Lola nodded and smiled. Jasmin entered the classroom. De la Mota was already sitting at his desk staring at his computer screen.

In the corner opposite De la Mota's desk, Jasmin's spaceship sat reminding her of the immense amount of work still pending on it. What they called Maya Explorer consisted of the shiny steel capsule. They still had to build the rocket portion.

"Let's make final adjustments for the test," De la Mota suggested. "And we'll invite everyone to join us this afternoon."

"I wish we could purchase the aluminum composites, titanium alloys, and silica tiles needed for the thermal shield. With a shield, my prototype could be the real thing, worthy of actual space flight."

"We have not built the rocket yet, so let's concentrate on what we have accomplished," De la Mota said. "Besides your grandfather has always told you the Maya Explorer would never leave the earth's atmosphere. Or even the patio for that matter."

Yet Jasmin dreamed about flying it. "After we build the rocket, maybe we can send it up five or six hundred feet above the shores of Lake Alchichica and retrieve the capsule in the middle of the lake."

"That's a good idea," De la Mota said, "as long as the capsule is unmanned."

"'Unmanned'? You must mean 'unfemaled.'"

De la Mota chuckled.

Over lunch, the professor invited Agustín, Leticia, and Lola to join them for the test.

Every critical system on the capsule had a backup to ensure functionality and to aid in survivability in case of an emergency. They were operated by switches built into the side of the seat and already had been tested. Mostly, they controlled the backup air and heating. Today's test would validate the backup systems.

Once the hatch would be closed, the air system inside the Maya Explorer would consist of 80 percent nitrogen and 20 percent oxygen, like air on earth. Jasmin had researched the NASA websites and found that for the Apollo program pure oxygen had been provided for the astronauts. The pressure in space is so great that regular air cannot be used for there would not be sufficient air to breathe. Spacesuits are equipped with pure oxygen. Jasmin knew that if she ever worked at the International Space Station and walked in space, she'd breathe pure oxygen. Inside the station the air is similar to regular air on earth.

They were also testing the larger fuel cells they'd built to generate electricity inside the capsule.

"Time to put your suit on," De la Mota said. "Throw your chewing gum away."

Jasmin heard the exuberance in his voice. She took a box from inside the capsule. It contained her spacesuit and helmet. She'd manufactured the shell of the helmet with the 3D printer and added air supply connections, communication devices, and cushioning material.

The spacesuit was another matter. She'd designed it and sent the specs to a seamstress in the village.

Excusing herself, she went into the bathroom to change.

The seamstress had sewn four fabrics into a pressure suit that resembled a crude version of an astronaut's uniform. The innermost layer of nylon tricot material felt smooth against her skin. The next layer, Spandex, made it snug. Of the next two pressurization layers, the inner one was made of urethane-coated nylon and contained bubbles, called bladders, that would partially fill with either oxygen or, in Jasmin's case, with air. The final and outermost layer was made from Dacron. It worked to retain the pressure in the finished outfit. She made sure the suit's umbilical cord was draped over her arm so she could keep it from dragging on the floor before stepping into her boots. Next came the helmet. She attached the umbilical cord that would provide the air supply. The cord was old technology left from the days of NASA's Gemini program, but they'd decided it was good enough for their purposes. The helmet also connected to the communication system. She put the gloves on and grabbed Alba to take into the capsule with her.

De la Mota already had his headset on. He had called their guests to come and watch. He'd placed a step ladder next to the capsule for Jasmin to use. With a spacesuit on, it was cumbersome to climb inside. She handed Alba to him.

Her mother's scorn came to mind every time Jasmin climbed inside the Maya Explorer. Today, that thought evaporated quickly. They were doing a full test of what they'd built. That was almost as exciting as going into space. She was probably the only astronaut who had built her own spaceship.

Before she got in, De la Mota handed her a life support backpack that would be secured under the seat.

"Just in case you decide to take a spacewalk," De la Mota said, joking.

Jasmin's helmet bobbed up and down as she laughed at his comment.

Once she settled into the seat and strapped herself in, the professor handed Alba to her. She secured her pink and purple companion in a little seat she'd attached to the edge of the control panel.

Next, she plugged the umbilical cord into the outlet in the seat. It started the flow of air. De la Mota's instructions filtered into her helmet perfectly. She was in the process of turning on the monitors when her grandfather peered at her through the open hatch. His handlebar mustache looked comical with the communication head-piece he had put on to talk with her.

"Is Mama coming out?" she asked.

Grandfather shook his head. "She's busy collecting rents and promises to be present next time we run a major test. Lola is here with us."

De la Mota closed the hatch. For safety purposes, it could not be locked.

"Capsule Communicator at Command Control to Astronaut and Space Traveler Jasmin Dominguez, can you read?"

"Roger, that's a positive, Command Control," Jasmin responded, echoing phrases she had learned from NASA videos.

For the next hour, De la Mota gave precise instructions for a series of tests. When he turned the air off, Jasmin flipped the emergency switch to get it flowing again. She was so elated when she felt the air gently tickling her nose that she tried to jump out of her seat only to be constrained by the seat belt.

The touchscreen monitors ran a video from a rocket propelling skyward looking back at the space center on the ground. She watched the earth recede and felt the sensation of what it would be like to launch into space. Except that Maya Explorer did not have a gravitational force simulator due to price considerations. They'd considered building one, but the cost would have been prohibitively expensive. In every other respect, the experiment, including the test on the new fuel cells, was performed without a single snag. They'd reached a milestone.

It was exhilarating!

That night Jasmin still felt intoxicated from the success of the full system test they'd run. Eventually she fell asleep.

The dresser drawer banged open and the diary flew over Jasmin's bed. Several heads popped out; their bulging eyes stared down at Jasmin. She awakened with a start. She could move this time. Ordering the monster and the sinister figures to go away, she was surprised when they disappeared. Once again, the afterimage lingered.

With hesitation she got out of bed, turned the light on, and opened the drawer. Taking out her mother's leather-bound diary, she crawled back in bed and leafed through the book.

The anxiety the nightmares provoked had kept her from opening the book for several years. Tonight, she found fragments of poems, snippets of thoughts, and doodles.

Just as she remembered, the poems spoke of love. Her mother had used the familiar Shakespearean sonnet structure for most of them. A line or two of doodles were often added below the rhymed couplet. She studied the scribbles more closely and discovered symbols she recognized. The more familiar ones, like two crosses, were repeated frequently. The script was not sophisticated like Egyptian hieroglyphics, yet she studied the repeated patterns and re-read the poems thinking they might serve as a kind of Rosetta stone to help decipher the doodles.

It did not take long to discover that the two crosses meant the priest and Mama had used the female symbol, a circle with a cross below it to denote herself. As Jasmin deciphered more, she could not understand what had been so secretive that it caused a permanent rift between her parents. She soon became bored with the writings and hid the diary in its usual place.

Would it make any sense to return it? Jasmin thought back to her mother's anger the day she'd discovered it missing. *No, Mama would ask me to leave. It's best to avoid a confrontation.*

Soon Jasmin fell asleep.

PART II

CHAPTER TWENTY-FIVE

The condo building in Mexico City sat at the edge of Chapultepec Park overlooking a wooded area replete with birds, snakes, rodents, and lizards. The plentiful cypress trees spread thick, fibrous, knotted root systems that spread along the surface of the ground before descending into the soil. Their wide trunks attracted a lot of woodpeckers. Jasmin's grandfather told her that the oldest of those trees were already there when Cortez arrived in 1519.

In the week since they'd arrived, she had come to love the panorama through the wall of windows. Yet she yearned for the family home in Ocotlán with its patio filled with fruit trees, jacaranda bushes, and flowering trellises. She missed Mama and Lola. She missed Ixchel and the stables the most. Her mare had played such an important role in her life that thinking about Ixchel made her sad.

Jasmin also longed for the zaguán. That wonderful gathering place of cats could not be reproduced in the condo. And Alonso, the oldest of the cats, had died a few days before they had left the village. She missed him. She couldn't decide if she missed Alonso or if it was the memories of all three cats eating on the zaguán that brought nostalgia.

She hummed "Ode to Joy" to feel better.

Deep inside, she felt that the worst part of moving to the big city was abandoning the spaceship project just when she would have started construction on the rocket. De la Mota and her grandfather had always told her it would never launch with her inside, but that hadn't stopped her from dreaming. Now she had to form new aspirations. De la Mota suggested she prepare for a career as an astronaut or an engineer for a space exploration company.

Her grandfather had hired a decorator to furnish the condo in rustic Mexican style furniture. In addition to their personal belongings, her grandfather had brought a few items from the casita, such as the buffet table. He placed it near the entry, with the picture of Leticia holding Jasmin as a baby and Anita standing with them on top of it. He claimed the table and the picture showing three generations of the women in his family made the condo seem like home. On their second day in the city, Grandfather had taken her to purchase a piano.

Gleaming white kitchen appliances had come with the condo, but since Lola had remained in Ocotlán, Jasmin wasn't sure who was going to use the new kitchen. Grandfather had arranged for a nearby restaurant to deliver meals to them. He and Jasmin took turns heating food in the microwave and loading the dishwasher. By the time they'd settled in, her summer semester was about to start.

She had brought her mother's diary to Mexico City and placed it in a drawer, as she had in Ocotlán, under blouses and sweaters. She feared her mother would find it if she left it behind. Alba the cat with her tiny helmet sat on a floating shelf along with her own helmet on the wall of her bedroom. The homemade spacesuit hung in the closet.

The following week her classes would start at the university. De la Mota was one of her advisors, and that made Jasmin feel good. Her grandfather had hired Gabriela, a graduate student in mathematics, to drive her to class and help with her orientation on campus. Jasmin assumed she was also there to protect her.

Jasmin felt excited about her first day of class and was happy when Gabriela arrived early at the condo to drive her to the university. On the streets, Jasmin was amazed by the endless flow of vehicles of all sizes, makes, and colors. The cars were so close together that they moved like a multi-colored blanket. Gabriela inched into the fray, and the momentum of the vehicles pushed them along. She eased toward a ramp and got on a loop around the city that she called the Anillo Periférico.

On campus, Jasmin admired the colorful murals on buildings they walked past on the way to her first class. Students were everywhere: groups standing around talking and laughing, others scurrying as if they were late, and more that seemed mindfully heading to a specific place. Gabriela took Jasmin up a few steps of a building to a landing with a glass-encased entrance.

Inside, Gabriela accompanied Jasmin to a small lecture hall and asked her where she wanted to sit. The room, equipped like a home theater, was reserved for graduate-level courses. She took Jasmin to the front of the room and told her she'd be waiting outside the hall when the class ended.

Another student was sitting on the row Jasmin selected. He stood and moved over a couple of seats. "You and your daughter can sit here."

Gabriela laughed, introducing herself and Jasmin, and added that she was not her daughter.

"I'm Akifumi Sato," he said, after apologizing. "Call me Aki." Of Japanese ancestry, Akifumi wore thick-lensed glasses and a shirt partially tucked into his pants. He sported a long, stringy ponytail.

The professor walked in shortly after Gabriela had left. Akifumi looked around the room and asked if Jasmin's friend would return before class started.

"I'm the student, not Gabriela."

He blinked several times in rapid succession. "How old are you?"

"Almost fourteen. I'll be fourteen before the end of the year." Jasmin sat up a bit straighter.

He nodded. "I'm almost twenty. I thought I'd be the youngest person in this class."

The professor welcomed the students to the summer session and asked them to sign up online for the required lab. Four lab times were scheduled, enabling students to pick the one that suited them.

Akifumi leaned over and asked if Jasmin cared to be in the same lab with him.

She nodded.

As the semester progressed, Jasmin and Aki talked about their lab projects. Soon they found themselves talking about their personal lives too. One day, Jasmin mentioned she was studying physics to make it possible to work for a space exploration company.

"Do you want to be an astronaut?" Aki asked.

"That's pretty much all I want," she replied.

"Really? I'd also like to go into space," he said. "Maybe someday I'll fly to Mars. Where are you planning to go?"

"The whole galaxy. And I want to see the golden spiral of the Milky Way up close. Figure out why it resembles the Fibonacci sequence and see if it's woven into the topology of space time."

"If space travel advances quickly, maybe you'll get to travel in the galaxy. To do it, time travel needs to be possible. Or using wormholes, like a water slide, to go where no one has gone before."

"Hibernation for humans on long journeys in space, like traveling to Mars, would make the trip easier and save energy," she said.

"I just read something about that," Aki affirmed.

In addition to sharing their lab work, the two students often met in the library to prepare for exams. One day Aki used a pen to make notations in a spiral notebook. He put the pen on the table. Jasmin picked it up and commented that it looked like white marble with a random gold-colored design.

"That's kintsugi," he said when he noticed Jasmin studying it. He passed it to her. "It's a ceramic pen that belonged to my grandfather. I dropped it and I put the pieces back together with liquid gold. Kintsugi's an ancient Japanese art form."

Jasmin handed it back to him. "It's very pretty."

"You can have it."

She shook her head. "It was your grandfather's. You should keep it."

"Okay, then someday I'll do a kintsugi for you."

Jasmin liked the idea of Kintsugi. *If only a little gold would repair my relationship with Mama.*

By the fall semester, Jasmin felt a bit more comfortable on campus. One day, De la Mota sent Jasmin a text asking her to visit him in his office. She was studying in the library, and she asked Aki to walk with her. She introduced her fellow student to the professor.

De la Mota told them he'd secured a television interview at Televisa, the large media conglomerate. They wanted Jasmin on a program devoted to news on science and technology. Apparently, the media organization was interested in the age she would be upon graduating with a master's degree in quantum physics.

"I'll ask Grandfather. Make sure he's okay with it."

"If you're interested, I'll call your grandfather," De la Mota said.

Jasmin told them she was not particularly excited about being on television.

"If they see a teenager like you mastering math and physics," Aki said, "you'll be an inspiration."

De la Mota agreed.

Jasmin asked him to wait a week or so before approaching her grandfather. She needed to talk it over with him.

Aki walked with her back to the library.

"You're the one friend I can actually talk with," she told him. "You remind me of my grandfather."

"Me?" Aki asked, surprised. He smiled and added, "must be my slanted eyes that remind you of him. But he's a lot older than me."

Jasmin's face reddened. "I mean that I can discuss stuff with you, and you seem interested in what I have to say. That's the way my grandfather is too."

Aki high-fived her.

"I'm still uneasy about life in the big city, and I feel lucky to have you as a friend," she told him. "You seem so comfortable with all the people around us. Just this university has a population of three hundred and fifty thousand students. It gives me the jitters."

CHAPTER TWENTY-SIX

J asmin became friends with Gabriela very quickly, but it was not the same as her friendship with Aki. Although Gabriela knew a lot about mathematics, she was not interested in theoretical physics, an important part of Jasmin's life, a part that she did share with Aki. Yet her governess fit right into the lifestyle Jasmin and her grandfather had. Gabriela often went on outings organized by Colonel Campos. Aki accompanied them at times too. And when he did, he and Jasmin spent hours discussing the latest findings in the various fields of physics while Gabriela talked with Agustín about politics.

With the cooler air of the fall season, Jasmin hungered to ride Ixchel and walk among her old projects. She wanted to see Lola. Relations with her mother had never been the greatest, but she thought things might have improved and Mama might be happy to see her. She asked her grandfather if they could visit Ocotlán.

Gabriela offered to drive them to the village.

Sunshine filled the morning as they traveled from Mexico City to the state of Puebla and eventually to the turnoff to Tlaxcala. With little visible pollution, the Popocatepetl and Iztaccíhuatl volcanoes offered splendid views. The scenery must have ignited her grandfather's memory, for he spoke about the beauty of Puebla and Tlaxcala, even mentioning the highlands of Puebla, where apples are grown.

"They're more delicious than the ones from our patio. And it would have been nice to attend the apple fair in the mountain village of Zacatlán de las Manzanas, but I cannot take both of you away for that long. I used to know a young woman who was from there. Her family gave me crates of apples. The best I ever tasted," he said with a nostalgic sigh.

They arrived in Ocotlán at noon, in time to chat with Leticia for the better part of an hour before washing up for lunch. Lola prepared tlacoyos, a pre-Hispanic predecessor to the taco made with thick corn masa, black beans, cooked cactus paddles, pork cracklings which Lola substituted for the turkey meat originally used by the native Mexicans, chile sauce, and a sprinkling of cilantro.

Jasmin was excited about being home. She'd brought her mother a small gift wrapped in a box.

"This one is an Aztec jaguar," she said when her mother opened it. It was as nice as a jaguar throne she had brought her mother from Chichén Itzá four years ago.

"Another cat," Mama said, turning it over.

"It's cuauhxicalli," Jasmin said, holding her breath, hoping her mother would like it.

"This one is not a throne, like the other one you gave me," her mother said. Then she gazed at Jasmin intently. "The Aztecs used cuauhxicalli as a vessel for holding the heart and blood of people, mostly young women sacrificed to the gods. Women about your age."

Leticia's words sounded chilling, even though she'd said them with a smile.

Jasmin could tell the gift had not pleased her mother. "You can put it in your office with the one from Chichén Itzá," she stuttered.

"Oh, that one broke and I threw it away. You should know I don't like cats." Leticia looked around the table, confirming everyone had finished their coffee and dessert. She mentioned Lorenzo could saddle horses for anyone who wanted to ride. She had organized a concert for that evening and had invited friends to listen to Agustín and Jasmin play the piano in the zaguán.

Jasmin was excited to show the stables to Gabriela. The second they stepped on the patio, a loud clanking alarm announced Gabriela's presence.

"Oops, I forgot about Zaggie." She asked her governess to follow her to the zaguán where she turned the alarm off and set Gabriela up on Zaggie's face recognition application.

As Jasmin looked around the patio, she saw everything had changed. She'd planned to take her governess to the pyramid and schoolroom after showing her the stables, but when she saw the broken trellises and the raspberry-colored bougainvillea wilting on the ground, she changed the plan. Outside the classroom door the Kukulkán temple had lost pieces of the rock facing and revealed raw wood in the underlying frame. The outside of the classroom looked like an abandoned camp.

"This is not the way we left it," Jasmin told Gabriela. She took her into the schoolroom first. "We'll do the stables later."

The colorful papier-mâché flowers inside Talavera pottery and papel picado designs hanging from the ceiling were gone. The room had reverted to uninviting, cold, white walls. It had fallen into decay, as if they'd been away for decades, not months. Jasmin felt overwhelmed with sadness.

She stopped and surveyed the desolate condition of the classroom. At that moment, she was thankful she'd taken her mother's leatherbound diary to Mexico City. If she'd hidden it in the classroom or left it in an empty drawer in her bedroom, her mother would have found it and she would probably never again allow Jasmin to visit the house and stables.

She walked toward her worktable and noticed the Purple Panther, the drone she'd built for the race in Puebla. It was thrown on the table next to jars of bolts and screws, plyers, wrenches, and soldering irons. Jasmin blew dust off the drone.

Her grandfather, looking sullen, joined them.

"Please keep my Purple Panther," she said, handing it to him. "We'll fly it in Chapultepec Park."

The Maya Explorer, her prized science undertaking, was so covered in grime it could be mistaken for a pyramid. Peeking through the hatch, Jasmin was shocked to see the monitors were gone and the 3-D printed interior paneling had been ripped to pieces.

Jasmin let out a muffled scream.

Grandfather rushed to her side. When he saw the devastation inside the capsule, his mustache quivered.

"It's a good thing we took our cats with us," he said, his eyes welling up with tears.

Seeing him cry was more than Jasmin could take. She hugged him. "Don't be sad. All great civilizations leave archeological sites worth visiting. This one is ours."

The three of them returned to the patio and stopped in front of the pyramid.

"Do you know that mathematics made the Maya the most advanced Mesoamerican tribe?" Jasmin asked.

Gabriela nodded.

"I'll have to tell De la Mota about the union of math and archaeology."

Her grandfather touched the tips of his mustache. "Only if you want to upset him."

"I can tease him that I'm thinking of a career in archaeology after all."

"That'll set him off," Grandfather said, chuckling.

Jasmin stared at the pyramid. She told Gabriela that during its construction, her grandfather hired a carpenter to build a wooden frame to lay the stones on. The pyramid had not been traditional construction, but her grandfather wanted to make certain the structure would not collapse and injure her. She and Arroyo had glued the rocks onto the wood like a veneer instead of using limestone mortar between the stones like the original pyramid builders had used. The effect looked authentic enough, but in the end, the pyramid was merely a replica. As for her spaceship, the blueprints were legitimate, but the Maya Explorer had been only a model.

De la Mota and Arroyo had clashed to gain Jasmin's loyalty to their respective disciplines. At times, she had felt like a fought after trophy on a military battlefield. But in the end, De la Mota won. Jasmin was studying physics and mathematics at the university, and he served as her thesis advisor and unofficial mentor. She kept in touch with Arroyo, and they'd invited him to dinner a couple of times, but he no longer influenced her studies.

Jasmin became introspective and Gabriela remained quiet.

"I'm sorry about all your treasures," Gabriela said, breaking the silence. "Don't worry, you'll build bigger and better things in the future."

"Let's make sure my mare is okay." Jasmin led the way to the stables.

Ixchel whinnied when she saw Jasmin.

The mare was not saddled. Jasmin ran to the moon goddess, threw her arms around her pet soulmate's neck, and whispered in her ear. She grabbed a handful of mane and pulled herself onto the palomino, riding bareback into the pasture. Mare and rider spent the next twenty minutes riding, trotting, and galloping. Then Jasmin coaxed Ixchel to the lower, easier portions of the obstacle course. After doing the easy jumps, she rode up beside her clapping audience—Gabriela, Grandfather, and Lorenzo. She told them she wanted to ride a bit longer but she was going to saddle Ixchel so she could do the entire obstacle course.

"It won't hurt my feelings if you've seen enough and want to return to the house."

When Jasmin remounted, Lorenzo handed her a helmet. Halfway through, she sensed her mare was gaining confidence with each jump. She took Ixchel through the entire obstacle course as if they'd done it yesterday.

Her audience applauded for the second time.

CHAPTER TWENTY-SEVEN

Afternoon sunlight in the zaguán glinted off the black lacquer of the piano. Grandfather lifted the cover and played a note. Somehow the tone sounded sad. Jasmin wondered if it was her imagination or if the piano had missed its patrons.

She left her grandfather fussing with the piano while she sneaked into the kitchen. Lola gave her a huge smile. Jasmin placed a finger over her lips to prevent Lola from speaking out loud.

"What happened to my pyramid?" she whispered. "Entire pieces are missing."

Lola sighed and signaled to step outside.

"Your mother has taken to putting bird seed on the pyramid. The birds, especially the crows, have pecked the seeds to the point they've damaged your pyramid. Then the rain and a couple of bad hailstorms have added to the damage."

"Why would she do that?"

"Leticia likes birds, mi niña, but I'm so sorry. I know how hard you worked on it."

"It's not just my pyramid. It's also my classroom. What happened there?"

"A few days after you left, she tore down all the papel picado. She set it on fire on the patio, then sat on the edge of the fountain and sobbed."

"I don't understand why Mama would destroy the very things I made to please her, to make her proud of me."

Lola touched Jasmin's arm. "She's jealous of you." She was about to say something else but looked away instead. When she glanced back, she added that Leticia built an even bigger fire with the papier-mâché flowers. Then she took buckets of mud into the classroom and hurled the sloppy mess against the capsule. Some of it fell through the hatch. Lola explained that she'd tried to clean it up, but Leticia had stopped her. "She took a wrench and ripped the monitors off. It was like your Mama wanted to destroy all the things that reminded her of your intelligence. Like destroying the obstacle to a good relationship with you."

"Why didn't you call us?"

Lola shook her head. "I couldn't. Your mother threatened to fire me if I mentioned it to your grandfather." Lola said that Leticia had seemed depressed after Jasmin and her grandfather moved to the city. "She'd walk back and forth between the zaguán and the main house, looking downcast and despondent. In fact, the first two weeks you were gone, she hardly ate a morsel."

"What have I done to Mama to make her hate me so much?"

Lola shrugged.

"It's like she was trying to obliterate the memory of me," Jasmin said.

"Yet she also seemed to be missing you. Maybe she was trying to overcome her guilt."

"Yeah, like I'd died, and she was mourning me," Jasmin murmured.

———

Playing the piano with her grandfather, Jasmin found the homage to Kukulkán was bittersweet. Chairs on the patio accommodated the sprinkling of friends Leticia had invited. After a rousing rendition of "Moonlight Sonata" by Beethoven, Lorenzo turned off the patio lights and switched on the strobe lights at the top of the pyramid. The light looked like animated snake bodies slowly slithering down the balustrade to connect with the snake heads Jasmin had chiseled out of stone.

When the performance ended, Grandfather thanked Lorenzo for his part in the show and asked the audience to show him their appreciation. Everyone applauded. The man's eyes lit up, but not as much as they did whenever he glanced at Leticia.

Gabriela told Jasmin she could not believe how the undulating strobe lights, crawling down the edges of the stairs, gave such a realistic appearance of two serpent bodies winding their way down to attach with their heads at the base of the replica. She'd loved the whole performance.

A few neighborhood cats had gathered for the concert. Lola anticipated they would remember the food they received a few times after recitals, so she'd prepared tidbits for them and fed them near the gate to the street to keep them as far away from Leticia as possible. Jasmin's two cats had remained behind in Mexico City, looked after by a cat lover in the condo building.

It was heartbreaking for Jasmin to be back. Yet strangely, it also felt good. She'd missed Lola and was happy to spend time with her. She'd been more of a mother to Jasmin than her mother had ever been. The next day Jasmin would ride Ixchel to her heart's content. She wished Aki had made the trip with them so he could see her mare.

The priest did not attend the concert. Jasmin was relieved to see he was not in the dining room either. *Maybe he and her mother had broken up?*

The table was laden, family style, with large platters of food. Lola's mole poblano was the main attraction. All fourteen people took their seats. It seemed Lola had intentionally put Jasmin on the far side of the table, away from her mother, in hopes of everyone enjoying a harmonious dinner.

Discomfort in Jasmin's stomach rose toward her throat. She needed to know why her mother had vandalized her classroom, the capsule, and her pyramid. She could not even look at her. Instead, she stared at her plate and moved the food around with her fork.

"Jasmin, would you prefer to eat outside with the feral cats?" Leticia asked.

Agustín quickly said something about cats liking music.

"It's the feeding of animals that I'm talking about," Leticia said.

Agustín gave Leticia a killer look.

"The cats may be feral, Mama, but they are more courteous than you," Jasmin said. She picked up her plate and headed outside.

Agustín stood and invited everyone to take their plates to the patio.

Much to Jasmin's surprise, her mother cooperated. Her grandfather saved the evening.

CHAPTER TWENTY-EIGHT

J asmin cried herself to sleep for a week after returning to Mexico City. Her relationship with her mother kept deteriorating. She wished she could speak about it to her grandfather, but they never discussed Leticia's behavior. She needed to understand why her mother didn't love her. She brainstormed ways to improve their relationship. She concluded that if she could gain her mother's respect, if not her love, she would be happy.

De la Mota had contacted her grandfather the evening before to tell him about the Televisa interview. And that was not the only good news he shared. Princeton University had offered Jasmin a fellowship. If she accepted, she could get a doctorate in quantum field theory. Or if she preferred, she could take a different career track in astrophysical sciences.

Jasmin was in the living room staring at the park below when her grandfather came in.

Sojón swiped at her grandfather's cane as he walked by. Jasmin immediately felt the warmth and love her grandfather radiated. Despite his age, he was in good health though he could be unsteady on his feet at times due to old military injuries which had left him with a slight limp. He now used a cane, inside the condo, to maintain his equilibrium. When he went out, he never took one.

He had about twenty canes, ranging from shillelaghs to ornate antiques that he liked to believe had religious origins or at least had been used by rabbis, Orthodox deacons, or imams. Regardless of their size or decoration, Sojón found them intriguing. When Agustín stopped by the sofa to talk with Jasmin, the cat laid on his back and used all four paws to nudge the cane as if his action would make the cane march on its own. In fact, he'd already scratched his signature into the base of most of them.

"A peso for your thoughts," he said.

Jasmin wondered if she should bring up the Televisa interview. Instead, she mentioned the fellowship offer.

"And what do you think?" he asked.

"If I decide on astrophysics, I could do research at the Princeton Plasma Physics Lab. It's world famous."

"Never heard of it," her grandfather said. "But I have heard of the Institute for Advanced Study. That's where Einstein worked."

"If I study quantum field theory, the letter hinted I could apply for postdoctoral work at the institute. There are no guarantees of getting accepted."

"Is that all they offered you?" he asked. He looked at his granddaughter with a profoundly serious expression. Not able to contain his serious demeanor, the tips of his mustache bounced with gusto, and he burst into happy peals of laughter. "My granddaughter at the same institute where Einstein was. That brings me such joy." He wiped the dampness that had formed in his eyes with a handkerchief.

Jasmin looked at him. He propped his cane against the sofa and rested a hand on her shoulder. Sojón poked at it and knocked it to the floor. Without her grandfather holding it in place, the cat lost interest in the cane and left the room.

"I'm so proud of you," he said.

"I'd have to complete the doctorate at Princeton before the institute would even consider me. Accepting the fellowship would be an easy decision if you agree to move with me. You speak perfect English, so you'd fit right in."

"Hardly," Grandfather said. "The institute is for people like you. And other brilliant minds, like Einstein's."

Jasmin could not contain her smile. Her grandfather spoke of Einstein as if he were still alive and of the institute as if it would offer them a place to live.

"I mean the town of Princeton, Grandfather. You'll love it there. And I can't go without you."

"Nonsense. You won't need me around. You're very mature for your age. Besides, I'm getting old, and I don't want to die away from home."

"You're not going to die for a long time. I won't go if you don't." Jasmin pouted to convince him.

"But I think you're side-tracking. You're also thinking about the Televisa interview. Are you not?"

Amazed at his ability to read her mind, Jasmin smiled. "The interview, yes. Why are you not enthusiastic about it?"

He smoothed his mustache and looked away for a few seconds, as if he were lost in thought. "You're about to be fourteen. An interview on national TV will give you a lot of visibility. I've always tried to protect you, but it's time to make sure you understand every action we take in life brings consequences. Some good, some bad."

Jasmin nodded.

"If you go on a live interview on TV, what do you expect from it?" he asked.

"To be a role model for teenagers. Get kids to realize there's more to life than videos and selfies posted to social media. That's so superficial and empty."

If she could recruit a handful of kids to study math and science instead of wasting their time on social media, she'd accomplish the goal she and Aki had discussed. She made a silly face, pretended to hold a smart phone in her hand, and posed as if to take a selfie.

Grandfather chuckled. "Some aspects of life are double-edged swords. You've expressed the good that can come of your interview. Think of the bad."

"Well, Mama could see me and scold us. She might say being on TV is one-upmanship. Hopefully, she'd be proud of me."

"I'm concerned about kidnappings," her grandfather said. "For safety reasons, it's best to keep a low profile, not make waves where the wrong people might target you. Appearing on television makes you more vulnerable."

Actions and consequences. Jasmin got it. Grandfather warned her of kidnappings all the time. She had to admit people did get abducted, like the young girl in Ocotlán. And there had been an attempt on her, yet she'd escaped. She hoped to convince him that influencing a few young people through a TV appearance would be a good thing. Besides, De la Mota would be disappointed if she declined the interview. And so would Aki. Both of them encouraged her to do it.

"Abductions happen in this city all the time," Grandfather continued. "Don't you hear the news?"

"It's all about shootings and corrupt politicians. But I have something I need to ask."

"Then ask," Grandfather said.

"When Mama first told you she had decided to send me to Mexico City, she said you were afraid your secrets might come out. That I might be kidnapped and you could lose me. What was that about?"

Grandfather shook his head. Stating he did not have Jasmin's excellent memory so he could not remember his conversation with Leticia. He returned to the topic of the interview saying that Jasmin should do what she considered best.

"Galileo called mathematics the 'language in which God has written the universe.' Since the interview is about both math and science, maybe I could reach a couple of brilliant kids out there and change their lives without even meeting them. It's worth trying."

Her grandfather glanced at her sideways, as if he were analyzing her thoughts. Was he concerned that she'd overheard the conversation he'd had with her mother about his secrets getting out? She couldn't tell, but he seemed worried.

"That may be true, or it may be wishful thinking. But I'm feeling more pragmatic than you are right now and I need to catch up on news of the world." Grandfather went to his desk. He put his reading glasses on and smoothed his mustache before settling into the online news.

Jasmin thought about her grandfather's secrets and wondered why he wouldn't discuss them openly with her.

CHAPTER TWENTY-NINE

Leticia announced she was getting married. Jasmin and her grandfather returned to Ocotlán for the wedding.

Lola and Jasmin stood, dressed in their finest, on the patio behind the apple tree she used to climb to retrieve Sojón. They chatted about the guests gathering for the ceremony.

Then Jasmin told Lola she'd been surprised to hear about her mother's wedding. "When Grandfather and I visited for the equinox less than two months ago, we were happy the priest wasn't around."

"Leticia and Alfredo," Lola said, using the former priest's name, "stopped seeing each other as a test to make certain they wanted to commit to marriage. Let's hope they know what they're doing."

Jasmin silently hoped Lola was right. But the family home would no longer feel like home to her. Her pyramid, completely dismantled, had been replaced by a pergola with a lattice roof supporting scrawny vines, probably set up specifically for the big event. Twinkling lights adorned the posts of the pergola, where the wedding vows would be recited in a few minutes. Japanese lanterns and dozens of ceramic pots with freshly planted white calla lilies livened up the patio. Jasmin wasn't sure if it was the number of guests, her missing treasures, or the unseasonably warm weather, but she broke out in a sweat.

Guests milled around waiting for the bride, drinks in hand. The noise level increased every time another couple arrived. Loud observations about the festive atmosphere annoyed her. Dr. Arroyo joined them, expressing sadness that the pyramid was gone. Jasmin found it hard to make small talk. Eventually she gave up trying.

"Five hundred fourteen thousand, two hundred and twenty-nine—"

Leticia, wearing a white lace gown, arrived on Agustín's arm. She looked beautiful.

Guests used words like ravishing, gorgeous, and stunning to describe the bride. Agustín walked her, to the rhythm of the music, toward the former priest and the judge waiting under the pergola.

After the marriage vows, everyone was seated at round tables in the patio for an elegant dinner. Grandfather joined Jasmin's table after carrying out his fatherly duties.

Lola had turned her kitchen over to the catering service that had prepared mountains of food. Waiters in white jackets topped off the feast with imported red wines from Argentina and whites from Chile. A variety of cheese and fresh fruit was served after dinner. The cutting of the wedding cake was followed by chilled champagne that the guests held up to toast the happiness of the newlyweds.

Three violinists, a harpist, and a couple of flutists struck up "A Thousand Years." Leticia and her new husband danced on the concrete slab surrounding the fountain. They gazed romantically at each other. A few of the guests, especially the women, were whispering among themselves.

"I can imagine what they are saying about this fallen priest," Lola whispered. "They can't understand what your Mama sees in him, but they suspect he's interested in her money."

Jasmin was about to respond when four hungry, meowing cats surrounded the newlyweds on the dance floor.

Grandfather tapped Jasmin's shoulder. "Look, they remember our concerts."

Jasmin could see he was smiling at the memory.

Leticia stopped dancing. "Lola," she shrieked, "take them away."

Lola ran to a side table and stacked leftover meat on a plate. She opened the gate to the corral and put the food down. Jasmin helped by picking up two cats. The other felines needed no further prompting and followed the food trail. Once all the cats were eating, Lola closed the gate.

Leticia looked furious. She stared at Jasmin as if it had been her fault the felines had circled round the dance floor. Jasmin knew her mother hated cats and now they had ruined her wedding dance.

Why does Mama blame me for things that go wrong? Jasmin wondered why her mother had insisted that she attend the wedding. *Wouldn't she have been happier if I hadn't been here?*

For a few seconds, Jasmin felt a perverse pleasure the cats had ruined her mother's dance. It was a small price to pay for the damage Mama had done to her school projects. The thought quickly evaporated when she glanced at her grandfather. He had a hand covering his mouth, yet his mustache quivered like it did when he laughed.

Her grandfather leaned over and whispered to her, "Leticia must think the cat species does not include domesticated felines; she obviously believes all cats are wild."

"She does not like jaguars either," Jasmin said.

CHAPTER THIRTY

It had been easier to return to Mexico City after her mother's wedding. Jasmin did not cry herself to sleep the way she had after returning from the first visit. She did miss Ixchel and was glad Lorenzo took such good care of her.

After Leticia's wedding, the best part was that Lola moved to Mexico City with them, claiming her religious convictions would not allow her to serve a household with a priest who had broken his holy vows to marry his teenage love.

Lola pampered Jasmin and Agustín in every way possible, especially with her cooking. This morning she burst into the room, cats at her heels, carrying a tray with coffee and freshly squeezed orange juice. She stopped by the dining room table to put the glasses of orange juice there.

"Breakfast will be ready in fifteen minutes," Lola announced. She placed Agustín's coffee at his desk so he could enjoy it while he read the news. For Jasmin, she'd prepared warm milk and honey with only a drizzle of espresso, saying her growing bones needed calcium.

Whenever Gabriela arrived at the condo, Lola also indulged her with cakes, cookies, and empanadas. Sojón and Sancho received their own special treats.

Gabriela worked whenever Jasmin's schedule required it. She and Lola became good friends. She took Lola shopping for groceries once a week and took Sojón to the veterinarian whenever he needed a shot of prednisolone for his allergies. Gabriela attended concerts with them at Nezahualcóyotl Hall on the university campus or the national auditorium at the opposite end of Chapultepec Park.

Agustín and Jasmin moved to the dining room for a typical Tlaxcalan breakfast of eggs baked in ramekins with chile poblano, cream, and Chihuahua cheese. This morning's preparation included a healthy side portion of fruit—mamey, zapote, and fresh figs. The aroma of freshly baked carrot-pineapple muffins permeated the dining room, making the condo cozier and more inviting than when Agustín and Jasmin had first moved to Mexico City.

"Most teenagers fear mathematics," Jasmin said, thinking about the television interview. "If they knew it's mostly a written language, not some alien mumbo-jumbo, they'd overcome their fright."

"Like music," Grandfather said. He swallowed a mouthful of eggs and chile. "Patterns of sound can be played from a musical score. Now you're telling me math is a score written in numbers to describe geometry, logic patterns, and differential calculus?"

"Mathematics is the fundamental way to understand the cosmos. It describes our universe through a jumble of formulas. Math, like history, repeats itself. For example, the structure of our galaxy is very similar to the Fibonacci sequence. It's called the golden spiral."

"You're becoming too philosophical for me. But I've changed my mind. You should do the interview."

"Thanks." Jasmin felt as if her whole body were smiling.

"When you do it, keep it simple. Don't get philosophical, like you do with me."

She gave him a big hug.

Like talking with Aki, it was always easy to talk with Grandfather, except when she wanted to know about family secrets. Her thoughts turned to the interview and hoped her mother would be pleased to see her on television.

At fourteen, Jasmin didn't know what a television interview would entail. She was nervous. Her palms were sweaty. Would there be an audience? How many people would ask questions? The idea of more than two people in the room sent tremors of terror down her spine. She should have listened to Grandfather and declined. She didn't like being the center of attention.

Aki drove them to the studio. He'd stay with Agustín, and they'd watch the interview on one of the monitors in the lobby. Jasmin was in a daze as a receptionist ushered her into a dressing room. A woman was already there. She explained she'd style her hair and put makeup on her. When Jasmin refused to let her smear gooey creams and potions on her face or apply lipstick or eye shadow, the stylist called the head cameraman.

"We only want to make you look good on camera," the man said. "Even the president has makeup applied before going on TV."

"He's an old man. He needs all the help he can get, but you're not doing that to me."

After another attempt to convince her, he turned to the stylist, "She's a stubborn one. Let her go the way she is. Just comb that mop of hair."

Jasmin felt nervous and recited a few numbers in her mind.

The cameraman left the room and stepped into the hallway.

"Spoiled little savant," he muttered.

Instead of hurting her, his words worked like a miracle. She stopped stressing about the people who would be in the interview room and focused on the fact that she'd managed to cope with ugly remarks before, even from her mother.

Aki hugged Jasmin after she finished the interview. He seemed elated, and so did Grandfather. Aki drove them to the condo and though Agustín invited him in, Aki said he had to get up early the next day.

Jasmin felt ecstatic when they entered the condo. Lola congratulated her and asked her to follow her into the kitchen. "Mi niña, you were extraordinary. Even I understood what you talked about on the show."

From the appearance of the kitchen, Lola had been in the process of cutting a few oranges into very thin slices, leaving the peel but removing the seeds. She pointed toward a crate of oranges that Leticia had sent with a friend who was visiting the city. The woman delivered the oranges while Agustín and Jasmin had been at the TV station.

They talked about the interview while Lola combined sugar, water, and the orange slices into a stainless-steel pan and stirred the ingredients together over the stove. Jasmin knew her grandfather loved orange marmalade and Lola probably wanted to surprise him. She asked if the marmalade would be served the next morning with freshly baked croissants. Lola smiled and asked Jasmin to keep it a secret.

"These types of secrets are the only ones that families should keep," Jasmin said. "Secrets that make people happy when they are revealed."

The next day, they were eating breakfast when De la Mota called. Jasmin put him on speaker phone.

He sounded overjoyed about the interview. "You brought the highest ratings this program has had all year."

"Not because of me," Jasmin said. "No one even cares about math or science."

"All because of you." De la Mota's voice sounded loud over the speaker, it reverberated off every surface, scaring the cats back into the kitchen. "The station had been announcing for three days prior to your interview that a young math genius would be presented. And it worked. You attracted a *huge* audience."

"Then it was the freak appeal," she said.

Her grandfather gently slapped her wrist.

"That interview will influence young people," De la Mota said. "The station told me several people have called to get more information about the university's offerings in mathematics."

Gabriela arrived and joined them at the table. She heard the end of the conversation with De la Mota. Lola brought coffee, a plate with homemade croissants, and marmalade.

Taking a bite, Agustín smacked his lips to show his appreciation for the homemade preserves.

"I loved your interview last night," Gabriela said, stirring cream into her coffee. "Don't be surprised if other stations want to interview you too."

"I hope the interview does some good," Jasmin said, "and brings a few science-minded students to the university. I didn't enjoy the fuss they made over me at the station, and I would not do it again."

Gabriela chatted with Lola and Agustín. Jasmin went to her room to finish getting ready for class. The laptop she used for taking notes was already in her overstuffed backpack.

As Jasmin and Gabriela walked toward the car, a familiar vehicle was parking on the street. Stunned to see her mother and Alfredo, Jasmin ran to greet Mama. Leticia cheek kissed her and brushed her aside.

"Did you see my interview on TV last night?"

Her mother gave her a cold look that sent chills down Jasmin's back.

"I never turned it on," she said. "I don't care to see you flaunting your intelligence to the nation." She asked about Grandfather in a venomous whisper.

"Fourth floor." Jasmin pointed toward the condominium building. She would have been more polite and taken them to the condo, but she didn't as it would make her late for class.

Her mother headed for the lobby of the condominium and Alfredo shadowed his wife.

Jasmin returned to Gabriela's car. She thought about the visit to Ocotlán when her governess had driven them. Leticia had been hospitable, but Jasmin knew her governess realized that mother and daughter had a challenging relationship.

"Your mother seemed angry with you," Gabriela observed.

Jasmin stifled the impulse to cry. She clamped her jaw shut and stared at the traffic on Avenida Constituyentes while Gabriela drove.

"She must be unhappy your grandfather allowed you to do the TV interview."

"I guess," Jasmin said.

Gabriela drove up the ramp to the double-decker Anillo Periférico, driving the rest of the route in silence.

CHAPTER THIRTY-ONE

Taking the usual seat at the front of the class, Jasmin removed her backpack. She retrieved the laptop and looked around for Aki. But he was absent. She was surprised when an older student sat next to her, a student she'd never seen before. Even the professor noticed.

Dr. Rojas stared at the man with laser-focused eyes. "I don't believe I know you."

The man shifted and cleared his throat, stuttering as he spoke. "My academic advisor suggested I visit your class to decide if I should register for it next semester."

"Very well then. Welcome," Rojas said, turning away to start his lecture. He projected a familiar equation onto the large overhead screen.

$$H(t)|\psi(t)\rangle = i\hbar \frac{\partial}{\partial t}|\psi(t)\rangle$$

"Today I want to discuss Schrödinger's equation, a partial quantum theory which did not take relativity into account."

Rojas looked back at the equation briefly and glanced at the students.

"And I will further discuss Paul Dirac's successful merging of quantum mechanics with Einstein's theory of special relativity and how this led to the full quantum field theory, as we know it today, sometimes mistakenly called the Second Quantization Revolution."

The man next to Jasmin squirmed and scoffed. She glanced at him.

"I've never heard of a revolution in mathematics," he whispered.

"Over the years," Dr. Rojas continued, "all subatomic forces, electromagnetism, and both the strong and weak nuclear forces have been included."

Jasmin figured by the man's continued fidgeting that this lecture was beyond his comprehension. He would not be signing up for Rojas's seminar. Surely he would not even meet the prerequisites.

When the lecture concluded, the man asked if she'd appreciated the professor's discourse. Something about this stranger made her uneasy. She remembered Grandfather's warnings of kidnappings. Apprehension ran down her spine.

Her response, as she tucked her laptop into the backpack, was that she considered Dr. Rojas a brilliant physicist.

"Ah, I thought you looked familiar. You're the young math genius who appeared on Televisa last night."

The man continued talking, but Jasmin paid no attention. Grandfather had warned her of the consequences of appearing on TV, but she'd never expected people to seek her out at a university lecture hall. It hit her that the intruder had attended this lecture to see her.

"I have to go," she said.

"Not so fast." He moved to block the steps to the exit. "We need to talk."

Jasmin looked around the small hall. Fellow students often remained to discuss fine points of the lecture or even approach Dr. Rojas to ask additional questions, but today all of them had vaporized. Worse yet, the one day she desperately needed Aki, he was not around. She was alone with this man, and she was scared.

Gabriela would be waiting for her at the library and would not miss her for another fifteen or twenty minutes. She figured her only defense was her smart phone, but it was lost at the bottom of the over-stuffed backpack.

"When I watched you last night, you looked familiar to me. I could not place you. But then I saw another girl's image flash across my mind," he said.

Her fear kept her from fully comprehending his words, but she realized his stuttering and throat clearing were gone. That's when she knew he was a threat.

"Excuse me, my governess is waiting. She'll soon come looking for me." Jasmin set her backpack down and dug into it. Desperate to find her phone, she felt around for it. When that failed, she decided to get outside as soon as possible. Her hands trembled. "Can you move, please?" Her voice squeaked.

"When I knew where I'd seen your face before, I went searching for proof of it," he said, ignoring her request to move out of the way.

The man dropped a large envelope onto the open backpack.

"I did not intend to scare you. You simply remind me of another mathematical genius. Take your time looking at the photos I've made for you." He walked up the steps and looked back from the doorway. "I'll see you again. Very soon."

Jasmin's heart pounded so fast she couldn't breathe. Finally, she took a deep inhale and let it out slowly. Her trembling hands gradually returned to normal, though the pit of her stomach felt queasy like a vacuum had sucked up the contents of her breakfast. She located the phone and set it on the desktop. The envelope was right there. She picked it up hesitantly. With even more hesitation, she opened it. Expecting photos, she was surprised to find three sheets of paper with color photocopies of her face.

Except it was not her face.

She moved the backpack onto the floor and sat down to study the images the man had left. They made no sense. Here were several photocopies of a teenager who looked exactly like her. "Another mathematical genius," he'd said.

Do all mathematical prodigies look alike, she wondered. She didn't know another math genius, except for Aki. And he was Japanese. *But could it be all Mexican savants physically resembled each other?* She realized that was a silly thought.

Studying the photocopies, she saw her resemblance to the pictured woman was almost exact. The dark brown hair, green eyes, olive-colored skin, the shape of the face, the features, all looked like her. The person was presumably a mathematical scholar. So what was this about? Had he photoshopped Jasmin's face? Was it a joke?

Then it struck her. Could she have a twin sister? Did Mama have twin girls and one went missing in early childhood? Is it possible she was abducted and never found? That might be the reason Grandfather seemed obsessed with kidnappings. And it could explain why Mama never seemed to love her. They took the wrong child. They'd abducted her mother's favorite. If so, that would explain everything.

Her grandfather would know. She'd ask him as soon as she returned to the condo. If she had a twin sister out there somewhere, she'd ask her grandfather to hire detectives to locate her and bring her home.

Gabriela rang and wanted to know if she'd been detained after class.

"No, I'll be along in a couple of minutes," Jasmin said. Ending the call, she stuffed the envelope into her backpack. She needed to collect her thoughts before meeting Gabriela.

Her grandfather had an obsession about actions and consequences. The consequences could be good or bad, he'd told her. He'd been wise for warning her about the risks involved in notoriety. His worry of kidnappings had to be rooted in more than the attempt on her.

When she would arrive at the condo later today, she would invite her grandfather to Chapultepec Park. He could watch her fly the Purple Panther. They had done that several times and that activity had not only relaxed them both, but it seemed to put her grandfather into a talkative mood. She would take that approach today and then she'd ask him about her twin sister.

CHAPTER THIRTY-TWO

J asmin unlocked the door to the condo. She heard Grandfather's angry voice and stopped cold, leaving the door open a crack so she could peek in.

"You divorced one man you were supporting to marry a second one who also depends on you financially. Salva was at least a father for Jasmin. Until you ran him off."

"Stop, don't go there—" her mother's voice said.

Agustín interrupted Leticia. "How many times must I apologize to you?" He sighed. "You never give Jasmin a chance."

Mama's face turned red with anger. "Always concerned for your Jasmin, aren't you? No one else counts." Her voice sounded hurt as well as angry.

"You know that's not true," Agustín said, "but you're hardly a mother to her."

"Why should I be?" Mama asked. "She flaunts her damned intelligence every time I speak with her. If she'd just be normal, like other kids. Why must she constantly remind me of who she is?"

Agustín moved across the living room. Jasmin could no longer see her grandfather, but she could still hear him.

"If you only *tried* to understand her. Salva always did. And your new husband, well, I don't think he's ever talked to her. Jasmin needs a father."

"She doesn't need one with you around," her mother said angrily.

Jasmin stepped into the living room. Mama turned and stared.

Jasmin waved.

Neither her mother nor her grandfather returned her greeting. Her heart ached. Not knowing what else to do she went to her bedroom and found Lola sitting on her bed. She stood and hugged Jasmin.

"What's happening?" Jasmin asked.

"I was waiting for you," she said. "Your mother is furious with Colonel Campos. He changed his will. It had your mother inheriting everything—unless she remarried. In that case, the assets would be split between you and her. That's the gist of it. Now Leticia has lost half of her inheritance. And she's enraged."

Jasmin grimaced. "She can have it all. I don't want her upsetting Grandfather that way."

"Your grandfather wants to take care of you. He feels your mother's marriage puts your inheritance at risk. He's concerned Alfredo would inherit everything if something happened to Leticia."

"Grandfather never did like Alfredo." Jasmin thought back to the day he'd wanted the priest exorcised from the house and played loud jazz to get him out. Yet Grandfather's jazz had not succeeded. Nor had Rossini's or Stravinsky's musical reproaches.

"Your grandfather is not alone in disliking that man. After all, Alfredo made a promise to God and reneged on it," Lola said.

"What else did Mama say?"

Lola looked away. "Well, she sneezed a lot, saying the cats aggravated her allergies. When one rubbed up against her leg, she screamed."

"But what did she *say* about me?"

"Basically, I've told you all I heard, mi niña. Leticia accused your grandfather of treachery. That's when Alfredo left, after Leticia and your grandfather started arguing."

"I've always known Mama does not love me."

"There was a time she loved you a lot," Lola said. "In a strange way, she still does."

Jasmin stared at Lola and tried to remember feeling her mother's love, but she couldn't think of a time she felt real affection. Since Jasmin loved her mother, she surmised they'd had a connection in the past.

"But that changed, didn't it?" Jasmin asked. "Tell me, how old was I when Mama became so distant with me?"

"It must have been when you were around four, maybe five years old. Something changed. Although she's always made sure you've had the best of everything. When you got sick, she'd be by your bedside. Once you recovered, she'd withdraw again."

"Can you think what happened to make Mama change? Why did she turn away from me?"

"At age three to four, it became obvious you were more clever than most ten-year-old kids. Maybe she didn't know how to handle your brilliance."

"That's when Grandfather hired tutors to teach me. When I was four, right?" Jasmin asked.

Lola nodded. "She's jealous of you. Of your intelligence. That's all."

Jasmin's shoulders slumped. Her mother wanted a normal kid, whatever that meant. She didn't even know how to pretend to be one. "Being smart is a curse, not a gift."

Lola squinted, as if trying to remember the past. "When your grandmother was still alive, something about your math ability made her angry."

Jasmin didn't understand why mathematics was an issue.

"Then there was the purchase of Ixchel," Lola said. "Your grandmother was furious with your grandfather. That's when she . . . well, she had a heart attack and she died."

Jasmin thought back to her therapist. She had memories of Teresa teaching her to talk to Ixchel as she groomed her, looking into the mare's eyes as she gave her a carrot, and learning the parts of the mare's body by touching each part while they sang. The moon goddess was barely five, a year older than Jasmin, when her grandfather had given Ixchel to her. Mare and child had grown up together, until Jasmin was sent to Mexico City.

"The therapist worked with you for almost three years. By using the mare, that woman taught you to interact," Lola said.

"Interact?" Jasmin felt perplexed.

"With people."

"You mean Ixchel made me interact with people? Well, it didn't help, did it?"

"Oh, yes, mi niña, it helped a lot. You didn't used to let people touch you. Now you love hugs. You couldn't look people in the eye. Now you can."

Jasmin felt bitter, thinking about her relationship with her mother. Lola's remark about Teresa, her equine therapist, brought her grandmother and her father to mind. She didn't remember much about her grandmother. Her earliest memories involved her grandfather. Images started sifting through her memory bank—her grandfather teaching her to groom and saddle Ixchel, sitting at the piano for her music lessons, coaching her in French and English, and listening as he read classical stories. As she grew older, she'd read the classics to him. But none of this explained why Mama resented her.

"Don't be so hard on yourself, mi niña," Lola said.

"Are you aware of secrets Grandfather has kept over the years? Secrets that could explain why Mama hates me?"

Lola shrugged. "We all have secrets, Jasmin."

"Did I ever have a sister?"

Lola blinked. She shook her head. It was not a negative movement, but it was definitely not an affirmative one either. She sighed and glanced across the room. Her expression changed from surprise to a quizzical look. "Not that I know of."

Jasmin stared at the food on her plate.

"I'm sorry your mother did not say good-bye," Grandfather said at the table that evening. "I was hoping she'd stay for dinner."

"She really didn't even say hello. I had planned on flying my Purple Panther, but my mother's visit ruined that."

Her grandfather put his hand on hers. "We'll go to Chapultepec another day and you can fly your drone."

Lola had gone out of her way to make up for Leticia's behavior by preparing Jasmin's favorite dish—chiles rellenos. If only Mama had not been so angry, she could be sitting with them enjoying Lola's culinary expertise.

Jasmin cut into a relleno. It melted into a luscious bouquet of flavors on her palate. Lola's cooking had a way of evaporating her worries.

She'd intended to ask Grandfather if she had a twin sister. But after her mother's tirade, her grandfather did not need to be troubled.

"The chiles are superb tonight," Jasmin said, trying to sound cheerful.

"Your Mama was very upset with me," Grandfather said. "It has nothing to do with you."

"That's not true. If not for me, she'd be happy."

He set his fork down. "I was afraid you might think it's about you, but it's not. She's been angry with me for years. I have not lived up to her expectations. Even when I explain my actions, she misinterprets. I ask her for forgiveness, but Leticia can't forgive."

"But it *is* about me," Jasmin insisted.

Grandfather took a sip of water and went on speaking as if he'd not heard her. He shook his head slightly. "I've made many mistakes in my lifetime. Every time I turn around, I've committed another unforgiveable offense in Leticia's eyes."

"Remember Mama doesn't make mistakes," Jasmin said, thinking about her mother's tendency to blame others. "Do those mistakes have anything to do with a kidnapping, like Mama said before we moved? Remember, she said your secrets might get out."

Sojón brushed up against Jasmin's pants and meowed. Whenever the vet gave him shots for his allergies, the venerable old blue-eyed cat would be energetic and famished for a couple of weeks. Gabriela had taken him in for his treatment and he was hungry, but their pets were not allowed to beg for food, so she ignored him.

"Secrets?" Grandfather shook his head. "I have no idea what your mother was talking about."

"Then tell me, why was she so angry this afternoon?"

"It was all about my will. I had it revised after your grandmother died. At that time, I left all my assets to Leticia. You were a small child. But I had the foresight to include a clause that if she ever remarried, you would get fifty percent of my assets. To avoid misunderstandings, I've rewritten the will to divide the assets between the two of you."

"She can have it all, Grandfather. I don't want her upsetting you."

He placed his hand over Jasmin's again. "No, ma petite princesse. I'll protect you for as long as I can. You'll have sufficient assets to continue your studies through a doctorate and post doctorate if I die."

Jasmin shook her head. "There's no reason to fight over money. I will have fellowships. And I can work." She knew she could give piano lessons or tutor students in math. There were so many ways she could earn money. If her mother wanted nothing to do with her, then moving to Princeton would be the perfect solution. "Tell me you're not going to die for a long time." Jasmin squeezed his hand tightly.

"You need to know this condo is yours. It's now in your name. When we go to Einstein's institute, we'll lease it to bring you additional income. The fellowship won't cover everything."

"It's not the institute, Grandfather." Jasmin laughed, knowing he was saying that on purpose—to keep her focused on the goal he wanted for her. "It's Princeton University."

"Hmm, after you receive your PhD, you'll continue at the institute." He smiled. "I'll stop waxing my moustache, leaving it wild and crazy. To look more like Einstein."

Jasmin twisted an imaginary mustache. Her grandfather laughed, and she was happy his playful disposition had returned.

For the next three days, Jasmin kept quiet about the experience in the lecture hall. Her encounter with the man of the photocopied images could wait until Grandfather had fully recovered from Leticia's unpleasant visit. Her mother's recent spiteful comments brought back memories of the diary and the nightmares. She picked up the habit again of touching the leather-bound book every night to make certain it was still hidden under sweaters and blouses at the bottom of her drawer.

She attended class, talked with Aki as they worked in the lab, and generally spent the evenings playing the piano with her grandfather after she fed the cats and cleaned their litter boxes. On two occasions, they went to Chapultepec Park where she flew her Purple Panther.

On Saturday morning, the fourth day after Leticia's unpleasant visit, her grandfather suggested an outing. Lola declined going with them saying she wanted to stay and bake homemade bread.

"Pablo Neruda, the deceased Chilean poet, once said, 'Mexico is in its markets.' And I agree," he said. "Let's go to Bazar Sábado and have fun today. See if the artists have anything worth buying. Later, we'll lunch on the patio at San Angel Inn and pretend we're back in Ocotlán."

"I'd like to visit the flower market and buy fresh flowers. They'll remind me of the papier-mâché ones Dr. Arroyo gave me." Jasmin loved fresh flowers, but they didn't last as well as the artificial ones. Dr. Arroyo had instilled in her a respect for the artisans, from villages all over the country, including Tlaxcala. He had taught her to find the artistic expression the women had woven into their flowers.

The two of them took a taxi to Bazar Sábado. For a couple of hours, they toured the art exhibits. Her grandfather bargained with the artist of a pen and ink drawing featuring the feathered serpent, Kukulkán. The figure was a man in a feathered headdress, drawn on vellum to resemble a Maya codex. The young woman reduced the price only slightly. She smiled, charming Agustín, who would have paid full price. As they walked away, he said that part of the fun was the good-natured haggling over prices.

"We'll frame it and hang it in your bedroom," he said.

"It reminds me of the trip we took to the Kukulkán temple in Chichén Itzá," Jasmin said. "That was such a wonderful trip. I loved talking to all those archaeologists. They actually understood me. I can talk to Aki. He's not very interested in ancient civilizations, though he told me he's reading about the Maya."

Leaving behind the lively music of the mariachi band in the park, they crossed the street to a colonial-style hacienda. The patio housed the flower market. Vibrant colors and the sweet smell of flowering jacaranda trees welcomed them into the courtyard of the former hacienda. Several couples sat at small tables sipping coffee and eating pastries in the courtyard.

Agustín stopped to study an old map exhibited in a glass case near the entrance. Jasmin continued to a long wooden bench with buckets containing an assortment of flowers. She selected a few to take home.

A loud yell carried across the courtyard. Pivoting, she saw her grandfather on the ground. She screamed and dropped the flowers. Two men, obviously his attackers, ran out of the courtyard and three men got up from the tables to help Agustín.

The shop owner rushed to Agustín's side as the café customers helped him to his feet.

Sebastián, the shop owner, thanked the three patrons and took Agustín and Jasmin inside a small office. He offered Agustín a bottle of water or something stronger, like tequila or a cognac. Agustín chose cognac. After pouring a couple of snifters, Sebastián pulled a coke from a small fridge and handed it to Jasmin. The shopkeeper refilled the snifters twice more. He and Agustín reminisced about a bygone era when life seemed better. The two were soon on a first name basis. Sebastián poured more cognac. By the time Jasmin and her grandfather left the shop, Agustín and Sebastián were both tipsy. The two men had become friends, planning their next get-together for lunch or a chat over coffee.

CHAPTER THIRTY-THREE

J asmin and Aki were working in the lab on Monday afternoon. Aki received a call. Dr. Rojas wanted him to work on a new project.

"Can Jasmin join me on it?"

Aki turned to her and asked if she'd be interested in collaborating on a project that had just been funded by the National Quantum Matter Laboratory. When Aki explained that they'd study ultracold matter and quantum information, Jasmin immediately accepted.

Her phone dinged. A text message from De la Mota asked her to visit his office the next day to talk about the drone race on campus coming up on Thursday. She texted back, glanced at her watch, and told Aki it was time for her to meet Gabriela.

On her way to the library, she saw the man who had given her the photocopies the week before. With the emotional upheavals of Mama's visit and Grandfather's assault at Bazar Sábado, she'd put him out of mind. Seeing him again made her apprehensive.

"Stop! Get away from me or I'll scream." Her voice quavered and she hoped he couldn't tell how scared she was.

He seemed surprised at her reaction. "I'm not going to hurt you."

She thought about her grandfather's assault. "You had hitmen attack my grandfather, didn't you? Are you trying to kidnap us?"

The man shook his head. "Makes me sad that you'd think that. Colonel Campos helped my family years ago though life's circumstances later separated us. If you only knew how much I respect your grandfather."

She told him to contact him directly. After all, he presumably knew Agustín. She started walking away.

"Does the name Rosana Huerta mean anything to you?"

Jasmin stopped and shook her head. "Why should it?"

"Visit the Panteón Civil de Dolores on Friday at 11 a.m. to find out why you should care. Agustín goes there to visit Rosana. Her ashes are interred close to the tombstone of Siqueiros, the famous muralist. If you go, ask your grandfather what he's doing there."

"Why don't you explain who Rosana is?" Before he could answer, Jasmin saw her governess walking toward her.

The mystery man noticed too and left abruptly. Gabriela asked if that man had bothered her.

Jasmin shook her head. But he'd mentioned the Panteón Civil de Dolores, and she wanted to see it. She asked her governess to drive her to the cemetery.

"Why?" Gabriela asked.

"Presumably my grandfather goes there every Friday. To visit the burial place of a woman called Rosana Huerta. And I want to know why. She's supposed to be buried near the Siqueiros tomb."

In the days when they still lived in the village, her grandfather left early every Friday morning to drive into Mexico City. He'd always told her that as a retired army colonel he carried out volunteer work in the city. And she'd believed him. Apparently, that was not the full truth.

"Ask your grandfather to take you if you want to see the tomb of the famous muralist. That way, you can check on anyone else buried close to him," Gabriela suggested as they walked through campus toward the car.

"Hmm, if I ask my grandfather to take me, he won't. My family holds lots of secrets. Even Grandfather keeps things from me. If we find him there, he cannot deny why he's there."

Gabriela looked hesitant. "Sometimes it's best to leave the dead in the cemetery. If you go digging up the past, you might uncover stuff you'd prefer not to stir up."

Jasmin shrugged.

They got into the car and strapped themselves in. Gabriela added that if this man were honestly trying to reconnect with her grandfather, he should approach him directly. "If this man can find you, he can certainly locate Agustín."

"Good point," Jasmin said, though she'd already considered the same thought.

"I can talk to your grandfather if you don't want to," she said. "I don't like that the mystery man has not told you what his name is."

Not that Jasmin had thought to ask him. "Let's keep this to ourselves," she said.

She convinced Gabriela to drive past the cemetery. It was between the second and third sections of Chapultepec Park, just a few blocks from the condo. In fact, it was within easy walking distance.

"Do you suppose Agustín purchased the condo to be close to this cemetery?" Gabriela asked. She now seemed intrigued.

"That's possible," Jasmin said. "See what I mean about my family's secrets?"

On Thursday, Jasmin arrived at the ecological reserve on campus carrying the drone under her arm and the backpack over her shoulder. Lola, Gabriela, and Grandfather followed her on the graveled path toward the Espacio Escultórico, a sculpture garden surrounding one of the petrified lava flows on campus. Lush plants and tall shade trees bordered the pathway. Occasional glimpses of the central library's muraled walls could be seen through the branches. If there was a time Agustín needed a cane, it was today. The pebbled walkway was slowing him considerably. But he wouldn't use one outside the condo.

Lola gawked at the gorgeous scenery. Student violinists rehearsed behind one of the two temporary bleachers set up for the drone race. Agustín cocked his head to listen to the students.

Aki was already there and waving for them to join him on the bleachers. Jasmin took everyone to the seats Aki was saving.

Jasmin looked around for Sebastián, the owner of the coffeeshop near Bazar Sábado. Agustín had invited him to watch the drone races. She waved at him and he joined them. Her grandfather and Sebastián had become good friends and got together once a week for lunch.

De la Mota, one of the sponsoring professors, had arrived early. Jasmin caught a glimpse of him standing in front of one of the slanted, massive, monolithic concrete slabs that formed a sculpture ring around a pit of volcanic rocks and a lava flow. The professor seemed to work the registration table while talking to a person in a brown leather jacket.

Jasmin's stomach cramped. She was looking straight at the mystery man.

Is this man following me? She tilted her head slightly signaling Gabriela to look in that direction.

Gabriela raised her eyebrows. Obviously, she recognized the man talking with De la Mota.

Jasmin sat next to her grandfather, pointed to the guy in the leather jacket standing by De la Mota, and asked if he knew the man. By the time her grandfather looked in that direction, students had surrounded the professor. The mystery man was nowhere to be seen.

Grandfather asked if he could use the extra pair of goggles, the set with a wide-field view. When she removed them from her backpack, she noticed the envelope with the photocopies. She pushed it further down into the pack and took out the goggles, adjusting the channel for him to watch. He'd gone with Jasmin several times when she freestyled the drone in Chapultepec Park, but he hadn't needed goggles to watch it fly around the trees. Plus, the Purple Panther was the only drone to watch in Chapultepec.

"My drone is racing against other drones. Since I'll fly the Purple Panther as fast as possible, you won't be able to see much. It will be going through a standard, measured course. That's how they'll score us."

"A course? You mean like a racetrack for horses or a speedway for cars?" he asked.

"More like an obstacle course at high speeds."

"Obstacle course, you said?" He seemed to be having trouble hearing her over the chatter of other people on the bleacher.

All the noise and people were starting to get to Jasmin. She felt flushed. Mentally she recited a few numbers in the Fibonacci sequence, until her grandfather interrupted her.

"What if I get dizzy?" he asked.

"First of all, stay seated. Or take the goggles off and let Sebastián or Aki use them."

Jasmin helped adjust the set to his head.

"Take care of Grandfather," she said to Gabriela, tilting her head as a message to remain vigilant for the mystery man.

With her quadcopter drone tucked under her arm and the remote control and pilot goggles in her backpack, she headed toward the registration table.

When she got there, she asked De la Mota about the man in the leather jacket.

"He's a professor from the Ibero-American University," De la Mota said. "Just another spectator."

How would that man know about the race, she wondered. *He's from another university*. Looking around, she didn't see him. She debated about leaving the competition and returning to the safety of their condo. In the end, she decided to sign in since she was already registered. It would be the only competition she had participated in since the one in Puebla when she'd built the Purple Panther. Most of her experience was freestyling, so she relaxed and prepared to have fun.

As the competition got ready to start, Jasmin felt the adrenaline pumping. Mere seconds after takeoff, she soared virtually through the trees and maneuvered Purple Panther into its first backflip. Her stomach felt the flip.

Speeding along the course made the competition thrilling. About halfway through, Purple Panther was in third place. That's where Jasmin hit the zone. An amazing feeling—she wasn't thinking, just flowing with her drone.

Close to the finish line, the two drones ahead of Purple Panther collided into each other. She passed through the final obstacle. She couldn't believe it.

De la Mota came over and hugged her.

"Beginners luck," Jasmin said. She and her mentor hugged again. Then he guided her toward a makeshift stage with two other participants. A man holding a microphone approached them and announced the first, second, and third place winners.

Until that point, Jasmin did not realize a television crew was recording the activities. A reporter with a cameraman came over to interview her. Her palms immediately became soaked with sweat. De la Mota stood next to her as the guy asked her how it felt to be the winner. He wanted to know about her preparation for the race.

De la Mota interrupted and informed the reporter that Jasmin had built the drone using a design she'd created on a computer program and had made the parts using a 3D printer. He went on to brag that she'd also designed and created the circuitry. After the reporter finished asking questions, Jasmin picked up her Purple Panther and ran toward the bleachers. She felt a racing high at that moment and could hardly contain her emotions.

"I won, Grandfather. I won!"

Aki grinned and high-fived her.

Gabriela tossed her head to one side as if her hair needed arranging. Jasmin looked in that direction and saw a familiar face. The mystery man was standing on the highest rung of the bleacher next to theirs. He jumped off the side and walked away.

"Did he talk to Grandfather?" she asked in a whisper.

Gabriela shook her head. "He never even looked this way."

With the race over, spectators were leaving the bleachers and joining the musicians who had now moved to the stage. A taco stand had opened and had a long line of hungry customers. Lola and Gabriela watched the spectators, musicians, participants, and acted as if they were visiting a colorful market.

Sebastián congratulated her.

"I'm glad you won," Grandfather said. He stood to embrace her. "I must say, I don't know how you control that little gnat of yours.

Together, the drones looked like a swarm of mosquitos. Neither Sebastián nor I could tell which one was yours."

"Did you wear the goggles?"

"I took them off," he said, "and sat on the bleachers. It was too dizzying to watch. I could not tell which drone had won the race until I saw you among the winners."

"What prize did you receive?" Sebastián asked.

"This," Jasmin said, holding up a piece of paper. "And the joy of winning."

"Really, that's it?" Her grandfather sounded disappointed.

Aki chuckled. He explained that, although the event was festive, drone racing doesn't generate much following, making it impossible to raise money for prizes. People attending the race were mostly family and friends of the competitors.

"It's funny to watch a race without a driver in the vehicle," Agustín said.

Jasmin laughed. "It's a *drone*, not a car."

"When I was involved in horse racing, I rode the animal myself, or sometimes hired a jockey. And car racing involves a driver in the vehicle. Drone-racing is so fast, it's mind-boggling." Agustín sighed. "If only a horse could gallop like that."

"But a horse isn't made from printed plastic and circuit boards," Aki said.

"True enough. Racehorses are bred, cared for as colts, with veterinarians treating them whenever necessary. Then when they're old enough, trainers turn them into winning horses. And that helps pay the bills of breeding, raising, and training."

For a few minutes, Jasmin and Aki listened while Agustín reflected on his younger days.

Sebastián kept nodding and agreeing that in the good old days, life was better. "If this were a horse race, your grandfather would be the winner."

"And I'd get a cash prize, not a piece of paper," Agustín said. Looking at the group, he added, "but to the Einsteins of the world, cash doesn't mean much. Does it?"

CHAPTER THIRTY-FOUR

Jasmin walked into the kitchen on Friday morning as Lola was placing cinnamon rolls on a baking sheet to pop in the oven for breakfast.

"Do you know of a woman by the name of Rosana Huerta?"

"Rosana Huerta?" Lola asked as she pushed the baking sheet into the oven. She pulled her hand back and ran cold water over a finger that had touched the hot metal rack.

"Yes, Rosana Huerta," Jasmin said. "Did you ever know anyone by that name?"

"Not that I recall." She looked pensive and shook her head. "Who is she?"

"That's what I'm trying to find out."

"Have you asked your grandfather?"

"No, and please don't tell him anything. Promise me. If anyone questions him, it should be me."

After breakfast Agustín announced he was going off to his volunteer work. He put a baseball cap on and left the condo.

When Gabriela arrived, Jasmin begged her to drive to the cemetery instead of the university. She needed to see if her grandfather was visiting Rosana Huerta's tomb. Reluctant at first, Gabriela eventually consented.

They parked the car and walked to the cemetery gate. An attendant pointed them in the direction of the Siqueiros tomb. Walking as silently as two cats on a hunt, they saw the sculpture marking the muralist's burial site. It loomed straight ahead. They stopped to take in the grounds, and a second later, Gabriela pulled Jasmin's arm to hide behind a mausoleum. Agustín was facing a wall with rows of brass plaques. Jasmin mentally counted the markers on each row. Several bundles of fresh flowers had been left at the base of the wall.

With his head bowed, Agustín seemed to be praying at one of the plaques. He placed a hand on each side of it. Then with his fingers, he rubbed the bronze as if he intended to polish it.

"Shall we join him?" Jasmin asked, whispering.

"And what do we say?"

"That we came to see the Siqueiros tomb." Jasmin walked up beside her grandfather.

He turned, surprised. "Jasmin? What are you doing here? You should be at the university."

Jasmin stared at the bronze plate. This woman was born the same year as her mother. Mama was approaching her thirty-seventh birthday. Grandfather's shoulder was obscuring the rest of the plate, so she was unable to see the year of the woman's death.

"Who is Rosana Huerta?" Jasmin asked. Her grandfather put his arm around her and suggested they walk around. As usual, whenever he left the condo, he never carried his cane. Jasmin had concluded he relied on canes as an affectation and used them around the condo as an excuse to build up his collection. Maybe he liked having them available for Sojón's playful antics.

He took the two young women by a grave and asked Jasmin to read the name.

"It's my grandmother," Jasmin said.

"She's buried here because she's the granddaughter of a very important military leader," Grandfather said. "I come by to see her and while I'm here, I visit others I used to know."

Ambling through other portions of the cemetery, he stopped periodically to point out the graves of famous people buried at the panteón. He especially noted the tombstones of the other three famous muralists—Diego Rivera, Juan O'Gorman, and Jose Clemente Orozco. And he motioned toward the tomb of Agustín Lara, the Mexican composer, whose music he loved.

They spent the better part of an hour walking through tombstones before Agustín asked Gabriela to drive Jasmin to class. The three of them headed toward the parking lot. Jasmin considered how cleverly he'd evaded answering her questions about the woman whose ashes were behind that plaque. She stood on the passenger side of Gabriela's car.

"I won't leave until you tell me who Rosana Huerta is."

"She worked for me. A wonderful young woman who died long before she should have. Your grandmother and I both knew her. Now run on to class."

He opened the car door for her, but Jasmin continued to push for a more complete answer.

"Mama is the same age as that woman would be if she were still alive."

"That's a keen observation, ma petite princesse. Now get on to the university. Ask your academic advisor if we can have a word with him next week. Maybe invite him to join us for dinner."

Gabriela was behind the steering wheel with the engine running. "Let's get going before traffic picks up."

Dejected, Jasmin realized she had to leave. Her grandfather sent her off with a kiss as she climbed into the car. She brooded over his evasiveness. He had treated her like a child, ignoring her questions about a woman who must have formed a major part of his life. Major enough to merit, like Grandmother, a weekly visit to her grave. Did he come to visit that woman and her grandmother just happened to be conveniently buried there? Then there was that mystery man who had mentioned Rosana Huerta in the first place. If her grandfather didn't answer her questions, she'd seek out that man and get answers from him.

Gabriela touched Jasmin's arm. "We'll figure something out. Don't forget I suggested leaving the dead in the cemetery. Now that you've seen him here, you should insist on knowing the truth. You can talk to your grandfather this afternoon."

Instead of walking together to the library where Gabriela would remain to use the computers and do her own research until Jasmin rejoined her, they walked all the way to the lecture hall. Gabriela told her to text when she was ready to leave.

Jasmin was late and Dr. Rojas was already lecturing about gravity. She slid into a seat at the back of the room.

"Gravity," he said, "has always been considered the most boring of the four fundamental forces but its mysteries, once unraveled, may prove to be the most interesting of all."

"Gravitational waves," Jasmin said, her voice echoing from the rear of the hall, "those ripples in the fabric of space time were predicted by Einstein's General Theory of Relativity. In 2017, three physicists, Weiss, Thorne, and Barish shared the Nobel Prize in physics for confirming those waves exist." Jasmin sat up straight, feeling satisfied about adding her bit to Rojas's explanation.

The professor glared. Despite the physical distance between them, his gaze bore into her.

"Would you like to give this lecture, Ms. Jasmin?"

She shook her head. Slumping into the chair, she felt her face get hot.

When class ended, Dr. Rojas asked her to remain behind.

"There's a time to speak up in class, but it's not when I'm lecturing. You've done this before. It must stop."

"I'm sorry."

"You're very bright, but you need to listen first and then participate when others can also speak up. Otherwise, I'll have chaos in my class. And no one benefits."

First her grandfather had brushed her off at the cemetery, and now she'd annoyed her professor. Even Aki had rushed off after the lecture.

Jasmin picked up the backpack and slung it over her shoulders. Her thoughts turned to the family secrets. If her grandfather would not explain who Rosana was, she would find the mystery man and get answers. Outside, she stood by the doors looking for the stranger.

Today, when she needed to speak to him, the man was nowhere in sight.

She paced in front of the entrance for another ten minutes. Even though her grandmother was buried in the same cemetery, she wondered what part Rosana Huerta had played in the family secrets. She could even be at the very center of it. She could not be Jasmin's twin sister, but perhaps she was Mama's twin. Since Jasmin only had the year Rosana was born, but not the date, it was impossible to know. And she didn't look like Mama at all, but they could be fraternal twins. But that could not be. Her surname was different than Mama's.

Another idea made Jasmin anxious. Recalling her mother's accusations, she wondered if Rosana could be Grandfather's love child. That would explain her resemblance to Jasmin. She thought she should check the diary to see if she found any clues. Since her mother had written scant and somewhat illegible notations, perhaps she could find a connection now that she had knowledge of this mystery woman called Rosana.

Her phone rang. Gabriela was on her way to meet her.

"Shall we have a late lunch before I take you home?" she asked. "How about Nube Siete? Our student IDs will get us a discount. Plus, it offers a veggie menu."

Jasmin agreed. Gabriela was a vegetarian.

Once they were seated, Jasmin started to take the envelope of photocopies out to show her, but quickly decided otherwise. Gabriela probably did not want to get more involved in the Campos family secrets. She'd taken Jasmin to the cemetery without her grandfather's permission. Maybe she should leave the governess totally out of the situation.

Jasmin opened the door to the condo and sensed a heavy atmosphere. Her stomach churned, anticipating the scolding she'd receive. Mama's constant tirades were one thing, but she didn't want a confrontation with Grandfather. He'd be upset she'd gone to the cemetery. But she had to know who Rosana Huerta was. Swallowing hard, she tiptoed into the entryway and placed the backpack on the buffet table that Grandfather had brought from Ocotlán. She took a second to admire the framed photograph of herself as a baby with Mama and Grandmother standing next to Grandmother's car. Wondering how far back the family secrets stretched, she could not shake the thought of Rosana being her grandfather's love child.

Lola came around the corner carrying a roll of gauze and a pair of scissors.

"Is one of the cats hurt?" Jasmin asked, thinking about Sojón and his tendency to get into mischief despite his old age.

"No, it's your grandfather. But he's okay. Just a few scrapes and a black eye."

"Black eye?" Looking toward the sofa again, Jasmin saw his arm draped over the back. She rushed to him. "Are you okay?"

He reached out to hold her hand.

"Do you remember those two men who assaulted me at Sebastián's coffee shop?"

Jasmin gasped. "They did this to you?"

Her fear evaporated. Anger replaced Jasmin's apprehension and an image of the mystery man flashed through her mind. She'd gone to the cemetery after he'd told her she'd find her grandfather there. It was a setup. He wanted to hurt or kidnap her grandfather.

"I'm certain they were the same guys, but this time they beat me up and took my wallet. Had it not been for the cemetery guards, it could have been far worse."

"When did it happen?"

"Shortly after you and Gabriela left the parking lot. Thank God you'd left. Otherwise, they might have hurt you."

A flicker of movement caught Jasmin's attention. She looked up and saw her mother sitting at the desk. Mama's expression told it all. Jasmin swallowed hard.

The moment Leticia looked at Jasmin, her face showed anger. "Why did you visit the cemetery?"

"Siqueiros is buried there." Jasmin mumbled almost incoherently. "I wanted to see his grave."

"That's a lie," her mother said in a hoarse whisper.

"A building on campus, the Rectory Tower, has a Siqueiros mural and I wanted to see where he's buried. Orozco, Rivera, and O'Gorman are also buried there."

"You're a student of science, not of the arts." Mama pronounced every word with emphasis. She insisted Jasmin was supposed to be at class, not dallying around with the governess.

Lola was silent as she cleansed Grandfather's wounds. He winced as she applied disinfectant ointment before bandaging him.

"Gabriela told me the campus is a UNESCO World Heritage site," Jasmin said, staring at the floor and taking an occasional peek at Grandfather. "Due to its history. And to the famous muralists who created the art on the buildings. They're buried at the cemetery."

"Cut your nonsense. I'll speak with Gabriela and if you are lying, I swear—"

"Did you come to visit me?" Agustín asked, lifting himself up to look at Leticia over the back of the sofa. "Or did you come to rebuke your daughter?"

"Why do you always defend her?" Instead of her ominous whispering when she was angry, she was now shouting. "She's incorrigible and you encourage her rotten behavior."

Leticia picked up a mug on the desk and threw it at Jasmin, who ducked. It crashed to the floor. The cats scurried to the safety of the kitchen.

Agustín sat up abruptly. "Get out of this house, Leticia. Right now." He glanced at the remains of his favorite coffee mug.

Mama scoffed. "This is my house. It's you and that bastard girl you protect who must leave."

"Bastard girl?" Jasmin repeated, staring from her mother to her grandfather.

Lola stopped tending Agustín's wounds and joined the cats in the kitchen.

"No, Leticia, you're wrong. This condo belongs to Jasmin. And you're the one who must leave."

Leticia started hyperventilating.

Grandfather stood and crossed the room. Picking up Mama's purse from the desk, he held it out for her, asking her for the third time to leave.

"This bastard girl has made you hate me," she screamed, "and now you're leaving everything to her."

"Mama, you're the only one who hates anyone," Jasmin said. Her voice sounded calm even though her heart was pumping so hard it felt as if it would crack her ribs. "You're the one who destroyed and burned my school projects."

"Burned your projects?" she repeated in an angry whisper. "Those miserable things you left behind. Projects you call them?"

Her words cut through Jasmin's heart.

"Why do you hate me?" Jasmin screamed. Her whole body was shaking.

"Ask your grandfather why I hate you," she said, snatching her purse from his outstretched hand.

"You can have the condo," Jasmin yelled. Her mother stopped near the door and looked back at her. Jasmin kept yelling. "You can have it all, but I need to know why you hate me."

"You're adopted. I was tricked into taking you," Mama said hoarsely. She stared at Jasmin with blazing eyes.

"Adopted?" Jasmin cried out. "That explains it all."

Leticia slammed the door as she left.

Jasmin fell to her knees. The living room was swirling around her. Sobbing, she dropped to the floor, her body sprawled out on the hardwood, scattering pieces of the broken mug. Her world had ended. Everything went dark around her.

When she opened her eyes, Grandfather was kneeling beside her. He gently smoothed her hair away from her face.

"Your mother is angry over issues having nothing to do with you."

"Don't you lie to me too," Jasmin implored through sniffles. The room still swirled but she detected the colors and fuzzy shapes of furniture in the room.

"I'm the one she hates." His voice was soft yet serious. "She's angry and takes it out on you, but trust me, I'm the one she despises."

"She has no reason to love me. I'm not her daughter."

"She does love you. This is all my fault and I'll work it out. I promise you." He pushed fragments of porcelain away so he could sit on the floor.

"Why bother? I'm not your granddaughter."

"Hush. You're my most precious granddaughter. Together we'll work this out. All families have issues, and this is ours. Life is not easy," he said. "You know how much I love you."

Tears slid down his face. Jasmin sat up and hugged him. After a few minutes of complete silence, she moved away slightly.

"If I'm adopted, why does Mama hate my math proficiency?"

He shook his head. "It's a long story."

"Does it mean I don't have Maya ancestry after all? I'm adopted, so I don't carry the Campos blood."

He glanced at Jasmin and then at the floor. He picked up a couple of porcelain fragments. "Help me gather them so I can throw them away."

Taking the pieces from his hand, Jasmin studied them and then gathered the remaining fragments off the floor. "I'm going to fix it."

"Just put it in the trash. We'll buy a new mug."

"I'll make it beautiful, better than new."

"That's impossible," he said.

Jasmin explained that by using a Japanese technique called kintsugi, it would be lovelier than ever.

"I've never heard of that."

"My friend Aki does this type of work. With gold."

Jasmin knew Aki would mend the mug for her. She'd pay him for the gold he would use to glue it back together. It didn't matter how much it would cost.

In the morning, she'd call Grandfather's attorney and transfer her assets into Leticia's name. That might fix their relationship. That could be her liquid gold.

CHAPTER THIRTY-FIVE

"**C**ome sit by me," Grandfather said. He patted the sofa for Jasmin to join him. "We should talk."

Jasmin sat down. Sojón slid through the cat flap in the kitchen door and jumped into her lap. Soon he was purring.

"Before you were born, a young woman worked for me."

"Rosana?"

Agustín nodded. "Her father and brothers were apple growers in the mountain region in the state of Puebla. A cartel was forcing farmers to pay protection money. Those were not big-time, international cartels like today's drug lords and human traffickers. But when farmers either couldn't afford to pay or were not coerced into paying, these guys would take their lands away."

Agustín stopped and stared out the window, trying to decide how much to confess. He stroked Sojón's head before continuing.

"Rosana asked me, in my capacity as colonel, to help her family save their land from the cartel."

He gazed at the blue-eyed cat and stroked Sojón's head again.

"I sent troops into the area to chase the cartel out. A couple of leaders were sent to jail. Another one was killed in a gunfight with my soldiers. All in all, the area was made safer because of my intervention."

He reached out to Jasmin's hand and sighed. "I'm sorry. I'll get this situation with Leticia fixed."

———————

Jasmin moved Sojón off her lap and got up to retrieve her backpack from the entryway. Returning to the sofa, she opened the bag and removed the envelope with the photocopies of the person who looked like her twin sister. She handed the pictures to him.

"Where did you get these?" her grandfather asked. His voice cracked.

"Is this Rosana?" Jasmin asked, staring at the floor.

Studying the images on the page, his hand trembled as he smoothed his mustache and nodded. He looked at the images again. "Where did they come from?"

"A man gave them to me."

"Where?"

"At the university."

"Stay away from him. Do you understand me?"

"Was Rosana my mother?" Jasmin asked, glancing at her grandfather without changing her expression.

He nodded.

Though Jasmin had lots of questions, she didn't think she could express them. Instead, she merely asked what Rosana's personality and nature had been like. It was obvious she resembled the woman in the pictures very closely, but she wanted to learn about Rosana's character.

"Very much like you—a beautiful woman and a math genius."

At the mention of Rosana's intelligence, she remembered Lola's story about Grandmother's anger when she realized Jasmin was too smart for a normal four-year-old. She surmised Rosana was the reason behind her grandmother's heart condition.

"How old was I when Mama adopted me?"

Her grandfather's voice faltered several times as he told Jasmin she had been a few days old when the agency turned her over to Mama and Salva. Rosana, he explained, had died in childbirth.

"And you arranged for my parents to get me instead of just any baby?"

He nodded and pursed his lips as if to contain his emotions. He added that he'd helped her family arrange for Rosana's cremated remains to be interred in the cemetery where she'd found him earlier that day. Four years later, he had Grandmother buried there too.

"Panteón Civil de Dolores is not a cemetery open for burials," he said, "unless you're a very accomplished person, which Rosana was not. Or if you have relatives already in that graveyard, like your grandmother did. Rosana also had family buried there. I helped the Huerta family get her remains accepted on that basis. She was very fond of the relatives who are interred there. They were cousins of Rosana's grandmother."

Gabriela had explained that morning that only important people such as politicians, artists, philosophers, and military leaders were buried there. Jasmin had been curious.

"Who were Rosana's relatives?"

"The O'Gorman brothers."

Jasmin was shocked. "O'Gorman? You mean the muralist-architect?"

Grandfather nodded. "And Edmundo, the younger brother. A historian, writer, and philosopher."

Jasmin started to piece the information into an understandable whole. The facts her grandfather revealed, combined with Rosana's loyalty as an employee, her devotion to him for helping her family retain their land from the mafia, had probably been too much for her grandmother to accept. Despite not ever having had a boyfriend, Jasmin understood her own feelings of jealousy when anyone took her grandfather's attention away from her for too long. And he was not her husband. She could understand why Grandmother had been upset.

"Did Mama know Rosana?" she asked.

He shook his head. "Grandmother did. After all, Rosana was my assistant."

"I guess Grandmother and Mama didn't know I was Rosana's daughter when I was first adopted?"

Grandfather looked at her and slowly nodded. "That's correct."

"But they realized who I was once I started showing my abilities in math, didn't they?" she asked, thinking back again to Lola's comment that her grandmother's attitude changed when she became aware of Jasmin's intelligence.

"You're so smart, my beautiful Jasmin." He reached over and patted her hand, his eyes showing anxiety. "But something concerns me. Tell me the name of the person who gave you these pictures." He glanced again at the photocopies laying on the sofa where he'd placed them.

"A mystery man. I don't know his name."

"How did you meet him?"

"He found me. Like you warned me, the TV interview could have consequences. He watched the program and attended my class one day."

On campus, walking with Gabriela and the bodyguard her grandfather had hired for added security, Jasmin asked to see the murals of the Central Library. Javier was tall, muscular, and serious. Jasmin tried to ignore this new person assigned to escort her everywhere.

Gabriela had been informed about the assault on Agustín at the cemetery. Her new instructions from the colonel called for her to stay with Jasmin at all times, even during lectures and labs. Jasmin resented the bodyguard and she also thought Gabriela now took her duties too seriously.

Stopping to admire the pre-Hispanic motif on the north wall of the library, Jasmin could envision Rosana being enthralled with the mural. She assumed Rosana must have admired O'Gorman's art if that's the connection Grandfather used to get her remains into the panteón.

She wondered whether Rosana would have loved her. Thinking of Mama, Grandmother, and the family secrets, a chill ran down her back. Those secrets centered on her and yet she'd been kept from knowing them. It all sucked in her mind.

"How did O'Gorman paint the mural?" Jasmin asked.

"With a technique called tessellation," Gabriela said. "Instead of paint, it's done with tiny colored stones from all over the country."

Gabriela continued talking about the architect-muralist who had constructed and decorated the library, although he had assistants on the architectural side and lots of workers who did the manual labor of setting the colorful stones in the mural.

"I should build a miniature replica. If only our condo had a garden where I could put it," she said as the three of them headed toward the lecture hall.

She thought someday she'd build a replica. After all, it wasn't just any old mural, it was created by someone who was her distant relative.

The three of them took seats in the front of the lecture hall.

Aki seemed surprised when they arrived. He asked Gabriela if she would move over one seat so he could sit next to Jasmin. "We share notes," he explained.

Jasmin was accustomed to people staring and she didn't care if there was one more reason to gawk. Grandfather told her the body-guard was for her own protection. All this vigilance impacted the one aspect she needed to explore—finding out what else the mystery man knew. Her grandfather had given strict instructions to Gabriela to keep the stranger away. That would complicate access to the man.

Normally, Jasmin was focused. Today she found her attention drifting away from Dr. Rojas's lecture to her family issues. When the lecture was over, she turned to Aki and opened the bag containing the fragments of porcelain.

"Can you beautify this broken mug?"

"Beautify?" Aki asked. "With kintsugi?"

"I'll pay you for the gold."

Aki looked inside the bag and brought out a handful of fragments to make sure he could work them into a coherent piece again.

"It's Grandfather's. It's his coffee cup, so make sure the gold and alloys are harmless."

"I'll return a piece of art," he said, placing the bag of fragments in his backpack. He brushed back the hair falling over his forehead and smiled. "I'll enjoy doing this."

Javier, standing close by and appearing uncomfortable, acted indifferent to the conversation, but Gabriela seemed interested in the gold-inlaid repair process and asked questions.

Aki seemed uncomfortable with Javier, even after being introduced to him. Jasmin told him her grandfather had been assaulted and Javier was there to protect them.

"Assaulted?" Aki asked, shocked. "Is he okay?"

"He has a few bruises, but it could have been worse. It worries me that this is the second time he's been attacked."

"There's a program called Ciudad Segura, safe city," Aki said. "Your grandfather can probably have one of their special agents look into the surveillance cameras and get information on what happened, where the assailants came from, or even who they are."

Javier agreed that was an option, although the assault had happened at a cemetery, and it might not be surveilled. He'd talk to Agustín about it. "The program's command center is called C4I4, and they do have good agents."

Aki left for the lab, telling them to be careful.

Gabriela and Javier escorted her to De la Mota's office. When they arrived, she asked them to wait in the hallway.

"Your thesis is progressing nicely," De la Mota said after she sat down. "I'd been skeptical. Tachyons are so controversial. There's no proof they exist."

"That's why I find them exciting. Einstein's theory of special relativity does not exclude the possibility of particles traveling faster than the speed of light."

"True," De la Mota said, "it only excludes them in the linear, real world we perceive."

"And that's good," she said, "or else we would see the effect of something before the cause was established, like the fragments of porcelain before the cup is broken."

That concept would disturb her grandfather, who said that all actions have consequences. He would never consider consequences that could occur before the cause. She smiled at the thought of discussing that point with him.

"And you plan to continue working on the theory that dark energy might be composed of tachyons?" De la Mota asked.

"For the mathematical model in my thesis, yes. Proving tachyons exist will take decades. Scientists will need to gather evidence where they occur. At supernova explosions."

"You'd need to create a way to measure them," De la Mota added. He used the palm of his hand to smooth his wing beard. "It'll take extraordinary evidence to prove them since they lie outside of accepted theories."

"Lots of previously unaccepted theories have been proven to be correct," she said, staring out the small window of his office. "Tachyons might explain the acceleration of our universe."

"That'll include inventing a new theory." De la Mota sighed, as if he wished to be directly involved in the research too.

"That's for sure. I think dark energy might be an undiscovered field, the way the Higgs field was until recently."

"Prove any of this," De la Mota said, "and you will join the ranks of the greatest minds in physics."

Roll over, Einstein, I'm joining you. She could envision her name added at the end of the string of great physicists—Galileo, Newton, Einstein, and Hawking. But what was the probability? Jasmin mentally reprimanded herself for thinking that would ever happen.

Once De la Mota discussed recommendations for her to consider in her thesis, he changed the subject. "Would you do another media interview? Huerta wants to invite you on his radio program."

"Huerta?" Jasmin stared out the window.

"The man in the leather jacket," De la Mota explained.

"Ah, *that man*," she said, swallowing hard. Thinking how she might get answers on her family secrets, she also thought it could be a ploy to kidnap her or her grandfather. "Did you say he's a professor?"

"He teaches communications at the Ibero-American University. He came by my office a couple of days ago saying he'd like to host you for a program on physics. It's the FM 90.9 station. You've probably listened to it."

"A professor of communications," she repeated.

I should meet with him, she thought. He shares the same surname as Rosana, but Grandfather would never approve. That's why there was a bodyguard in the hallway. Yet it would give her the opportunity to speak with Huerta if she could wiggle away from her guardians.

"I'll meet him here in your office," Jasmin said. "But only if we keep it a secret between us. Grandfather does not like any notoriety around my scholastic abilities."

"Would it help if I spoke to your grandfather?"

"No," she said emphatically. "First let's speak with Mr. Huerta."

"He's Dr. Huerta."

"If you can bring him here, we'll talk. That way, the bodyguard can stay in the hall. And Huerta will have to hide here so he can't be seen."

Jasmin stood to leave. Her thesis advisor didn't know about the new research project she was involved in, and she thought she should mention it.

"Ultracold matter and quantum information?" he asked. "Won't that take you away from your thesis writing?"

She shook her head. "I'll manage. Plus, Aki and I are working on cold matter together."

CHAPTER THIRTY-SIX

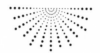

Mr. González, Grandfather's attorney, called Jasmin on the way home. She asked Gabriela to pull over so she could step out of the car and have privacy.

"I received your message, Jasmin. I regret to tell you, but I cannot change your assets into Leticia's name. You're underage and cannot make those decisions."

Not exactly the response she had wanted, but she got back in the car as Javier held the door open for her. It was uncomfortable having a person watch over her so closely.

When she arrived at the condo, she opened the door and heard Grandfather on the speakerphone with her mother. Jasmin stood by the entrance and listened. He told Leticia that Jasmin had contacted his attorney, without his knowledge, to change her assets into Leticia's name.

"I'm trying to tell you that Jasmin is so hurt that she called González to have the assets in her name transferred to you. You don't understand. She's seeking your love."

Mama's voice was breaking up, but not from bad communication lines. She sounded emotional, and Jasmin couldn't understand what she said until the very end. Her mother told Grandfather that *he* could certainly change the title of the condo and other assets back to her.

"You've missed the point, Leticia. I'm telling you how much you've hurt her. And I'm not providing you with an opening for requesting revisions to my will or the assets I've already placed in my granddaughter's name."

Jasmin entered the living room. Lola, with the cats trailing behind her, came through the kitchen door.

"You're very selfish, Leticia. You should learn from your daughter," her grandfather said.

Leticia apparently hung up on him. He put the phone down and glanced at Jasmin.

"Colonel Campos," Lola said softly, "no wonder there's bad blood between Leticia and Jasmin when you make comparisons like that."

Her grandfather, obviously angry with Mama for hanging up on him, would have been incensed with Lola's comment, except he caught sight of the tray of coffee, scones, and marmalade she was carrying. His mood immediately lightened up.

The three of them took a seat at the dining room table. Lola did not always join them for snacks, but Jasmin was glad she did on this occasion. Mama had rejected her again. Despite everything, Jasmin loved her mother, though she was giving up hope there would be a chance to gain Mama's love. It simply would not happen.

Pretending not to let the conversation injure her feelings, she took a bite of scone. It stuck in her throat, and she couldn't swallow. She coughed. Coughing again, she got it up and spat it into a napkin. Both Lola and her grandfather jumped to help her, but by then she was wiping her lips.

The air in the room seemed heavy and stale. They sat in silence, not eating. Lola gathered the dishes. Jasmin held the kitchen door open and followed her.

"Lola, why didn't you tell me I was adopted?"

"It wasn't my place," she said.

"So, you knew it?"

"That's always been Colonel Campos's dilemma," she said, looking at the floor. "It was not my business. I'm sorry. Plus, your grandmother made me promise I'd never tell you."

"Everyone knew but me." Jasmin's indignation swelled in her chest. "Do you know how depressing it is to learn everyone knows I'm adopted except for me? You should have told me. I asked you why Mama didn't love me. You knew the answer but kept silent."

"Listen, mi niña, your grandmother would have fired me. After she died, Leticia made the same threat. I would have been devastated to lose you if they'd asked me to leave. I've always loved you. And so has your grandfather."

"You should have told me," Jasmin repeated. Her face felt hot. "You protected them."

"Don't accuse me of deceiving you," Lola said. "You're not the only one who's been hurt."

Glaring at Lola, Jasmin started to answer. She saw the housekeeper was about to cry. Instead, Jasmin apologized. "I should not take my anger out on you. Mama and Grandmother should never have threatened to fire you. And I love you too. You know that, right?"

Lola nodded. She wiped the tears away with her apron and loaded the dishwasher. "It's best not to get upset over situations we can't control. Don't let this get you down. You have a whole life ahead of you." She suggested that Jasmin go to the living room and play the piano.

She played "Ode to Joy," hitting the keys forcefully. Grandfather always suggested singing Schiller's poem acapella as a warmup before playing the musical adaptation, but she didn't feel like singing. Her grandfather had always encouraged her to play it for its upbeat tune. Yet "Ode to Joy" had been a protest anthem. She played it again, hitting the keys more forcefully than the first time.

The cats gathered around the piano. Lola leaned against the kitchen doorframe to listen while her grandfather, at his desk, tapped his foot in rhythm. She played the piece over again, feeling every note. When she finished, she felt much better.

Jasmin headed for the kitchen with the cats following her, anticipating they would be given tasty rewards. Once she'd fed the felines, she felt the happiest she'd been in weeks.

CHAPTER THIRTY-SEVEN

After the lecture ended, Jasmin told Aki about the meeting with her academic advisor and that she'd skip the regular lab once again, but she'd put extra time into the ultracold matter. She headed, her guards in tow, toward De la Mota's office. She felt apprehensive, as though her brain might explode like a supernova, yet she had to hide her emotions from her governess.

De la Mota greeted her at his door and asked Javier and Gabriela to wait outside. He closed the door. As planned, Huerta was already there, seated in a corner so Jasmin's entourage could not see him if the door were opened.

Her mouth went dry. "Five million, seven hundred two thousand, eight hundred and eighty-seven—"

"Jasmin, I hope you'll understand what I'm about to tell you," De la Mota said, scratching his wing beard.

She took a deep breath and gazed at the floor.

"Before you were born, I became an assistant professor of advanced mathematics here. I had a wonderful student. Her intellectual capacity was similar to yours. Her name was Rosana Huerta. Do you know who she was?"

Nodding, she continued staring at the floor. "Grandfather told me a few days ago."

"This man is Segundo Huerta," De la Mota said.

He and Rosana share the same surname, Jasmin thought.

"He's Rosana's brother," the professor said, "and your uncle."

Looking at Huerta, her thoughts swirled with confusion. This man may have been responsible for the assaults on Grandfather, yet he was related to her. "Why didn't you tell me?"

"Until the television interview, I didn't know you were even alive. Seeing you—"

"You didn't know I was alive?" Her stomach churned.

"When Rosana died, the doctor informed us her baby had also died," Huerta said. "Watching that program was a serendipitous coincidence. It was like seeing Rosana alive again."

Huerta's claim shocked her. Maybe it wasn't a good idea to be here. But with Gabriela and Javier in the hallway, all she had to do was scream. Her mind felt like a battlefield of conflicting emotions, and in that sense, she felt like Schrödinger's cat, in a box where she had no control over people who were observing her inside the box. She took a deep breath. To uncover family secrets, she needed to listen.

Jasmin looked at Huerta suspiciously. "But you know my grandfather."

"True, but we had no idea his daughter had adopted you," Huerta said.

"You came looking for me instead of Grandfather. Why?"

"To learn the truth. We lost contact with Agustín after he retired and moved. We eventually accepted Rosana's death and life moved on. After seeing you on TV, I did a little research. Fearing that your grandfather would not want to see me, I contacted you. I did follow your grandfather for two weeks and found he goes to the Panteón de Dolores every Friday, and visits Rosana's grave."

"She worked for him," I said. "My grandmother is also buried there and he visits her grave too."

Huerta looked at her intensely. "After Rosana died, my family asked Agustín to arrange a niche at the panteón for her ashes. As a teenager, she had loved going there to see the O'Gorman graves. She loved their work."

De la Mota asked Huerta why Rosana had been cremated.

"I was furious that she'd been cremated without our approval, but the doctor gave us a document signed by Rosana. It clearly stated her wish to be cremated and have the ashes turned over to her family."

"But the doctor must have concealed something," Jasmin said.

Huerta stood briefly and grabbed a ballpoint pen from a mug on De la Mota's desk and glanced at her. "Yes, he concealed that you were alive. It appears Agustín also covered it up."

The room went silent.

Huerta started clicking the pen on and off. He recounted that Agustín had recommended taking the physician to court, but later convinced them not to file a complaint since that would not bring Rosana back. "After that, Agustín disappeared from our radar. He deceived us. You were alive and he kept it from us. That's why I contacted you and not him."

Jasmin noticed Huerta was staring at the floor. Periodically, he'd close his eyelids as if he found this conversation difficult. The pen clicking continued, and she wanted to reach over and take the ballpoint from him. The noise was so irritating she wanted to scream.

"We're the ones who should have raised you. We're your family," Huerta said. He flung the pen against the floor.

De la Mota looked straight at Huerta and asked what the doctor had told the family about Rosana's baby.

Huerta struggled to speak. The doctor told them the baby was also cremated; the ashes commingled with Rosana's. "Shortly after my sister died, Colonel Campos moved. Later we heard he'd retired. We had no reason to stay in contact with him. I can't believe he deceived us all this time." Huerta pounded a fist on his thigh.

De la Mota looked surprised. He glanced from Huerta to me. "I recommend running a DNA test to confirm you and Jasmin are related."

"Why? She looks exactly like Rosana." Huerta picked the pen up off the floor and fidgeted with it again.

"To confirm you're related," De la Mota repeated.

"Did you know Leticia adopted me?" Jasmin asked De la Mota.

"Not initially." He explained it had first occurred to him after he'd been tutoring Jasmin for a while. "You look so much like Rosana, at times I felt myself in a time warp, teaching Rosana all over again. Mathematical responses or insights rolled off your tongue. I remembered Rosana doing the same at the university."

"You've established who my biological mother was—"

De la Mota reminded her that DNA confirmation was pending. He shifted in his chair, appearing nervous.

"Who's my father?" Jasmin asked, looking at Huerta. "He's been as absent as Salva, my adopted father, after he and my mother were divorced."

"Rosana was unmarried. She kept the father of her baby a total secret. The family figured it could have been one of her professors," Huerta said, looking at De la Mota with a questioning expression. "In fact, we did not know about the pregnancy until she could no longer hide it."

Jasmin stared out the window. Secrets abounded on both her biological and adopted sides of her family. The universe concealed mysteries, too, but at least these were open for exploration and research through science and math. Once a theory had been proven, science opened previously undiscovered secrets for the entire world to study. If she lived long enough, the scientific method would reveal the unification of the four fundamental forces of physics, the work initially started by Galileo, which continued through Newton, Einstein, and Hawking. *Science needs a woman to add her name to the four great pillars of modern physics*, she thought. *I'll be that woman.*

De la Mota must have noticed how quiet Jasmin had become and asked if she was okay.

"Can we find my father through DNA testing?" she asked.

"You're underage," Huerta said. "Your grandfather or Leticia must give approval. Plus, anyone who might be your father also needs to be tested. That might be hard to do."

De la Mota and Huerta exchanged ideas on how to carry out the testing, concluding that Leticia had to give her permission since she had legal custody. And then there was the problem of whether possible fathers could either be tested or could be found in a database.

"My mother will never agree," Jasmin said.

"Could we find a doctor who will run the test for us without getting Leticia involved?" Huerta asked.

De la Mota immediately dismissed that suggestion, but he offered to check with one of the university attorneys. He emphasized that whatever they did had to be legal. Even if Huerta had to threaten Leticia with a lawsuit to get her consent.

Jasmin knew the law would work against her, a minor, just as it had prevented her from legally registering her condo in Mama's name. The law would surely prevent her from obtaining tests to determine her blood relatives. Unless her mother could be convinced.

The two men discussed several more issues to follow up on and they agreed to meet in another week. Huerta crouched in the corner like a thief when De la Mota opened the door. Gabriela sat by herself. When De la Mota asked about Javier, she said he was running an errand and would catch up later.

CHAPTER THIRTY-EIGHT

Jasmin sat at the piano with only her music and the cats to keep her company. Gabriela had driven Agustín and Lola to the grocery store and to pick up tacos al pastor for lunch. It was a lazy, overcast Saturday morning and her grandfather had suggested Lola take the day off from cooking.

Jasmin played Mozart's "Magic Flute." The music fit her recent mood swings, from the playful melodies of the bird catcher, Papageno, to the more profound themes expressed by Tamino, the prince, in his search for love and the meaning of life. The cats paced, tails in the air, around the baby grand, and periodically one of them would slink by the stool and rub against Jasmin's pants as if to remind her to feed them.

The doorbell rang. Grandfather was probably signaling they had returned with lunch. They had a key and would let themselves in. She continued playing the piano until the doorbell sounded again. She answered the door.

"A concert so early in the morning?" Salva Dominguez asked.

Jasmin was shocked speechless. After he and Mama divorced, it didn't take him long, by Mama's account, to marry a rich lawyer in

Madrid so he would not have to work for a living. She thought her mother was wrong though. Her father was teaching history at a university in Spain.

"You're a young woman now," he said. "And so beautiful. Do I get a hug?"

Salva had been a loving father. He'd tried to keep in touch, but over time the phone calls dwindled until they'd stopped altogether. His jovial personality that contrasted with Mama's severe outlook on life had made Jasmin gravitate toward him when she was a child. She'd been devastated when Salva moved far away to Spain. She'd always felt guilty about her parents' separation. *I wonder if Mama's diary was the reason they divorced.* Grandfather had filled the emptiness and made up for the loss she'd felt when Salva left.

Opening the door wide, she stepped up to hug him. "Come in. Grandfather is away but should be here shortly with lunch. And you must stay. He's bringing tacos al pastor."

Salva rolled two suitcases in. He unzipped one and removed a gift-wrapped box and handed it to her.

"I understand you're quite the math genius. You always were so smart. Fortunately, you didn't inherit my total lack of understanding of the subject." He laughed, joking how math had eluded him completely. In fact, he thought math was a profane word until he was an adult. That's when he realized it was essential to business, science, and just about any worthwhile endeavor. "It was my own little Jasmin at age five who made me aware of the importance of it." He hugged her again.

She opened the gift and found a mug inside. The six most important world-changing mathematical formulae were superimposed on a geometric tessellation background reminiscent of Escher's periodic tiling. She stared at it and started to cry.

"If it makes you sad, let's throw it away," Salva said.

"It's beautiful and I'm happy to see you. That's why I'm crying." Pointing to a formula, she explained Newton's second law of motion, and moving her finger to the next one, she spoke about Newton's law of universal gravitation. By the time she placed her finger on Einstein's mass-energy equivalence, Salva's eyes were glazed over. She was disappointed not to expound on the complexities of Schrödinger's wave function notation, but she could already hear her grandfather telling her Salva didn't need boring lectures on physics.

At that moment, she heard footsteps outside. "Grandfather has arrived with lunch," she said, excited.

Instead, her mother and Alfredo walked through the open door.

Leticia walked in, protesting that the cats would aggravate her allergies. Then she saw Salva. Mama's defiant expression dissipated.

"What the hell are you doing here?" she asked.

"Thanks for the warm welcome. You haven't changed much since I last saw you," Salva said. "I've come to visit my daughter and Agustín."

Mama introduced the two men to each other.

Stress was palpable in the air and Jasmin relaxed when Grandfather arrived with the tacos. He would know how to handle everyone in the room. Walking straight to Salva, Agustín gave him a hug, welcoming him like the prodigal son.

Gabriela and Lola laid out the cartons of food and drinks on the dining room table and placed stacks of napkins in several spots.

"Can we all sit down to enjoy the tacos before they get cold?" Alfredo asked.

When Leticia objected to eating street food, her husband took her hand and asked her to join them at the table anyway. She did as he asked, but with a rigid scowl.

"My favorite street food," Alfredo said as he opened the boxes with roasted shaved lamb and beef, small containers of guajillo chile sauce, onion, pineapple chunks, and cilantro. He passed them around the table.

"My favorite too," Jasmin said, surprised she agreed with Mama's husband.

"That's three of us," Salva said.

"Make that four," Agustín added, selecting a taco from the box being passed around.

"What brings you to Mexico?" the former priest asked Salva.

Salva wiped his mouth before answering. "Colonel Campos invited me. He said Jasmin is growing up and I should see her before they move to Princeton."

"Princeton?" Leticia jumped from her seat as she said it. "Why hasn't anyone told me?"

Alfredo reached over and took his wife's hand. "That's a wonderful opportunity for your daughter." He asked when they were planning to leave.

"As soon as she finishes her thesis. After this semester is complete," Agustín said.

"It'd be better if she moves sooner," Leticia said in a tone that made everyone cringe.

"Why?" her husband asked.

"So she can be the genius among geniuses." Mama's tone became more conciliatory. "But before you leave," she said, turning to Agustín, "you must know she is meeting in secret with De la Mota."

"De la Mota is my advisor." Jasmin clipped her words and glared at Gabriela who had stopped eating a vegetarian taco and looked as if she were about to get sick.

"You also met with a man by the name of Segundo Huerta," Mama said. "At De la Mota's office."

"You're spying on me." Jasmin was so angry she wanted to stomp out of the room, yet she controlled her temper and stared at her mother. "You not only keep secrets from me, but you also snoop into my personal life. You're not fair." Then glowering at Gabriela, she added, "And I know who the tattletale is."

Gabriela stood and excused herself to leave.

Agustín frowned at her. "No, Gabriela, please stay."

She slinked back into her chair.

"Sounds as if I came at a very good time," Salva said, chuckling and shaking his head in amazement. "I don't know what secrets anyone is keeping. Why don't we talk things through?"

"I second that idea," Alfredo said.

Mama stared at Salva. "Jasmin found out she's adopted. That's the secret. So now she's doing stupid stuff."

"It's true," Salva said, looking at Jasmin, "that you're adopted, but you are so lucky to have such a wonderful family. We love you; you're our daughter. We've all had our share of problems but tell me what family does not have its issues. I'm the one who is guilty for not being around."

"It's all the other things you've kept from me," Jasmin said, looking straight at her mother. "I'm old enough to know. Like maybe who my father is."

"I'm your father," Salva said.

"I mean the biological one," she retorted.

The table went silent.

"Does it really matter?" Alfredo asked, breaking the silence. "You have Salva. You have your grandfather. And now you're stuck with me, though we don't really know each other very well yet. What are you lacking?"

"It's Mama. She doesn't love me," Jasmin mumbled.

"Your mother does love you," Alfredo said. "She doesn't express her love easily."

"That's right. I'm very stern," Leticia said with a grim expression, exaggerating it until everyone realized she was joking.

Jasmin never remembered her mother having a sense of humor. Maybe her new husband was a positive influence.

"I want DNA testing to know the truth. Who my mother is. Who my father is."

"If you want to know, we can probably ask the adoption agency to disclose that information," her mother said.

Leticia finally reached for a taco and started eating.

"No, I want DNA testing."

Her grandfather cleared his throat. "The agency should provide facts we can use for follow up."

"No! That proves nothing," Jasmin spat out, interrupting her grandfather. If Mama could get Gabriela and Javier to report on her visits to De la Mota's office, she could convince the adoption agency to provide bogus data.

"Is there any harm in DNA testing?" Salva asked in a tentative voice. He looked around the table at everyone.

"Only that a stranger has been influencing her," Leticia said. "Segundo Huerta. He's putting ideas in her head."

"He may be my relative," Jasmin said forcefully.

"He's a stranger to you," Mama said, pointing at her. "He could want money, or he might hurt you. Even kidnap you."

Lola gathered empty food containers and soiled napkins. Gabriela helped her and both women headed toward the kitchen, their arms full of throwaway items.

"Look, Leticia," Grandfather said. "If Jasmin wants to have her DNA tested, she can do it. I'll take her on Monday."

Leticia scoffed. Appearing shocked at first, her expression changed to indifference. She stood and gazed directly at Jasmin. "How do you know Segundo Huerta is not the person who had your grandfather beaten up?"

Salva's jaw dropped. "Beaten up?"

Briefly explaining the two incidents with the assailants, Agustín dismissed it all as nonsense.

Salva looked concerned. "Did they steal anything?"

"Only my wallet."

"Anything else?" Salva asked.

Agustín shook his head and looked away.

"He did not even report the assaults to the police," Alfredo said.

"Unless the police are less corrupt than when I left," Salva said, "that's a good idea."

"They are more corrupt than ever," Leticia added.

"That's enough." Agustín glanced at Salva and invited him to the DNA lab on Monday.

"I have custody of Jasmin," Leticia said, "without me to sign the paperwork, the tests won't be run."

"So Salva, Leticia, Jasmin, and I will leave for the lab at eight a.m. this Monday morning," Grandfather said. "Does anyone else want in on this party?"

When no one answered, Salva suggested moving into the living room to listen to Agustín and Jasmin play four hands at the piano. He picked up Agustín's guitar and said he'd be happy to join with classical guitar if he knew the music.

Grandfather put his arm around Jasmin and whispered in her ear.

"Salva has come all the way from Spain to visit you. Don't hurt his feelings by saying you want to know who your real father is."

"You're right. It's not fair to him. Should we cancel the DNA test?"

"Not at all," Grandfather said. "You won't be happy until you have the results, but don't offend him in the process. All I'm saying is to take other people's feelings into consideration."

CHAPTER THIRTY-NINE

At the lab Mama signed documents allowing them to compare Jasmin's DNA to the university's database to find matches. Still, if her father wasn't in the database, they wouldn't find him. Jasmin's group was the noisiest among the clientele that filled the waiting room. Lab personnel buzzed around doing their work, adding to the chaos. In Jasmin's entourage of seven only Gabriela and Javier kept quiet.

Talking, giving opinions, and asking questions, they attracted attention as they walked down the corridor. The phlebotomist seemed overwhelmed when everyone decided to cram into the tiny work-station.

"Are you sure the needle is sterile?" Salva asked.

"Let me see the package before you open it," Agustín demanded. He used the antiseptic handwash dispenser mounted on the wall to clean his hands before he inspected the small package.

The phlebotomist prepared to take the blood sample and an eerie silence pervaded her lab station. Jasmin suppressed her urge to pick up the Fibonacci sequence. The clinic's odor of disinfectant overpowered the alcohol the technician used on Jasmin's arm before inserting the needle into her vein. Everyone watched while the blood was drawn.

Since she wanted the test done, Jasmin felt she had no choice but to be brave despite feeling queasy.

The results would be available in ten working days, the receptionist told them as they left. Everyone departed to their next location: Mama and her husband to Tlaxcala, Salva to visit friends, and Agustín back to the condo in a taxi. Jasmin and her bodyguards headed for the physics department.

Aki now seemed oblivious to Jasmin's security detail. As soon as she sat down, he handed her a package.

She took a quick peek and gasped. "It's a masterpiece."

"Did you see where I wrote his name?"

She took the mug out. *Agustín Campos de la Vega* was inscribed in gold across the top.

She squeezed Aki's hand and told him she was anxious to get home and present it to her grandfather. "How much do I owe you?"

"It's a gift."

After class, she and Aki worked in the lab. Gabriela did research on her tablet and Javier, looking bored, mostly sat. Periodically he would stand, pace the hallway, and return to the bench in the lab.

Aki asked Jasmin if she'd decided about Princeton.

She shook her head.

"It's fun working with you," he said. "It's like having a little sister who understands theoretical physics. I'll miss you if you leave."

"Why don't you apply to Princeton?" she asked. "We could work together there."

Aki frowned and turned away slightly, pursing his lips. Then he looked at Jasmin and nodded.

For the next two hours, they ran experiments, calculations, and Jasmin documented their work. She took a break and went into the restroom to text De la Mota.

I can't make the next meeting. My bodyguards reported the last one with you & Huerta to Mama and she's ordered them to keep me away from him.

Had DNA done. Tell Huerta to test his DNA at the university labs.

She erased the texts and returned to the lab.

A somber Salva met her at the door when she got home that evening. He hugged her. "Your mother is here. We're having a little meeting with your academic advisor and Segundo Huerta."

Jasmin's demeanor changed. "Did De la Mota report the text I sent him?" she asked.

Salva shook his head, though he had not understood what she said.

After she placed the backpack and the package with the mug on the buffet table, Salva guided her to the sofa. Leticia, De la Mota, and Huerta were already sitting. Alfredo stood next to the piano. Her grandfather was missing.

"You've told us you're old enough to know all the secrets in this family," Salva began, holding her hand. Taking control of the conversation, he explained this was a situation they could not keep from her.

Everyone looked glum.

"Where's Grandfather?" she asked in a squeaky, terrified voice.

"He took a taxi from the lab, but he never made it home," her mother said, sniffling. It was obvious she'd been crying.

"We'd barely arrived in the village when we received a call," Alfredo said. "From kidnappers. They asked for ransom. We contacted Salva and drove back here."

Salva cut in. "Agustín's assailants at the cemetery might be connected to a military engagement years ago, when he sent troops to protect the apple growers in the highlands of Puebla." Glancing first at Jasmin and then at Huerta, Salva told everyone that when he'd arrived from Madrid, one of the first things Agustín discussed with him was that military incident. "Call Segundo Huerta if anything happens," Colonel Campos had said. Salva added Agustín told him the apple farmer intervention had protected Huerta's family from the cartel extortionists.

Huerta glanced around the room before speaking. "After the cemetery incident, Agustín contacted me to locate the whereabouts of those troublemakers who had gone to prison. We discovered that one of them, El Lencho, had been released. He could be the one who abducted Agustín."

Jasmin listened in astonishment. Grandfather had never mentioned being in contact with Huerta. On the contrary, she'd been told the bodyguard was to protect her from people like him. She felt a pang of anger that family secrets were still being kept from her. Turning to Huerta, she asked if he'd seen her grandfather at the cemetery the day he was beaten up.

Huerta shook his head. "If I'd witnessed it, I would have come to his rescue. I learned about it when Agustín contacted me."

"Grandfather said the assailants at Bazar Sábado were the same ones at the cemetery. So what are we going to do to get him back?" Silently she recited the Fibonacci sequence to remain in control of her emotions.

When Alfredo mentioned the ransom amount, Leticia gasped. Jasmin wasn't sure what upset her mother more—her father being kidnapped or the possibility of having to pay out a small fortune.

"Look," Jasmin said. "Let's call González, Grandfather's attorney. Maybe he can find a way to sell my condo and pay them off."

Salva shook his head. "First, we need assurances Agustín is alive, and then we'll negotiate."

Mama started hyperventilating. Alfredo put his arm around her shoulders and whispered instructions to let out long exhales. Lola brought a box of tissues and placed them on the coffee table.

"Cool heads need to prevail if we are to get Agustín back alive," De la Mota said, speaking for the first time.

Her family was not religious, and she didn't know how to pray, yet Jasmin started a silent prayer thinking it couldn't hurt. That would also be better than reciting the Fibonacci sequence. She also thought that Mama's husband should lead them all in a prayer. Concentrating on asking God to return Grandfather unharmed, she asked forgiveness for flaunting her intelligence, for thinking she might actually be a genius of such magnitude that she could carry forth the tradition of the greatest minds of physics. She was sorry about telling Einstein to roll over like a dog.

When she finished her conversation with God, a thought came to her. "We must contact C4I4."

"And what is that?" Salva asked.

"It's the command center for Ciudad Segura, the city's urban security program. My friend Akifumi told me about it. My bodyguard said it has good agents working there. Plus, I researched it online."

Salva looked stupefied. De la Mota agreed it was an idea worth considering. He described it as the center for urban surveillance and crisis response. With more than thirteen thousand cameras set in strategic spots throughout the city, it also included a network of police patrolling city streets and environmental sensors to capture data related to seismic activity and various other types of emergency events.

"Are police part of this program?" Salva asked, sounding hesitant, as if he were analyzing an idea he didn't like.

De la Mota nodded. "Mexicans don't have much love for the police, but if you want to save Agustín, we might have to get them involved."

For several minutes, they discussed their misgivings about involving law enforcement. And once again, De la Mota told them it depended if they wanted to save Agustín or not.

"Does Colonel Campos carry kidnapping insurance?" Salva asked.

When Mama responded affirmatively, Salva suggested calling the insurance. Instead of the police, they would send a negotiator to the condo.

"Why don't we also contact González, the attorney?" Alfredo asked. "At least for his advice regarding both C4I4 and the insurance people."

Lola walked to the kitchen to prepare coffee and Jasmin followed her. The two cats stayed with her as if they knew something was amiss. Feeling sad, she sat on the cold tile floor to be next to them. Sojón stood on his hind legs, placing his front paws on her arm. Sancho climbed into her lap. The most important person in her life was in terrible danger and the cats seemed to sense something was wrong and acted as if they were consoling her.

"Lola, what are we going to do? I feel guilty that I've been so self-ish. That I've thought myself so smart."

The aroma of Lola's freshly brewed coffee filled the kitchen.

"We can all be more humble," she said, cutting slices of poppyseed cake to take to the living room with the coffee. "And we can pray too."

Agustín sat on a cot and looked around a small room. It smelled moldy. A filthy blanket covering the single cot was full of holes. A stained and disgusting chamber pot took up the far corner. He had been blindfolded until they brought him into the room.

We must be in the Puebla highlands. Perhaps in the apple growing area, he considered, though the room had no windows. A single bulb in the middle of the ceiling provided dim light. The handcuffs had been removed, but his arms still ached. They'd also taken off the tape from his mouth when they dumped him in this hellhole. He was tired and hungry.

Two men wearing ski masks had held up the taxi on his way to the condo. They'd taken him, blindfolded him, taped his mouth, and cuffed his hands behind his back. They walked him to what he assumed was an SUV. The taxi driver had remained silent. Agustín figured the man was either scared out of his wits or he was an accomplice. As soon as there had been a chance, the taxi had sped off.

Agustín's two abductors had hardly spoken during an interminably long ride. One had driven the SUV and the other one had sat in the back seat with him. The radio had blared out ballads about narcos.

Agustín heard someone unlocking the door.

The same two men with ski masks entered.

"Sancho," Agustín said, "So good to see you. Have you taken care of Rocinante? My faithful horse needs food and water after our long ride."

"¿Que mierda estás diciendo?" the short, stout man asked.

"I'm appalled at your language, Sancho. Don't speak such foul words. We must be chivalrous."

"There's only one way to deal with this shit," the taller one said.

He stepped toward Agustín and punched him in the jaw.

The blow knocked Agustín off the cot. He struggled to get up. Back on the edge of the miserable cot, he stared at the stout man.

"Sancho, your friend is a bad influence. Where did you meet him?"

"Chingados, está loco el hombre. Piensa que es el Quijote," the stout one said. "Shit, this man's crazy. He thinks he's the Quixote."

"Si, yo soy Don Quijote de la Mancha," Agustín said, introducing himself and extending his hand in greeting. "I'm Don Quixote of La Mancha."

CHAPTER FORTY

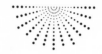

S alva called González, the attorney, and asked him over to the condo to discuss Agustín's abduction.

González listened to the family's idea of involving either the insurance negotiators or C4I4, at times nodding and occasionally shaking his head.

Salva was the most reluctant of all about involving law enforcement.

"Due to the circumstances," González said, "I recommend the family work with C4I4. They have more resources."

After a short discussion, the family agreed. Salva asked González to report Agustín's kidnapping to central command immediately.

In less than an hour, an overweight man, Detective Serna, arrived to handle negotiations. He informed Salva that he would remain at the condo for the duration of the case. With labored breaths, the man explained the personnel and equipment assigned to finding the hostage. The goal, he emphasized, was to recover Colonel Campos alive and unharmed. Using the guest bedroom, he interviewed each person, asking specific questions and reminding them that all details, no matter how insignificant, would be important. Two hours elapsed. When he completed his interrogations, De la Mota and Huerta were allowed to return to their homes. He called Gabriela and Javier in for questioning.

After the detective released Gabriela to return home, Salva thanked her for her cooperation. "Don't mention Agustín's kidnapping to anyone. We're trying to keep this quiet."

"The detective told me the same," she said. "It could potentially endanger Agustín. And others too."

Javier had been interrogated the longest of anyone.

"The detective has asked me to remain at the condo until further notice," Javier told Salva after Serna released him. The order seemed to rattle the bodyguard's nerves.

Salva understood his apprehension. After all, Detective Serna from C414 had called him in for an interrogation and then asked him to stay with a family he hardly knew. Salva asked Lola to set up a makeshift bed in the entryway for Javier to sleep on.

"I'll set up an inflatable mattress," she said.

The detective remained in the guest bedroom to make calls to his office on what he called his secure phone. Then he gathered Salva, Leticia, and Alfredo, in the bedroom. "I've done a background check on Javier and found nothing suspicious. I'm recommending he stay at the condo to guard you."

<hr />

Jasmin was surprised when Detective Serna announced he would also stay at the condo. Yet she was not surprised, given his weight, that the detective soon learned Lola was not only an outstanding chef, but that she was also motivated to cook.

The more Lola fretted, the more frenzied she became in the kitchen. She cut, diced, boiled, grilled, baked, and fried. Then she would turn her attention to cleaning and scrubbing the pans, banging them as if that added to their cleanliness. Savory specialties, regional dishes, spicy sauces, pastries, and tortes kept accumulating in the kitchen.

"Do you think we're gathered for a wedding rather than a kidnapping?" Jasmin asked.

"Don't make a wisecrack," Lola said. "I'm keeping busy to endure the stress. Plus having the former priest with us isn't easy." Then she admitted Alfredo was not such a bad person after all.

Lola had voiced her opposition to C4I4 to Jasmin in private. Like Salva, Lola had favored using the insurance company's private negotiators. Every time Lola complained about the detective's food intake, Jasmin felt sick. She felt responsible, since she'd been the first one to suggest bringing in the city's security group. What if the insurance negotiators had been a better option?

Serna prepared to sleep on the sofa, but not before giving the family an update that he needed to sleep to remain alert throughout the crisis. If there were any developments in the case, his mobile phone would awaken him. Judging from the snoring that came from the living room that night, Jasmin figured he was the only one to get any sleep.

The men holding Agustín captive returned with a bowl of beans, two corn tortillas, and a cola.

"Sancho, what delicacies have you brought me?"

Neither man answered. They put the food and drink on the cot and left, locking the door behind them.

Agustín's jaw hurt, but he ate. When he finished, he put the bowl on the floor. A cockroach scurried toward it. He stomped on it and pushed it into a corner using the tip of his shoe.

He slept restlessly, startled awake several times by the feeling of cockroaches crawling on his body. When he checked, there were none, but he knew that wherever there were cockroaches, there were likely to be rats. Worse yet, his kidnappers could come in the middle of the night and beat him again.

The next morning Agustín awakened to three masked men standing by his cot. The third man, he figured, was the leader. He seemed older though it was hard to judge through the ski mask.

"We have a score to settle," the leader said.

"Hand me my lance, Sancho. For this man is our enemy."

The leader backed away slightly. "Knock some sense back into this hijo de puta."

The tall man stepped forward and punched Agustín in the jaw, knocking him flat on the floor. Then he kicked Agustín in the stomach.

"Hey, don't kill the bastard. Not yet. I want to collect the ransom."

"Don't worry," the tall man said. "He's only pretending to be unconscious."

After about thirty seconds, Agustín opened his eyes.

"How about that? The Quixote's alive," the leader said sarcastically. "Clean the blood off his face and get him on the cot."

He stood in front of Agustín. "Where's Rosana?"

"Who?"

"That young woman that worked for you."

"I've never had a young woman working for me. I only know Dulcinea and she's a princess."

The leader slapped him. "You know Rosana didn't die that night. She went to the US, and we lost track of her. The man I work for is asking where you've kept her over the last several years?"

Agustín held up his hand and spoke to the short, stout man. "Don't get involved in this battle, Sancho. You're not a knight and it'd be improper for you to defend me."

"Cut the bullshit, pendejo." The leader slapped him again, harder this time. Agustín's nose dripped blood. "You're going to pay for your intervention with the apple growers years ago. You spoiled our business here and your soldiers killed one of our captains."

The tall one asked if he should force Agustín to talk.

"Not now. Leave el pendejo to think about his responses. I'll be back tomorrow, and you can make him talk then."

At the door, the man laughed and told his accomplices that they'd put the knight errant on a burner phone the next day to call his family. "He'll order them to pay the ransom. If he keeps talking crazy, I'll kill him." He touched the gun at his waist and closed the door when they left the room.

Salva, having been asked by Leticia and Alfredo to be the lead family member to coordinate with the detective, immediately joined the man when a call from the command center came in at four in the morning of the third day.

"An anonymous tip was called in about the location where Agustín is being held," Serna told Salva. "I need to be there to help in the rescue." He reviewed a few precautions they were to follow in his absence.

Before leaving, the detective went to the kitchen and helped himself to a slice of chocolate cake and a cup of coffee for the road. Salva watched Lola, who like everyone else, had hardly slept. She was standing by the refrigerator holding a wooden spoon, slapping it against the palm of her other hand as she watched the detective cutting the cake.

When he left, Lola mumbled that she hoped his phone call was not a ruse.

Without the detective around to feast on Lola's cuisine, food piled up in the kitchen, though the pantry shelves were getting bare. The cats meowed more than ever, making Leticia irritable.

Salva and Jasmin fed them small portions of the meat and fish dinners to quiet them. Other than the cats, Javier was the only one still eating.

The rest of the group were too stressed to eat much.

Every time the phone rang, they all sprang to answer it. When Huerta called, Leticia invited him and De la Mota to come back and await any news.

Salva, worried about his daughter, asked Jasmin how she was doing.

"I'm talking with God, asking for Grandfather's safe return and begging forgiveness for my past transgressions. I've even promised God I won't use my intellect to feel better at the expense of others. And not to get into arguments with Mama."

"You've never had transgressions."

"Ahh, yes, I have. It was my fault when you and Mama separated. I took her diary and hid it in my room, and she blamed you for its disappearance. I should have returned it long ago. Everything would have turned out differently. I feel so guilty."

"That was not the reason your mother and I separated. I can assure you, our marriage had lots of issues." He embraced Jasmin, telling her to forget about the diary.

The doorbell rang and Salva answered. He escorted Huerta and De la Mota into the kitchen.

"There's a lot of food and it's too good to throw away, so please help yourselves," he told them.

Lola had dishes and flatware set out, buffet style, on a kitchen counter. On another counter, pastries, cakes, and breads Lola had baked, were lined up. The men helped themselves. Huerta looked guilty about eating given the tense situation, but he got over it quickly and returned for seconds. Javier was on his third or fourth dessert and seemed oblivious to be eating with the very man he'd been told was out to kidnap Jasmin. De la Mota was the one who seemed genuinely concerned about Agustín.

About four that afternoon, Detective Serna called.

The group held their collective breaths. Gathering by the dining room table, Salva placed the phone on speaker.

"We think Agustín is still alive. But someone must have tipped them off about our rescue mission."

"How could that be?" Leticia asked, angrily banging her hand on the table. She was hyperventilating again.

Alfredo asked Lola to take his wife to Agustín's bedroom.

Salva demanded an explanation from the detective.

The phone vibrated on the table each time the detective spoke in his loud baritone voice. The plan, he explained, was to call off the rescue mission until investigators had a new lead. After the detective told them he'd return to the condo to stand by in case of further ransom requests, Salva ended the call.

Jasmin's legs shook. She leaned against the wall to steady herself. Then she inched down the hall to check on her mother. Mama was leaning against pillows propped up against the headboard with her legs stretched out on the bed. Lola massaged her feet. When Jasmin walked into the room, Lola asked her to rub her mother's feet so she could make a cup of chamomile to soothe Leticia's nerves.

By the time Lola returned, Leticia had fallen asleep. Lola placed the steaming cup on the side table and signaled Jasmin to follow her. In the living room, Salva and Alfredo were sleeping on the sofa. Apparently, exhaustion had hit them too. The other three men—De la Mota, Huerta, and Javier—were in the kitchen finishing the chocolate cake.

Lola looked at the men in the kitchen. "How can you explain that through mathematics?"

"There's no theorem to cover humanity's ability to eat chocolate," Jasmin said. "That's plain gluttony. But as far as the probabilities of rescuing Grandfather alive, I don't want to think about it."

"I'm sorry, mi niña, I thought we could use a light moment in the face of this tragedy. That was thoughtless of me."

De la Mota put his plate down and walked to Jasmin and took her hand. "Agustín is going to be all right."

"How can you say that?"

"I can feel it in my bones," he said.

Jasmin felt so sad she paced up and down the hallway, praying as she walked. She took her grandfather's mug out of her backpack, took it to her bedroom, and placed it on the bookshelf next to the cup Salva had given her.

She stared at the cups and wondered if her prayers would be answered. She hoped that her grandfather's safe return was not merely wishful thinking on her part.

CHAPTER FORTY-ONE

Jasmin was drifting off to sleep on her bed when she heard the doorbell ring. She ran down the hall as Javier opened the door. Her grandfather stood next to the heavyset detective. Was it really her grandfather standing there? Or was she delirious from lack of sleep?

She hugged her grandfather and let out a sigh of relief when she realized he had made it home safely. Everyone crowded around, even Leticia. Salva and De la Mota high-fived Agustín.

Leticia became spitting-fire angry and turned to Detective Serna. "You damned bastard, why didn't you tell us he was safe? Have you no idea the suffering you caused us?"

Alfredo took his wife's hand. "Be thankful your father is back. The detective helped in the process."

"The phones in this house are not secure," Serna said. "We could have endangered Colonel Campos. They'd hidden him in a very isolated part of the Puebla highlands. I couldn't risk an ambush if they'd had collaborators tracking our calls."

Grandfather looked gaunt. One eye was bruised and swollen. He had stitches along the jawline and a bandage on his forehead. White stubble covered his cheeks. He smoothed his mustache and passed his hand over the whiskers. "I'm safe. That's what counts. Thanks to all of you and especially to Detective Serna."

The detective brought everyone up to date on the rescue. After soldiers surprised the men at the compound where Agustín was held, they took control of it. A helicopter, with Serna in it, was waiting to make the final rescue. Both men were flown in the chopper to the command center's clinic where doctors examined Agustín. They tended to his cuts and bruises, and they administered glucose, potassium, and other nutrients intravenously for dehydration.

"Then we had a police escort here," the detective said. "He needs to rest. He'll be in fine condition in a day or two. The worst part was being badly dehydrated."

Even though they were all exhausted, the joy of seeing Agustín made their adrenalin pump. They all marched into the kitchen and piled food high on their plates, and they listened to Agustín's tale of his abduction.

"It wasn't so bad," he said. "I acted crazy, pretending to be Don Quixote de la Mancha."

Everyone laughed, except for the detective.

"It could have seriously backfired," Serna said. "That was El Lencho, just out of prison. He's Rodrigo Alvarado's henchman. Alvarado is a dangerous guy. We've been searching for Alvarado for years."

Jasmin didn't listen too closely. She was engaged in a conversation of her own—with God—giving thanks for her grandfather's safe return.

When the group's talk turned to the more serious topic of safety, she listened.

Her grandfather told them that C4I4 had apprehended the kidnappers when they rescued him. "They'll investigate and notify me of their findings. They think it's the same group that attempted Jasmin's abduction. And the kidnapped girl who was never found. At the time of those incidents El Lencho was still in prison."

Lola invited everyone to retire to the living room. She remained in the kitchen preparing coffee to serve with dessert.

Jasmin ran to her bedroom and grabbed the mugs. Returning to the kitchen, she filled them with coffee and carried them to the living room. She handed the Kintsugi cup to her grandfather.

"My name is written on it. What a piece of art," he exclaimed. Upon examining it closely, he added, "I can't have coffee from this. It's too beautiful."

Jasmin held her mug high. "Salud, Grandfather. Enjoy your coffee from a masterpiece."

CHAPTER FORTY-TWO

J asmin had missed a full week of class and lab work. Three days after Grandfather's rescue, life was settling back into a routine. Leticia and her husband had returned to Tlaxcala. Even Lola's kitchen was back to normal with her pantry fully restocked. As Detective Serna had prepared to leave, Lola had hugged him and handed him a chocolate cake on a paper plate to take home with him. Javier had devoured all the leftover food. For the last few days, Lola had been busy cooking Colonel Campos's favorite meals, breads, and desserts.

"You need to gain back the weight you lost," she said.

Agustín spoke to Gabriela and Javier about varying the routes and times of day to drive Jasmin to and from the university.

When Jasmin finally returned to the lecture hall, Aki seemed overjoyed.

He confessed he'd thought she was avoiding him. "I tried calling you and you never answered. I left several messages."

"The C4I4 detective told me to turn my phone off and not turn it back on until Grandfather was rescued." She described the ordeal they'd been through since she'd last seen him. He shook his head and mumbled about how terrible it must have been for all of them.

"The beauty of your kintsugi helped me get through it." She mentioned where she'd placed her grandfather's cup in her bedroom shortly before the detective brought him back to the condo. "I prayed for the first time in my life. Maybe that helped."

Aki stepped forward and hugged her. "I'm glad you're both okay."

On their way to the lab, she received a text from De la Mota. He asked to meet her in his office immediately. She told Aki, Gabriela, and Javier that issues had come up in her thesis and her academic advisor needed to speak with her. Aki continued toward the lab by himself.

De la Mota closed the door to his office leaving Gabriela and Javier in the hall.

After inquiring about Agustín he nervously mentioned a couple of minor items about Jasmin's thesis.

He cleared his throat. "May we discuss the DNA tests?"

"There's nothing to talk about," Jasmin said. "The results won't be available for another couple of days."

"That's the point. You need to know I'm also being tested."

"You?" Jasmin blinked. "Why?"

"I was in love with Rosana," he said. "We even discussed getting married. One day she told me she was pregnant. That's when she broke off our relationship."

"My god, you could be my father."

De la Mota nodded.

Jasmin looked dumbfounded.

"In fact, I'll be very disappointed if I'm not," he said.

"Why didn't you marry Rosana?"

"When she told me she was expecting a child, I wanted to marry her right then. But that's when she disappeared from my life, and I never saw her again. Unfortunately, I don't know if I'm your father."

Jasmin stared at him.

He spoke about the grief he'd felt when Rosana died. An event, he claimed, made even more sad since she'd broken off all communication seven months before.

Several years later, the university administrative office told him a certain Colonel Campos de la Vega wanted to hire a tutor for his granddaughter, a math prodigy. He vaguely remembered that name but thought nothing of it. Expecting to encounter an overly enthusiastic grandfather, De la Mota had made the trip to Tlaxcala out of curiosity.

"After all, I had a full-time job teaching. Taking on private classes would add considerable work to my schedule. The minute I spoke with you, I recognized your ability. You'd already had a tutor from age four, but your grandfather understood your talent and wanted a college professor to teach you."

"Please, let's not speak of my ability," Jasmin said. "It's hindered me and kept me from enjoying a happy life. Mama always wished for a normal child and I'm not normal."

Stopping to study her for a second, De la Mota said her gift was exceptional. "I'm not a religious man, but your gift is God given. Don't waste it."

He'd accepted the tutoring job on a whim, intrigued by a child with such a command for both abstract and applied mathematics. By the time Jasmin was ten she resembled Rosana so much that he considered the possibility she might not only be Rosana's daughter, but his own as well.

"That's when I contacted Segundo Huerta," he said. "When I dated Rosana, I'd met her younger brother. Rudely, he dismissed the whole idea that I'd found Rosana's child. Both mother and baby had died. The Huerta family blamed me for Rosana's death. They thought I had not been responsible enough to marry her after getting her pregnant."

"I thought Huerta was your friend," Jasmin said. "You arranged for me to meet him."

De la Mota nodded. "After your television interview, Huerta came looking for me. Said he'd discovered a teenager who resembled his sister, someone who sounded like Rosana—her voice, her inflections, her way of expressing mathematical ideas. He asked if you were the child I'd taught, and he apologized for his earlier behavior."

"He stalked me on campus," Jasmin said. "He scared me."

"Huerta has difficulty relating to people."

Jasmin wanted to know if Rosana had interpersonal issues.

"Rosana was very nice, though she could be blunt when she felt strongly about something. Once she made her mind up, that was it."

"Why did you convince Mama to send me to Mexico City?"

"Selfish, I know, but it was so I would not lose contact with you." He chuckled. "Besides I could not let you waste your brilliance on archaeology."

"If I were your daughter, why would Rosana not marry you? I'd think she would have wanted a father for me. Or was she planning to put me up for adoption?"

De la Mota glanced at her with a sad expression. "I don't think she considered giving you up for adoption. She was happy to be pregnant. After she broke off with me, I thought many times that she knew I was not the father. Even though I love you like my daughter, I've been careful not to display my feelings."

"Display your feelings? At times you gave me the impression you were drilling through my brain to see what I was thinking."

"Maybe I stared too intensely trying to find something of myself in you," he said. "I'm sorry."

"Whether you're my father or not, I love you like one," Jasmin said.

"Other than your grandfather, I hope I'm the most important father figure in your life. We've assembled drones together, built robots, and designed spaceships. Like a daughter bonding with her dad."

On Thursday the lab called. Agustín and Jasmin stopped by to pick up the results. She asked him not to take an entourage. For such a private issue she wanted to keep it quiet. Gabriela and Javier waited in the car.

The results were printed on three pages. The first one showed

Jasmin's maternal lineage. Segundo Huerta showed an extremely high probability of being related to her, proving that Rosana was her mother. The second page had a completely negative paternal test.

Agustín looked at it. His hands started shaking. "Your academic advisor thought you might be his daughter?"

Jasmin explained about De la Mota's relationship with Rosana.

Agustín stared at the results, unable to speak.

"What's wrong?" she asked.

"How could I possibly have hired a professor who thought he might be your father? Is this a bad joke?"

"It's simple," Jasmin said. "He's a mathematician. Rosana studied with him, and they dated. When you needed a professor to teach me, you recruited him yourself. The universe of mathematicians is small. There's nothing unusual about it."

"Let's see if they found who your dad really is." He flipped to the last page. "Negative."

Jasmin felt disappointed.

De la Mota was saddened to know he was not the father of Rosana's baby. Jasmin was not his daughter after all. He looked across the desk.

"As you said, Jasmin, we can still be close." The professor folded the results of the paternity test. "I'm sorry to learn the truth, but mathematics and physics will continue to provide a bond between us."

"I wanted you to be my father."

De la Mota nodded. He patted her hand with a faraway look. "Your mother was brilliant. But you are even more talented than she was. Rosana had a sweet disposition. The main difference between the two of you is your determination. You'll accomplish great things."

"I'll take you to Stockholm when I win the Nobel," Jasmin joked, and immediately added, "I take that back. I don't mean to be arrogant."

"Why? It's great to think in those terms," De la Mota said.

She told him that when her grandfather was abducted, she vowed to stop flaunting her intelligence.

De la Mota, in a fatherly tone, explained that there was a difference between being boastful and setting goals to achieve aspirations in life. "Without objectives, we'd never achieve much," he said. "There's nothing pompous about having goals."

"Are you sure?"

"So sure, I'll start packing for the trip to Stockholm."

Jasmin laughed and soon De la Mota joined in too.

She looked serious again and asked him if she seemed to lack consideration for people or their feelings. Her grandfather had corrected her many times, telling her she needed to be more considerate of others.

"Let me address two sides to that question. First, you are someone with laser sharp focus. When we worked on the spaceship designs, it occurred to me an earthquake could rumble through and shake the classroom and you would not have been aware of it until the roof caved in."

"And that's unusual? You mean I get too wrapped-up in my thoughts?"

"That's right. By concentrating on the task you have at hand, you forget other people's feelings. Yet, if we want to find negativity, we can turn every quality you possess into something undesirable."

"Like getting buried under the rubble because I'm too concentrated on a project? I think you're saying I should learn to balance life a bit more."

De la Mota nodded. He talked about how much he'd seen her mature over the last two years and gave Agustín credit for developing a deep sense of responsibility in her.

"Child prodigies, like Mozart, often behave in immature ways, due in part to the intensity of their concentration and isolation from their own age group," he said to her. "People often misunderstand true brilliance." Though he did not say it directly, he insinuated Leticia neither understood nor appreciated her daughter's intellect.

"Lola has told me she thinks Mama is jealous of me."

He continued talking about the importance of socialization, explaining that it brings about understanding and empathy for others. He delved straight into the second point he wanted to discuss. "Sports teaches us to collaborate with others and become team players. You were never in a situation where you could learn to relate to kids your age. It's a shortcoming you should work on."

"For sports, I rode Ixchel," Jasmin said. "And I did the drone competitions with you."

"But that is not really being part of a group working together."

"I'm part of two lab teams. Aki and I work very effectively together. And don't forget the teamwork you and I shared in the drone races. We designed them, purchased materials, and built them. The same for the robot and spaceship."

"Those are great memories," he said, smiling wistfully.

De la Mota wanted to know if Agustín had contacted Huerta to discuss the DNA results. When she shook her head, he suggested a meeting would be good.

"Grandfather may be afraid Huerta will try to take me away."

"That cannot happen because Leticia and Salva adopted you."

CHAPTER FORTY-THREE

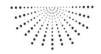

Agustín called Salva, Huerta, and De la Mota to a meeting about his abduction. He included Jasmin too. She held Sancho in her arms and followed the men to the living room.

First, he talked about the deplorable conditions of the room where they'd held him and the inhumane treatment he'd received. He'd pretended to be Don Quixote since he thought it'd anchor him to withstand whatever they'd do to him. He didn't know if it had worked or not, but he figured it may have bought more time before they would have forced him to speak to his family on a burner phone about paying the ransom; additional time that he felt in retrospect had been important to his rescue. He glanced at his granddaughter. Acting like Don Quixote, he told them, had given him a connection to Jasmin and that kept his resolve focused on surviving.

"One always learns things, no matter the situation. What I learned from my kidnapper," he said, turning once more toward Jasmin, "is that Rosana did not die the night Jasmin was born."

Jasmin dropped Sancho. The cat landed on his feet.

"Rosana is alive?" Huerta asked incredulously.

"I didn't say that. All I know is that the guy called El Lencho believes Rosana did not die that night and he assumes I know where she is," Agustín said. "Yesterday, I spoke with a nurse who helped the doctor when he performed the cesarean. She said no one died that night. At least not while she was there."

"That's ludicrous," Huerta said.

"How did you find this nurse?" asked De la Mota.

"Through a detective."

"Detective? Really?" Huerta raised an eyebrow. "A fly-by-night for sure."

"Not at all. Serna, who handled my abduction case, put me in touch with an investigator from the command center."

"And he came up with an unknown nurse whose testimony you believe?" Huerta asked.

"The detective knows what he's doing. Besides, if Jasmin is alive, her mother could be too," Agustín said. "We don't know where she could be. Maybe she's in the US. El Lencho mentioned that. Maybe Mexico. Who knows."

"She may not even be alive. You're putting hope in the heart and mind of a child when you have no proof," Salva said in a heated tone of voice. He shook his head and turned to face Jasmin. "What are you thinking?"

"It seems like a twisted telenovela," Jasmin said, "but if there's a chance Rosana could be alive, I want to look for her. I want to talk to the nurse."

The four men continued talking about the possibility. In the end, they decided much more information was needed.

For security purposes, Salva suggested Agustín, Jasmin, and Lola move to Princeton immediately since their visas were already issued. Other than missing two weeks of lectures and completing the thesis for her master's degree, which could be done from anywhere, they could spend the late spring and summer in New Jersey. Or visit him in Spain.

Salva told them he could spend another ten days with them before returning to Madrid. He offered to help with moving arrangements. When Lola heard this remark, she burst into tears, saying she was uncertain about moving to a country where she did not speak the language. She had accepted going with them but told them she was having second thoughts and would search for another job in Mexico City.

"What do you fear?" Salva asked.

"I'm afraid of being picked up by US immigration and being deported," Lola said. "I don't speak English."

As part of his household, Agustín explained, Lola had been issued a temporary resident visa. For as long as she remained a member of his household and Jasmin was a full-time student at Princeton, Lola would be a legal resident. No one could deport her.

Agustín reminded Lola they'd planned for her to move with them to Princeton. He was getting older and needed her help. Everybody would be happier if she went with them. After all, she had no other family. At fourteen, Jasmin was underage and needed a female role model.

Salva suggested that after six or eight months, if Lola was unhappy in Princeton, she could return to Mexico.

"Now that I've found Rosana's daughter, she's being taken away from me," Huerta interjected, anger flowing through in his voice.

"To Princeton?" Salva asked.

Huerta nodded.

De la Mota seemed surprised and shook his head. "Would you rather she did not have the opportunity to attend a great university?"

"Now Salva is telling them to leave immediately," Huerta said, looking indignant. "Why so soon? Taking Rosana's daughter out of the country, all of you are, instead of letting her spend time with my family."

Salva told him the reason for the quick move was to keep Agustín and Jasmin safe.

Huerta remained silent for a few seconds. "Makes it look like Agustín is running away."

"Would you have them stay and run the risk of getting kidnapped again? Or worse?" De la Mota asked testily.

Huerta looked at the professor. "You've got a point."

"The detective told me the kidnappers are in jail awaiting trial," De la Mota said. "You know they're pissed about being locked up."

"Don't forget that criminals can order kidnappings and assassinations from prison," Salva added.

Jasmin whispered the Fibonacci sequence, but only Salva heard her over the loud voices of the men.

Salva realized the chaos had rattled Jasmin's nerves. It all had been too much. Now that she knew her mother might be alive her emotions were fluctuating. She was further shaken by the ensuing argument over the move to Princeton, Lola's sudden reluctance about relocating to the college town, and Huerta's demands that Jasmin not leave Mexico City.

Salva picked up the guitar and asked Jasmin to join him at the piano. When he strummed a couple of notes of "Ode to Joy," she sat on the bench. He played a few more notes. She didn't attempt to play. Instead, she sat at the piano looking glum.

"I'll miss hearing you play when I return to Madrid."

With that, she started playing the piano.

Lola interrupted the music when she put a tray of coffee for the men and café con leche for Jasmin on the dining room table. A platter of cinnamon rolls filled the house with a mouthwatering aroma. Even Huerta smiled when he saw Lola serving the rolls on individual plates. He picked up a fork, ready to jab a roll.

Lola announced she'd thought about the move again and decided she would definitely go to Princeton. Her announcement plus the coffee and sweet rolls improved everyone's mood. Jasmin returned to the piano and played "Ode to Joy." Agustín joined her and started playing. In a matter of seconds, Salva picked up the guitar again. Music filled the room and Huerta started singing. He had a resonant bass voice.

As they harmonized together, Salva thought about the bond forming in the group that only music can produce. He glanced at Jasmin, and she smiled at him. She was surrounded by the men of her family, Salva thought, guys who half an hour before had been at each other's throats.

After an hour or so, the music stopped.

Jasmin turned to Salva. "You told me I have the most amazing family. And you're right."

CHAPTER FORTY-FOUR

J asmin and Salva drank coffee and talked after breakfast. He encouraged her to go forward with the move to Princeton before he left.

"I can't leave Mexico," she said, "without speaking to the nurse who claims she delivered me. She may know more than she's said. Rosana could even be in this country."

"What about the university?" he asked.

"It can wait. Until the fall semester anyway."

"The kidnapper told your grandfather Rosana had moved to the US. Why do you think she might be in Mexico?" Salva suggested he'd take her to the adoption agency he and Leticia had worked with and maybe they could provide useful information. Soon they were in front of the condominium, waiting for a taxi.

In the adoption agency's lobby, Jasmin and Salva talked, read magazines, waited impatiently, and ate chocolates they'd bought at a little shop across the street after the taxi had dropped them off. After the long wait, the administrative office claimed that legally they could only reveal the name of the doctor who had turned the baby over to the agency and suggested they contact him. For three more days they tried to locate the gynecologist. The doctor's office had closed fourteen or fifteen years ago, the building manager told them. Salva made phone calls after compiling a list of people with the doctor's name. They did searches on the computer, but the man had simply vanished. Salva concluded he'd either retired, moved, died, or left the country.

Jasmin asked her grandfather to set up a meeting with the nurse that Huerta and Salva would attend with them. Even Leticia would not know about it. Huerta offered to drive them to the nurse's apartment.

They interviewed the nurse. A thin woman, she looked older than Agustín. When one of them asked a question, she often prefaced it with the words "that was almost fifteen years ago, and my memory may fail me." Despite her assertion, she described a young woman who was brought to the doctor's private clinic and prepped for a caesarian.

"The doctor said this woman was not only a student that showed great promise in mathematics, but that she had powerful people around her. Some of them wanted to protect her while others wanted to harm her. The doctor made me promise I'd never tell what happened."

"So what did happen?" Jasmin asked.

"The doctor administered a strong sedative, though she looked like she'd already been drugged. He had a document for her to sign. That's normal for surgery, but this was not the normal consent form."

Salva asked her to explain.

"It requested cremation if she died," she said. "And for the baby too."

"That was prepared in advance?" Huerta asked.

"Go on," Salva said, scrutinizing the woman.

"After the baby, a little girl, was born, I was told to leave. Seemed like a normal caesarian with a normal baby delivered. What occurred after I left, I cannot say." The nurse looked at Jasmin for a few seconds. "Are you that woman's child? You're about the right age."

Jasmin half nodded.

Agustín asked if Rosana was alive when she'd left.

The woman wrinkled her brow. "I can only assume she was. There had been no complications as far as I could tell. All I can say is that after the delivery, the doctor was adamant that I leave. The way I was threatened if I spoke to anyone about it made me think they were up to no good. Otherwise, why have the young woman sign a cremation request?"

When Huerta asked about the doctor, she said he acted scared that night. Like someone had forced him to do a secret caesarian. "He performed it in his private clinic, but he did not deliver babies or perform c-sections at the clinic. Those he did at the hospital."

"Do you know who could have threatened him?"

"A woman," she said. "A woman in an expensive car. A Mercedes, I think. She and her pistolero."

"A gunman?" Grandfather shifted his stance. "Did you see either one?"

"Only the car. The woman never got out. I only saw her silhouette. The pregnant one was carried in by the doctor and the pistolero. Even though it was at night, the pistolero wore a hat, low on his head. As I said, the young woman had already been drugged. I never got a good look at the man's face, but he carried a gun in a holster."

"What about the car? Any distinguishing features that you remember?" Agustín asked.

"I remember a hubcap missing," she said. "It's so strange to remember that detail when obviously the devil was at work that night. I remember being very scared."

Huerta shook his head. Then wondered out loud how a missing hubcap could be noticed at night.

"The streetlight fell on the driver's side of the car. The front tire had a shiny hubcap and reflected the light. That's when I noticed the rear tire did not have one," she said. "But that was so long ago, it does not make any difference now. It might have if I'd told the police back when it happened."

"Why are you talking about this now?" Salva asked.

"The doctor is dead. And I'm growing old."

Salva climbed into the back seat of the SUV and sat next to Jasmin.

"I'm thankful they saved you," he said. "But if they wanted to kill Rosana, why did they deliver the baby?"

Agustín sat in the front.

"To make money on the black market," Huerta said, settling into the driver's seat. His fist slammed against the steering wheel. "Obviously, they deceived us saying the baby had also died."

Salva protested that he and Leticia did not adopt Jasmin through the black market. They'd done it legally and they had been extremely lucky to get such an incredible child. He squeezed Jasmin's hand.

"I'm not accusing you. That agency got a baby through illegal means. I will visit them tomorrow with my attorney," Huerta said, anger creeping into his voice.

Huerta dropped Agustín off at Sebastián's coffeeshop where the two friends were going to have lunch. He took Salva and Jasmin to the university where they'd meet with De la Mota.

Jasmin sat next to Salva in front of De la Mota's desk. She told the professor that they'd spoken with the nurse.

Her thoughts slipped into the past, projects she'd done with the professor. He'd been a father figure to her after Salva left. Her grandfather had been her surrogate father. *What do I care if Mama did not love me? I had three father figures who've been there for me.* She couldn't ask for more. It was time for her to stop whining about what she lacked and start appreciating how lucky she really was.

De la Mota's voice brought her back to the conversation in the office. He was looking straight at her.

"There's no reason for you to remain here to search for Rosana. She's probably in the US anyway, and Princeton is waiting for you. Both Huerta and I will do whatever we can to locate her if she's still alive. I will notify you if we find her."

"Keep me updated," Jasmin said. "Maybe Grandfather and I can help."

"If Rosana is alive, why do you think she's stayed completely away from her family, her friends, and even from the child she gave birth to?" Salva asked.

De la Mota contemplated the question for a few seconds. "If she's alive, and that's a big if, something or someone threatened her. Why sign a cremation request? She was obviously scared enough to do it."

"From what the nurse told us, Rosana had been drugged before she signed," Salva said. "It shows she didn't sign of her own free will."

Both De la Mota and Salva continued speculating on why Rosana had signed her own cremation paperwork. And Jasmin's too.

"We must find out who that woman was. The one who drove her to the doctor's office," the professor said.

PART III

CHAPTER FORTY-FIVE

TWO MONTHS LATER

Jasmin's grandfather rented a duplex in Princeton on Stanworth Lane, within walking distance of the university. Small, with two bedrooms and two baths, the building had been a family home converted into a duplex. Its beige vinyl siding was totally different from any home Jasmin had lived in before. On the front side a quaint and inviting veranda, with a wooden deck and a white railing held in place by sturdy white pillars, ran the length of the duplex. Steps leading from the sidewalk to the covered veranda guided them to the front door, painted bright red.

Inside, the central cooling system worked wonders in the summer heat. Jasmin and Lola shared a room with twin beds, while Agustín had the smaller bedroom. The kitchen, living, and dining areas formed an open floor plan making the place appear bigger than it was. A small upright digital Yamaha piano set next to unpacked boxes. Jasmin had never played a digital instrument and was anxious to try it. Even when she played a guitar, it was the classical instrument, not the electric version.

In Mexico City, Jasmin had packed her own belongings and she'd told Lola that she'd unpack the box containing her precious books on physics and mathematics herself. Her copy of *Don Quixote* was in it as well as her wooden cat, Alba. The leather-bound diary, still wrapped in the decoy book cover, was tucked into the bottom of the box.

Jasmin no longer had nightmares about the diary growing into a monster and she rarely gave her mother's book much thought. She'd tried to talk about it with Salva after her grandfather had been abducted, but he hadn't seemed interested. She thought maybe it was better that way, to forget about it, though she did reflect periodically on the terror it had caused her when she was younger. Since she shared a room with Lola, she taped the plastic bag, with the calculus book cover peering through, to the back of the dresser she would use. Although she'd kept it, she was not sure what she'd do with it. If she returned the diary, Mama could no longer ask her to leave; Jasmin was already far away from the family home. She wondered if her mother even remembered it.

Jasmin was happy that Lola seemed to be adjusting so quickly to the move. As had always been the case, Lola was absorbed in creating a happy home environment. Urging Agustín and Jasmin to explore the town, she unpacked their clothes and hung them in closets or folded them into drawers. Lola had also ventured out by herself to two grocery stores, La Mexicana and Lupita, a short distance away. She told Jasmin that they carried the spices and ingredients she would need for her cooking. After discovering a vibrant community of Mexicans and Guatemalans, she announced she was not going to be lonely at all.

"Princeton is beautiful, mi niña. I stopped at the Catholic Center to find out about English classes. I've bought magazines so I can start to read the language and I'll learn pronunciation from watching television."

Jasmin and her grandfather familiarized themselves with the historic town while Lola shopped for produce and spices for her kitchen and attended her first language class. A week after their arrival, they walked to Einstein's institute, as her grandfather called it. Since it did not offer tours to the public, all they could do was stroll through the grounds. They walked along Stony Brook, admiring the clean, clear water in the creek as it flowed toward the Millstone River. The fresh air held the sweet scent of grass and flowering bushes, a nice contrast to Mexico City's pollution. It was tempting to throw a rock into the brook, but the grounds were so peaceful that Jasmin controlled her impulse. Her grandfather sat by the edge of the creek and seemed absorbed by its beauty.

The peaceful setting reminded her of the star-forming region in the Carina Nebula. NASA had released the Webb Telescope's first images that morning. Excited about the pictures, she called Aki to discuss her thoughts about the previously invisible star formation area revealed by the new space telescope.

She asked him if he had seen the Webb photos.

"It's humbling," he said, "to think about the insignificance of the human race in light of the vast universe."

"We stand on the frontier of uncovering the mysteries in the cosmos," she said. "Our combined lifetimes will not suffice to study a few of the infinite number of secrets it holds. I wonder how many golden spirals are spread throughout the universe."

"Enough to keep you traveling in space for a long time," Aki joked.

She ended the call saying how good she felt about being in Princeton and hoped he could find a post-doc fellowship or research position at the Plasma Physics Lab.

She hated to pull her grandfather away from the institute's meditative grounds, but she had to return to the condo to finish unpacking her personal belongings. Making their way back to the duplex, they passed Einstein's house on Mercer Street. Agustín stopped on the sidewalk, roughed up his hair and mustache, and opened his arms skyward.

"What are you doing?" Jasmin asked, laughing.

"If I look enough like the great man, his intelligence might find its way into my brain. That way, I might be able to converse with you in the language of the universe."

"That language speaks in numbers which are both simple and complex," Jasmin said.

"For me," he said, "you must keep it simple."

They continued walking along Mercer Street toward the university campus. Agustín was unusually quiet. When they reached Nassau, they turned left to walk toward Bayard Lane and took that street until they arrived at Stanworth. Opening the door to the apartment, they realized Lola was away.

"What's troubling you, Grandfather?"

"You can read me like a book," he said.

"Are you sad to be here instead of Mexico?"

He shook his head. "Let's sit down."

Not imagining what could possibly be on his mind, she thought the atmosphere of the institute's grounds had made him melancholy. It had affected her that way. She felt awed by the names of people who had served there, not only Einstein, but also people like Gödel and van Neumann, and more recently, Edward Witten, a great mathematician doing work in string theory. What she noticed was that the majority of researchers who had worked at the institute were men. How could she possibly expect to one day work among the most brilliant minds the world offered when she was female? Thinking about the Webb telescope images again, she considered she could have a chance at the institute if she accomplished the right things in her doctoral work. Her grandfather, she knew, was quite certain she would join the institute someday.

"I've hired a private investigator from Miami to track Rosana," Grandfather said, interrupting her thoughts. "To see if she's alive. I wanted more information before I mentioned it, but I can't keep this secret. De la Mota has not found a trace of her in Mexico."

Grandfather's mind was on a totally different topic, an issue even more important to her than her university studies or the fantastic Webb images.

"Have you learned anything?"

"Not yet," he said. "It's interesting how many people share the same name, but when you add Rosana's maternal surname, as we do in Latin America, it narrows the field. So I'm hopeful."

"It'd be nice if something came up before my semester starts."

The cats had not yet acclimated to the apartment. Jasmin could sense they'd resented the move they'd been put through. Especially Sojón.

"I'm glad we can reason through the move better than those two," Jasmin said, looking at Sojón pacing around Sancho sprawled on the floor catching the sunrays coming through the window. She was unpacking the final two boxes of personal items.

As Jasmin worked, Lola mentioned to her that someone at the Catholic Center had told her it takes two years after a move to feel you belong to your new community.

"By then, mi niña, you will have completed your studies and we will be returning to Mexico. The cats will be unhappy at being moved again. Or maybe you will be on your own, working as an astronaut somewhere."

"Not likely. Getting my doctorate will take four or five years."

"But you're a genius, mi niña. It won't take you that long."

"I wish," Jasmin said, glancing at the knickknacks and family photos she had unpacked and temporarily had placed on the countertop. Reaching for the mug Salva had given her, she placed it next to her grandfather's mug. Admiring Aki's masterful Kintsugi artwork, she noticed that the golden script spelling the colonel's name sparkled in the light. She picked up the silver framed black-and-white photograph taken of her a couple of weeks after her birth. She was in her mother's arms and Mama was standing next to Grandmother. Memories of her grandmother had faded, and she found it difficult to remember anything about her.

Then she saw it. Her heart skipped and she dropped the photo. Grabbing it off the floor, she rushed to the veranda where her grandfather sat in a rocking chair reading *The Quantum Theory of Fields*. She'd given him the book in hopes that it might give him an inkling for what her studies would cover.

"Explain this to me," Jasmin said, handing him the picture.

"It was taken about two weeks after you were born. Your mother is holding you."

"Not the people. Look at the back wheel," she said. Her heart was palpitating.

His mustache quivered. He looked up at her. "It's missing the hubcap."

Agustín called Leticia and turned the speaker on before asking her if Anita had ever mentioned using her Mercedes to take Rosana to a clinic in Mexico City.

"I don't know anything about the car that took that woman to a doctor. For God's sake, that was so long ago." Leticia bitterly enunciated every single syllable over the speaker on Agustín's phone. She stopped to catch her breath and added, "Besides, I never knew your secretary."

"All I want to know is what your mother might have told you, if anything, about going to the doctor the evening Jasmin was delivered."

Leticia wanted to know why he would even ask a question like that.

"I've discovered it was Anita's car that transported Rosana to the clinic that night," he said.

Leticia continued her tirade, accusing Agustín of being responsible for her mother's death. Unable to reason with her, Agustín hung up.

He glanced at Jasmin. "Your mother keeps accusing me of causing Grandmother's death." He repeated what he'd always told Jasmin. Anita died of a heart attack. She'd had a bad heart for several years and had taken medication for it. "As for Rosana, she lit up my day, every day at the office. Her sweet personality had that ability—to bring joy to everyone who encountered her."

"Not everyone liked Rosana," Jasmin said. "Someone hated her enough to want to kill her."

"And I promise you, ma petite princesse, that is what we are going to find out."

The next phone call was to De la Mota.

Agustín explained that his wife's car had apparently been used to take Rosana to the doctor. "As best we know, the doctor was the last one to see Rosana alive. If she survived that night, he would have known her fate. But he's probably dead, so we must start from scratch."

He asked the professor to fly to New Jersey so they could discuss the matter in person.

When De la Mota asked if Huerta was aware of the new information, Grandfather said he'd prefer to leave Huerta out of it for now. "He can be unreasonable about anything related to Rosana."

On Thursday Agustín took Jasmin with him to the Newark airport. De la Mota came off the plane with carryon luggage and they went straight to the car. When Agustín got into the driver's seat, the professor glanced at Jasmin sitting in the back.

"I thought you'd be driving by now."

"In New Jersey I can't even get a student permit until I'm sixteen. More than a year away."

When Grandfather steered the car onto the turnpike, De la Mota turned toward her. "I trust you'll give me a tour of Princeton."

"And the grounds of the institute and Einstein's house," she added.

"Einstein's institute," Agustín said, correcting her. He tousled his hair, making De la Mota laugh. "We'll inhale the atoms and molecules outside the genius's house in hopes of acquiring his brilliance."

After a late lunch at the duplex, they sat on the veranda.

Lola brought coffee and dessert for them. She pointed out a clump of phlox growing between the veranda and the sidewalk. The colorful flower tops peered over the railing. Jasmin invited her to sit with them, but Lola excused herself to tidy up the kitchen.

Agustín sipped his coffee, dabbed his mustache with his napkin, and cleared his throat. "Rosana's father contacted me fifteen years ago, right after the doctor notified the Huerta family that their daughter had died. In my attempt to help them, I suggested bringing a malpractice lawsuit against the doctor. Two days after Rosana's death, her father and I went to see him to pick up the ashes. We threatened him with litigation. As soon as I returned to my office, the doctor called me. We set up a time to meet privately."

De la Mota finished his coffee. Agustín was silent, trying to put his thoughts together.

"Surely this is not all you had to say when you asked me to fly here?" De la Mota asked. He seemed anxious to learn what Agustín had to share with him.

Agustín shook his head and rubbed his eyes, trying to recall the important details he wanted to discuss. Speaking slowly, he explained the doctor had suggested talking in an elevator, to ensure privacy, at the Marriott Hotel in the Polanco area of Mexico City.

"The doctor found me after I'd been riding up and down one of the elevators for fifteen minutes. He spoke quickly, saying his life had been threatened and he wanted to warn me to refrain from investigating anything or else I, too, would be in grave danger. And anyone else looking into Rosana's death would be killed."

Agustín stopped for a second, looked up, and sighed before continuing. "A member of the mafia from the apple region in the Puebla highlands forced him to perform the cesarean, kill Rosana, and dispose of her body. He'd been told to hand the baby over to a person from an orphanage that would collect her at the clinic a week later. The doctor hired a nurse to take care of the baby girl. He'd been directed to inform the family that both mother and baby had died. The gynecologist emphasized repeatedly that anyone investigating Rosana's death would be killed."

"Then you knew the baby had not died," De la Mota said.

Agustín nodded. "That's when I learned the baby was alive."

"And you acquiesced to the doctor's request?" De la Mota asked. "You kept the family from filing a criminal injunction?"

Agustín nodded with a spasm-like robotic movement.

"How could you?" De la Mota asked. The words coughed up from his stomach like a growling dog.

"If the Huerta family found out the baby was alive, the mafia would have killed the newborn," Agustín said. "Don't you understand I had to do it, or Rosana's infant daughter would have been murdered. And the rest of the Huerta family too."

Jasmin listened to her grandfather without speaking, as if she were numb from the words she had heard.

"I know the truth seems too terrible to contemplate," Agustín said.

Clouds had blown in obscuring the sunlight on the veranda. Agustín lowered his head and covered his eyes. "Rosana was already gone. I could not bring her back." His words were a mere whisper. De la Mota leaned in closer to be able to hear Agustín. "But I could make sure a good family adopted her daughter."

"Leticia and Salva had already applied at an agency for a child," De la Mota said. "Is that correct?"

Agustín's face had lost its color. Keeping his eyes closed, he nodded. "And the doctor and I scrambled to pay off the other orphanage before they reported not getting the promised baby. I got my lawyer involved to negotiate the payoff to the clandestine orphanage to avoid direct contact with them. That would have endangered Jasmin eventually."

De la Mota took out his phone and uttered a few words to be recorded in a notetaking application about finding out if the man currently held in custody for Agustín's kidnapping was responsible for Rosana's abduction years ago.

"If that were the case, he would not have asked me where Rosana was," Agustín said.

"Of course," De la Mota said. "How could I forget?"

Agustín was so upset, he couldn't speak. He asked Jasmin to take over.

"It won't help anyone if you fade away on us," De la Mota said. "You must help us strategize."

Jasmin told the professor they'd already widened the search for Rosana, her grandfather had hired a private investigator from Miami who specialized in locating missing people. She worked internationally, so the search would not be limited to the US. They'd provided the PI a list of names. "The investigator told us that wherever Rosana is, she's probably changed her name."

De la Mota raised his eyebrows. "Under the circumstances, wouldn't you?"

CHAPTER FORTY-SIX

Jasmin's first semester was nearing, and she'd already attended a couple of orientations and met with two of her professors. The university had issued an identification tag, and she put it to good use by visiting the rare book collection at Firestone Library. Deep in climate-controlled tunnels under the campus, it was a good place to spend a few leisurely hours. Enjoying these relics was much better than staying around the apartment. Even though she was impatient to start her research, the idea of finding Rosana was always present. Whiling the hours away with nothing to do was not her style. She had to keep her mind busy. Otherwise, she'd ponder family secrets, wondering how much was still being kept from her.

One afternoon when she returned from the library, she found Grandfather, wearing an old men's fraternity T-shirt, napping in his rocker on the veranda. The book on quantum theory of fields had obviously put him to sleep. It had fallen to the deck. Sojón had joined the old men's fraternity and was sleeping on his lap. Her grandfather opened his eyes when she placed the book on the table by his chair.

"I'm glad it's you, ma petite princesse. That nightmare of the student uprising has returned. I didn't sleep well last night, and I was catching a few winks."

"Tell me about your nightmare."

"It's the student uprisings before the Olympics in 1968. The noise, the guns, the horror of it all. I see the tanks moving into Tlatelolco."

Kissing him on his forehead, she told him next time his dreams tormented him, to tell them to go away. Permanently. "Mind over matter. I've read that it works on the unconscious mind and relieves people of their bad dreams. I made it work on my own nightmares."

"I hate to tell you, Jasmin, but I'm only on page twenty of this book and I'm totally lost," he said, changing the subject. "You didn't warn me it's written in cuneiform. Maybe the ancient Egyptians could decipher the author's writing, but I cannot. I'm afraid you must navigate through your studies without having me understand your field."

"You mean that Einstein's brain waves have not penetrated yours? We must visit the institute more frequently."

They laughed. Turning to more serious topics, they briefly reminisced about Ocotlán. Jasmin knew that Lola was at her English class and took advantage of her absence to ask her grandfather a question that nagged her.

"How did you manage to get the adoption agency to turn me over to Leticia and Salva?"

Grandfather smoothed his mustache; the tip of his tongue swept his upper lip as he sat up straighter.

"Whether it was true or not, the doctor told me Rosana had died. And I believed him. But her baby, he told me, was alive and well. I saw the opportunity to negotiate with him. I'd stop Rosana's family from suing him, but in exchange, he had to give the baby to the adoption agency Leticia and Salva were using. I spoke with the agency director, and he turned you over to Leticia without mentioning any circumstances."

"And that made you my grandfather."

He nodded, but his gaze was far away.

"All these years have passed, and I never suspected your grandmother had colluded with the mafia," he said, petting Sojón. "If only I'd suspected, our lives could have turned out so differently."

"But Grandmother figured out I was Rosana's child. My math ability gave it away when I was three or four."

He nodded again. "I couldn't bear the thought of any harm coming to Rosana's baby. Leticia and Salva were already working with an adoption agency, so I arranged for them to get you. Your grandmother never suspected anything. No one did. Until you were older." He looked at Jasmin intensely. "My biggest fear was that you'd end up on the black market. Or that you'd grow up in some unknown household, God knows where. Or in an orphanage."

They sat quietly on the veranda for a long time. Jasmin held his hand. After about an hour, he fell asleep again.

The big day came when the semester formally started. Excited, Jasmin was leaving early for campus. On her way out the door, Grandfather's phone rang. It was De la Mota. Her grandfather told him he was on speaker so Jasmin could listen. He objected, but Agustín convinced him that she shouldn't be left out of any family secrets.

De la Mota was hesitant saying the stuff would be hard to swallow.

"Go ahead," Jasmin said. "I'm prepared."

De la Mota told them Agustín's investigator at the central command center had extracted information from Agustín's kidnapping suspect, El Lencho. The man was in custody at the federal prison awaiting trial. "In hopes of getting leniency, he gave up the name of the mastermind behind your abduction."

"Mastermind?" Grandfather asked. "I thought El Lencho was the mastermind." He leaned on the breakfast counter as if to steady himself.

"El Lencho works for Rodrigo Alvarado."

Agustín said he did remember Serna, the detective, telling him that El Lencho worked for a dangerous cartel boss, Rodrigo Alvarado.

"The Federales have been after Alvarado for a long time," De la Mota said over the speaker. "Alvarado was apprehended and is now in federal prison. Our contact informed me the prison detectives got him to talk."

"What did they find out?" Agustín asked. He fidgeted impatiently, rearranging Lola's magazines on the counter.

"Alvarado claims he hired a woman in Mexico City to look after Rosana for two months in a condo he provided. Once she recovered from the cesarean," De la Mota's voice broke up. When he spoke again, it came back as a painful mutter, "Rosana was sold to a human trafficker."

"Is there a name for this trafficker?" Agustín asked.

"Yes, Gustavo Molinari. I have not been able to find anything out about him. Who knows if he's even alive."

Grandfather scribbled the name on one of Lola's magazines. After hanging up, Agustín called the PI working for them. She assured them her office had contacts in the murky world of human trafficking. Warning them not to get their hopes up, she added if Rosana was somewhere in Mexico or the US, her office might be able to find her. But then she added that many trafficked women only survive a few years. "If she's still alive, she will not be the same person."

Lola came bouncing into the apartment with an armful of flowers she'd probably purchased at McCaffery's grocery market. Seeing Agustín's expression, she dropped them on the coffee table and rushed to them.

"What's happened?" she asked.

"Those I love have been punished for my sins," Agustín said. He sat on a bistro stool and laid his head on the counter and wept.

For the following six weeks, Jasmin attended seminars on quantum fields and string theory. One afternoon, her advisor called her to a meeting. Nervously she walked to his office thinking she was going to be asked to leave the PhD program. That she was not up to the standard the university expected. Her grandfather would be so disappointed. His dreams centered on her studies.

What occurred instead would make him very proud. The department offered Jasmin a research assistant position. Since she was underage, she could only work a few hours a month, but her advisor told her that being an assistant would open opportunities to learn more about the university and the various programs in her field.

On the way to the duplex, she called Aki to give him the news. They talked about his application to Princeton and the Plasma Physics Lab. He expected to hear from them soon. She ran home to tell her grandfather about her student research position.

"They know what a gem they have in you," he said. "Let's call De la Mota. He'll be so pleased."

They were talking with her mentor in Mexico City when another call came in. She told De la Mota they'd call him back.

The PI had found a woman she thought might be Rosana. "She's reluctant to speak about her past. At first, she totally refused, but when she learned her daughter was searching for her, she relented."

"Where is she?" Jasmin asked, excited about the news. "When can we meet?"

Agustín turned the volume up.

"Not yet, Jasmin," the PI said. "She's concerned for herself and for you even though she's never seen you, not even when you were born. She remembers being anesthetized. When she regained consciousness, the doctor told her she'd had a little girl. And she was threatened the baby would be killed if she ever tried to find her."

"Will I be able to talk to her?" Jasmin asked.

The PI explained they had to take this slowly for two reasons. First, she needed to verify the woman was Rosana. She would order DNA tests to prove the blood relationship. The second reason was to protect everyone involved.

"That's understandable," Agustín said.

"It might help if her brother speaks with her," Jasmin suggested. "She might talk to him."

Grandfather made a negative face at that suggestion, but she defended her position, saying it had been Segundo Huerta who had made her aware of her biological mother.

"The good news is she has agreed to undergo DNA testing," the PI said. She hesitated before adding, "There's something else. Rosana wants you to know she's built a life for herself under a different name. She wants to protect herself and her son."

"Her son?" Agustín repeated. His voice was a mere whisper. "So she's married?"

"No, she's never married. It's complicated. I think it's best if she explains it once we prove she really is Jasmin's mother," the PI said.

The initial excitement of meeting her biological mother dissipated thinking that her mother had another child. Jasmin's stomach rumbled in anguish.

"If the DNA test is positive, we can move forward and arrange a meeting," the PI said. "I'll set it up. I can be present, if needed."

Jasmin interrupted her saying she'd already had DNA testing done in Mexico. "Can't we use that?"

The PI said the tests had to be done through a lab with AABB accreditation. "That's to make sure the sample collection is done correctly, and it follows an established chain of custody."

Jasmin sighed and resigned herself to being jabbed by a needle again.

Before she finished talking, the PI told them about visiting the nurse who assisted in Jasmin's delivery.

"You went to Mexico City?" Agustín asked, surprised.

The PI told them they went to other countries to interview people, if necessary. She laughed. "Don't worry, you'll get the invoice covering my time." Returning to serious business, she told them the gynecologist had disappeared two weeks after Jasmin's birth. He was never seen again, and the nurse presumed he was dead, that he'd been killed.

Agustín gasped. "Why didn't she report it? I met with him the day after Jasmin's birth. And we worked together for a week getting Jasmin to the adoption agency."

"The nurse told me she'd never informed the authorities or anyone else about Rosana for fear she'd be the next one to disappear. Until you spoke with her."

Agustín appeared to be assimilating the information. "Why is the nurse talking now?" he asked after a few seconds.

"She's got cancer and wants to die with a clear conscience," the PI said. "Everyone needs to be careful. Don't forget your own kidnapping a few months back."

When Grandfather said the culprits were in prison awaiting trial, the PI countered with another warning.

"Prisoners have people on the outside." She told them she'd be in contact when the DNA test was set up.

"Can you add an ethnic ancestry analysis for me?" Jasmin asked.

She sounded confused about Jasmin's request.

"I want to know if I have Maya ancestry."

She agreed she'd ask for it.

"We can't discuss this with anyone else. Here or in Mexico," Grandfather said once the call ended. "That means not even Lola."

CHAPTER FORTY-SEVEN

When Leticia and her husband arrived in Princeton for a short visit, Jasmin thought their purpose was to restore harmony after the way her mother had lost her temper over the phone. And she was sure the conciliatory effort had been Alfredo's idea. The former priest now worked as a professor of philosophy at the University of the Americas in Puebla. He had taken a week off to make the trip.

Her grandfather acted distrustful of their intentions. Yet, he gave them his bedroom and he slept on the sofa in the living room.

The early October weather was turning cool. Maple trees in front of the duplex contrasted with the golden leaves of the honey locusts, making the maples look a brighter red. Lola suggested they gather on the veranda to enjoy the fresh air and fall colors. Mama and her husband, each with a glass of wine, soon engaged in animated conversation with Agustín. The house phone rang, and Lola jumped to answer it.

As Lola entered the house, the cats escaped and joined the guests on the veranda. Sojón took one look at Leticia and backed away, finding a spot with the last bit of sunshine. Sancho rubbed against Leticia's leg. She quickly pushed him away with her foot.

Lola returned saying the labs had called to set up Jasmin's DNA tests.

Mama immediately asked what that was about. After all, she reminded everyone, she was the custodial parent. When Agustín was unable to give a quick answer, he suggested they have a DNA party and all of them have their blood tested. "That way, we can determine our ancestry," he said. "We may all be Neanderthal."

"Certainly not Jasmin," Mama said. "She's way too smart."

Alfredo agreed it was a fun idea to test for their origins. "Neanderthals were a lot smarter than they get credit for," he added. "And a lot of people have a trace of Neanderthal in them."

Mama kept insisting there was an ulterior motive to having the test run again so shortly after it had been done in Mexico City.

"It's to find Rosana," Jasmin blurted out.

In an instant, Leticia's expression turned from questioning to anger. She faced Agustín. "I see you're setting things up to exclude me from your will altogether. You've already spent more on your granddaughter's education than I will ever inherit from you."

Alfredo put his hand on Mama's thigh. "Hey, Leticia, remember we came here to leave confrontations behind us."

She ignored her husband and stared at Agustín. "Why don't you and I have a DNA test done to prove your paternity?" she whispered angrily. "I want to prove I'm your daughter."

Grandfather shrugged. "Fine. If that's what you want."

Sancho rubbed Mama's leg once more. She kicked the cat for a second time. Alfredo whispered to her, probably trying to sooth her outburst. Soon, the conversation returned to its earlier conviviality, although Sancho, like Sojón, now kept his distance.

By the time they went to the lab a couple of days later, the additional tests for Leticia, Alfredo, and Grandfather were set up. The former priest would obviously not be related to any of them, so it sufficed to check his sample for ethnicity.

After they returned from the lab, Lola was busy in the kitchen cooking. Jasmin helped by cutting vegetables. Lola told her she was offended by not being included in the DNA party.

"Now I'll never know if I'm part Neanderthal," she said.

They both laughed.

The next day, Leticia and her husband took the train into New York. She wanted to attend Broadway plays and Alfredo planned to visit the Metropolitan Museum of Art. From there, they would fly back to Mexico.

Jasmin walked home from campus thinking that everyone had forgotten about the DNA tests. Her grandfather sat on the veranda reading and Lola was at her English class. Excited to tell him about her research project, she prepared iced tea and joined him outside.

She chatted about her project. The phone rang and she jumped up to answer. The PI was calling with the DNA results. Jasmin handed the phone to her grandfather who immediately put it on speaker.

"You'll be happy to know Rosana is indeed Jasmin's mother." The PI took an audible breath. "What's more interesting are the other results. Your daughter Leticia is not your daughter. And you hadn't told me Jasmin is your child."

CHAPTER FORTY-EIGHT

"I'm your daughter?" Jasmin asked in a whisper, as if the news should continue being shrouded in secrecy. "Did you know it?"

"I've always known you were my child," Agustín confessed. "It's the reason I arranged to have Leticia and Salva adopt you. That way you'd grow up in my household."

"You've kept the truth from me. That's not fair." Jasmin paced the veranda. "I can't believe you did this. You, you told me not to eavesdrop. You taught me to tell the truth. You always said that actions have consequences. Yet you don't follow the rules you set up for me!"

"In retrospect, I wish I could have been truthful back then," Agustín said. "Don't forget I knew you, and others, were in grave danger if anyone found out you were alive. Plus, Anita would never have accepted you in the house if she'd known. That's why I handled it the way I did. I'm sorry."

"Grandmother figured it out anyway." Jasmin felt her face flush with anger. "Now I understand why she kicked you out of the big house."

Agustín reached for her hand, but Jasmin pulled it away. She reflected briefly on the other information the PI had provided.

"Did you know Leticia was not your daughter?"

He shook his head. "No, but I raised her, so that makes her my daughter too," he said in a sad tone. "It's Anita who betrayed me, not Leticia. All the way back to colluding with that scum, Rodrigo Alvarado, when you were born."

Her grandfather—oops, Agustín, papa, father, whatever she should call him seemed too preoccupied with finding Rosana to pay much attention to the fact Leticia was not his biological child. Now he faced the complication of telling Mama about the DNA results. If Jasmin felt upset, she imagined her mother's hostility when she'd receive the news.

"Maybe Grandmother is the one who should have moved to the casita. She was unfaithful long before you were."

"That's all in the past," Agustín said. "Let's forgive what happened and focus on the future."

"As long as you live by the rules you set for me. Don't keep secrets from me," Jasmin demanded.

It was impossible for Jasmin to switch overnight to calling Agustín either father or papa after calling him grandfather all those years. He'd always treated her like a daughter, especially after Salva left. For years she'd wondered about family secrets, ever since the day she'd overheard Mama taunt him, and even before that, when she tried to figure out why her mother didn't love her. This had to be the biggest of those secrets. The revelation of Agustín being her father should not have shocked her so much. On the contrary, she felt immense joy, for nowhere could she have found a better father.

"Once the PI arranges a meeting with Rosana," he said, "we can talk about the test results with Leticia. I'll invite them to New Jersey. I'd rather break the news face-to-face."

"I dread an emotional scene," Jasmin said.

"With Leticia?" he asked. "We cannot keep it from her. I simply want to avoid a supercharged meeting until after we've met with Rosana and can honestly tell Leticia everything."

"What about the other tests?"

"Which ones?" he asked.

"The ethnic ancestry."

"I'll pick the results up at the labs later this week."

The PI called three days later to inform them that Rosana lived in Niagara-on-the-Lake in Canada. She used the name Vanessa. She'd agreed to meet them after hours at the restaurant where she worked as sous chef. To make it easy, Agustín suggested eating dinner at the same restaurant. The PI could inform Rosana they would be discreet with the wait staff to avoid giving away their reason for being there.

The PI suggested taking time to speak by phone before heading to Canada for an in-person meeting. And getting a psychologist involved could be useful.

Agustín disagreed. He wanted to set the meeting up as soon as possible. No phone calls. No psychologists. Just sit together at a table and figure things out.

The PI suggested taking an album with Jasmin's photos to break the ice.

Agustín asked the PI to set the meeting up for Thursday evening.

Agustín awakened Jasmin at five on Thursday morning to travel to Ontario. The meeting was scheduled for that night. If things did not work out with Rosana, they could exchange the Amtrak tickets and return immediately. Agustín felt nervous and thought Jasmin must be too.

At Princeton Junction, they boarded Amtrak for New York's Penn Station with a transfer to Niagara Falls on the Canadian side, a total of twelve-hours. Twelve long hours of thinking, anticipating, question-ing, and perhaps regretting the decision to meet Jasmin's biological mother.

"The scenery will be so beautiful, you won't even have time to get nervous," Agustín said, reading Jasmin's mind.

His promise did not materialize, at least not initially. It was dark outside, and the train sped through industrial sections of town and dilapidated neighborhoods. Jasmin looked out the window. Black and white scenes rushed by like a science fiction film about forgotten people in a dystopian world.

Once the train departed Metropark in the Woodbridge area, rays of light played off the tops of buildings on the New York skyline, creating areas of feathery light that contrasted with the darkness below. Electric lights shining through windows punctuated the lower, darker parts of the buildings. Gazing south of Manhattan in New York Harbor, Jasmin pointed out the silhouette of the Statue of Liberty in the distance for her father to see.

Signs inside the crowded New York station were confusing, but if millions of people who used it regularly could figure it out, Agustín thought a Princeton grad student and her father could manage the transfer.

Agustín reached for her hand and squeezed it.

They elbowed their way through the halls to the platform they needed, dodging people during the peak rush hour who were scrambling to get to work on time.

When they found their seats, they took their coats off before settling in. He handed her an envelope with the DNA findings on her ancestry.

"You have plenty of Maya in you," he said, smoothing his mustache. "Seventeen percent. You must honor it by doing great things in math."

She peaked at the results and placed them in her carryon. "I hope someday to do great things that will benefit our planet. That should honor my Maya ancestry."

Agustín cleared his throat. "I've always thought your brilliant mind is like Einstein's and I've pushed you in that direction. Maybe I've been wrong. You should fly your own spaceship into the unknown."

Jasmin looked at him incredulously as if she couldn't believe what she'd heard. "To launch my homemade spaceship was a childish dream, especially with me in it."

"As determined as you are, you'll fly one someday. Or you'll have a company of your own taking scientists and tourists into space," he said.

"Oh, don't say such things because I don't want to disappoint you."

He patted her shoulder. "You've never disappointed me, ma petite princesse. Not ever."

Once the train was speeding through the Hudson Valley, bright sunlight that fell on the maple trees rendered them aflame. Traveling further on, they witnessed an explosion of color, as if pigments had been painted on the leaves that covered thousands of trees. Agustín was riveted to the sight, thinking that neither one of them had ever witnessed such gorgeous foliage—a kaleidoscope of deep burgundy, bright red, sunlit yellow, and burnt orange glistening and shifting in the sunlight.

"Remember when we read *Jane Eyre?*" Jasmin asked. "When Charlotte Brontë wrote about the colors of fall leaves."

Agustín sighed. "She called them 'congealed relics of autumn, russet leaves, swept by past winds in heaps.' I think I've got the quote right."

The words sounded philosophical, like a comparison to life and death. It made him think of the books he and Jasmin had read together over the years. She continued looking out the window as if she were mesmerized with the brightly colored leaves.

Jasmin's phone rang. Aki wanted to break the news he'd been accepted at the Plasma Physics Lab in Princeton for his post-doctoral work. "I've missed our great conversations," he said over the speaker. "We'll be able to continue them once I'm there next spring."

Agustín saw her joy upon knowing her fellow student would be moving to Princeton. "Don't forget Aki is six years older than you."

"I know. He's like an older brother to me and he's one of the few people close to my age I can talk to. He understands me and we discuss lots of ideas."

As the train raced further north, the trees became bare. They traveled for endless hours. The sun disappeared on the western horizon, and everything went dark outside the window again.

"I think I'll take a nap," he said.

Jasmin took his coat and covered him with it. He squeezed her hand in appreciation.

CHAPTER FORTY-NINE

The train stopped. In anticipation of crossing into Canada, Jasmin awakened Agustín and pulled their passports to present to immigration officials. They disembarked at the West Depot Avenue station and picked up a rental for the remaining hour's drive to Niagara-on-the-Lake. If they followed the GPS without making a wrong turn, they'd arrive at Rosana's restaurant at seven-thirty, just in time for the dinner reservation.

"No time for a shower," Jasmin said, regretting not being able to change into fresh clothes after traveling all day.

Rosana's restaurant was inside the Prince of Wales Hotel. The maître d' walked them to their table, past paintings that looked like museum pieces. He seated them in chairs with plush dark blue velvet upholstery. On the wall behind their table was an oil painting in a carved gold leaf frame. It depicted a white-washed village with red tile roofs that contrasted with bluish-purple mountains in the distance. Agustín took a seat along the wall under the painting and placed a bag on the chair next to him.

The maître d' handed menus to them.

Jasmin looked around the room. Despite the antique décor, splashes of greenery from strategically placed ceramic pots provided a feeling of airiness. Her father's quote from *Jane Eyre* earlier in the day came to mind as she contemplated the furnishings. The setting seemed appropriate for Charlotte Brontë's Victorian novel, yet the restaurant was not stuffy as she had imagined the homes of noble families of the nineteenth century to be. Laughter and chatter came from two larger dining halls filled with people, but the small room where they were seated was empty, except for them.

Agustín opened the menu. He glanced at Jasmin and told her a tasting menu, featuring an assortment of appetizers to be served before the main course, seemed appropriate for the evening. The entrée offerings were wild-caught salmon and venison. He picked up one of the wine glasses and held it up. His eyes twinkled. "If I order a wine pairing, will you have a sip?"

Jasmin nodded. "What if she's changed her mind about meeting us?"

"If she has, she has. We'll simply enjoy our dinner, spend the night in the hotel, and if she doesn't contact us, we'll return home. Or I'll call our PI to intervene."

"I wouldn't want to beg her." Jasmin's hands were sweaty. She silently recited numbers in the Fibonacci sequence.

Her father's expression turned serious, and he stood up.

Jasmin turned to see what had caught his attention. A woman wearing a stiffly starched, full-length white apron was leaning against the wall observing them, making her forget the Fibonacci sequence. Jasmin felt like jumping out of her skin. The aproned lady now walked toward their table. As the woman got closer, she thought Rosana appeared to be nervous.

Courage, she told herself. Swallowing hard, she smoothed her hair and stood.

"This is Jasmin, your daughter," Agustín said, touching Jasmin's shoulder. "Our daughter."

A wall of silence settled on them. Jasmin's head began spinning as the three of them stared at one another, each waiting for the other to speak first.

"She's beautiful," Rosana said after a few seconds, reaching out to hug Jasmin. "I never dreamed this moment would ever happen."

"We assumed you were dead," Agustín said. "If we'd only known—"

"It would have been dangerous to look for me. Nor could I search for Jasmin. I did not want to put her in danger," Rosana said, looking at Agustín. She glanced around the room. "I'm not even sure we're safe now. I've had to hide for years."

Clumsily, Agustín handed Rosana the package he'd brought. "Photos. All of them of Jasmin. She looks so much like you, beautiful, like you."

"A gift?"

Agustín nodded.

"I'll take them home with me. Right now, let's talk." Rosana sat down, leaning the package against the leg of the chair. "I've rehearsed this in my mind for years, all the time knowing I would probably never get a chance to tell you."

Jasmin and Agustín also sat. Rosana briefly glanced at Agustín before focusing on the place setting in front of her.

"When I asked you to save my family from the poachers who threatened to take our land, I was not completely truthful. That was only part of it."

She raised her eyes and looked at Agustín again.

"I'll tell you everything. I've lived with such fear that I'd go to my grave without ever seeing you again or meeting my daughter." She looked at the top of the table as she continued. "The man behind the threats was Rodrigo Alvarado, a bully from our town in the Puebla highlands. If I would become his mistress, he told me, he'd forgo my family's land and instead take me. He already had a wife and grown children, plus he was not a good man. An extortionist, he'd taken orchards from other families in the area. I was scared. You were a colonel in the army, and I worked for you. When I begged you for help, I never mentioned Rodrigo's threats to me personally.

"After you took the army in and cleaned up the mess, Rodrigo left the area, some of his men were jailed. One died. Confiscated lands were restored to their rightful owners.

"But there's more." Rosana sighed. "What I also kept from you was that Rodrigo's son was a seventeen-year-old student at the university during the Tlatelolco uprising in 1968. The son was killed, and Rodrigo blamed you. That incident happened years before I met you."

"I never knew Rodrigo Alvarado. Nor his son," Agustín said.

"He blamed you for the entire student massacre."

"I was a mere captain in the army during that uprising and I followed orders. That's what an army officer does," Agustín said. "Do I regret that awful situation? Yes, but I was not responsible for the decision to quell the demonstration with bullets. What makes him think I killed his son?"

"A fellow student told Rodrigo that you climbed out of an army tank just as his son rushed toward you shouting, 'We don't want the Olympics, we want revolution!' According to the student bystander, you opened fire and killed Rodrigo's son at point blank. Presumably the incident happened in front of the Chihuahua building at the Plaza de las Tres Culturas."

Agustín turned pale. His hands trembled. "That boy rushed toward me. Gunfire was ricocheting all around. The kid reached for his waist. I thought he was pulling a gun." Agustín took a deep breath. "I've had nightmares all my life over that incident."

Rosana squirmed in her chair as if trying to get comfortable. "Years after the Tlatelolco uprising," she continued, "when you were a colonel and you moved the army into my village, my family heard Rodrigo swear he'd get revenge against you." She glanced at the table and shifted the position of the wine glasses in the place setting next to her.

Jasmin held her breath. Secrets, it seemed, pervaded her family. She had not necessarily expected a happy reunion, but still she had thought it'd go better than this. She clasped the stem of a wine glass.

They listened as Rosana spoke about details she'd obviously kept bottled up for years. She never broke down, but at times her voice became almost inaudible. "Four years after you cleaned up the mess in the village, I returned. Rodrigo had not been seen. And I wanted to be by my mother's side when I gave birth. You'd offered to leave Anita or even set up a house for me, whatever I preferred. I did not want it on my conscience that I'd broken up a marriage, and even though I loved you, I was not going to live as anyone's mistress.

"Rodrigo had contacts in the village. He found out I was pregnant, that I worked for you, and that it had been you, four years earlier, who had brought soldiers to the highlands to protect the apple growers. He figured you had to be the man whose child I was expecting. Instead of confronting you or me, he contacted your wife."

"Anita?" Agustín asked, looking as if the very earth had been moved from under him.

"They kidnapped me. Rodrigo pointed a gun at my head. Anita injected me with some sort of drug, and they dumped me in the back seat of a car. He got in behind the steering wheel and your wife sat next to me. The next thing I remember was signing a piece of paper at a doctor's office," she said, snapping the stem of the wine glass. A couple of drops of blood appeared on her thumb. She glanced at Agustín and then at Jasmin. She cleaned the blood off with a napkin and proceeded to tell them about other details she remembered from that fateful night.

"If I did not sign, my baby and I would both be killed, they told me."

The wall of silence returned.

A server started toward them carrying a basket of bread and a crystal pitcher of ice water. Rosana held her hand up in an apparent gesture to stop the server, who turned and left the room.

Agustín mumbled a few words of apology, saying it was all his fault.

"I think it was the next day," Rosana said, "Rodrigo picked me up. They had kept me drugged because I was semiconscious. He took me to a condo in Mexico City and brought a woman to take care of me. I was locked up in a bedroom for two months." She hesitated. "This is terribly painful to talk about. Rodrigo sold me to a sex trafficker, saying I was a—"

She turned toward Jasmin and winced, apologizing for the terrible descriptions, but continued by emphasizing it had to be told.

"He said I was a whore, and I was getting what I deserved."

She stopped momentarily and glanced at the mountains in the painting on the wall behind their table. Shifting her chair, she touched Jasmin's arm and looked straight into her eyes. "A monster like Rodrigo is not capable of understanding the purity of the love Agustín and I shared. We loved and respected each other. When reality set in that Agustín was married, I chose not to live in a 'casa chica.' I was not going to be the mistress in a secondary house. If only I had known what horrible things would happen, I would have let Agustín divorce his wife."

CHAPTER FIFTY

Over the following two days, Jasmin and her father learned of the suffering Rosana had endured after she was brought to the US as a sex slave. She called it her misfortune.

"Others have suffered even more than I, so why should I complain?" she asked.

On the second day after their arrival, Rosana took the day off work. She picked them up at the hotel and took them for a drive along the Niagara River on the Canadian side. At first Jasmin thought she was merely trying to entertain them, but as they traveled south on the Niagara River Parkway, she showed them where she'd crossed into Canada. She parked the car at a designated picnic area, Locust Grove, wedged between the Sir Adam Beck Hydroelectric Reservoir and the river. The three of them stepped out. Rosana pointed to the US side.

Gazing across the river, she started talking. "First, I'd been trafficked in the Houston area. That was for the weekdays—Monday through Thursday. On Fridays, I'd be flown into New York City to work the weekends. About every six months, Rodrigo would show up in Houston. He'd threaten me and demand money from my pimp for my work. You see why I could never escape and try to find my little girl."

That day in Princeton when the PI informed them Rosana had been sold to a trafficker, Jasmin had never seen such anguish on Agustín's face. He had cried for the suffering he'd caused those who were being punished for his sins. But today his expression was even more pained.

"One day I was sold again. To a sex trafficker in Buffalo. Then I became pregnant. I knew they would take this child away from me too. I'd dreamed of breaking away, but I'd been too fearful. Getting pregnant changed everything. It made me determined to fight."

Agustín had often worked with Jasmin on the issue of empathy. For years he'd told her to bring her head out of the clouds and feel the pain of others. Right now, she wished she could experience less empathy. Her heart ached so much, she felt it would shatter into a thousand pieces. And there would not be enough gold in the world to put it back together. She realized Rosana was still talking, so she listened.

"I didn't have much money," Rosana said, "but I got the name of a taxi driver in Niagara Falls on the US side. When I escaped from my trafficker, the cabby arranged to get me into Canada."

Agustín looked as if the slightest breeze could knock him over.

"I stayed with his family until I was almost due. I started having labor pains. He drove me to the river where a man with a canoe paddled me across the border. All of this for a fee, of course. Before the canoeist disappeared into the night, he called an ambulance for me."

Rosana looked serene for the first time. Maybe a load had been taken off her shoulders. She signaled for them to climb back into her car.

"Wasn't it dangerous to wait until you were in labor before you crossed the border?" Agustín asked.

"Yes, yet that was the only way to make certain I was not deported before I delivered my baby."

Rosana drove to the Greater Niagara General Hospital, and she pulled into the parking lot.

"This is where the ambulance brought me. An hour later, a cesarean was performed, and Campos was brought into the world."

"Campos?" Agustín blinked. "My surname?"

"I wanted to honor you that way," she said, keeping alert to their surroundings.

"After all the suffering I put you through?" he asked.

Sitting in the backseat, Jasmin could not help but compare Rosana and Leticia. Rosana did not blame anyone for her misfortunes. Mama, by contrast, cursed everyone around her and blamed others for all her troubles.

Jasmin's thoughts were interrupted as Rosana told them they would drive to Niagara-on-the-Lake and pick Campos up at school. On the return trip, she told them that four weeks after Campos was born, she took him with her to immigration. She explained she'd crossed the Canadian border illegally looking for protection for herself and her then unborn child. She presented herself as an asylum seeker. They told her to file refugee claims for herself and her baby.

"I had to pass an exam. It was a breeze. I scored out of the ballpark in mathematics. They classified me as a skilled worker, better for my citizenship application to be approved. Soon I was working as a teacher's assistant at the Niagara Falls Secondary High School. But I wanted to cook. I took a job at a restaurant as a dishwasher and from there I moved up."

"You make it sound so easy," Jasmin said.

"Not at all, it took years of hard work, but I loved every minute of it. I was free. Someday I'll be a full-fledged chef. For that, I'll have to complete my studies at the culinary institute."

Jasmin had plenty of time, as Rosana drove, to envision all sorts of scenarios about her half-brother. Would Campos accept her? What would he look like? Did he also excel in mathematics? Did he know about Rosana's past? What would he think of Agustín, the man he was named after but not related to? It nearly drove her crazy.

She was pleased to find that Campos seemed like any well-adjusted ten-year-old. *He was the child Mama would have wanted*, she thought, *not a genius, just a good-natured kid*. When he was introduced to Agustín, he shook hands very formally.

"I've heard so much about you," he said, breaking into a wide smile. "My mother has always told me of the love she has for you and that's why I was given your name."

"I'm honored," Agustín said, choking up.

Campos turned to Jasmin and gave her a hug. "I like the idea of having a big sister, as long as you're not too bossy."

CHAPTER FIFTY-ONE

When Jasmin and Agustín returned from Canada, Lola seemed overjoyed and wanted to know all about the reunion with Jasmin's birth mother. The two women talked about it for hours. When Lola started fixing dinner, Jasmin went to her bedroom to change clothes. She opened the bottom drawer to grab a sweater and heard a thump behind the chest. The leather-bound diary had fallen. She picked it up and leafed through it. She noticed the inside of the back cover was coming unglued and a slight bulge was evident.

Jasmin took the edge of paper that was unglued and pulled it. It lifted easily to reveal a folded paper underneath, which she removed. Opening it, she saw a handwritten letter her grandmother had written to Leticia. Her hands trembled as she read it.

I'm distraught that my husband deceived you and me both by bringing that baby into our household. This is not a coincidence. Agustin obviously arranged it. If he will take such a monstrous step, he will disinherit you if given a chance. You must stop that girl from taking it all away from you. Besides, she's not normal. Her ability in math proves she's Rosana's daughter. I suspect she may be your bastard half-sister. Now that you know it, I trust you'll do everything in your power to keep her at a distance. She's not worthy of your love.

Jasmin stared at the letter not believing what she'd read. It was obvious Mama knew all about Rosana's relationship with Agustín. It also explained why she and Mama did not have a good relationship. How could they? Her mother and grandmother had been very close. It was her grandmother who had hated her, and Leticia had obeyed by keeping Jasmin at a distance.

What could she do with the letter now? She wondered if she should discuss it with her father. She didn't want to upset him with details from the past when he still faced the hurdle of revealing the DNA tests to Leticia. In the end, she folded it and stuck it inside the diary.

Agustín had invited Leticia and Alfredo to Princeton. She sat on the sofa and pouted that she'd been forced to make the trip to discuss the DNA results. In contrast, her husband seemed happy for the opportunity to visit. Even the cats, hearing the commotion, came out from the back bedroom to join in the reunion. Sojón brushed up against Alfredo's pants in a friendly gesture. He picked Sojón up and placed him on his lap. The old cat purred for a few seconds until he lifted his head and noticed Leticia on the sofa. He jumped down and left the room.

Prepared to lead the discussion, Agustín glanced at the envelope he held in his hand. It contained the test results.

Lola had made a punch with orange, pineapple, and lemon juice spiked with Jamaican rum and grenadine. Alfredo had complimented her on the punch during his last visit. It seemed Lola was making peace with the former priest. She served everyone a glass, including Jasmin.

Looking at Leticia, Agustín informed her the DNA results showed he was Jasmin's father.

Leticia scoffed. "My mother always suspected you were. So that's why you made me travel up here? To tell me your beloved grand-daughter turns out instead to be your most beloved daughter. You should not have wasted the money." Holding her glass of punch, she stood up and scowled at Lola. "Serve lunch so my husband and I can return to Mexico this afternoon."

"Sit down," Agustín said with the tone and snap of a military command.

Leticia seemed shocked as she slumped back onto the sofa. She took a sip of her drink.

"I called you here primarily to tell you the tests revealed something else," Agustín said.

In a mocking tone, Leticia said she was listening.

"You're not my biological daughter," he said in a tone of authority, yet much softer than his previous statement. He stepped toward Leticia and handed her the envelope.

"I knew it. You're trying to disinherit me. This isn't true and I want these tests run again." She choked on the words and started coughing. Once her coughing spell was under control, she glared at Jasmin. "You provoked this, didn't you? You've schemed to take it all away."

"Look at me, Leticia," Agustín said. "You're the one who wanted a DNA test to prove I was your father."

"That's not true," she said, spitting the words out with venom.

In a gentle voice, Alfredo reminded his wife that she had in fact requested the DNA tests on their last visit.

"So now Jasmin will get everything, just as my mother predicted." She held the punch glass and looked around the room as if she were searching for the right target before she threw it.

Alfredo held Leticia's arm and took the glass, spilling punch on the sofa. She whispered unintelligibly but it was her expression that showed her rage.

In two or three minutes, Leticia's outburst subsided. Agustín explained he was leaving his will intact. Leticia scoffed, saying she did not believe him.

"It's because you believed Grandmother," Jasmin said. "It was she who hated me and told you I was not normal and to keep me at a distance because I'd take it all from you. And that's not true! I won't take anything from you."

Leticia stared angrily at Jasmin. "You stole it, didn't you? You stole my diary. I should have known it had been you and not Salva." Leticia turned and screamed at Agustín. "You see. She's already stolen from me. She took my diary. Can't you see that proves she's out to take everything from me, like my mother always told me."

Alfredo calmly asked Leticia to follow him outside.

Lola had been setting up lunch, buffet style, on the kitchen counter. She put it on hold.

It took almost an hour for Leticia and Alfredo to return. When they did, Leticia apologized for her behavior and said they were ready for lunch.

Everyone sat at the dining table after serving their plates. Leticia still appeared sulky.

No one spoke. Eventually, Agustín asked if the apple trees had been pruned in Ocotlán. Alfredo told him they were still waiting for colder weather and would do it in January.

"Who do you suppose my father is?" Leticia asked, poking her fork into the brisket Lola had slowly cooked for several hours with dark ale and vegetables.

"You tell me," Agustín said.

She responded that if she knew, she wouldn't ask.

Jasmin couldn't help herself and suggested it might be Rodrigo Alvarado.

"Who is he?" Leticia demanded. She stared at Lola, sitting next to Jasmin. Lola stared back without saying a word.

Agustín felt uncomfortable. "He's the man who helped your mother kidnap Rosana and take her to the doctor in Mexico City who delivered Jasmin," he said. His discomfort had translated into a soothing voice, as if that would soften the blow of what he revealed.

"You can run your own DNA test with him," Jasmin said.

"And where can I find him?" Leticia asked. Her voice had become meek.

"At the Altiplano federal penitentiary," Jasmin said.

Leticia gasped, probably at the thought of being the offspring of a common criminal.

"That's enough, Jasmin." Agustín was visibly upset. He had rarely used such a cutting tone of voice.

Agustín hoped to make Leticia feel better by suggesting that she run tests with Lorenzo, the stableman.

"How can you be so cruel? Both of you," she said. She walked away and locked herself in the bathroom.

Everyone could hear her crying. And of course, they'd stopped eating. The leftover food would probably be fed to the cats over the next week.

Jasmin felt numb and could not move. Alfredo turned to her and suggested she apologize to Leticia.

"But she's hurt me for over ten years, and she's never apologized."

"Two wrongs don't make a right," the former priest said. "We must start forgiveness somewhere. A bit of kindness toward your mother after the disturbing news she's heard would be the right thing to do."

Agustín agreed. "Empathy, Jasmin. Don't put salt on your Mama's wounds. You've had your issues with her, but Leticia is not a bad person. She's insecure and tries to cover it with aggression."

Alfredo added that Leticia was a very emotional person who found it difficult to express herself. "She suffers from intermittent explosive disorder and she's receiving treatment for it. We should be supportive of her."

Agustín excused himself, asking Jasmin to follow him to his room. He closed the door and suggested she reflect on her own good news from the DNA testing plus the blessing of finding Rosana and Campos.

"By being compassionate to your mother, whose personality is insecure and fragile, you might benefit as much as she will if you'll apologize." He left the room, leaving Jasmin to meditate on her actions.

When she returned to the living room a half hour later, Jasmin felt genuinely contrite. Leticia sat next to her husband on the sofa. Jasmin took a seat and expressed remorse for what she'd said. "I'm also sorry I stole your diary. That was wrong of me. It caused your divorce from Dad."

Leticia nodded and took Jasmin's hand. "You need to understand that I didn't know my mother did those terrible things to Rosana. After she discovered you were Rosana's child, she filled me with anger and hatred. I took things out on you. On her deathbed, she told me about the letter she'd written. I hid it in my diary, the letter you obviously found. That's where she told me you were probably my bastard half-sister. She carried on as if you had leprosy. On her deathbed, she made me promise I'd keep you at a distance. And yet I still loved you, but I felt disloyal to my mother whenever I tried to express my love for you. You asked me a long time ago, why I had destroyed your pyramid and your spaceship."

Leticia stopped speaking but still held Jasmin's hand.

"I felt angry at the world, and I was jealous that you were so much smarter than me. I thought if I destroyed them, I could get rid of the evidence that you are so much more intelligent." Leticia sniffled. "I'm sorry, that was so wrong of me to destroy the projects you worked so hard on."

Jasmin told her adopted mother that she had tried to excel on the projects in an attempt to gain her love. "I guess we both did things we should not have."

Leticia leaned toward Jasmin and hugged her.

"I have something else to share with you," Leticia whispered. "Alfredo and I called Lorenzo a few minutes ago. When I asked him if he might be my father, you cannot imagine how happy the old man sounded. He could not stop telling me how much he loved me and was glad to know the secret he'd kept to himself for thirty-eight years was no longer a secret. We'll run tests when we return home." She looked at Jasmin with sad eyes. "Now I wish with all my heart that I were your half-sister. I'm not even that."

"You'll always be my mother," Jasmin said. "Let's build a good relationship going forward." She offered to get the diary and return it.

"It should be burned," Leticia said. "Or torn up and thrown away."

After Agustín's revelation of the family secrets, Leticia's tantrums, and their mutual apologies, Jasmin was exhausted. She glanced around the living room. Everyone appeared calm, seemingly unperturbed.

Jasmin thought about the day she'd seen the priest kiss her mother. Lots had changed since then. Glancing at her family again, she realized that without any drama going on, life was pretty good. She loved the feeling. If only Aki were here, that would make it even better.

Lola hummed a song as she cleaned up the kitchen. Leticia leaned on her husband's shoulder while they watched a documentary on jazz. Agustín stood over the counter cutting leftover brisket for the cats. Jasmin opened a can of cat food and mixed it with the brisket.

Jasmin and her father walked to the veranda to feed the cats. She watched as both pets followed Agustín with the typical quiet movements of felines. Feeling a slight twang of possessiveness over the cats she had taken care of, she was surprised they followed her father when she was carrying their food. Jasmin filled their dishes, but they did not leave her father's side. Sojón meowed incessantly. She bent down on a knee and picked up the loveable old cat and placed him in front of the food. He immediately returned to Agustín's side.

"They like you better than these gourmet treats," she said, smiling up at him.

Her father's face was gray, and his forehead glistened with beads of sweat. Alarmed, Jasmin stood up as Agustín crumpled to the ground. She tried to catch him, but it was too late. He hit the veranda floor.

Jasmin screamed. Those inside the duplex came running. Alfredo assessed the scene and rushed inside to call an ambulance.

Lola and Leticia helped Agustín to his rocking chair. Jasmin kneeled beside him and held his hand. When Alfredo returned to the veranda, Agustín asked his son-in-law to make sure the family resolved their troubles in the future.

"I want all of you to get along. Including Rosana." His shortness of breath made the words sound like a whisper. He relaxed into the rocker.

The paramedics couldn't find Agustín's pulse. Jasmin and Leticia climbed into the ambulance for the short ride to the Princeton Hospital. Agustín, her grandfather, her father, and her best friend was declared dead on arrival. The most beloved person in Jasmin's life was gone. She was numb.

As soon as they returned to the apartment, Jasmin called Rosana. Alfredo called Salva, De la Mota, Huerta, and Sebastián. After the extended family members were called, Jasmin spoke to Aki. Everyone agreed to convene in Princeton for a memorial service.

CHAPTER FIFTY-TWO

Two weeks later a small group, including the out-of-towners —Leticia and her husband, De la Mota, Huerta, Salva, Rosana, Campos, Aki, and Sebastián—attended Agustín's memorial service at the Catholic church. Salva sang "Ave Maria." And the church allowed them to break with tradition and add "Ode to Joy" to the music selection. They all cried, especially when De la Mota and Salva eulogized Agustín. When the service was over, they hugged each other and walked in the chilly weather down Nassau Street to Bayard Lane to Stanworth. They walked in silence as if the blanket of cold air prevented anyone from speaking.

Stepping inside the duplex, the aroma of food warmed them instantly. Lola had prepared everyone's favorites, including tres leches spiked with Kahlúa for Huerta. Not having previously cooked for the Canadians, she took a guess and prepared duck pâté en croûte. For Aki, she'd made bite-sized chicken on skewers, called Yakitori. But most of all, she aimed to please the former priest, who had become one of her favorite people. She'd made rum punch for him.

They served their plates and squeezed together at the table while Huerta and Salva stood near the buffet laid out on the counter.

Everyone mingled a few laughs with their tears as they told stories about Agustín. Jasmin and Aki were the quiet ones.

"It must be awkward to be with my family," Jasmin said to Aki.

"I want to be here," he said. "You're my friend and I admired your grandfather. Umm, I mean your father."

Leticia and Campos hit it off so well, she asked Rosana if he could spend the summers at the house in Ocotlán.

"Only if he will be safe," Rosana said.

When Huerta overheard her comment, he immediately gave everyone the news he had apparently been waiting to share after the funeral. "Rodrigo Alvarado was assaulted by fellow inmates a week ago. He's in the hospital having suffered severe head trauma that put him in a coma. He's not expected to live. His physical injuries hurt his spine, and if he survives, he may never walk again. Hopefully, he will no longer pose a threat."

"It appears," De la Mota added, "that sorry criminal has a lot of enemies inside the prison."

"There's more," Huerta said. "Alvarado ordered Agustín's kidnapping. He'd tried to get Jasmin when she was a little girl. Despite the intervening years since his own son was killed at the Tlatelolco uprising, he intended to carry out his threat to kill Agustín. He also wanted to track Rosana down. He'd lost track of her when she escaped to Canada. It seems as if he wanted to punish them forever."

Jasmin gasped. "My father always taught me that actions have consequences. If I'd turned down the TV interview, my father would not have suffered the abduction." Her stomach felt as if it'd been gripped in a vise.

"Agustín thought he was going to be kidnapped when he was assaulted," Huerta said. "That's why he contacted me to help after he was attacked at the cemetery. In case they tried again."

"Things happen for a reason," Alfredo said. "If Agustín had not been kidnapped, he would not have learned through his abductors that Rosana was still alive."

"Alvarado is an old man. Let's hope he cannot carry out any more threats," Salva added. "We want Jasmin and Rosana to be safe."

Despite everything, Jasmin felt guilty about her father's abduction.

Salva must have sensed the grief she was feeling. He sat next to her, put his arm around her, and whispered in her ear. "You were Agustín's greatest joy in life. He told me that many times. He'd want you to live free from the harm a madman could inflict on you and Rosana. Be happy that he'd be happy for you."

Jasmin told him she had to apologize to him again for stealing her mother's diary years ago. "I was wrong to do it and I'm sorry I did not admit it immediately after taking it. It might have saved yours and Mama's marriage."

Salva told her it would not have mattered. His marriage to Leticia was already over. The diary incident had merely served to bring it out in the open.

"I didn't appreciate the family secrets maintained by everyone else. Yet I did the same thing. I hid the diary for ten years." Jasmin had trouble breathing for a few seconds until her emotions settled down. She told Salva she would try not to feel guilt over the stolen diary anymore. "I've also learned Agustín was my biological father and that fills me with joy."

Huerta spoke to Rosana and Jasmin turned to listen.

"With renewed safety, you can revert back to your original name."

Rosana shook her head.

"My name was officially changed when I became a Canadian. All of you can continue to call me Rosana, but I have the legal documents to prove my name," she said. "Plus, I love my name, so why change it?"

"And what, may I ask, is your full name, sister?" Huerta asked.

"Vanessa de la Vega. And my son is Campos de la Vega."

"Campos de la Vega?" De la Mota repeated. "You used both of Agustín's surnames? You must have loved him a lot."

"Immensely," she said, nodding. "And now, I can get to know our daughter."

Jasmin noticed Leticia cringed when Rosana referred to Jasmin as her daughter. She was fatigued, but she felt compelled to reassure Leticia. She nudged in between Campos and her adopted mother and hugged her.

"I'm Rosana's daughter and that makes me enormously happy, but

I'm also *your* daughter. We have the papers to prove it. Besides, I like having two mothers," Jasmin said. "And I love having a brother too." She pulled Campos in for a three-way hug.

"And if you need a surrogate father, I'm around," De la Mota said, walking up and pulling Jasmin into a standing position.

"That makes two of us," Alfredo said, echoing the sentiment.

"Jasmin also has me," Salva said. "And that's on paper!"

Aki looked at Jasmin and then around the room. "I'm not old enough to be her father. I used to think of myself as her brother, but now she has Campos. I guess I'm just her friend and study companion."

Sebastián seemed overwhelmed by Agustín's death. He had kept quiet except for saying that he and Agustín had forged a wonderful friendship. "If you ever need anything, Jasmin, please know that you are family to me. I'll help in any way that I can."

At that moment, Jasmin felt very loved. Her father figures were important in her life. Aki was a good friend. As for Agustín, she would miss him so much, in ways she could not even begin to imagine yet. Life would be different without her closest ally.

If only he'd lived to enjoy his friendship with Rosana now that he'd found her. Jasmin was happy her biological father had found a good friend in Sebastián. She knew they would all miss Colonel Campos.

Jasmin had often thought of the young girl who had been kidnapped in front of her. She asked if the investigation into her father's abduction had uncovered anything about that incident.

"One of El Lencho's henchmen did it. It's been proven recently through a sample of DNA submitted years ago that matched up to a man El Lencho identified as the perpetrator," De la Mota said. "The sample came from the scab that you, Jasmin, pulled off the man's arm years ago."

Jasmin asked if the girl had been found.

De la Mota winced. "I hate to say it, but she died several years ago. El Lencho stated that and the detective who found the nurse followed up. Unfortunately, he confirmed it."

"You can feel good," Alfredo said to Jasmin, "about justice being done. El Lencho is now in prison, and it appears Rodrigo has received his punishment too."

Feeling overwhelmed with all the news, Jasmin walked to the digital piano and pulled back the keyboard cover. Hesitant, she sat on the bench and started playing "Ode to Joy." Across the room, De la Mota began singing. Salva joined in, and before long, everyone in the room was singing. Even the cats tiptoed around the piano, knowing they would be fed after the concert. Jasmin's thoughts flashed to her childhood years of playing the piano with her grandfather.

When she finished the piece and people quieted down, Huerta asked what she planned to do now that she was fifteen and Agustín was gone.

Before responding, she walked to the center of the room and glanced at Aki. They would both be in Princeton for the spring semester. Rosana and Campos would be in Canada. Princeton was where she wanted to live for now.

She looked at Huerta. "As a child, I was idealistic and wanted to travel into space in my own spaceship. My father encouraged me to walk in Einstein's shoes, doing research. Recently he said maybe he'd been wrong and suggested I follow my dream and fly into the cosmos."

"You can do anything you want," De la Mota said.

"My early desire to fly a spaceship was a childish dream. As I've added a few years to my age, my feet are more firmly planted on the ground. For now, I'm staying in Princeton to complete my doctorate. After that, who knows? The institute, a space exploration company, astronaut training, or something I have not yet considered will be waiting for me."

Aki took her by the hand and led her to the upright digital piano. He took the Secondo, or left side of the bench, and asked her to join him in playing "Rhapsody in Blue."

"You take the Primo position," he said, "and play the high notes."

She ran her fingers across the weighted ivory keys that felt as good as those on an acoustic piano. Everyone listened, even Sojón and Sancho.

They played Gershwin's jazzy rhythms and integrated the tempo perfectly with the more classical aspects of the piece. When they finished, Jasmin told Aki she was amazed that he not only knew his way around the keyboard, but also that he had such a wide repertoire.

"Wait till next semester," Aki said. "We'll share a lot more interests than just theoretical physics and music. There's so much to do in this area and we might even check out the golden spiral when we travel through the galaxy."

A NOTE FROM KATHRYN

Thank you for reading *Stolen Diary*. If you enjoyed this work of fiction, please write a review so others may also find Jasmin's story. The best way to reward authors is through honest and thoughtful reviews.

Amazon: amazon.com
BookBub: bookbub.com/profile/kathryn.lane
GoodReads: goodreads.com

If you would like to learn about my new releases and other news, please sign up for my newsletter at kathryn-lane.com

Happy reading!
Kathryn

WAKING UP IN MEDELLIN

CHAPTER ONE

If only Manuel Del Campo would speak to me, I could be on my way.

I sat in Del Campo's plush office near Medellín, Colombia, waiting for him to answer a few questions. Fidgeting with my nails, I was having second thoughts about the job, but it was too late. Now that I was on-site, it was better to get on with it.

It was exasperating to wait on him. The man's bombastic voice gave final instructions to a subordinate in the hallway at my back.

"Tell them we can ship to Singapore and have it there in six weeks. Or they can pay for air freight if they want it sooner."

I twisted in my seat and saw Del Campo standing outside the double doors of his office. The molding of the oversized doorway framed his muscular and impeccably dressed physique. He wore a crisp, highly tailored, bone-white suit—appropriate to the climate, yet contrasting conspicuously with the concept of steel mills.

I'd flown in last night. A weather delay before I left Minneapolis, plus the five-hour flight to the José María Córdova Airport in Medellín, gave me ample time to think about corruption in Latin America—corruption so widespread that individuals across the work-force, from police on the street to low-level government officials in back offices, supplemented their incomes inappropriately. When dishonesty exists so openly, it emanates from the top and permeates all of society. In countries like Colombia, drug-related crime adds layers of complexity. To their credit, the Colombian people had fought against traffickers. And I was fortunate not to be investigating the trade. I was only here to probe into possible mismanagement of a steel mill.

I turned toward his desk again. A photo of Del Campo, wearing the same bone-white suit he sported today, stared back at me from a gilded frame. Suddenly the man entered the room, lowering his voice to apologize for his delay.

"I have time," I said, thinking he probably kept business appointments with men promptly.

He walked behind his carved mahogany desk, preceding our meeting with pleasant Latin platitudes as he flipped open a cherrywood humidor, his initials engraved on the top, and selected a seven-inch Churchill. He cut the cap with a double guillotine cutter and lit a narrow strip of Spanish cedar with an old-fashioned butane lighter he retrieved from the top drawer of his desk. Cigar in mouth, he slowly rotated it in the spill's flame as he pulled air in gentle puffs to ensure an even burn. The spicy-sweet aroma of good hand-rolled tobacco mingled with the scent of the burning cedar, making me crave a cigar. But Del Campo was not about to offer one to a woman, certainly not to a lowly auditor. The man could ignore the ban on indoor smoking that worldwide headquarters in Minneapolis had issued. After all, Medellín is a long way from Minneapolis.

He rolled the cigar between his fingers. Without lifting his eyes, he abruptly turned the conversation to the purpose of my visit.

"So you're here to investigate me." His voice hardened.

"I'm here to investigate allegations of wrongdoing reported to headquarters," I said.

"I'm completely transparent about managing this company." Del Campo puffed on his cigar. "Everything here is on the up-and-up, like in a fencing bout."

"Fencing? What does that have to do with managing a company?"

"You don't go for perfection," Del Campo said. He puffed on his cigar, blew out three smoke rings, and stared at me as the rings slowly dissipated. "You just go for solid returns."

"I don't know much about fencing. But let me ask a few routine questions about the mill."

"Women would understand business if they learned the art. In the context of fencing, it's all about the frame you set up." He angled the photo of himself so it sat straight ahead of me.

"Frame?" I asked, confused.

"Let me explain. If you tell yourself your opponent is weak, you create a psychological advantage. On the contrary, if you are afraid of your opponent, you will see yourself ambushed."

"That sounds true to life. In the weeks to come, you can explain fencing to me. Right now, though, I need to get some information from you about the company."

"I'm at your service," he said, leaning back in his chair.

For the next hour, I asked a lot of questions. He lit up a second cigar. The more he spoke, the longer he drew on each puff. He held the Churchill between his thumb, middle, and index fingers, clearly an aficionado. I continued probing. He continued blowing smoke rings.

"If everything is aboveboard, as you say, why did your employees call the corporate security office to report misappropriation of company assets?" I asked.

He switched the cigar to his left hand. The inch-long ash fell in one piece on the highly polished mahogany. His right hand, fingers cupped, pushed the ashes across the desk in a semicircle and onto the floor in one sweeping motion.

"It's probably a disgruntled employee trying to discredit me. Or a competitor," he said.

"You think one disgruntled employee would be so persistent?" I asked, my voice firm.

"Why believe a caller who won't give his name?" Del Campo asked, his tone playful.

Almost immediately, he swiveled his chair, moved forward, and looked me straight in the eye.

"Look, Ms. Corporate Auditor Nikki Garcia, I'm tired of your insinuating questions. I find your tone accusatory. If corporate headquarters is not happy with my performance, they can fire me. They can trust me and stop this goddamned investigation, or they can fire me. You tell them that."

His voice heated and his face reddened. He looked at me as if it was all he could do to control his anger. If I'd been a man, I think he might have taken a swing at me.

"I thought fencing was about dealing psychologically with the opponent," I said.

He took what remained of his cigar and crushed it against the ashtray with such force I thought it would break. His face purple with anger, he stood, signaling our meeting was over. As I got up, his demeanor relaxed. He escorted me out of his office, smiling like a man accustomed to getting his way through temper tantrums. He cleared his throat, as if the cigar had irritated it.

"If you need anything while you're here on assignment, Nikki, just speak with my assistant. She'll arrange it for you. We want to make your visit to Medellín as pleasant as possible." He closed the door to his office, officially ending our conversation.

I stood by the door, once again livid with the corporate policy of informing high-level executives when they were the object of a review for fraudulent activity. No one ever told lower-level employees when they were the target of an audit, a tactic that ensured they didn't have time to cover up or destroy evidence. *So why inform executives?*

That man, manipulative as he seemed, had been president of Amazonia Steel for twelve years. He had taken control of a small company that manufactured for the Latin American market and grown it into a vast enterprise that exported around the globe. And he had been relentless in building his empire. His name had been tossed around at headquarters as a successor to the aging worldwide CEO, but Del Campo himself had taken his name out of contention, preferring, he claimed, to live in his native country.

I looked at the lavish furnishings in the office Del Campo's administrative assistant occupied. I'd met Theya, his assistant, that morning before she left at noon for personal reasons. The entire building was impeccable, but the elegant setting of the executive suite made me feel as if I were in upscale offices in New York.

I walked to the window to calm my anger at corporate policy before I talked with anyone else. Five floors up, I had a splendid view of an artificial lake that sparkled in the sunlight. Feeling queasy, I moved slightly away from the window, where I could better appreciate the view. A bridge curved gracefully over the lake, ending at a small, tree-lined parking lot near the front entrance to the building. Trees shaded a path around the lake. Beyond the lake and across the highway were low, rolling hills. The vacant land, lake, and neatly tended lawns around the company gave the entire complex a country club atmosphere. The steel mills were tucked out of sight half a mile away.

Amazonia Steel was one of the most profitable affiliates in the Globan family of companies. Globan International, where I worked, had worldwide holdings in steel, mining, energy, and large-scale construction. I'd been sent to "la ciudad de la eterna primavera," City of Eternal Spring, after the Globan corporate security office received fifteen anonymous phone calls on the Sarbanes-Oxley hotline claiming the president was defrauding the company.

Sarbanes-Oxley was the law that resulted from several large accounting and fraud scandals in corporate America, including giants like Enron, Tyco, and WorldCom. Though the law is complex, multinational companies instituted telephone hotlines as part of their internal policing function to comply with a small part of the legislation. Employees could report malfeasance anonymously on these hotlines.

Calls to Globan's corporate security office hotline gave few details on the accusations against Del Campo. *I could be chasing a hoax.* Yet that thought quickly evaporated as I focused on the man's behavior at our meeting. Still gazing out the large window in Theya's office, I glanced at my watch. It was time to call it a day.

My driver maneuvered slowly through the evening rush-hour traffic. I appreciated having a chauffeur, leaving the driving to him while I organized my thoughts. I pondered Del Campo's responses to my questions, the same routine I go through with employees suspected of deceitful practices for personal gain. The most prevalent frauds involve accounts payable or accounts receivable supervisors who add themselves, under fictitious names, as vendors or suppliers and send fraudulent invoices to the company. Or shipping and receiving clerks, where internal controls aren't enforced, caught stealing merchandise or supplies. The most classic fraud of all is perpetrated by payroll managers who pad the number of employees while collecting the salaries of nonexistent personnel.

This particular assignment was in another league. The president was being investigated. The benefits of being president—the seven-figure salary, cash bonuses, stock options, and perks—are not usually risked by getting involved in scams or swindles. At least, reasonable people wouldn't risk it. But I had seen corruption many times, including at high executive levels.

We arrived at the Intercontinental Hotel, an old property in the prestigious El Poblado area in southeast Medellín, which had been recently renovated. A garden with flowering shrubs and trees graced the driveway leading to the spacious portico, like an old Southern mansion. The lobby was open and airy, typical of hotels in temperate climates, with flowers everywhere in colorful ceramic pots. I could even imagine Rhett Butler lounging by the bar, sipping a mint julep. But glancing over at the lobby bar, I didn't see any interesting men. I wondered where Colombian men hung out. Before that thought evaporated, a tall man in uniform, his thick biceps bulging through crisply ironed shirt sleeves, handed me a long-stemmed red rose.

"I'm Juan, the concierge," he said. Surprised, I stared into his dark-brown eyes. "This is my card. Call me if you need anything during your stay."

I thanked him and continued on my way. The fragrant aroma of cut flowers arranged in elaborate vases followed me across the lobby to the elevators. My suite was compact yet cozy. I kicked off my high heels even before I locked the door behind me. Taking the computer out of its case, I locked it in the safe inside the closet, a practice I'd followed for several years now. An extra stash of three disposable mobile phones was also stored in the safe. And the one I always carried, my secure phone—a petite model with a high-powered battery, good German encryption software, and a GPS system. But I always used a throwaway for local calls.

I could reach Ian McVey, head of corporate security, with the touch of a button any time, day or night. Even Sarah, my assistant at headquarters, was accessible to me twenty-four seven. Paul Harris, my boss, was vice president of the audit department, but I worked much more closely with McVey from security, a man who styled himself my unofficial mentor.

I dialed Sarah from my secure phone and left a voicemail telling her all was quiet in Medellín. In the middle of the room, I stretched up on my toes and back down several times to relieve the pressure from the spiked heels, all the while craving a good cigar. Healthier thoughts soon took over, and I slipped into my swimsuit.

Small waves, created by three children playing in the water, rippled along the width of the pool, breaking gently onto the mosaic tiles of the pool's rim. The scene brought to mind images of Robbie, my son. He had loved to swim. By the time he was twelve, his coach told me Robbie was Olympic material. And then his death. It was over six years ago now, but the pain was as sharp as if it had happened yesterday. My nightmares persisted, interrupting my sleep with horrifying images. Malevolent figures snatched Robbie out of my arms. I could hear his screams, and they would wake me. Then I'd realize they were my own screams, which left me sweating, shaking, and sleepless.

After Robbie's death, I'd found solace in the swimming pool. We'd talked a lot as I drove him back and forth to swim meets. People told me time heals everything, but I was still mourning. I'd buried my head in work, becoming a workaholic. To counter the long hours, I took up exercise, training at times as if I were preparing for a triathlon.

Diving into the pool, I took up a butterfly stroke. The sweeping movement of both arms coming out of the water and moving toward both thighs with my legs close together as I kicked created a soothing wave effect throughout my body. I focused my mind on swimming and forgot the rest of the world.

After showering, I ordered dinner at the open-air café and savored a margarita while focusing my thoughts on the job at hand. McVey had asked me, on short notice, to perform the review in Colombia. It meant I'd not had adequate time to prepare, so I would have to intuit my way, especially at first. McVey thought this job would be easy, and I'd be home in a week. McVey also knew I enjoyed working in exotic locations. But I'd had second thoughts about this job. I hated being in a country that still produced and exported cocaine and other illicit drugs. My feelings against them were so strong, it was almost a phobia.

While I mentally worked on a strategy for this assignment, my waiter offered me limoncello instead of coffee after dinner.

"Señora, it's the perfect digestivo to follow the osso buco and risotto you enjoyed. An Italian meal must be finished off with an Italian liqueur. That way, everything is complete, a la Italiana."

I agreed to the drink with a nod, but his suggestion sparked an idea. I couldn't rely on my sixth sense alone for finding fraud. I needed reason, too. My waiter had given me the answer when he paired an Italian liqueur with Italian food. I was investigating a steel operation, so I should review the steel manufacturing process instead of focusing exclusively on financial data.

At Amazonia, there were two mills, side by side. One produced steel, and the mini-mill rolled steel and made specialty products. From the little bit of research I'd had time to do before leaving Minneapolis, I knew Del Campo was tripling the size of the plant. Construction projects often provided opportunities for fraud to occur, but the steel mill's processes would be my primary focus.

Now I had a plan. I leaned back into my chair and enjoyed the rest of the limoncello.

"Buenos días, señora." My chauffeur greeted me with a warm smile.

"Good morning," I said.

We drove several miles without conversation. I gazed out the window, noticing how densely populated and disorganized the city was compared to Minneapolis. We drove through busy city streets, then on highways leading to industrial parks beyond the suburbs. People teemed everywhere—walking, waiting for buses. Desperate folks competing for rush-hour taxis, others riding bicycles or motorbikes, and the lucky ones in cars, honking at every obstacle that threatened their foot on the gas pedal.

By contrast, the company's administrative office building, where Del Campo's office was located, sat opulently in the middle of the meticulously landscaped campus, with the artificial lake and bridge that I'd viewed yesterday from Theya's window. This sumptuousness was precisely the show of wealth that headquarters did not approve of. A line of trees, set back at least a quarter of a mile on the left side of the property, partially obscured the large steel mill from view. The additional steel processing plant was needed to meet the demand for the Asian export market, Del Campo had told me yesterday. I could see construction cranes towering over the site.

After passing the guard station, my driver stopped the Mercedes sedan at the main entrance. He jumped out and briskly walked around to open my door. At the reception desk, I presented my temporary pass to the security detail. She phoned Theya to inform her I was on my way up. Instead of taking the elevator, I made my way through the five-story atrium to the spiral staircase, a graceful curved sculpture that echoed the opulence leading to the main entrance. The staircase connected the ground floor with the wide mezzanines of each of the four floors above, all open to the lofty atrium. Some employees stood around, while others, engaged in animated conversation with their coworkers, sat in the open café on the ground floor, sipping coffee before taking the elevator to their offices to begin their work for the day. Everything was serene and beautiful. It was difficult to believe I was here on a high-level investigation. As I entered my temporary office to set up my computer, Theya walked in with coffee and biscotti.

"The biscotti are baked on the premises, different flavors every day. They're delicious," she said.

Theya—a tall, attractive woman in her mid-thirties—dressed, looked, and spoke like an executive. She had been hired by Del

Campo when he came on board. She spoke several languages and had moved to Colombia when she married. Her Spanish was flawless, and her English was spoken with an elegant British accent, a status symbol for Del Campo. What did not make sense to me was why a woman of her education and polish was an administrative assistant when she could have been an executive herself.

"Thanks, Theya. Do you have a minute?" Without waiting for an answer, I added, "I interviewed Señor Del Campo yesterday afternoon. When I finished, I lingered in your office to enjoy the view. It's magnificent. Especially the rolling hills across the highway. Is there any plan to use that land in the future?"

"Señor Del Campo likes to look at those wooded hills from his desk, so I doubt it, but you should ask him. He's the one who makes those decisions."

"You know, Theya, I was wondering why you're working as his administrative assistant. Your boss should recognize your abilities and place you in marketing or public relations."

"Funny you should say that. He's tried to promote me, but it's my choice to stay where I am. You see, I have a son who was born with CP."

"CP?"

"Cerebral palsy. It's difficult with all the medical attention and therapy he requires. Señor Del Campo gives me the time off I need to take care of him. In fact, that's where I was yesterday, taking him to the neurologist. We have a full-time nanny, but I'm the one who takes him to doctor appointments. My husband travels with his job, and I want to be home every evening with my son. This job doesn't require travel, but as soon as I move to an executive position, travel becomes a must. I can't say I'm not tempted to have a more exciting career, but I'm a mother before anything else."

"How old is he?"

"Twelve. We celebrated his birthday a couple of months ago. He was so beautiful and so perfect when he was born. We didn't notice anything wrong until five months later. That's when he showed signs of something wrong. It was devastating."

"I can imagine your pain," I said, thinking of Robbie.

"We've adjusted. Now I wouldn't know what to do with my life if it were not for him," Theya said. "Thanks for your concern. Regarding work, is there anything I can do for you today?"

"Yes, I'd like to see the mill director, if you could arrange a meeting for me."

I dunked the biscotti in the coffee. It was delicious, as promised.

She returned almost immediately with a young man, maybe late twenties, with jet-black hair, brown eyes, and a winning smile. His smile reminded me of the way Robbie beamed at swimming meets he'd just won.

"This is Luis Ceballos. He'll escort you to the mill and introduce you to our plant director, Ramón García. Also, here's Señor Del Campo's mobile phone as well as my own number, in case you need us," she said.

Theya walked us to the president's private elevator. Luis and I took it down to the ground level, walked outside, climbed into a golf cart, and headed toward the mill.

"Is this your first visit to Amazonia Steel?" Luis asked as he drove the cart across the manicured lawns toward the mill.

"Yes. I'm looking forward to working here for a few weeks. I'm certainly enjoying the warm weather. Minneapolis is such a cold place. Even our summers are too short," I said. Changing the subject, I added, "How long have you worked here?"

"Eight years," Luis said. "I started straight out of college, although I'd done a summer internship before I graduated, so I knew that it was a great place to work."

I took advantage of the ride to input Del Campo's and Theya's phone numbers in my throwaway mobile.

The mill director, Ramón García, was a short, stout man with glasses that slipped down his bulbous nose. He had assembled, on short notice, a small army of people for me to meet. They were amazed I was fluent in Spanish. I explained that, growing up in Minneapolis, I'd spent the summers with my grandparents at their small ranch a couple of hundred miles south of Mexico City in the state of Oaxaca. My abuelita tutored me in Spanish, and my abuelo taught me to ride horses. What I did not mention was that at age sixteen I'd lost my parents in an auto accident. I lived with my grandparents in Oaxaca for two years before they sent me back to Minnesota to study at the University of St. Thomas.

With the exception of Ramón, none of the assembled personnel were fluent in English. Ramón had pulled together a formal slide presentation, complete with video clips, probably from one he'd given recently. He was going all-out for the meeting. I would have preferred a less formal approach, without the dog-and-pony show, but it was part of the game. It was the price of their cooperation with my audit. And it gave me a chance to see the group interacting.

"When was the decision made to add the mini-mill?" I asked. Someone had enough strategic vision to have complementary mills operate side by side.

The manager for the specialty products started to answer, but Ramón, adjusting his glasses with the middle finger of his left hand, cut him off in mid-sentence.

"When Señor Del Campo was hired as presidente, he brought in the concept of the mini-mill. The specialty products are very lucrative, so it's been a very wise decision."

"Tell me what you make there?"

"There's normal rolling of plate, but custom engineered products, proprietary tank or vessel requirements, bring in the money. We work with orders from water treatment facilities that are upgrading or repairing their equipment," he said.

Again, his middle finger propped up his glasses into their proper position. He did this several times while he talked.

"The tank and vessel products are also used in the petrochemical industry. Worldwide, these markets are worth billions of dollars. We're already an important player in the Americas. We are positioning Amazonia to become the leader in servicing these worldwide markets ten years out. That's the reason for the expansion project."

"Tell me about the expansion," I said.

"It will triple the size of the mill. We will have the construction complete by the end of this year."

"Who is the contractor? I asked.

"Zambrano Construction Company," Ramón responded.

"Why aren't you using an affiliate of Globan for construction?" I asked.

"We received a better bid from Zambrano. It's the biggest construction company working in Colombia. They are also the most reputable. Your corporate offices vetted them and approved them before we signed the contract." He sounded defensive.

After an hour of more questions, Ramón conducted a tour of the mill. It was an impressive operation. Robotics and automation were so prevalent that only twenty or so employees worked in each of the production areas. Mills are mills. They aren't the cleanest operations around, but this mill was spotless.

"The engineering offices are equipped with the latest technology," Ramón said. He adjusted his glasses again.

We walked through a wing of product design and planning offices. Then Ramón instructed Luis to conduct the rest of the tour and bring me to his office when we were finished.

The mill was enormous. It took over an hour for Luis to show me the remaining sections, including the manufacturing floors, where I wanted to see a few details the director had not shown me. Nothing of what I'd seen so far seemed out of the ordinary, but I had a gut feeling that, contrary to what McVey thought, this job was not going to be easy.

Back in Ramón's office, I told him I'd start running computerized audit programs the next morning.

"I'll need a technical person to work with me to pull reports off the computer system. I'll also need temporary office space."

"Luis can help you," Ramón said. "He's very knowledgeable on the accounting and procedures of operations. He knows the flow of production, and he's practically an expert on our computer system. I'll make sure he's assigned to assist you."

I noticed a hint in Ramón's attitude, courteous as he was, that he felt this female auditor in her mid-thirties posed no threat at all. If I had assessed his attitude correctly, I would use it to my advantage. I knew every step I made, every action I took, and every word I said would be reported to Manuel Del Campo.

The next two days slipped like sand through my fingers. I became familiar with the company's processes and procedures. I relaxed into a routine. Luis was an excellent assistant, and we worked effectively together. For production reports on raw material used in the manufacturing process or documentation for a quality assurance inspection, he showed me how to pull the information from the computer system. When I requested an overly long report to be printed, he suggested doing it overnight. He volunteered to come in early and pull the supporting documentation.

"Let me look at the report first thing after I arrive tomorrow, and I'll select a sampling of items," I said.

I wanted Luis to assist, but I did not want to provide opportunity for documents to be destroyed, altered, or instantly produced. Also, I intended to check the items I selected all the way through the production batches into inventory and through the shipment process to customers. I also wanted to trace the raw materials back to receiving reports confirming the arrival of the raw material lots at the factory.

On the job the next day, every single item I selected from the computer reports checked out to original documents or procedures. I was beginning to feel I had fallen into a perfect make-believe world, where errors never occurred.

Finally, it was Friday—the conclusion of the first week on my assignment. No discoveries of wrongdoing, no suspicious transactions, nada. Nothing except for Del Campo's aggression toward me in his office earlier in the week. I thanked Luis for his help.

"It's been a pleasure to help you, Ms. Nikki. Feel free to call if you want a tourist guide to show you the city." He handed me a business card with his personal phone number handwritten in.

I packed my computer and dialed Theya.

"I just want to let you know, my driver is already at the mill to take me to the hotel. I'll coordinate my pickup on Monday with him if I'm going to have the same driver next week."

"I'm so glad you called," Theya said. "I was just going to call you. Señor Del Campo is having a dinner party at his home tomorrow night, and he would like for you to join them. He has a friend who's a sculptor, and it might be nice for you to meet him. We'll send the driver for you at seven p.m. And yes, Tomás will be your driver the entire time you're in Colombia. He will even be available on the weekends, if you need him."

Del Campo, inviting me to a dinner party at his home? I was flabbergasted. My first thought was to decline the invitation, even though it sounded like a command performance. I could turn it down, being an invitation to the home of the person I was investigating. On second thought, he probably calculated it as part of his psychological fencing strategy. I'd be able to see where he was headed with the frames. From a work perspective, I'd have a firsthand look at the lifestyle of this individual—an opportunity not to be refused. Lifestyle analyses cost tens of thousands of dollars, and I was being offered the chance to obtain one totally free.

"Theya, thanks, I'd love to meet a Colombian artist," I replied. I thought Del Campo was probably attempting to help a starving artist by introducing him to people in the community who might purchase his work. I just hoped I was not expected to buy a piece of art. "What is proper attire?"

"A cocktail dress."

"Cocktail dress?" I asked. I was unable to hide my surprise at the apparent formality of the event. "I don't bring cocktail dresses on assignment. I'll need a boutique where I can buy one."

"I will have Tomás pick you up tomorrow morning, say ten-thirty, and take you to a couple of nice places. I'll call tomorrow afternoon to make certain you found a dress you like. If not, I'll take over two or three of my own. We are about the same size," Theya stated in a polished, professional voice, as if she were dealing with a head of state.

The lush gardens behind the hotel, beyond the pool, tennis courts, and open-air café, were as beautiful as any I'd seen. I needed to check in with McVey. What better place to do it than among the colorful flowering shrubs and aromatic orange and lime trees. Besides, it seemed like a very safe place to call from. No bugging devices dangling from rosebushes. McVey answered on the second ring.

"How's it going?"

"Not much to report. Del Campo got angry when I questioned him, but as far as the records are concerned, everything I check is absolutely perfect," I said.

"Angry? About what?"

"Well, he said corporate should review his record and decide if they want to keep him or fire him."

"And you haven't found anything wrong?" McVey asked.

"No, but that makes me feel uncomfortable. For a fraud auditor, it's a dead end. I need errors, exceptions, problems, or strange items requiring further investigation."

As I spoke, I plucked a little blossom from the orange tree where I stood and almost dropped my secure mobile phone.

"Are you ready to come home, or do you want to spend another week there?" McVey asked.

"I think I should check a few more things out."

"Yeah, good idea," McVey said. "It's probably nothing more than a jealous competitor or disgruntled employee falsely accusing Del Campo. You can wrap the job and fly home early."

Did McVey say disgruntled employee or jealous competitor? Funny, Del Campo had used those exact words.

Tomás was waiting for me outside the hotel when I came out after a leisurely breakfast at the poolside café. He opened the door for me. He was an efficient driver, well-mannered and well-dressed. He had a distinguished look about him. In fact, he was much more distinguished looking than the mill director. Probably in his late thirties, he was in excellent shape. He looked as if he worked out regularly. We had exchanged a few pleasantries during the week as he drove me to the company and back to the hotel. Now it was time to find out more about my chauffeur.

"How many years have you worked for the company?" I inquired.

Tomás expertly maneuvered the car from the quiet hotel grounds into the heavy street traffic.

"I've been at Amazonia longer than Señor Del Campo himself. I've worked here for sixteen years. It's my second home."

"Who hired you?"

"Mr. Sweeney, an American who was president before Señor Del Campo. Mr. Sweeney set up the original plant. Mr. Sweeney was a great manager."

"Do you know anything about the party at Señor Del Campo's home tonight?" I asked.

"It's a reception for Señor Pacheco, one of our famous sculptors," he said. "You see, Señor Pacheco lives in Spain and only spends three months a year in our country. Señor Del Campo has a party for him every year. Pacheco is not quite as well-known as our other famous sculptor, Botero, the one who does the fat people."

This conversation was already proving to be useful. The guest of honor was no starving artist. To host a world-famous sculptor was quite a feat for the president of any company. I was relieved not to be obligated to buy something.

Back at the hotel after a marathon of trying on dresses and shoes, I looked at the charges on my credit card slips and was amazed my full attire had cost over six hundred dollars. More money than I would have liked to spend, but I needed to dress the part. I also knew that my attendance would cause rumors to fly around the company on Monday morning that the auditor was being bought out by Del Campo. Not a bad thing, as long as someone at the company approached me on the strength of those rumors. I had no leads yet, no evidence at all of any wrongdoing, so I had to take a bold step—in a six-hundred-dollar dress.

The phone rang.

"Did you find a cocktail dress?" Theya asked.

"I did. Royal blue georgette with an accent of sequins and little cut crystals along a V neck."

"I just wanted to check that you felt comfortable with your attire," she said.

"Comfortable? The dress is a bit sexier than I'm accustomed to wearing."

"You'll look beautiful. Besides, you're in Colombia. Women dress much sexier here than in the States."

CHAPTER TWO

The lights of Medellín glittered as if decorated for one of the many festivals that had made it a favorite tourist destination in recent years. Though still overcoming a bad reputation from the days of Pablo Escobar—the drug lord who became one of the world's richest men—Medellín was a modern city with universities and a lively cultural scene. It was also a top producer of steel and exporter of flowers, products so different from the coffee and gold that made it prosper before the Medellín drug cartel threw the city into chaos decades ago. I asked Tomás about the industries in his city.

"In my youth, I never guessed Medellín would become a leader in pharmaceuticals and health care. I should have studied chemistry or become a lab technician," Tomás said. "That's where the jobs are."

"So what did you study?"

"History. I have a master's degree, but I earn more money as a driver for Amazonia than I would as a high school teacher, so I continue as a chauffeur, the job that paid for college."

The night air was cool. Medellín's subtropical, humid climate, high elevation, and surrounding wall of blue-green mountains made the weather more temperate than other cities at the same latitude. Tomás drove past Botero Square, a large downtown park permanently displaying twenty or so large sculptures donated by its namesake. He was the most prestigious of Latin American sculptors, far better known than the one I was meeting tonight. I had once seen about fifteen Botero sculptures in a temporary exhibit running the length of the Magnificent Mile in Chicago, where the sculptures had appeared out of place and the massive proportions of the bodies rather grotesque.

I had googled Pacheco and his work so I could converse intelligently with the famous painter-turned-sculptor. In New York, I realized I had seen Pacheco's monolithic steel sculptures—a few with straight beams rising out of the ground with angular crossbeams, others with polished curved surfaces like giant wombs. My own taste ran more toward Pacheco's modern pieces than those obese people molded in bronze by Botero.

"We have arrived, señora," Tomás announced.

I was unprepared for what I saw. If the company was in an opulent setting, this was an even more impressive site. On a smaller scale, of course, but that human scale was precisely what made it more attractive.

At the entrance, four guards stood by a two-story house that looked more like a wooden Swiss chalet than a guard shack. Inside the grounds, the driveway curved and wound around the property like a maze. Tomás drove me slowly through the gardens, where purple, orange, and red flowers planted next to dark-green shrubs grew in carefully planned landscaping, like a scene from an English countryside. He continued past an artificial lake, encircled by graceful vera-wood trees covered in orange-yellow flowers. A dramatic, cascading waterfall reflected the last rays of sunlight at the farthest end of the lake, where the terrain rose into a gentle hill. In the middle of the lake, a Pacheco sculpture sat imposingly on a tiny island. The steel structure was wrapped in the golden light of a fading sun, making it appear in harmony with the surrounding nature. We drove past three splendid homes as we made our way to the mansion.

"What are these other houses on the grounds?" I asked.

"That first house is for Señor Del Campo's parents, and the second one for his in-laws," Tomás explained. He pointed at two brick homes. "The third one in the back is a guest house. The stables and an equestrian field, where la señora practices dressage, are beyond the guest house, at the back of the property. Señor Del Campo's stables are considered the finest in the country."

"What types of horses does he own?"

"Thoroughbreds, señora. That's what makes his stables famous. Señor Del Campo has told me his horses have pedigrees traceable to three stallions imported into England in the 1600s and 1700s. That bloodline was introduced into Colombia in the late 1800s. He races them. And he breeds for other disciplines—show jumping, dressage, and polo. He exports polo ponies to Argentina, England, and Dubai. He's crossbred his Thoroughbreds to have a line of quarter horses that he also exports."

"How does he have time to devote to such a complex activity?" I asked.

"Señor Del Campo has ten or twelve employees who care for the horses, including a full-time veterinarian."

"Is it a profitable enterprise for him?"

"That I cannot say, señora, but Señor Del Campo tells people that horses are his passion."

"Quite a hobby," I said. I was looking for the stables, but instead I saw a helicopter.

"Does the señor own a helicopter?" I asked, pointing toward it.

"Oh, sí, señora. It is a Sikorsky S-76C, a beautiful machine."

I didn't know much about helicopters, but I did recognize Sikorsky as a major manufacturer, the one that builds the Black Hawks used by the military.

"Does Señor Del Campo deliver fillies in the chopper?" I asked.

"Fillies?"

"Sorry, Tomás, bad joke. Where does he fly it?"

"He doesn't fly it himself. He has a pilot," Tomás said.

"And where do they fly?" I asked again, trying to sound indifferent.

"I don't know. To call on customers, he says."

This evening, thanks to my driver, had turned into an informative one, and it was just beginning.

We arrived at the front entrance, and Tomás opened the door of the Mercedes so I could step out. He took my arm, and we climbed the steps to the extra-wide double doors. He continued to politely hold my arm until we stepped inside a grand vestibule with marble floors. A bronze Botero sculpture, dwarfed only by the size of the foyer itself, was placed in the center of this show hall, and a grand piano was offset against the farthest wall of the two-story atrium. Twenty or so guests were standing around, engaged in conversation in groups of two or three. Manuel Del Campo himself stepped forward to greet me as my chauffeur doubled back to the car.

"Welcome, welcome to my home," he said with a smile.

Del Campo, reframing himself as the charming host, placed his arm around my shoulder, as if I were an old friend. His wife approached, and he introduced us. I had seen photos of her in my brief research into the man and knew her name was Clara Iglesias.

"Manuel told me you grew up around horses," Clara said.

"Only in the summers, when I visited my grandparents. My grandfather was an avid horseman, so yes, I grew up loving horses."

I had not mentioned a word to Del Campo about horses. That rumor had filtered up from my meeting at the mill with Ramón and his management group.

"We have stables, and if you'd like to ride, you're more than welcome to come out while you are in Medellín," she said.

"Thank you, Clara. I haven't been on a horse for almost seven years," I said.

I thought back on the last time I rode a horse. We were on vacation in Colorado, a few months before Robbie died. Robbie had loved horses, too.

"There's always time to start again," she said.

"And I'm looking for a person to manage my stables," Del Campo said. "I need someone with an international business background and language skills." A small grin emerged on his face, as if what he said was humorous.

Looking away and pretending to ignore the suggestion, I made small talk with his wife, but Del Campo put his hand on my arm. He maneuvered me around the vestibule, as if I were a filly on a short rein, introducing me to a businessman and his daughter, a neurosurgeon with a wife young enough to be his daughter, and several other couples. We moved through another set of oversized double doors into a well-appointed parlor, where five people gathered around a distinguished looking, gray-haired gentleman. I recognized him from my internet search. Del Campo guided me right up to the famous artist, ignoring the other guests.

"Francisco, this is Nikki Garcia. She's visiting us from the States. I promised her that you'd take her around the house and show her my art collection," he said, interrupting Pacheco in mid-sentence. "And don't forget to show her my collection of fencing equipment in the library."

Pacheco smiled and excused himself from his admirers.

"Será un placer. Let's start with the Renoirs in the dining room," he said.

A waiter in a tuxedo stopped us and offered me a glass of champagne, which I was glad to accept, although my head was already spinning.

"Our host appreciates Renoir's diffused palette, although I personally prefer bolder statements and definition of line, like Goya or Velázquez. Or Picasso, to name a more modern painter," Pacheco said as I followed him.

The dining room had nineteenth-century French cherry and walnut burl cabinets with ivory inlay and gilt bronze details. A grand mahogany table was formally set for dinner, surrounded by four smaller round tables, also set for tonight's dinner. The wall directly across from where we stood had four floor-to-ceiling windows overlooking the lake, which was resplendent in artificial light as the encroaching darkness surrounded it. Long brocaded curtains accented each side of the window frames. The Renoirs, four of them, brought a sense of serenity and quiet elegance to a room that could easily have been overdecorated.

I had hardly uttered a word, other than the usual pleasantries during introductions.

"Are these real?" I asked out loud.

"Most definitely."

"Where did he purchase the Renoirs?"

"From the Impressionist auctions at Christie's and Sotheby's in New York," he answered. The artist selected a chicken liver wrapped in bacon from the tray of hors d'oeuvres offered to us by another tuxedoed waiter.

Not liking chicken liver, I took a miniature cheese puff. Pacheco suggested we move to the next room to see the Monet water lilies.

"The water lilies are his favorites," he stated.

"Monet's water lilies? Really? I like those, too," I said, trying not to sound flabbergasted or stupid, the way I'd sounded over the Renoirs.

Next we visited the library. Two life-sized mannequins in full fencing regalia stood on wooden stands. Each mannequin was encased in a Plexiglas bubble, like those in museums covering antique pottery or other valuables, only these enclosures were large enough to cover the mannequins.

Pacheco pointed toward one of the fencing figures.

"Look at those hideous mannequins. How can you not see them? They dominate this room. I guess he's proud of the fact he was an Olympic fencer."

Then Pacheco steered me toward two rather large, brightly colored paintings displayed on the only wall space not covered by volumes of books, arranged on built-in bookcases.

"These are the most worthwhile assets Manuel owns—two of my original paintings. Early work. Look at the vibrancy of those colors."

Listening intently as he described his own art, I commented on how the near photorealism of his oil paintings differed from his modern abstract sculpture.

"Styles change over time," he explained. "It would be boring to work the same themes in the same style for too long. Like a man married to the same woman all his life. Can you imagine how dull that would be? It's the same in art. You have to keep reinventing yourself."

Since he appeared to be by himself at the party, this led me to believe he was between wives or women friends. Changing direction in the conversation, I asked him how long he had known Del Campo.

"Oh, for the last eight or nine years. He contacted me for advice on purchasing art. We hit it off. We work together on my favorite charity here in Medellín. As you know, he has a lot of influence in the business community of this country."

I wondered to myself if Del Campo had inherited great wealth, but it was not a question to be asked here. It would have to wait until next week, when I was back at the company.

We walked and talked our way through two more roomfuls of exquisite art, including a Degas ballerina. We returned to the foyer, where a quintet of mariachis was finishing a rousing rendition of Mexican music. The mariachis and their Mexican folk songs seemed out of context in the elegant surroundings. Pacheco must have seen my perplexed look.

"Mexican music and soap operas are very popular in Colombia. Everybody listens to mariachis, and all the women, rich and poor alike, watch the telenovelas," he said. I sensed a facetious tone in his voice.

Continuous lines of waiters in matching tuxedos still offered wine and champagne, as well as the tasty hors d'oeuvres. Over the murmur of voices engaged in small talk, I began to hear soft music, either a violin or another string instrument, streaming in from the dining room. The soft melody was far more appropriate to the ambiance than the earlier mariachis had been.

Del Campo, with Clara standing next to him, requested that his guests join them in the hotel-sized dining room. Name cards had been placed above the plates. Pacheco found my seat with his name at the next place setting.

"I know a gentleman here who is far more interesting for you to sit next to than this old man," he said, looking around.

I started to protest, but he was waving his hand at a very handsome man I hadn't seen until now. The stranger approached us.

"Eduardo, this is Nikki Garcia from the US. She's here on business, and I think she would be much more interested in hearing about your charitable foundation and your research department than listening to this viejo carry on about the inequities of the art world," Pacheco said.

I was embarrassed by the switch in companion, but I reached my hand out to the stranger. He took my hand in his and smiled.

"Eduardo Duarte." He followed up very quickly with the usual, "A tus órdenes." Repeating "At your service," he pulled the chair out for me to sit down.

The first course, seared tuna on a bed of greens, had already been served prior to the guests being seated. When everyone was settled, Del Campo and his wife picked up their forks at the main table. All guests, including me, followed suit. Such formality is inconceivable today in the United States, except for state dinners at the White House, perhaps. I suspected that, with the exception of very formal events, it is not seen often even in the finer homes in Colombia. Not many people anywhere lived the lifestyle the Del Campo family obviously enjoyed.

The same tuxedoed waiters from earlier were now serving wine, taking away dishes, bringing the main course, and offering bread rolls with the precision of the robotics I'd seen at the mill. They seemed programmed to bend in stiff formality at the same moment. It felt surreal, out of a science fiction script. Was Del Campo an obsessive-compulsive man who orchestrated the robots at the mill? Demanded the inconceivable cleanliness of the mill's floors? And still had time to command the performance of telerobotic waiters serving us, or at least controlling them through carefully devised instructions for attending to his guests? Could he really have his nose in everything?

Eduardo sat to my left. To my right was the neurosurgeon I'd met earlier, conversing with his young wife. That was fine by me. Eduardo was far more interesting. A harpist played soft music from the back of the room. Eduardo mentioned that South America produces a lot of modern music for the harp, and the piece being played was written by an Argentine composer.

The main course—filet mignon in a delicious wine sauce, mashed potatoes, and five or six giant asparagus tied, like a bundle of logs, with a strip of red pepper—was so good that I ate every morsel. I passed on dessert in a feeble attempt to save my figure after having stuffed myself with all that continental-style food. Four waiters with carts moved effortlessly around the tables, tending to each guest individually. I'd seen this in restaurants but never in a private home. The waiters offered a selection of cheese, both local and imported, and served the cheese and crackers with coffee, poured into dainty demitasse cups. I could tell I was getting tired because the waiters were beginning to resemble penguins in their tuxedos. Or perhaps I was feeling the effect of the wine and the altitude.

"May I ask what plans you have for tomorrow?" Eduardo's tone was formal.

"I'm working for a while, and then I'll swim an hour to get rid of the calories I've put on tonight."

"Work? Really? On the weekend?"

"It's typical for me to work on weekends," I said.

"Would you consider a better offer?"

I simply stared at him. My hands gripped the napkin in a nervous gesture. I hoped he hadn't noticed.

"I'd like to take you on a tour around Medellín," he said. "If you want to swim, then we'll go to my house. I can grill a steak or seafood. You can work in the morning, and I'll pick you up after lunch."

"Don't you need to check with your wife before you invite me out?"

"I don't check with her now that she's divorced me," he said. "How about you? Are you married?"

"No, I'm divorced, too."

"What time would you like for me to come by?" he asked.

I'd enjoyed talking to him over dinner. He was handsome. He was charismatic. But as a Latin man, he was probably a notorious womanizer. I didn't need trouble, but maybe he could offer insights into Del Campo's background or social standing that might prove useful.

The sunlight was bright around the outer edges of the draperies I hadn't bothered to close properly last night. I looked at the clock radio on the nightstand and was startled to see it was almost nine-thirty. I jumped out of bed, went to the bathroom, and turned on the shower. My mouth tasted awful. So tired last night I'd gone to bed without brushing my teeth, I brushed them while the shower warmed up. Comforted by the spray of warm water, I stepped out, rubbing the towel vigorously over my body. I put sweats on over my swimsuit and headed downstairs to swim those laps I'd promised myself.

Lingering over coffee at the poolside café after breakfast, I analyzed the extravagant lifestyle Del Campo and his family maintained. It's customary in Latin America for business executives to have chauffeurs, a house full of servants, and other luxuries. It's also customary for various members of a family to live in a compound with several homes, but the attention-getter was the lavish lifestyle Del Campo and his family enjoyed. The helicopter, complete with pilot, the exquisite art collection, the first-rate stables with accompanying equestrian field, the full-time veterinarian on the payroll—all these extras were definitely over the top.

But there was more. I had a gut feeling a lot more was under that luxurious veneer. *How could Del Campo run everything with such a tight rein that robots seemed to surround him during his lavish entertaining? Why did employees of the company seem to act on cue and not of their own free will? What about the way he tried to intimidate me at his office and then turn around to treat me as a longtime friend at last night's party? And his stupid offer of a job at his stables? And his comments on the art of fencing? What did all that mean?*

Tomorrow I'll phone Sarah, I thought as I waved at my waiter to bring me fresh coffee. My assistant was very efficient at running the office and attending to the requests of junior auditors when I was on assignment. She was also excellent at following up on the most unusual requests I often burdened her with while I was performing a special review, such as this one. This job was going to require delicate investigative work, and for that, I would have her contact the private detective firm we had used on several occasions. Security Source, based in Miami but with international pull, would be able to dig up whatever Del Campo was trying to bury.

Back at the desk in my suite, I opened the computer and listed the items for Security Source to work on:

1. Search for bank accounts in US, Canada, Caribbean, Panama in Del Campo's name

2. Search for bank accounts in US, Canada, Caribbean, Panama in Clara Iglesias's name
3. Investigate Zambrano Construction Company for corruption
4. Investigate possible related party links between Del Campo and Zambrano Construction Company

A second list contained items for Sarah to investigate, such as helping me put together a lifestyle analysis on Del Campo.

Inflow:

1. Compensation, cash bonuses, stock awards, stock options
2. Investigate any special benefits or deferred compensation plans where he received advances
3. Stables—income—I will follow up and submit data to you

Outflow:

1. Personal home, paid in full or mortgaged?
2. Household expenses, including full-time gardener, groundskeeper, housekeeper, and staff
3. Helicopter—Sikorsky S-76C, paid in full (how much) or mortgaged?
4. Helicopter—Sikorsky S-76C, operating expenses for a year
5. Helicopter—pilot salary and benefits for one year
6. Stables—expenses—I will follow up and submit data to you
7. Art collection—investigate sales of Impressionist art sold to Latin Americans through Christie's and Sotheby's websites and catalogues, especially the works of Monet, Renoir, and Degas—go back 10 years

I finished a memo to Sarah, instructing her to purchase the catalogues from all auctions of Impressionist paintings held in New York and London for the past ten years and overnight them to me. With physical catalogues in hand, I might identify, during moments of leisure at the hotel, specific pieces of art hanging on Del Campo's walls. If we could prove the authenticity of the works through his accounts at auction houses, we could include the millions he'd spent on art. It was obvious to me there would be a colossal gap between his known income and his expenditures. I was not a forensic accountant. I would need additional help, especially since we'd be doing it without Del Campo's knowledge or cooperation. We would have to rely on estimates in a few areas. I'd personally handle the stables through Security Source and have Sarah plug that information in later to complete the analysis.

Just a casual observation of how that man lived convinced me there was wrongdoing at the company. His abrupt change in attitude toward me also made me suspicious. Apprehension stirred in my stomach. I'd have to be cautious in everything I did, even in submitting files to Sarah. I should not send sensitive data from the company premises, and I suspected that transmitting from my hotel room was not safe, either.

The phone rang, interrupting my thoughts. I wasn't expecting a call on the room phone from anyone. I answered, thinking it might be housekeeping since I'd spent most of the day in the room and the bed remained unmade. Instead, it was Eduardo, apologizing for calling early.

"The weather is so beautiful, I thought I could pick you up an hour earlier," he said.

The scent of flowers wafted through the lobby thirty minutes later, reminding me I was in the flower capital of Latin America, and Eduardo walked toward me the minute I stepped out of the elevator. His arms open in the traditional Latin embrace he was about to give me, he blew a kiss on the side of my face. He was wearing white pants, a yellow polo shirt, and men's Prada wrap-style aviator sunglasses. Several people in the lobby turned to look at us as we walked out.

The weather was indeed gorgeous. Eduardo opened the door to his

Audi R8 for me. Driving with the top down, the warm breeze felt good through my hair.

"There was a time when we could not drive a car like this because of the drug cartels. We've made so much progress in the fight against illegal drugs that we have transformed our country," he said with obvious satisfaction.

"It seems to me that Colombia only exported its drug cartels to Mexico," I said. I hated to dismiss his gratification about his country's war against drugs, but it was the truth. "Colombia may feel it won the war, but drugs are just as plentiful now as they were in the 1980s and 1990s. The violence Colombia experienced then has gripped Mexico this past decade."

"Unfortunately, you're right. Colombia is safer, but Mexico is suffering," he said.

"And the use of illicit drugs continues unabated, causing innocent people to die, whether it's by gang warfare or overdoses."

"How much of the city have you seen? I don't want to waste time on what you have already visited," he said, tactfully changing the subject.

"My chauffeur, Tomás, gave me a tour of the business district and Botero Square."

"Then we'll head to Nutibara Hill to get the full view of the city and continue on to the top so you can see a replica of a typical Colombian village called Pueblito Paisa. We'll return to see the cathedral and the historic part of the city. Then we'll go to my condo, and I'll cook dinner for you."

"To save time, why don't we just return to my hotel and grab a salad or a sandwich? That way I can get a little more work done tonight," I said.

"If that's what you prefer. Would you allow me to change dinner to a restaurant that serves typical Colombian fare, instead of eating at the hotel? That way you can experience how the other side of Colombia lives. I'd hate for you to return to the US with the idea that all Colombians live the way Manuel does." He stopped at a traffic light, took off his Prada shades, and looked at me.

I laughed, out of nervousness. "Very few people anywhere in the world live as lavishly as he does. I know his lifestyle is not your typical Colombian household. How long have you known Del Campo?"

"About seven years, when he helped Niños del Parque, the nonprofit foundation I started. He has served on our board of directors. He's donated both time and money to bring street children into orphanages," he said.

I seized the opportunity. "Does Señor Del Campo come from a wealthy family?"

"Not real wealth, not the kind of wealth he has now. He comes from an upper-middle-class family, though. Why do you ask?"

"Just curious."

"The auditor in you is assessing his lifestyle?"

"Well, yes. You have to admit, it's a bit extravagant," I said, trying not to show my surprise at his question.

"To my knowledge, he made money in a joint venture before he joined your company. He sold his interest to the other party, and rumor has it that it was for a very tidy sum of money. At least that's what he tells people."

I was about to ask that, if Del Campo had made so much money, why was he working as president/general manager for a multinational conglomerate when he could have a company of his own, or merely live the life of a philanthropist? But the curvy, windy road to the top of Nutibara Hill gave way to a lovely, typical little Spanish town, with whitewashed walls and red tile roofs. I was too distracted to pose the question.

Eduardo parked and rolled up the top of the Audi. We strolled down the main street in Pueblito Paisa, open only to pedestrian traffic. I felt as if I were floating on air, like a cotton candy princess, light and fragile, unable to feel my legs as I walked the cobblestoned street with this handsome man.

In the city for dinner, Eduardo ordered arepas, unleavened cornmeal patties, as an appetizer and the most typical Colombian food, bandeja paisa, as the main dish. It turned out to be a stew with meat, beans, rice, egg, sausage, and plantain.

"The word paisa is slang for peasant or folksy," he explained. "But the people from this region are also called paisas. A lot of the local culture incorporates the word paisa, like the village we visited and the stew we just ate."

I was anxious to inquire more about Del Campo but decided not to raise suspicions. Eduardo must have read my mind.

"I guess you're here investigating Manuel. And I know he probably looks guilty by the way he lives, but keep in mind that anyone who is as successful as he is abounds in enemies as well as friends, even enemies that pose as friends."

I smiled. "So you invited me out this lovely afternoon to pick my brain about the assignment that's brought me to Colombia. All this time I thought it was because you wanted to show a foreigner your beautiful city."

Eduardo leaned toward me. "Well, first of all, I don't know if he is guilty or not, though I would prefer to think he's innocent. I'd hate to lose my biggest contributor to the foundation."

"He's your biggest contributor?"

"As we say in Spanish, 'no voy a meter las manos al fuego por él,'" he whispered. "I'm not going to put my hands into the fire and defend him. You want to know the real reason I invited you out? Well, I'm trying to find out why an attractive woman like you does this type of work."

"You don't approve of my work?" I asked, nibbling on another spoonful of the Colombian stew.

"That's not it. It's all about your personal life. What kind of life, what kind of personal relationships can you build if you're always traveling from one country to another, working your life away?"

"I love to travel, see new places, experience new cultures, and meet new people."

"Meet new people? Really? You don't have time to meet people when you work weekends."

I smiled at him. No man was going to pry into my life. In defense, I flipped it over.

"Why don't you tell me about yourself," I said.

"What do you want to know?"

"Why did you start a foundation for street children? How do you spend your leisure time? Do you have time to do your own research when you're also running a research department?"

"Wait a minute," he said. He laughed, but his eyes were smiling more than his lips. "I'll have to invite you to dinner during the week to answer all those questions. Is Tuesday good?"

"Actually, Wednesday is better. I have plans on Tuesday."

"Dinner on Tuesday?" he asked. The grin faded from his lips. "Who's the lucky guy?"

"Two guys. The local CPAs in charge of the Amazonia account. The external auditors," I said.

"Then I'll settle for Wednesday night. I'll come by your hotel at six o'clock. There's more of the city I'd like to show you."

We both ordered fresh fruit for dessert and lingered over coffee, talking much more than I'd planned. Eduardo spoke of his childhood, of losing his father when he was young. He also talked about his scholarship to Harvard Medical School. He promised to tell me, at our next outing, how he got the idea for the foundation for street children.

I brushed my teeth and got ready for bed, reflecting on my afternoon with the Colombian philanthropist. Medical doctor from Harvard, masculine and handsome, founder of a charitable organization to save street children in Medellín, Eduardo was quite a guy. He could stand to lose about twelve pounds, but it was evident he exercised.

Why did he invite me out? Not that I had low self-esteem, but really, why had he taken the trouble to take me out? Was his humanitarian side feeling sorry for a woman, all alone in a foreign country, carrying out an investigation? Or was it the worst-case scenario, that Del Campo had asked him to distract me from the job? In time, perhaps I would know the answer.

CHAPTER THREE

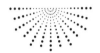

That blasted wake-up call. It always came too early, especially after a night when I'd slept so badly. I'd struggled to fall asleep after a nightmare. Monsters stole Robbie away again. Between the lack of sleep and the hangover of regret and fear caused by the nightmare, I didn't feel well. I'd set the call half an hour earlier today because I needed the extra time to phone Sarah and submit my files to her.

I wanted to avoid using my own suite, in case the place was bugged, and instead use a separate room in the hotel. As I engaged in debate about this with the front desk clerk, Juan, the concierge, walked over.

"Can I help you?" he asked.

"The phone in my room is not operating properly, and I'd like to borrow an empty room so I can make a rather urgent phone call," I said.

I looked at his muscular physique, wondering how Juan could keep himself in such great shape when he worked all the time.

"Our business center is available, or my office is at your disposal," Juan informed me.

"But I need privacy, and I only need a room for a few minutes," I pleaded, biting my lower lip, a nervous habit I'd tried many times to break.

Even though the files were encrypted, if my phone line was tapped, they could hear my conversation with Sarah. Also, I feared they could retrieve the transmitted files and, to my mind, the encryption we used was not foolproof. Too many technical articles indicated that a lot of off-the-shelf encryption really wasn't.

Juan told the clerk to give me a key to a vacant room. He also told her to have maintenance check out the phone lines in my suite. I ran upstairs, grabbed my computer, and went to the loaner room. Working as fast as possible, I connected to the net and accessed email to submit the files I'd prepared yesterday with Sarah's to-do lists. I signed off and, using my calling card, I dialed Sarah at the office and kept my fingers crossed she would answer. Her voicemail greeted me. I left a message, informing her "the weather was chilly," code words we used so she could inform McVey I had a hunch a cover-up might be occurring, a cover-up I could not yet confirm.

McVey had developed the codes so we could talk without raising suspicions over telephone lines. With the codes, I could also call him directly, twenty-four seven, and in an ordinary and innocuous conversation, let him know the status of the job, including if I felt in any danger. It was a backup method to be used when not communicating over a secure line or if there were other people present.

I closed the door to the loaner room, took the elevator to the lobby, dropped off the key with the front desk clerk, and walked outside to my waiting car.

Theya welcomed me with a big smile. "How was the dinner party?" she asked.

"Magnificent," I said.

"I can imagine. Señor Del Campo knows how to do things right." Then Theya added, "Señor Del Campo will not be in the office today. He's calling on customers in Bogotá."

I decided to take advantage of Del Campo's absence. Lunch with administrative assistants might prove more productive than the routine work I'd planned. Meeting other staff members might be helpful, too. Luis could run reports I'd formatted, print them, and give them to me midafternoon. He had proven to be such a good worker, I thought I'd approach him, once this job was complete, for a job rotation in the States. His fluent English and attention to detail, in addition to being an accountant with expert knowledge in computers, would make it easy for me to recommend him for the rotation program. That he reminded me of my son also made it easy to think of offering him opportunities to further his professional development.

Late morning, I took a stroll down the impressive, open mezzanines that served as hallways around each of the four floors that were open to the full five-story atrium occupying the center of the building. Steel railings on the inner rim around the circumference of each mezzanine kept absent-minded employees from falling off the edge to the ground floor five levels below. Still, I kept my distance from the railings. Fear of heights made me instantly dizzy if I got too close.

Looking around as I walked down the center of the mezzanine, I noticed for the first time a large number of paintings in various sizes and themes hanging on the spacious walls. On the floor along the walls, oversized, colorful glazed urns contained white and purple orchids, streaming profusely over the sides of the urns. The open, airy spaciousness of the mezzanines, the abundance of colorful orchids, and the paintings exhibited on the walls contributed to a relaxing atmosphere, which resembled an upscale Miami art gallery rather than an office building in the middle of an industrial park in Medellín. Del Campo's office suite looked more New Yorkish, but the mezzanines looked like Miami's best design. Del Campo, without a doubt, had good taste.

My plan was to meet a variety of employees. They needed to see me and know I was accessible, if they chose to talk. This tactic had worked for me at other operating companies. An important key to unraveling fraud at a company was having an insider talk. I had not yet found any leads, so my hope was to find a whistleblower. Or could it simply be, as Eduardo stated yesterday, that Del Campo had enemies who might be trying to sabotage him? *Was I jaded by other fraud audits and looking for culpability where none existed? Was I on a witch hunt?*

As I walked down the mezzanine on the fifth floor, I headed for the office of the chief financial officer, a man I had met at worldwide meetings but who was currently out on medical leave. He had undergone major surgery for lung cancer the week before I arrived and was not expected back for at least two months. I walked to his office to speak to Elena, his administrative assistant. She was plump, mid-forties, and wore her black hair, accented by a few gray strands, in a swirl pinned at the back of her head with a decorative comb. Bright-red lipstick matched her bright-red fingernails. I asked her if she had any lunch plans.

"I brought my lunch from home and plan to eat at my desk today," she said.

"Well, I'd like you to join me for lunch in the cafeteria instead. I also want you to ask a couple of other administrative assistants."

I could tell from the perplexed look on her face that she thought my invitation was strange. She repeated my request to make certain she had not misunderstood me.

"Yes, that's correct. I want to have lunch with administrative assistants because, you see, I started out my career as a secretary," I lied. "And at every company, I like to keep in touch with that line of work, in case I get tired of working at what I'm doing." I must have sounded convincing because Elena now had a smile on her face. "What time do you normally go to lunch?"

"One o'clock."

"Is that the time most people go to the company cafeteria?" I asked.

She nodded affirmatively. Good. I wanted to be in the cafeteria during the peak hour to have as many employees as possible see me at lunch with the assistants.

"Fine. I'll return here, and we'll walk down together," I said.

Like a seasoned politician, I walked all the way around the oblong mezzanines on all four floors waving, smiling, stopping to shake hands, and speaking with as many employees as I could. I was still walking around, introducing myself and talking, when I realized it was time to return to the fifth floor to meet my group of administrative assistants for lunch.

Elena had invited only one other woman to join us. Claudia was tall and attractive, with curly brown hair that fell to her shoulders. An accounting clerk from the finance department, she was young and had worked for the company for two years.

When we approached the cafeteria, heads turned. And more so as we took our place in line and got our lunches. Then we sat down at a table in the center of the cafeteria where everyone could see us. I asked each of the women to tell me a little about themselves, but they were more interested in knowing how I'd learned to speak Spanish if I lived in the US.

"My parents left Mexico City and moved to Minneapolis when they got married. They were seeking a better life. We spent our summers in Southern Mexico with our grandparents. My dad reasoned we would have a competitive advantage as adults if we spoke both languages fluently, so we spoke Spanish at home. And he's been proven right. I wouldn't have this job if I didn't speak Spanish."

I did not mention that my brother and I lost our parents when we were teenagers.

I told them a couple of stories, to break the ice, about getting the languages confused with comic consequences when I was a kid. I wanted the two women to feel perfectly comfortable with me. Soon they were laughing at my anecdotes, and employees at surrounding tables could see we were having fun.

I asked them what they liked about their jobs, and when Elena asked me the same question, I had the opening I was hoping for.

"I'm a CPA with an auditing background. At corporate headquarters, a group of junior auditors report to me that perform work at our US companies. A predictable routine without much excitement. Two supervisors assist me because I also perform fraud investigations," I said.

"Fraud investigations?" Claudia asked. Her eyes were wide, and she moved closer to me, as if eager to hear more.

"Yes. Last year I was in South Korea, reviewing our affiliate there. Top management at the Korean mill was involved in a fraudulent scheme. I was able to crack the case because two of the local South Korean employees talked to me about what was going on."

"What happened?" Claudia asked.

"We fired them," I said.

"You fired the employees who talked to you?" Claudia asked. Her voice whispered in horror as her shoulders rounded, as if to hide within a protective shell.

"No, no, they still work at the company in Seoul," I answered. "It was the executives involved in the fraud who were fired."

"Oh, okay," Claudia said. Her shoulders straightened a bit.

"I've also done several fraud investigations of high-level executives in the US and Europe," I added. I wanted to make certain the word would be out, beyond doubt in anyone's mind, that I was here investigating top management. I also hoped it would serve to counteract the effect of rumors that were probably raging in the hallways that I had attended a party at Del Campo's palatial home.

Elena looked around the room. The cafeteria was clearing as people returned to their offices.

"I must get back to my desk," Elena said. "My boss had a radiation treatment today, and I promised his wife I'd call to get a report on how it went."

Elena lingered at the table and looked over her shoulders. She moved a few inches closer to me.

"I think my boss got cancer because of the stress Señor Del Campo puts on him. Señor Del Campo asks my boss to cover up things," she said in an almost inaudible whisper.

"What sort of cover-up?" I asked.

"Look, I really must go," Elena said. Her lips quivered ever so slightly, and she stood up abruptly and left the table.

I asked Claudia if she could stay a little longer. It seemed to me from her body language that she wanted to open up. I made small talk until employees in the cafeteria had essentially cleared out, at least all the tables around us. Then I took a direct approach.

"Claudia, do you have something you want to say?"

"No, not really. But you should know that not everything is as wonderful here as it appears to be," she said.

"Can you explain?" I asked.

"What I mean is that the company may not be such a wonderful place to work as some people try to make it out to be."

"Are you unhappy here?" I asked.

"It's hard to get good jobs in Colombia, even when you are very qualified, so I want to keep my job." She fidgeted with a bracelet on her left arm.

"If I could assure you that you will keep your job, even if you tell me what's on your mind, would you trust me?" I asked.

Claudia was now looking at the top of the table and running her right index finger in little circles or figure eights over the ceramic top.

"It's just that I'm afraid walls listen," she said.

"That's not going to happen. I always keep confidential the names of people who supply information to me. I have corporate behind me. I will make certain you don't lose your position."

"I don't know that there was anything wrong, but I think it was strange, the way things happened."

"About what?" I asked.

Claudia looked around the room. Then she looked straight at me. "All I can say is that a friend of mine, a coworker, Oscar Fuentes, died here."

"Died?"

"Yes. It was an accident. That's what the company said. They had an investigation, and that's what the investigators said, too."

"But you don't think it was an accident?" I asked.

"It's hard to tell. I don't know, but I have always been suspicious that it wasn't." Claudia looked around again, her nervousness apparent.

"Can you tell me more?" I asked.

"It's all I can say. Maybe you can investigate it, but promise me you won't do it today or tomorrow because everyone saw me having lunch with you today. I need my job." She looked very tense.

"Can you at least tell me how he died?"

"He fell at the mill."

"Fell?" I asked.

"Yes, from the catwalk."

I kicked off my high heels as soon as I opened my hotel room door. Then I put the computer bag on a chair, took the Mac out, and locked it in the safe where my extra throwaway mobile phones were stashed. I was trying to sort out my thoughts on the information Claudia had given me.

A death at the company? He fell to his death from the catwalk? What was he doing that caused him to fall? Could foul play be involved? Claudia's nervousness certainly pointed to it. Elena had insinuated a cover-up in the financial data, but that was a small deal compared to the bombshell Claudia had laid out that a death had occurred. One that might not have been accidental.

After twenty minutes on the treadmill and a few laps in the pool, I returned to the suite for dinner. The phone rang as I picked up a dessert spoon to scoop up my first bite of ripe, red raspberries. Hesitating slightly, I popped the raspberries in my mouth before picking up the receiver.

Sarah's voice greeted me with a cheerful, "Your number one, handy-dandy assistant is calling."

In reality, this was the code to let me know she had received my first email message, the one I'd sent that morning from the borrowed hotel room.

"The Miami Dolphins had an excellent practice this week," she said in code, confirming the private detectives from Security Source in Miami had been instructed to search for bank accounts and investigate Zambrano Construction. "They will practice for two full weeks before the playoffs."

I interpreted her words to mean it would be two weeks before we might have any news from the detectives on the success or failure of their search for overseas bank accounts Del Campo might have. Obviously, their investigation would track large or unusual flows of cash.

"Is the weather still chilly?" Sarah asked.

"Enough to need a light wrap when I go out at night." Words to let her know the status of the job—suspicions and minor leads, but nothing concrete. I purposely did not mention anything about a death at the mill, not on the hotel telephone she had called me on. We chatted about a couple of routine office issues before we said goodbye.

Sarah's call was the only one I received. I'd hoped to hear from Eduardo, but that was wishful thinking. I was kidding myself if I thought he was unattached. I was kidding myself even more if I thought he was interested in me in a romantic sense. But it was fun to dream.

CHAPTER FOUR

Most of Tuesday morning I spent at a computer terminal at the mill, checking various items I'd marked for review from yesterday's online reports. I decided to pay a visit to Isabel, the filing clerk, and request several files—just to appear busy until I was able to investigate Claudia's lead on the accidental death at the mill.

"Come in, señora," Isabel said. She spoke Spanish with the soft accent of the northern coastal area of Colombia. She looked to be in her late thirties with a beautiful olive complexion, green eyes, and thick, wavy, brown hair that swept across her forehead in a stylish cut. She wore a gold chain with two dangling fourteen-karat-gold profiles of children. Traditional among many Latin mothers, these silhouettes announced how many children they had. She was responsible for paper files, which still constituted a warehouse of paperwork, despite the ability to go green. Many government export documents were still handled in hard copy, and companies stored them for legal and tax purposes.

After we exchanged a few pleasantries, I provided her with a list of original documents I wanted to inspect—customs forms, export paperwork, and receipts from the trucking companies used to transport the finished product. To be thorough, I would check for domestic deliveries as well as international ones. I was hoping to stumble across suspicious items, though I was also creating busywork to avoid anyone thinking I was here spending corporate money to take a break from the cold climate in Minneapolis.

Isabel said it'd take five minutes to get the files I needed. I glanced at my watch. Almost one o'clock. After I returned to my office, files in hand, I asked Marisa to bring me a sandwich so I could review the files over lunch. While I was eating, the phone rang. It was Theya, who asked me to return to the main building. Del Campo, back from his trip to Bogotá, needed to have a word with me.

"I'll jump in the golf cart and be there in fifteen minutes," I said.

Entering the administrative building, I walked up the spiral staircase because it provided an opportunity for me to remain visible to the employees who were now walking down to lunch. Once past the second floor, I started experiencing vertigo, even though I was holding the hand railing, so I moved to the middle of the wide staircase to steady my nerves and avoid letting the dizziness get a stronger hold on me.

I'd been fighting vertigo since that night in Minneapolis at the Abbott Northwestern Hospital, on the sixth floor. I had been standing near the wall of windows, overlooking the lights of Minneapolis, praying for Robbie's life, when two doctors came to speak with Robbie's father and me. Robbie was dead, they said, and my whole being fell into a dark chasm. I started screaming, hugging and scratching the wall of glass. Beyond the windows, the city lights flickered like a thousand candles, all lit for Robbie.

My eyes had caught sight of an ambulance approaching the emergency entrance, like the one that had brought Robbie here. From this height, its flashing lights were a harbinger of death, not a hope for life. My mind was swirling, caught up in the red and white flashes, and the sudden impulse to hurl myself through the glass to the gyrating lights six levels below was overwhelming. My life wasn't worth living without my son. Like an earthquake, my body started trembling. The building itself had started shaking all around me. I was sick to my stomach. My head was spinning. Then everything went black.

When I awoke, I was on a stretcher in a room behind the nurses' station. The faces of the two doctors, the ones who had broken the news to us, loomed above me. They were asking me what my name was.

"I'm Robbie's mother," I had sobbed. "Robbie's mother."

Walking into Theya's office in a daze from the memories of that night when I'd lost Robbie, my head was still spinning, but her voice grounded me in reality again. The door to Del Campo's suite opened, and he stepped out with a short man of dark complexion with piercing, jet-black eyes and graying hair around his temples. Del Campo, cigar in hand, walked straight over, gave me the cheek kiss, and introduced his companion.

"This is Roberto, my pilot. He's worked for me for eight years. Before that, he flew helicopters for the Colombian Department of Defense, when the war against drugs was being fought so hard in the mountains. He'll take you up for a ride sometime. He's also a good fencing partner."

I extended my hand to Roberto in greeting, but he hardly acknowledged me. *An odd attitude for a Colombian man, not to be more attentive upon meeting a woman.* He shook my hand limply, nodded, turned, and left the room without uttering a word. I checked the front of my blouse and then touched my hair, wondering if there was something wrong with my appearance.

Del Campo motioned for me to follow him into his office suite. After small talk about the party, he asked how the investigation was proceeding.

"There's nothing to report," I said.

"You're not going to find anything," Del Campo affirmed, taking a long puff of his cigar. "I've already told you, I manage this company with complete transparency and high ethical standards."

"And I'm just doing my job," I said. I surprised myself, sounding like a bureaucrat.

He returned to small talk about the party. "I noticed you and Eduardo seemed animated in conversation during dinner. My wife and I are taking the helicopter up to Cartagena this weekend. I have a fencing match. Clara suggested we invite you and Eduardo to come along with us. We plan to rent a yacht on Sunday."

"You know I'm here to work. How can you expect me to jet-set around, having a grand old time, instead of doing my job?" I asked. I could only imagine the rumors that would fly through the company if I toured Cartagena over the weekend with Del Campo and his wife.

"We're just trying to keep you from being bored," he said, smiling. "And the weekend should be your time."

"You know corporate headquarters would not approve."

"You can always take the job at my stables," he said in a serious manner.

What the hell was that? Was he trying to insult me? If he was using fencing psychology, what was he trying to achieve? Undermine my self-confidence? I pretended to ignore it, as I'd done at his home when he made a similar remark. Instead, I decided to go on the offensive.

"While I'm here, let me ask you a question. Why do you need a helicopter?" As I waited for his answer, I pushed my right shoe off with my left foot and stretched the toes of my bare foot.

"It's a convenient way for me to travel around the country to call on customers without wasting time in airports. I also use it to fly to Venezuela, where we have significant pipe sales to the government and the oil industry there."

"I understand it belongs to you personally. Yet you use it for business purposes."

Del Campo looked surprised. "Ah, yes," he said. "I purchased it and hired Roberto. I rent it out on days when I'm not using it, which pays Roberto's salary. I get reimbursed for the business use of it, just as you get reimbursed for car mileage in the US. You're the auditor. Check the records yourself."

"Thanks. I will," I said.

I slipped my shoe on and stood up to exit the room, but I was seething. *How could that man invite me to join them for a weekend at a resort? Was Eduardo a willing accomplice to this?* The whole trip smacked of bribery. And that offer to work in his stables was ridiculous. Even if Del Campo wasn't an embezzler, he had an attitude that he could buy anyone.

Perhaps he was assuming too much because I'd accepted the invitation to his house. I noticed my teeth were clenched as I walked down the spiral staircase, but I told myself it wasn't worth getting so upset. Instead, I breathed slowly to calm down. Still not sure what game Del Campo was playing, I realized that, so far, he had managed to set up plenty of tension for me.

I was still on the stairway, almost at ground level, when a woman's scream echoed through the atrium. I froze, clutching the railing. Yelling erupted from the top floor—first a woman's voice, then several tumultuous voices, nervous and horrified, shouting orders, all overtaken by hysterical crying coming from one person. An alarm sounded, then a siren.

The screams and the siren brought back my pain of the night Robbie died, but I was not the one screaming this time. Instinctively, I started running up the stairs toward the commotion.

Paramedics with a stretcher got off the elevator near the office of the chief financial officer. I ran down the hallway to where people gathered. The paramedics, four of them, were ordering people to move away. A defibrillator in hand, one of them started working on a body sprawled out on the floor. A decorative comb and long, black hair that had come loose lined the carpeting near the downed woman's head.

Elena—what happened to her? My heart pounded so fast I thought it would rip my chest open. Two paramedics kneeling over her stopped working and placed her on the stretcher; three of them picked it up, while the fourth medic moved toward the elevator.

By this time, coworkers who had gathered were completely silent. Manuel Del Campo walked up. He asked people to remain calm, pray for Elena, and await further notice of her condition. He informed everyone he would personally contact the director at the hospital where she was being taken, and he would join Elena's family at the hospital.

I lingered for a little while, taking in the scene. Elena's desk seemed normal. A busboy arrived to retrieve the tray of unfinished food.

"What happened to Elena?" he asked.

"No news on her condition," I said, "but news travels fast."

"Ms. Theya called to have the tray taken back to the cafeteria," he said.

A young man with humped shoulders came up behind me, cleared his throat, and asked me to excuse him. He leaned in toward Elena's computer and turned it off.

I walked to Theya's office, and she was standing in the doorway.

"What happened?" I asked.

"We don't know," Theya said, "but Elena suffers from a heart condition. She may have had a heart attack. We won't know much until she's evaluated at the hospital."

"Is she even alive?" I asked.

"I don't know any more than you do. I'll notify you as soon as we have an update."

"Why did you order the food tray removed and the computer turned off?" I asked.

"To keep things tidy. The computer for security purposes," she said. "Is there anything wrong with that?"

"No, just wondering," I said.

Outside, I jumped in the golf cart I'd driven over, turned the key, gripped the steering wheel as if I were in heavy freeway traffic, and headed toward the mill, wondering whether Elena was still alive. Glancing across the acres of manicured lawn and grassy hills, I guessed Del Campo was not a golfer. Otherwise, he'd already have put in an eighteen-hole golf course on company grounds—the way he controlled everything. It was beginning to look as if he even controlled life and death at the company.

Could Elena be one of his victims? If so, what kind of beast would want to kill an employee like Elena?

Continue reading Waking Up in Medellin on Amazon

ALSO BY KATHRYN LANE

The Nikki Garcia Mystery Series

Waking Up in Medellin

Danger in the Coyote Zone

Revenge in Barcelona

Missing in Miami

Audiobook: *Waking Up in Medellin*

Box Set: *The Nikki Garcia Mystery Series: Box Set*

Translated into Spanish: *Despertando en Medellín*

Other Books by Kathryn Lane

Backyard Volcano and Other Mysteries of the Heart

AWARDS AND PRAISE FOR KATHRYN'S BOOKS

WAKING UP IN MEDELLIN (NIKKI GARCIA MYSTERY #1)

Waking Up in Medellin was named "Best Fiction Book of the Year—2017" by the Killer Nashville International Mystery Writers' Conference and also won Killer Nashville's "Best Fiction—Adult Suspense—2017." It was also a finalist for the Roné Award—2016.

DANGER IN THE COYOTE ZONE (NIKKI GARCIA MYSTERY #2)

Danger in the Coyote Zone won first place in the 2018 Action/Adventure Category of Latino Books into Movies Award; named a finalist in the Thriller Category at the 2018 Killer Nashville International Mystery Writers' Conference, and was a finalist in the 2018 Book Excellence Awards.

REVENGE IN BARCELONA (NIKKI GARCIA MYSTERY #3)

Revenge in Barcelona won first place in Latino Books into Movies-Latino Themed TV Series Category 2020; won the Silver Medal in the Mystery Category 2020 by Reader Views Literary Awards; Finalist in the Eric Hoffer 2020 Book Awards; Finalist for Silver Falchion in the Best Suspense by Killer Nashville; Finalist in the Suspense Category by Next Generation Book Awards; Finalist in the 2020 International Latino Book Awards; Awarded Five Stars by Readers' Favorite.

MISSING IN MIAMI (NIKKI GARCIA MYSTERY #4)

Winner of Best eBook Fiction at the 2022 International Latino Book Awards; Distinguished Favorite in the Mystery Category of NYC Big Book Awards of 2022; Honorable Mention in the Best Novel in the Mystery Category of the International Latino Book Awards of 2022.

BACKYARD VOLCANO AND OTHER MYSTERIES OF THE HEART (SHORT STORY COLLECTION)

Backyard Volcano and Other Mysteries of the Heart was named "Best Short Story Collection—2018" by the Killer Nashville International Mystery Writers' Conference.

ACKNOWLEDGEMENTS

Stolen Diary is a departure from the norm for me. It's a coming-of-age and family life story with a hint of mystery sprinkled in. I hope readers will enjoy it.

I am indebted to many individuals who kindly share their thoughts, expertise, and words of encouragement with me. I'd specifically like to thank the following:

Bob Hurt—my husband, buddy, and ally—for his unconditional love and his support of my writing. His belief in this project is beyond my capacity to thank him.

Philip Calkins—my son—whose suggestions on technical issues are right on.

Lowell Mick White—mentor, critic, and friend—for his critical review included on the back cover.

My expert readers—Rosa Herst, Carol Ann Martz, Harry Martz, Norman Parrish, David R. Stafseth, and Jorge Lane Terrazas—for their thoughtful feedback.

Maureen Donelan—graphic designer for the Tortuga Publishing, LLC logo.

My Houston/Austin writing group for their suggestions.

Friends and book club members, too numerous to list, who provide the support and encouragement that inspires me to continue writing.

A big thanks to my team:
Sandra A. Spicher—my editor for her valuable advice.
Danielle Hartman Acee—my book interior designer for her excellent insight.
Tim Barber—for the beautiful book cover.

To my readers—I could not and would not do it without you!

ABOUT THE AUTHOR

Kathryn Lane is the award-winning author of the Nikki Garcia Mystery Series.

In her writing, she draws deeply from her experiences growing up in a small town in northern Mexico as well as her work and travel in over ninety countries around the globe during her career in international finance with Johnson & Johnson.

Kathryn loves the Arts and is a board member of the Montgomery County Literary Arts Council. Kathryn and her husband, Bob Hurt, split their time between Texas and the mountains of northern New Mexico where she finds it inspiring to write.

Kathryn's Website
Kathryn-lane.com

amazon.com/~/e/B01D0J1YES

bookbub.com/authors/kathryn-lane

goodreads.com/kathrynlane

facebook.com/kathrynlanewriter